ALSO BY CELIA LASKEY

So Happy for You

Under the Rainbow

Cover Story

Celia Laskey

GCP

GRAND
CENTRAL

New York Boston

Grand Central Publishing
Hachette Book Group
1290 Avenue of the Americas, New York, NY 10104
grandcentralpublishing.com
@grandcentralpub

First Edition: March 2025

Grand Central Publishing is a division of Hachette Book Group, Inc. The Grand Central Publishing name and logo is a registered trademark of Hachette Book Group, Inc.

The publisher is not responsible for websites (or their content) that are not owned by the publisher.

The Hachette Speakers Bureau provides a wide range of authors for speaking events. To find out more, go to hachettespeakersbureau.com or email HachetteSpeakers@hbgusa.com.

Grand Central Publishing books may be purchased in bulk for business, educational, or promotional use. For information, please contact your local bookseller or the Hachette Book Group Special Markets Department at special.markets@hbgusa.com.

Print book interior design by Marie Mundaca

Library of Congress Cataloging-in-Publication Data
Names: Laskey, Celia, author.
Title: Cover story / Celia Laskey.
Description: First edition. | New York : GCP, 2025.
Identifiers: LCCN 2024039942 | ISBN 9781538765609 (trade paperback) |
    ISBN 9781538765616 (ebook)
Subjects: LCGFT: Romance fiction. | Queer fiction. | Novels.
Classification: LCC PS3612.A853 C68 2025 | DDC 813/.6—dc23/eng/20240830
LC record available at https://lccn.loc.gov/2024039942

ISBNs: 978-1-5387-6560-9 (trade paperback), 978-1-5387-6561-6 (ebook)

Printed in the United States of America

LSC-H

Printing 1, 2025

*For the public figures who've been told to hide
and the everyday people who wish to see them*

Cover Story

1

Before, Ali woke up every morning to her partner Natalie throwing open the bedroom door to let in their scruffy black-and-white terrier mix, Glen. He'd bound onto the bed and stand on Ali's chest, licking her face and panting his warm trash breath. Natalie would kiss Ali and recount the details of Glen's walk: which route they took, which neighborhood dogs they saw, whether Glen had been in an agreeable mood or had been obstinate, and the quality and number of his poops. Natalie was an early riser and loved taking Glen out in the morning, which was fine by Ali, since she preferred to sleep as late as possible. After Ali had heard all about Glen's walk, she would usually recount a catastrophic dream she'd had: a flood, an earthquake, getting kidnapped by a murderer, Glen getting hit by a car. She'd look at Natalie and Glen and sigh, relieved that all was well.

But now the catastrophe is real. Ali still wakes up to Glen, but not returning from his walk—he's been next to her, trying to rouse her for at least an hour. When Ali's alarm goes off and she finally, begrudgingly, opens her eyes, she immediately cries—this is how she has started each day since Natalie died exactly one year ago. In books and movies, grieving characters always say there's a fleeting peaceful moment after waking up when they forget what happened, but Ali never experiences this. The instant she's conscious, the knowledge is present, nauseating her like a form of morning sickness—not for a new life, but for a lost one.

Bright sunlight cuts through the blinds, and birds outside chirp blithely. Ali wonders if birds stop singing when they're grieving—if grief is even an emotion they feel. Maybe what sounds like happy warbling to Ali is, in fact, a bird screaming into the void or calling out for a lost loved one. If she were a bird, Ali would fly straight up, like a rocket, until she reached the blackness of space. That's where she feels like her mind is now: in the blurry, indistinguishable line between the blue sky of life as we know it and the darkness of the great mysterious beyond.

But Ali's physical body is in sunny Los Angeles, where the weather never gives her the courtesy of matching her mood. It insists she get up, get over it. Glen would also like her to get up. He emerges from under the covers to lick the tears from her cheeks and look at her hopefully with his human-esque hazel eyes. His face is two-thirds white on the left side and one-third black on the right, with the black fur curving around his eye like a wide letter *C*. On the white side of his face, his ear is also white, with faded black spots like a dalmatian. This spotted ear is Ali's favorite feature of his, and she leans over to kiss it.

"I'm sorry, buddy, we'll go soon." Ali removes a thick night guard from her upper teeth and places it in a plastic container on her nightstand, which is covered in stacks of books (mainly short-story collections by Alice Munro, James Baldwin, Lorrie Moore, ZZ Packer, and

George Saunders), a box of Cheez-Its, stray earplugs, and a value-size container of ibuprofen for the headaches that debilitate her four to five times a week. This morning, she can already feel the pain poking at the base of her head, slightly above where her hair starts growing and just right of center—the spot where massage therapists sometimes press their thumb like it's a magic button that releases all the body's tension. If someone could keep their thumb pinned on that button twenty-four hours a day, Ali thinks she could feel like a functional human.

Instead, she stretches her neck to either side, then pulls her mouth as far apart as she can to rotate her jaw in circles, pressing her pointer and middle fingers into the corner joints that connect her upper and lower jaw. Ali has ground her teeth at night since she was a teenager, but in the past year, she's chewed through four different night guards touted by their respective companies as "indestructible." She swallows two ibuprofen for the headache, a probiotic for her irritable bowel syndrome, a vitamin D for her body's deficiency thereof, and a birth control pill for her ovarian cysts. (The fact that she, a lesbian, must take birth control always strikes her as annoyingly ironic.)

On top of ZZ Packer's *Drinking Coffee Elsewhere*, Ali's BlackBerry vibrates with a text from her best friend, Dana: Thinking about you. Remember to be kind to yourself today, and I'll see you tonight for dinner. Ali doesn't reply to the text and instead opens her Dell laptop to check her work email, her stomach surging and chest tightening as she prays no catastrophes have struck since she went to bed. Ali is a publicist at a well-known firm that specializes in public relations for celebrities, and you never know what kind of trouble they're going to get into. Plus the whole PR culture is to treat everything as a matter of life and death—a recent career survey ranked public relations executive as the eighth-most-stressful job, behind actual life-or-death occupations like soldier, police officer, firefighter, and airline pilot.

Ali doesn't view her work with such gravity—she sees her position as that of a glorified babysitter with a laptop, managing the moods and bad behavior of adult children. She never would have chosen this career, but her first job out of college was as a receptionist at a PR firm, and she ended up ambivalently climbing rung after rung on the publicity ladder due to her outsize student loan payments and what bosses called her "knack" for the job, which Ali thought was simply having a modicum of competence and responsibility. It was like a wave had carried her to the shore of a land where she'd never intended to live, and she'd stayed simply because it was easier.

She always used to tell herself she would quit and find a job that suited her better, but no career consists of reading and writing short stories, which is all she truly wants to do, so any job would likely feel as pointless to her as PR. Besides, thirty-five is a little late to switch careers and climb the ladder all over again, and most days Ali is resigned to her fate. The job provides stability and excellent health insurance, and for a person with an untreated anxiety disorder and a side of hypochondria, stability and excellent health insurance are necessities.

Shockingly, this morning her inbox contains no emergencies, which is so rare it's like the blooming of a corpse flower. Instead, it's the usual trash heap of press requests, pitch responses, and media inquiries. She checks the weather: seventy-six degrees currently, with a high of eighty-nine, which makes her groan. It's early September, which for most places in this hemisphere would mean cooling temperatures, but in LA, they're still hitting the high eighties or the nineties, and this will continue well into October and maybe even November. NASA scientists recently said 2005 was on track to be the warmest year in over a century.

Ali can't believe people continue to deny climate change when Hurricane Katrina hit New Orleans only days ago. Photos of the disaster flood the news: people sleeping on their roofs while waiting to be rescued, brown water only a few feet below them; cars floating in streets turned to rivers, street signs nearly submerged; a shaft of sunlight beaming through a hole in the Superdome roof after it was emptied of thousands of survivors. Ali pictures a skinny polar bear stuck on a jagged ice floe, the pier in Santa Monica underwater, fires that make it "snow" even in Los Angeles. The fires will start any day now, marking Ali's least favorite season, when blazes rage in all directions for weeks on end, making the air unbreathable and her anxiety unmanageable.

Glen nudges Ali's laptop with his snout, then stands on her chest and pants into her face.

Ali grimaces. "God, it smells like someone had diarrhea into a fish tank, then fell *into* the fish tank and drowned, and after the body rotted and the diarrhea molded, you took a long drink."

Glen pants harder.

"Okay, okay. You wanna…?"

Glen raises his ears.

"Go for…?"

Glen wags his tail.

"A dental cleaning?"

Glen cocks his head.

"A colonoscopy?"

Glen cocks his head the other way.

"Or…A WALK?" Glen jumps from the bed and shoots out of the room.

* * *

Glen pulls Ali down the street and she struggles to keep up. She hates waking up this early, but once they're outside, she has to admit it's a nice way to start the day, and she can see why Natalie loved it. They're in the Silver Lake hills surrounding the reservoir, meandering past magenta mounds of bougainvillea spilling over doorways and agave plants with what resemble towering stalks of asparagus growing from their hearts. Walls of jasmine bushes carpeted with white pinwheel flowers release an incredibly sweet perfume, and the white bark of eucalyptus trees sags and ripples, like the skin of a hairless cat, where the trunks meet the branches. All of it makes Ali cry again. She can't decide whether being surrounded by such beauty is a blessing or a curse—it makes her both thankful and resentful to be alive without Natalie. If she lived in the arctic tundra, or a parched desert, would she feel more or less depressed, or exactly the same?

A few streets later, as they're huffing up a steep hill, a coyote casually trots out from a yard about twenty feet ahead. Coyotes are a common sight in Silver Lake, especially near the reservoir, but they always send a chill up Ali's spine. This one is German shepherd–size with a thick coat of fur, as opposed to the fox-size, scraggly ones that look like less of a threat. When Glen notices it, he kicks into gear, barking his head off and straining against the leash. The coyote stands there calmly blinking at them, like *Go ahead and try it, little guy*. Another coyote appears, bigger than the first, and Ali's heart starts to beat double time. Her instinct is always to turn around and run, but she's read that with coyotes, you should stand your ground and make as much noise as possible. She waves her unleashed hand above her head and stomps her feet while yelling, "I'm really sorry we humans are displacing you! I'm terrified of you, but I have to act like I'm not, so you won't attack me! La la la la la!" At this, the second coyote takes a step toward them, and now Ali's heart beats triple time. She puts her hand on the pepper spray clasped to her shorts pocket, which she carries not only for coyotes but also for violent dogs who might attack Glen (which has happened before) and men. At this point you're supposed to throw something. She grabs a smooth, warm stone from a rock garden and tosses it at the coyotes, aiming just to their left. When it thunks near their feet, they finally trot off across the street and disappear.

Ali breathes in relief and squats down to comfort Glen, who coughs repeatedly from how hard he was pulling on his harness. "Yes, you're a very big brave boy, you definitely could have taken those two seventy-pound wild animals, yes you could have," she coos, petting his head. Her heart rate slows and sweat slithers down her stomach. Another day, another potential death narrowly avoided.

On days when Ali doesn't have any after-work commitments, she takes Glen to the office with her, but today she has a doctor's appointment and dinner at Dana's, so she drops Glen off at his dog walker/sitter's house on the way home because she thinks he gets anxious when left alone for longer than five hours, even though in reality, it's Ali who gets anxious, picturing him curled up on the couch alone. If it were up to her, she would never be separated from him.

She has time for a quick cold shower before running leave-in conditioner through her shoulder-length, naturally straight black hair and throwing on a pair of lightweight black slacks, a black-and-white-striped T-shirt, and a pair of black leather sneakers. The striped T-shirt is about as wild as Ali gets, fashionwise. She prefers basic cuts in neutral colors like black, white, navy blue, and gray, which she'll tell you is her favorite color when pressed to pick one. She never wears makeup, which she can get away with thanks to her even-toned, pimple-free skin, high cheekbones, and ridiculously long and dark eyelashes. Her one beauty ritual consists of dabbing a recently purchased "rejuvenating cream" under her eyes, an attempt to lighten the dark circles that have become more and more bruise-like over the past year.

Then Ali calls a cab to take her to her office in Hollywood. Ali has always found driving in LA to be a terrifying endeavor (see: merging onto a highway only to be forced to immediately merge over five lanes through a churning sea of traffic to get onto a different highway, trying to make a left-hand turn with no protected light and a steady stream of traffic whizzing by, other drivers who purposefully run red lights and whip U-turns with abandon and text on their phones while going seventy-five miles per hour), but two years ago, she got into a bad accident on the 10—a guy in a Mercedes merged right into her, resulting in a broken left arm, nerve damage in her neck and back, and ultimately PTSD so bad she stopped driving.

When Natalie was alive, Ali would ride to work with her, since Ali's office was mostly on the way to Natalie's, and whenever they ran errands or went out, Natalie would drive. After she died, it became clear how dependent on her Ali had been, how circumscribed her life had become. All her choices revolved around how far away activities were and how many cabs she'd have to take in a day and what it would cost her. She told herself daily cabs couldn't be much more expensive than a monthly car and insurance payment, but that wasn't true. Months ago, Ali had vowed to tackle her fear and be back on the road by now, but so far she'd only written down the names of a few driving schools, cognitive behavioral therapists, and, in a moment of desperation, hypnotists.

Today Ali's cabbie is a chatty man in his twenties who drives like he's auditioning for another *Fast & Furious* sequel. Ali takes measured breaths in and out as he barely taps the brake pedal at stop signs, weaves in and out of lanes like he's forming fabric, and honks at anyone who takes more than .01 seconds to hit the gas after the light turns green, all while droning on about the screenplay he's writing: "a futuristic *Groundhog Day* set in space." Ali believes the personalities of cities in the US can best be summed up by how people drive in them, and people in LA drive with such urgency and disregard for traffic laws, you'd think someone were giving birth in every passenger seat. But no, they're all just selfish idiots who do whatever they want, whenever they want, no matter how it affects anyone. Is it possible to like a physical place but hate almost everyone in it?

Ali grew up in North Dakota, in a town with a population of two thousand near the Canadian border. Her earliest and most enduring memories are of being cold: pressing her numb fingers and toes to the barely warm heater, making endless mugs of tea that would go lukewarm almost instantly, sleeping in three sweaters and a face mask. "Only people who sit still are cold," Ali's parents would say before making her scrub the bathtub or shovel the walkway or wash the dishes. At least the water was hot on her hands. When she got into UCLA on a full scholarship, she yelled, "I'm never going to be cold again!"

Ali has now lived in LA for sixteen years. For the last few of those, due to the aforementioned selfish idiots and the traffic and the wildfires and the earthquakes and the rising rents and temperatures (Ali doesn't want to be cold but she doesn't want to sweat through her clothes every single day, either), she and Natalie sometimes daydreamed about leaving, but realistically, Natalie's job prevented it. She was a TV writer, and therefore it was necessary for them to live in LA. When she died, she was about to show-run her first series—a dramedy about a fictionalized WNBA. It had been her life's dream to finally oversee her own show.

But now, with Natalie gone, moving seems unthinkable. How are you supposed to decide where to go all by yourself? How do you make friends as a grieving loner? At least in LA, Ali has Dana, her oldest friend from childhood, who moved here after college, and a "successful" career, albeit one she doesn't want. So for now, she's staying in LA, even though she just watched a car drive over a median to pull a U-turn, all to avoid a line of traffic at a red light.

2

After a minute of deep breathing in the parking lot, Ali passes a dense crowd in the lobby waiting for elevators and takes the stairs. It would be a reasonable choice if Ali's office were on the second or third floor, but it's on the tenth. Shortly after Natalie died, Ali watched a report on the eleven o'clock local news about how half the elevators in Los Angeles hadn't been inspected for over two years. After that, Ali stopped taking them, no matter which floor she was going to. Her choice was validated when, a couple of weeks later, a woman in a downtown office building was killed by a malfunctioning elevator. The woman had put one foot in when it suddenly lurched up, the doors still open. She was dragged by her ankle between the elevator and the wall until her body was crushed. So if Ali is sweaty and winded by the time she reaches the tenth floor, so be it.

"Good morning, work wife," says Ali's coworker Namisa, who's passing by as Ali swings open the door to the stairs, huffing and puffing. The greeting is a bit they do every morning, using a Valley girl baby voice to mock the Paris Hilton types who work in PR and sincerely use expressions like "work wife." Even though Ali and Namisa use the term derisively, it *is* accurate to describe their relationship—Namisa transferred from the London office five years ago, and Ali doesn't know how she ever survived at the agency without her. They get along well because like Ali, Namisa loathes the job, even though she's very good at it. They discreetly roll their eyes at each other and mime shooting themselves in the head during meetings, and they bust into each other's office yelling things like "Code red! I need one hundred and fifty cc's of blood, STAT!" or "He's flatlining! Hand me the defibrillators!" to make fun of all the other employees acting like they work in an emergency room instead of a PR office. Just as Ali would rather be writing short stories, Namisa would rather be choreographing modern dance routines. Before her career in PR, she was on the path to becoming a professional ballet dancer, but at twenty years old she fractured a bone in her left foot, which subsequently fractured her dreams.

Ali takes a moment to catch her breath. "Spin class kicked my ass today," she says to Namisa in the same affected voice. "Spin class" is what she calls her ten-story climb to the office.

"My ass is getting fat 'cause my fiancé keeps cooking me extravagant dinners." At the word *fiancé*, Namisa holds out her left hand and admires an imaginary hunk of diamond on her ring finger. "I need to go on a juice cleanse ASAP."

Ali scoffs. "No way, girl, your ass looks *fab*. My ass is the fat one."

Namisa gives her a playful shove. "No, mine is!"

Ali shoves her back slightly harder. "No, mine!"

"Mine!" Namisa pushes her hard enough that Ali stumbles backward.

"MINE!" Ali gives Namisa a don't-fuck-with-me look.

Namisa holds up her hands. "Okay, whatever, we're both fat-asses. Love you, wifey." She kisses the air next to Ali's cheek.

"Love *you*, wifey." Ali kisses back, completing the bit before they duck into their boss Victoria's office for the morning rundown.

Victoria eats a bowl of Lucky Charms while bent over what she calls an "adult coloring book," which Ali has never heard of but Victoria claims will be "huge" in a few years. She designs them herself before coloring them in, and the only differences Ali can discern between children's coloring books and Victoria's are that Victoria's are slightly more intricate and sometimes contain naughty pictures or words. You could say she has some arrested development issues. Her great-uncle founded the chain of stores that became Wal-Mart, so her family is extremely rich but also extremely fucked up. By the time she was twenty-one, she had already been to rehab three times, and when sobriety finally stuck, she reverted to a state of childlike innocence. She bought the firm a year ago to try to bring purpose to her life, having chosen it because she loved celebrity gossip, but she didn't know anything about running a company, not to mention PR. During a meeting one day, Ali honest-to-God caught her googling "Define publicity." Sometimes Victoria's incompetence drives Ali nuts, but usually it results in Ali being left alone to make her own decisions, which she likes.

"Morning girls, help yourself to brekkie." Victoria gestures to the boxes of Cookie Crisp and Cap'n Crunch and Froot Loops and Cocoa Puffs and Apple Jacks in her kitchenette. "How were your weekends? What did you both do?"

"I went on two *fantastic* dates," says Namisa. "One of the blokes picked up his leftovers with his hands and put them in

his trouser pockets—needless to say, I'm seeing him again."
The reason Namisa transferred from the London office five
years ago was a divorce from a husband who'd turned out to
be a sex addict. After that, she decided she needed a significant change of scenery. Ali can't believe Namisa has stayed
in Los Angeles—if Ali were facing the prospect of dating
local men, she'd be on the next plane out. The women here
are bad enough, and she tries not to think about how, in the
future, if she doesn't want to be alone for the rest of her life
(which she has not technically decided yet), she'll have to
start dating, too.

"I, uh…watched a bunch of TV and deep-cleaned the
bathroom," says Ali, pressing her thumb into the back of
her skull where her headache is still pulsing, despite the
Advil she took earlier. These days, Advil might as well be a
placebo.

"Wow, I don't know who I feel worse for," says Namisa,
"you or me."

"Well, you probably know what I did." Victoria finishes
her bowl of Lucky Charms and smacks her lips.

"Disney?" Ali and Namisa say at the same time.

Victoria beams. "We rode Splash Mountain five times
and ate Dole Whips till we nearly puked."

"Disney and dates," says Ali. "Between the two of you,
my nightmare weekend is complete."

"Okay, hit me with some good news." Victoria flips open
the Lisa Frank stationery she special-orders from eBay, pois-
ing a strawberry-scented glitter gel pen above the first line.

"People are going absolutely wild for Jen's *Vanity Fair*
cover," says Namisa. "Everyone has been dying to hear
her side of the split from Brad, and the article definitely
delivered."

"The internet is also getting a real kick out of the

paparazzi photos of Paris in her Team Jolie shirt and Nikki in her Team Aniston shirt," Ali says, pretending she cares. This was hard enough to do before Natalie died, but since then, the pretending has felt especially sapping. Ali feels like a cell phone you've had for a few years too many that can no longer hold its charge, and the second you perform one task on it—like replying to an email or playing a game of *Snake*—the thin line of low power appears. She wishes there were an outlet she could plug herself into.

"And Britney has agreed to do a *People* cover about the birth of Sean Preston," Namisa chimes in.

"Excellent," says Victoria. "Bad news?"

"All the gossip blogs are running those paparazzi photos of Lindsay Lohan with a boob falling out of her tank top," says Namisa. "Fucking crikey, I miss the good old days." The good old days being only a few months before, when media was mainly relegated to print or TV and all the major outlets were in publicists' pockets. Most published stories came directly from publicists, and if they didn't want certain information covered, all they had to do was threaten to cut off access or sue. On the rare occasion a scandal *did* come out, publicists at least had days to get in front of it. Now these online gossip blogs can publish stories in minutes, and publicists find out at the same time as the general public. The tipping point was around May, when Perez Hilton (previously known as PageSixSixSix), YouTube, the *Huffington Post*, and a US version of *OK!* all launched, and when camera phones started to outsell brick phones. Suddenly civilians could catch celebrities doing anything from picking their noses to leaving clubs wasted to cheating on their significant others. Over the course of 2005, the number of blogs has skyrocketed from ten million to twenty-five million, and for the first time ever, news seemingly moves at the speed of light, reaching countless people in a flash.

A prime example was Tom Cruise jumping on Oprah's couch to declare he was in love with Katie Holmes. Thanks to YouTube, short clips from the show almost immediately whizzed around the internet with titles like "Tom Cruise kills Oprah." Most people sharing the clips hadn't even watched the full episode, in which the crowd was even more hyped up than Tom, and Oprah was goading him into talking about his personal life. In context, while the interview was being conducted, it seemed more like he was playing along, but without the context, it looked like he had lost his mind. After that, it was all downhill for Tom, and no publicist could control it.

"Re: Lindsay's boob…" Victoria's eyes light up with one of her terrible ideas. "Could we say it was a stunt to increase awareness about breast cancer?"

Ali kicks Namisa under the desk.

"I think we're better off just letting it fizzle out," says Namisa. "By tomorrow the blogs will move on to something else."

"You're probably right," says Victoria. "Is there more bad news?"

"Perez is threatening to out Lance Bass again," says Ali. Pre–gossip blogs, they never had to worry about celebrities being outed. But since gossip bloggers have no relationship with publicists and thus nothing to lose, plus Perez himself is gay, one of his missions seems to be outing closeted celebrities. "If you know something to be a fact, why not report it? Why is that still taboo?" Ali doesn't believe anyone should be outed against their will, but she does kind of see Perez's point—how will gayness ever stop seeming like a shameful secret unless the media stops treating it like one? As an out lesbian with no shame about her own sexuality, she hates the hypocrisy involved in counseling her gay clients to stay in the closet, and she wishes things were different.

She still remembers the first time she learned an A-list celebrity was gay and hiding it. Ali had just started as an assistant at her first PR agency—she was twenty-three, and it was 1993, before any celebrities had publicly come out. She'd been backstage at a movie premiere, struggling to hold about ten different purses and clutches, when she saw ██████ ███, an actress in her early thirties with two Academy Awards, lean toward a woman standing next to her, someone Ali didn't know, and plant a casual kiss on her mouth.

Ali dropped all the purses and clutches and grasped her coworker Sharon's forearm. "Did you see that?" Ali gasped.

Sharon appeared completely unruffled. "Oh yeah, that's her longtime partner."

Ali blinked repeatedly. "I'm sorry, *what*?" A waiter passed by with a tray of champagne flutes, and even though they weren't supposed to drink at events, Ali grabbed a flute and took a big gulp.

Sharon laughed and pulled Ali into the corner, away from the celebrities giving press interviews. "I always forget you newbies don't know anything yet. But you couldn't have thought it was statistically possible for one hundred percent of Hollywood to be straight, right?"

"I guess I never really thought about it before." Ali kept her eyes on ████████, who now had her hand on the unknown woman's lower back. "So...everyone knows she's gay?"

"Everyone in the industry and mostly everyone in the media. The only people who don't know are the general public."

Ali took another gulp of champagne. "Isn't she afraid someone will say something?"

"No way. Everyone knows that's the one thing you don't leak. DUIs, drug use, prostitutes, abuse, hetero cheating—that's all fair game. But not someone being gay."

"Huh. That kind of seems like a double standard. Why is it the one verboten topic?"

"Because it would ruin their career." ███████ was now talking to someone from the press, and her partner was still standing beside her, although they had stopped touching.

"More than an actor being caught with a prostitute?"

"Oh yeah. Most of these closeted celebs are total heart-throbs for the opposite sex." Sharon pointed across the room at an A-list actor. "Housewives in the middle of the country would lose their shit if they knew ███████ sucks dick. And then he'd never be cast in anything again, because they'd only see him as a big homo."

"Wait. ███████ is gay?" Ali studied his chiseled jaw and killer smile and remembered how her mom had always joked she'd leave Ali's dad for him.

"The gayest."

"Oh my God. Who else?"

Sharon rattled off a list of very recognizable names who were frequently in blockbusters and on the covers of magazines. Half of them were backstage at the event.

"Holy shit." Ali drained the rest of her champagne. "But ███████ is married to ███████...How does that work?"

"Beard marriages, honey. They're a dime a dozen, and they've been around forever. Cary Grant and any of his five wives, Rock Hudson and Phyllis Gates..."

"Wow. Are the two people in a beard relationship always both gay?"

"If the gay one is more famous, sometimes a straight beard will do it, in the hope they'll get more famous. Or just for money."

Ali shook her head, her eyes as wide as quarters. She felt like she had been living in a gay version of *The Truman Show*, sailing along in the straight world's boat when the bow suddenly pierced the dome's painted sky. Underneath the pure shock of it, Ali felt something else she couldn't quite put her finger on. Was it anger? Yes, but underneath that, there was something more specific. Betrayal. Her whole life, she had been lied to. Because of those lies, she'd spent twenty-two miserable years thinking she was straight. Black holes started to eat through Ali's vision and she crouched down, blinking rapidly, images appearing behind her eyelids.

The boy on the playground with the buzz cut and Kool-Aid-stained mouth whom she'd always had insult contests with. One day he'd called her a lesbian and Ali hadn't known what it meant, so she'd asked her mom and her mom had told her not to worry, that the word had nothing to do with her.

The boy with spiky bleach-blond hair she'd made out with at the movies, just to get it over with, after her mom had taunted her about being "sweet sixteen and never been kissed." The whole next day, she'd hidden in her bedroom thinking she had the flu, she felt so sick.

The white, chalky liquid she'd swallowed at seventeen that made her insides glow and revealed she didn't, to her disappointment, have an ulcer. The doctor recommended Ali be sent to counseling, and to Ali's surprise, her no-nonsense, pull-yourself-up-by-your-bootstraps parents had agreed. The counselor had asked a lot of questions about Ali's mother.

She never once asked Ali about her sexuality. It didn't occur to Ali—even in her diary, even in her most private, hidden thoughts—that she might be a lesbian.

The foamy, neon-yellow bile Ali had puked up after losing her virginity to a man she was half-heartedly on-and-off dating her first year of college. Much like her first kiss, she'd done it to get it over with, not because she had wanted to. There hadn't been an ounce of pleasure to be found in it.

She'd written anguished entries in her diary questioning her intense fear of sex and relationships. About how she "fell" for completely unavailable guys and then cried when they didn't like her back. And when they *did* like her back, she found some other reason to end it. She trapped herself in the perfect catch-22, ensuring her loneliness and sadness. She had fiercely close relationships with her female friends and always felt inordinately betrayed when they found boyfriends.

Every single time Ali slept with a man, she puked afterward. Men literally made her sick, and it still didn't occur to her that she might be a lesbian. She thought she was just really picky, or hadn't met the right person yet, or was commitment-phobic, or had some kind of emotional problem, or just wasn't a very sexual person, or was asexual—all these things occurred to her, but the simplest and most obvious option did not.

But then a year after graduating from college, Ali met Natalie. The puking and the doubts and the fear stopped, and were replaced by comfort and happiness and pleasure. And then love. The first time Ali called herself a lesbian out loud, her whole body vibrated with confirmation. She couldn't believe it had taken her so long to figure it out—looking back, it was wildly obvious. But when society lied and told you everyone was straight, you assumed you must be straight, too.

Backstage at that movie premiere, Ali finally realized what her bottommost emotion was underneath all the shock and the anger and the betrayal: grief. For those twenty-two torturous years, and for the happiness she might have found sooner had she known the truth about how many people were actually gay.

Her coworker Sharon put a hand on Ali's arm. "Oh, honey. You look like I've just told you Santa Claus isn't real."

Even worse than realizing how all these closeted celebrities had indirectly affected Ali's life was thinking about how they would *directly* affect it. Ali's stomach churned. "As publicists, we probably play a part in all this, don't we?"

"A huge part. We arrange all of it, usually."

Ali swallowed a mouthful of sour spit. "Doesn't that feel...wrong? To actively lie like that?"

"It's our job to protect these celebrities' public image. So that's what we're doing."

"Couldn't we do that without lying, though? Couldn't we just tell closeted celebrities to say their private lives are off-limits, and that'd be that?"

Sharon guffawed. "You've been to a grocery store, right? With all the gossip magazines at checkout? The general public is *obsessed* with stars' private lives. Trust me, that would *never* be that."

The churning in Ali's stomach increased. The champagne she had drunk bubbled up her throat, acidic and hot. She swallowed it down. "You know I'm gay, right? I don't think I can be involved in this kind of thing." Ali thought about quitting the next day, but she was living paycheck to paycheck thanks to her rent and student loans, both astronomical. It had taken her months just to land the reception position that had preceded her promotion to assistant.

"I think it'll be impossible to avoid," said Sharon.

"I think I'm going to be sick." Ali held a hand over her mouth, trying to quiet the gagging sensation in her throat.

"Aw, Ali." Sharon rubbed her back. "You'll get used to it."

Eventually, as the years went by and Ali slid yet another beard contract across the table, or arranged yet another staged paparazzi shoot, it did start to feel normal. Still terrible, but normal. Her need for a paycheck always outweighed her moral disgust. She told herself she was just a cog in a machine and there was nothing she, personally, could do to change the closeted culture of Hollywood. Every year, she told herself LGBT acceptance would get better: In 1997, Ellen was essentially the first celebrity to come out, and Ali was so excited, assuming it was the drop that would bust the closeted dam open, but it ended up tanking Ellen's career. For years after, no one was willing to be next. Ali thought the new millennium meant stars would *have* to be allowed to live their truth soon, but it wasn't until 2002 that Rosie O'Donnell came out, and two years after that, in 2004, that Cynthia Nixon followed in her footsteps. In August of this year, Portia de Rossi came out, bringing the Hollywood grand total to four celebrities who were willing to risk their careers for the sake of being honest about their sexuality. It was too early to tell how it would affect Portia, but neither Rosie nor Cynthia had worked on anything notable since coming out. Many would say it was just a coincidence, but Ali knew better. Four out celebrities weren't enough to move the needle in a significant way, and they weren't enough for Ali to change the way she did her job. Even if it did make her sick.

What Ali doesn't tell anyone she works with, other than

Namisa, is that she lies awake at night picturing all the people who, like her past self, don't know they're gay due to the lies she helps to propagate. While tossing and turning, Ali rehearses her resignation speech and the op-ed she'll write calling all publicists to stop counseling their clients to stay in the closet, and the business plan she'll craft for her own agency, where she'll help any client who wants to tell the truth about themselves and/or the industry. The fleeting moments when Ali enjoys her job always relate to her clients speaking out about something: a personal struggle they've been through, activism they're involved in, or prejudice they've encountered in the industry. Ali believes the general public would actually relate *more* to stars if they were completely honest about their experiences and opinions, but she's probably the only publicist who thinks so.

"What if, with Lance…," Victoria says, pulling Ali back to the present, "we film a sex tape of him with a woman and 'leak' it?" She makes air quotes around the word *leak*. "Then no one could say he's gay!"

Ali blinks, using all her willpower not to catch Namisa's eye. "I think it'll be enough for Lance to be photographed out and about with a female celebrity," Ali says. "All the legit magazines will speculate on whether they're dating, and no one will believe Perez."

"Yeah, I guess that's easier," says Victoria. "Speaking of keeping the gay cat in the bag, I have some new business. Have you girls heard of *Real Love*, the movie that's coming out in a couple months?"

"Something to do with sims, right?" says Ali. "Based on the YA book series?"

Victoria nods and reads the logline from her computer screen. "When a female gamer from the future falls in love with a sim, she enters the simulation to be with him."

Namisa laughs. "I'd enter a simulation right about now if it meant I could find a decent man."

Ali would enter a simulation if Natalie were there—even a facsimile of her. Ever since Natalie died, Ali's real life has felt like a simulation anyway. She wanders around like a robot controlled by an ambivalent gamer, completing meaningless tasks and thinking *Why?* and putting food in her mouth and thinking *Why?* and staring at screens and thinking *Why?* and falling asleep and dream-thinking *Why?*

"The movie is supposed to be a *huge* romance block-buster," says Victoria. "Produced and distributed by Para-mount. Like *Titanic* or *The Notebook* but with sims. The lead actress is Cara Bisset. Ever heard of her?"

Ali and Namisa shake their heads.

"Exactly. This is her breakout role, and the studio says she needs help with her 'public image.'" Victoria rotates her laptop so Ali and Namisa can see the screen, then clicks through a series of grainy camera-phone photos of two women passionately kissing. In one close-up, both their tongues are visible. "They requested you have lunch with her tomorrow, Ali."

Ali's headache needles the back of her skull. "Of course they did. If you get the gay publicist to tell the gay actress she can't be out, it doesn't look homophobic!" Just last week, Ali sent ▮▮▮▮▮▮ and ▮▮▮▮▮▮▮ to a PDA-filled dinner at Spago, where the paparazzi were always waiting like vultures, to fend off rumors about ▮▮▮▮▮▮ and a gay porn star.

Death by a thousand beard cuts.

Back at her desk, Ali takes more useless Advil and conducts internet research on Cara. She's so unknown she doesn't have a Wikipedia page yet, but through a few interviews Cara did for *Refrain*, the indie movie she was in before *Real Love*, Ali learns Cara grew up in the Valley with a single mom who worked for a cleaning service that specialized in celebrity homes. Her mom couldn't always afford day care, so sometimes Cara would accompany her, running from room to room, admiring the sheer amount of space and the glamorous decor and the awards lining the walls. When Nicole Kidman was home, she'd run lines with Cara, saying the same sentence seven different ways with a different emotion or emphasis each time, and that was when Cara decided she wanted to be an actress, too.

Cara's first job was as Teen Number Three in a Hot Pockets commercial. Then she landed the role of a dead girl on *Law & Order: SVU*. Her big break came at age eighteen, when she played the daughter of a judge and a lawyer on a family sitcom called *Overruled* that ran for five seasons. *Refrain* came a year later, in which she played the daughter of an addiction-prone musician.

And now she's about to be catapulted to fame in what critics are calling "the most romantic movie of the year."

After work, Ali has a doctor's appointment for her head-aches. The one she woke up with has gotten progres-sively worse throughout the day, like a Chia Pet of pain. What started at the bottom of her head spread to the right side, then the left, until it wrapped around her entire skull like an extremely tight headband. It's now pulsing like a techno beat in a club, vibrating through her whole body. Ali has found that coming up with similes to describe the head-ache helps distract her from the pain.

Tonight, though, the similes don't work—all she can think about is her headache. The fluorescent lights in the office seem laser-targeted directly at her pupils, so she squints until her eyes are barely open while Dr. Chernov, a Russian woman in her fifties with zero bedside manner, stands next to her, reading her chart. Ali started seeing her because she had the best online reviews for female primary care physicians within a five-mile radius, although after Ali's first appointment, she had to question why. She's been mean-ing to find a new doctor for ages, but after Natalie died, items on the "should-do" list moved to a "never-going-to-happen" list.

Usually Ali goes to a walk-in clinic in Hollywood because they're able to see her at the last minute when she's panicking about a skin rash or heart palpitations or a new lump in her breast or ovary pain or heavy spotting between periods or vertigo or persistent stomach cramps or numbness in her hands or ringing in her right ear or what she was convinced was a tumor in her throat but turned out to be a condition pejoratively named "globus hystericus," the sensation of having a lump in your throat when there's nothing there. The printout the nurse gave her mentioned it was especially common among young women.

"You've been having...headaches?" Dr. Chernov says, like a headache is the most trivial problem a person could have.

Ali nods and swears she feels her inflamed brain knocking against the sides of her skull. "Can-barely-get-through-the-day headaches."

Ali can't tell whether Dr. Chernov rolls her eyes or simply glances at the ceiling. "Where are they? What do they feel like?"

"They start in the base of my head. Here." Ali touches the spot. "At first it feels like concentrated tightness and pressure. Then it spreads to one side of my head, usually the right, or both if it's a really bad one, and it usually throbs. I have one like that right now. Sometimes they get so intense I can't tolerate any light or sound or smells and I feel like I'm going to puke. Nothing from the drugstore helps."

The doctor makes a note. "What you're describing isn't a headache; it's a migraine."

"I thought those involved auras like flashing lights and stuff."

"Not for everyone."

"I didn't know I was having *migraines*. That sounds serious." Ali hopes Dr. Chernov will finally take pity on her.

"Not really. Plenty of women have them." *Pathetic, weak women*, she might as well have said. "You previously said you grind your teeth at night. That can cause migraines." The doctor squints at Ali, sizing her up. "You're clenching your jaw right now. And your shoulders are scrunched up near your ears. And you're making fists with your hands. It's like you're braced for impact. What are you so afraid of?"

Ali tries to release her jaw, but it recoils right back to its clenched position like a rubber band. A lightning bolt of pain surges through her head. "Dying. People I love dying."

Dr. Chernov shoots a short, judgmental blast of air out of her nose. "No use being afraid of that. It's going to happen. Better to accept it."

Ali scoffs. "Oh sure, that's easy. I'll just accept it."

The doctor glances at the clock. "You seem like you have a lot of stress, which can contribute to both bruxism and migraines. Was anything particularly stressful happening around the time the migraines started?"

Ali bites her lower lip, trying to stop it from wobbling. "My partner died," she croaks.

"What?" Dr. Chernov says. "Speak up."

Ali forces herself to meet the doctor's eyes, even though hers are brimming with tears. Her headache screams. "My partner died," she says, so loud it's almost a yell.

"Your…partner?"

Ali comes out to this doctor every time she comes in. How difficult is it to make a note in a chart? "Yes, my romantic partner. Of over a decade."

For the first time, Dr. Chernov's face softens. "Oh. I'm sorry for your loss."

Ali's teeth scrape against each other and she wills herself not to blink, keeping the tears at bay.

The doctor clears her throat. "I can write you a prescription for a stronger pain reliever—"

"Do you have anything I can take right now?" Ali asks. "The pain is really bad."

Dr. Chernov opens her mouth—Ali guesses to say no—but seems to remember Ali's dead partner and instead opens a cabinet and rifles through it. She hands Ali a condom-size packet labeled "500 mg naproxen."

Ali tears open the packet and regards the tablet, which is much bigger than an Advil. "I have a hard time swallowing pills this big."

Dr. Chernov throws up her hands. "That's all I have. Take it or leave it. And you'll have to see a neurologist for actual migraine meds."

"Great," Ali says. "How long does it take to get an appointment with one of them?"

"Usually about three to four months," says Dr. Chernov. "Minimum."

After her appointment, Ali goes to the bathroom and closes herself in a stall, working up her nerve to take the pill. She places it on her tongue and takes a swig of water. She repeatedly tosses her head back, waiting for the right feeling to strike before she swallows, but it doesn't. A trickle of water sneaks down her throat and she panics, heart racing, gulping before she meant to, and she's afraid she'll feel the pill scraping at her throat, but thankfully she only feels the water. She breathes out.

All she wants to do now is go home and lie down in her quiet, pitch-black bedroom, but if she cancels dinner, Dana will pester her with repeated Are you sure you're okay? texts. Better to go over and continue pretending she's holding up fine. At an earlier point in their friendship, Ali would have cried and told Dana everything on her mind, but that point was years ago, before Dana had kids. Now Dana is constantly distracted, saying "uh-huh" too often to actually be listening as she watches three-year-old Arlo tear around the room, or grimacing as she breastfeeds six-month-old Cayenne. Even if they go out without the kids, Dana still stares at her cell phone like it's a pot on the brink of boiling, waiting for a call from her husband, José, or the babysitter about a calamity—and there almost always is one. A fever or a fall or a meltdown. Ali and Natalie were firmly in the anti-kid camp forever, and Dana was, too, until her mother died from a sudden heart attack. Her grief made her sentimental for a more traditional kind of life, so she used the money from her mother's life insurance to buy some sperm from the most desirable donor at the bank (because José is trans) and a three-bedroom bungalow in Pasadena.

As Ali arrives, she steels herself for the squalor inside. The house was nice enough when they bought it, but now it's covered in what Ali calls kid grime. Surfaces sticky with indeterminate substances, Goldfish cracker crumbs embedded in the carpet, and tonight's pièce de résistance: a toilet-training potty filled with yellow pee next to the couch. Ali tries not to think about the dirt and germs hiding in Dana's vegan three-bean chili as they sit around the sticky dining table, eating.

"How's work, Al?" Dana asks, her eyes on Arlo as he pushes a toy truck around his bowl. She's wearing tan overalls stained with red splotches, one strap undone as she nurses Cayenne—it seems like the baby is never *not* nursing.

"Have you heard of this movie called *Real Love*?" Ali says.

"Uh-huh," Dana says in the vacant way that means she's not listening.

"Really, you have?" Ali says.

Dana shakes her head. "Sorry, I just remembered all the cloth diapers are dirty. I can't forget to do a load after this." She taps her temple with her pointer finger. "Self, remember to do laundry. I swear, new-mom brain is worse than five-bong-rips brain. I'm sorry, Ali. What were you saying?"

"Well," Ali plows on despite how pointless it is, "this movie *Real Love* is coming out in a few months, and—"

"Fuck!" Dana yells, spiking Ali's headache. No, not her headache—her *migraine*. Dana winces and pulls Cayenne away from her huge, swollen breast. "Sorry, she bit my nipple, and they're already so tender from being infected. No one tells you how absolutely excruciating breastfeeding is."

"Do you want the nipple ointment, babe?" José asks, looking up from his phone.

Dana narrows her eyes at him. "Not *while* I'm feeding her, babe. Anyway, go on, Ali."

Ali waves a hand in the air. "It's not important, really."

"Of course it is," Dana says. "Go on."

"Well, the star is this up-and-coming actress, and—"

Arlo drives his toy truck into his glass of soy milk and it spills dramatically across the table.

"Whoopsie, whoopsie, whoopsie," Arlo says.

José springs up to get a towel, and Cayenne scream-cries at the commotion. With each scream, Ali's migraine pulses in tandem, like it and Cayenne are communicating.

"Great." Dana widens her eyes. "Literally crying over spilled milk." She gets up and paces back and forth, trying to get the baby to stop crying. José mops up the mess and Arlo keeps saying "whoopsie" over and over, obsessively.

"It's okay, bud," José says to Arlo. "I'm cleaning it up. No need to freak out. Sorry," he says to Ali. "He gets like this lately whenever the smallest thing goes wrong. Like he can't let it go."

Ali regrets her choice not to cancel. "It's okay. I should be getting home anyway, and you guys clearly have your hands full."

"No, you can't go yet!" Dana yells over the crying. "We've barely gotten a chance to talk." She holds out Cayenne to José. "Can you take her so I can talk to Ali for a few minutes?"

José takes Cayenne and Dana leads Ali out to the front porch, which is covered in pots of half-dead herbs. She sighs dramatically. "Oh, I feel terrible. I invited you over to try and make your day better, and it's been a complete shit show."

"Honestly, I do feel a little better." Ali realizes the naproxen must be helping, because she hasn't thought about the pain in her head for a whole minute. "I don't know how you do this. I would go insane."

Dana gestures to herself: her unwashed hair in a chaotic bun, her dark-circled under-eyes, her stained overalls. "I *am* going insane, isn't that obvious?" She laughs maniacally until it turns into crying. "And now I'm crying like a selfish twat on the anniversary of Natalie's death."

Ali rubs Dana's arm. "It's okay. I'm not the only person going through stuff."

Dana wipes at her eyes. "Next time I'll make José watch the kids and we can go somewhere. Really talk, you know?"

"Okay," Ali says, though she knows it won't really make a difference.

They hug, both reluctant to let go and face the reality waiting for them.

Ali ends her day the way she started it: in bed with Glen, crying. She wishes Natalie were here to massage her head like she used to every night while listening to Ali talk about her day. If Natalie were here now, Ali would tell her about the squirrel that ate an entire avocado while perched on the fence outside her bedroom window, the Canter's pastrami sandwich that helped her not hate her life at least while she was eating it, how meaningless her job is, how the last line from the Alice Munro story she reread between meetings about the old woman with Alzheimer's who forgets her husband absolutely destroyed her, how depressing it was seeing what Dana's been reduced to.

The only way Ali has been able to fall asleep for the past year is by watching *Frasier* DVDs on her laptop—she has a box set of every season. She usually watches one episode, then turns the screen brightness all the way down and simply listens to another, and then sometime during the third one, when she's gotten enough distance from the real world, she'll doze off. There are eleven seasons, and when she's finished them all, she starts back at episode one and repeats the process. The show is as comforting to her as a bowl of velvety macaroni and cheese eaten underneath a warm, weighted blanket, and it keeps her thoughts from looping around the usual anxiety running track.

What if a wildfire starts late at night and Glen and I die in a raging blaze?

Are the circling helicopters searching for a serial killer who's been breaking into the apartments of single women and killing them by peeling off their skin and wearing it as a flesh suit?

What if the big earthquake finally hits and the ceiling fan above the bed falls right on me but doesn't kill me, and miraculously I can reach my phone to dial 911, but all the cell towers are down and I die a slow, agonizing death from internal bleeding?

And so on and so on and so on...

Instead she watches *Frasier* overcome insignificant problems, like competing with Niles to become "Corkmaster" of their wine club or choosing between two equally attractive women. Tonight, Frasier becomes a local hero after he assaults a rude customer at Cafe Nervosa. It's also the episode where Daphne gets a punk song stuck in her head called "Flesh is Burning," and the entire episode, she and Martin shuffle around the apartment singing, "Flesh is burning, na na na na na na." This bit always makes Ali laugh uncontrollably, and for a fleeting moment she forgets Natalie is dead, and that she herself will die, and all the possibilities of how. Then she remembers how she and Natalie would randomly text each other Flesh is burning, na na na na na na, guaranteed to make the receiver crack up during a client meeting or while sitting in traffic.

Don't go down the grief rabbit hole, she tells herself.

In Ali's mind, anxiety is a rubberized running track you visit at predictable times, looping around and around. Grief, however, is a dark, endlessly meandering tunnel you can fall into anytime you're not looking.

4

The next morning, Ali spends two hours calling every female neurologist who accepts her insurance in Los Angeles, and Dr. Chernov was right—they all have wait times of three to six months. Ali worries her head might literally explode by then, but she makes an appointment for February fifteenth—over five months from now—with a neurologist named Rebecca Joyce, who mentions in the "About" section of her website that she can empathize with her patients since she's a migraine sufferer, too. In her picture, she has a remarkably kind smile.

At lunchtime, Ali sits in the succulent-lined, geometric-tiled back patio of an insufferably trendy restaurant in West Hollywood, fruitlessly fanning herself with a menu while she waits for Cara Bisset, who is twenty minutes late. Ali, as usual, was ten minutes early. The space between two white canvas umbrellas creates a triangle of sunlight that scorches Ali's forearm—the high today will be ninety-one. She regrets forgetting her lightweight linen overshirt as she rubs SPF 100 onto the spot on her arm. The two young women sitting next to her have used the word *retard* three times so far: "OMG your boyfriend is such a retard"; "This salad is so good it's retarded"; "You don't know how to parallel park, you retard?"

As Ali fantasizes about lecturing the young women about their word choice, Cara saunters in, unhurried. What strikes Ali first is Cara's outfit: She's wearing a threadbare white tank top, the kind that comes in a Hanes six-pack, and underneath it a visible gray sports bra with the trademark Calvin Klein band around the rib cage. On her bottom half, she sports black Adidas track pants with the white stripes down the sides and, bizarrely, a pair of sleek brown leather loafers. Cara raises a hand to her eyes to shield her vision from the blinding sun, revealing a robust patch of underarm hair, and she scans the crowd for Ali, who reluctantly waves.

Cara slides into the chair across from Ali and tips her chin upward. "What's up," she says, drawing out the *u* with vocal fry. She has short, bleach-blonde hair with an inch of greasy brown roots at her scalp, drowsy lichen-colored eyes, a pronounced cupid's bow at the top of full, albeit noticeably chapped, lips, and a jawline so defined it could be an entry in the dictionary. On her chin is an expansive red pimple; it looks to Ali like the kind that never pops no matter how much you squeeze it. Despite the pimple and chapped lips and greasy hair and mismatched outfit, Cara is objectively one of the most attractive people Ali has ever seen. There's also something strangely familiar about her, which makes Ali wonder if she's seen her in something in the past—a commercial or a guest spot on a TV show—or maybe even met her before.

Ali extends her hand across the table. "Hi, Cara. I'm Ali."

As Cara shakes Ali's hand, she gives her a bemused,

knowing look that makes Ali ask, "We haven't met before, right?"

"I don't think so, but I have this weird feeling…"

"Me too! Maybe we've just seen each other around. We probably frequent a lot of the same spots. Like…Akbar?"

"I hate their 'no Madonna' policy, but I love their cheap drinks. Tiki Ti?"

"Ooh, gimme a Ray's Mistake. Casita del Campo?"

"My roommate does drag there! Plus the enchiladas aren't bad. Plus—"

"The stained glass!" they both say at the same time, then laugh.

"That must be why we look familiar to each other," says Ali.

"Yeah, must be." Again, Cara gives her a funny, penetrating look. "Anyway, sorry I'm late. I totally overslept." A pillow crease cutting diagonally through her cheek seems to confirm this.

"You're just waking up?"

"Yeah, my friend's band had a gig and they didn't go on till midnight. Then I met up with this girl I'm kind of seeing and we got in a major fight that lasted hours, and then we had to make up for hours." She pauses, giving Ali a suggestive eye roll. "So I didn't go to bed until after the sun rose."

"Ah, youth," says Ali. "How old are you?"

"Twenty-five," says Cara.

Before Cara can ask how old Ali is, Ali says, "Twenty-five and on the brink of superstardom, huh?"

Cara makes a pouty face. "It doesn't really feel like that yet."

"You should cherish this time when no one knows who you are. In a few months, you won't be able to walk down the street without being ambushed."

Cara smiles goofily. "That sounds sick."

"Trust me, it will not be sick," Ali says as the waitress approaches to take their order. Ali decided in the thirty minutes she spent waiting that she was getting the Cobb salad, mainly because it's relatively easy and fast to eat. Ali could probably win the Guinness World Record for slowest eater, since she's paranoid about choking and chews her food to a fine paste while taking frequent sips of water to help her swallow. A bready sandwich or a dry chicken breast could take her a full hour to get through, so during client lunches, she sticks to salads, soups, and saucy pastas. After glancing at the menu for two seconds, Cara orders the burger, then tells the waitress her tattoo of cartoon-esque clouds on the inside of her wrist is "dope."

"May I?" Cara places her thumb and pointer finger on the waitress's wrist and pulls it closer.

The waitress doesn't protest.

Cara rubs her thumb across the tattoo. "They remind me of the clouds from *Super Mario Bros.*"

The waitress's mouth falls open. "No way, that was totally my inspiration for them! No one ever notices."

"I'm *very* observant." Cara slowly roves her eyes up the waitress's body and holds eye contact.

The waitress giggles, her cheeks reddening.

Jesus Christ, Ali thinks, grinding her teeth. This is going to be a much harder job than she thought. Underneath the annoyance, there's another squirmy feeling, one she can't quite pinpoint.

"Excuse me, miss," says a man sitting nearby to the waitress. "I'm still waiting for my fries."

"I'll be back," the waitress whispers to Cara, and Cara squeezes her wrist before letting go and watching her walk away.

Ali clears her throat, trying to commandeer a sliver of Cara's attention. "See, *that's* the kind of thing you won't be able to do anymore once everyone knows who you are."

"What?" Cara says innocently.

"Flirt with women, make out with women in public, et cetera."

"Why not?"

Ali leans back in her chair and crosses her legs. "What did the studio tell you about this lunch?"

"They said you're going to help me with my 'public image.'" Around "public image" she makes air quotes.

"You don't know what that's code for?"

Cara shakes her head.

"It means you're starring in a highly anticipated movie about a man and a woman falling in love, and viewers have to believe the two of you could actually *be* in love for the movie to do well."

Cara guffaws. "Are you saying I have to pretend to be straight?"

"You don't *have* to. Let's just say it's highly recommended."

"But being gay is, like, my whole personality." Cara vaguely gestures to herself. "There's no off switch."

Again, Ali curses the difficulty of this upcoming assignment. "That's what I'm here for. I'll help you find...not the off switch, per se, but the input button for a different mode. You can still have your private, personal life, but you'll also have your public persona."

Cara shakes her head violently. "No way. I'm not going to lie about who I am. Didn't the studio tell me *you're* gay? Don't you think this is all, like, morally sketchy?"

Ali remembers how disgusted she was that first time backstage at the movie premiere, how sure she was that she'd never participate in such a thing. It feels both very far away and like yesterday. She feels bad to be the one telling Cara Santa Claus isn't real and wishes she could spare her, but alas, this is the terrible reality. Ali takes a drink of water and fans herself with the menu before giving her standard answer: "If it was up to me, no one would have to hide their sexuality. But my job is to help my clients achieve the most success possible, and being out doesn't help that. Let me ask you a question. Where do you see yourself in five years?"

Cara smiles seductively at the waitress as she hurries by with an order. "Standing at the Oscars podium, accepting my golden statue."

"What about ten years?"

"Standing at the Oscars podium, accepting my *second* golden statue. But this time for directing."

"I hate to tell you this, I really do, but that level of success just won't be possible if people know you're gay. I hope we'll get there someday, but today is not that day."

Cara dips her fingers into her water glass and fishes out a piece of ice, then sucks it into her mouth and crunches it loudly, open-mouthed. "Come on, it's 2005. Didn't the California State Assembly pass the same-sex marriage bill this week? And hello, *The L Word* exists! Ooh, what do you think is gonna happen in season three? Will Bette and Tina stay together?"

Ali gives Cara a dead stare. "Who gives a shit about Bette and Tina?"

"That's the correct answer." Cara gives Ali a high five.

Ali laughs. "I'm here for Dana and Alice. I really hope they don't break up."

"Same. Hey, any chance you can introduce me to Sarah Shahi, the chick who plays Carmen? God, she's hot."

Ali's heart stings, and she wonders if it's acid reflux or

something else. "No!" Ali sticks her pointer finger in Cara's face. "We're here for the exact opposite of that. And we've gotten off track." She takes a deep breath and puts on a serious face. "Despite *The L Word* and the same-sex marriage bill Schwarzenegger's never going to sign, we are not in a coming-out place right now. Trust me, I wish we were. How about I give you the phone numbers of a few of my other clients? People the public believes are straight who are 'married' with 'babies' and have an entire room in their mansion for all their awards. Maybe you'll believe them."

In a cab back to work, Ali asks the driver to turn off Santa Monica Boulevard before they pass the dive bar where Ali met Natalie twelve years ago, but he can't merge into the right lane in time, and when they drive by it, Ali is forced to remember all the details of that night.

The bar hosts a weekly comedy night that Ali used to attend religiously in her early twenties. A male comic had just made a nonjoke about "fake rape—you know, the kind where the woman secretly likes it," and above the laughter, a woman with purple hair and a pierced nose yelled out from the crowd, "Fake rape doesn't exist," to which the comic responded, "Any guys in the audience want to put that to the test?" The woman stormed out, and Ali felt compelled by a magnetic force to follow her.

Outside, the woman faced away from the door, lighting a cigarette. The back of her jean jacket had the word "VULVA" printed in all caps in a Gothic-looking font.

"Are you okay?" Ali asked.

"Yeah." The woman turned toward Ali and exhaled a stream of smoke. "I just can't stand that shit. It's not even a joke. It's just misogyny, you know?"

"I know," said Ali, who at that point in her life had never said the word *misogyny* out loud. "I'm glad you said something. I wanted to, too, but I just freeze in situations like that."

The woman flicked ash from her cigarette. "Fight, flight, or freeze. I pretty much always choose fight."

Ali tried to think of a way to keep the conversation going. "I like your jacket."

"Oh yeah?" the woman said suggestively, like Ali had said she liked vulva.

Heat pricked Ali's cheeks. At twenty-three years old, she had never had a boyfriend or an orgasm given to her by a man, but she still considered herself straight. Until this moment, being a lesbian hadn't occurred to her as an option, mostly because a woman had never flirted with her before. Especially not a woman who looked like Natalie, with her deep brown doe eyes, long, elegant nose, and full, shapely lips. Underneath her jacket, she was wearing a white T-shirt tucked into black, high-waisted jeans that showed off her curves and red high-top Converse sneakers. It was an alluring mix of femininity and punk energy. Ali also liked that the woman was so outspoken—since this was a trait Ali lacked, she found it especially attractive.

Before Ali could come up with a response, the woman said, "You want to get a drink? Somewhere other than here?"

They talked until the bar closed, about how they were both assistants (Natalie for a TV showrunner, Ali for a publicist) and all the inane, inappropriate tasks involved with their jobs: Ali had to fill out adoption papers for her boss and frequently clipped her toenails. Natalie had to pick the red gummy bears out of packages because it was the only color her boss liked and procure him weed. One night, Natalie's boss had dragged her to a strip club, where a dancer did a bizarrely artful and sad routine to Whitney Houston's "I Will Always Love You." Afterward, still completely naked, she sprayed down the mirror she had been rubbing against to clean it. "Someone really did have to unbreak my heart after that," Natalie said. "I still think about it all the time." Natalie talked about growing up in Albuquerque, the quintessential image of tan adobe against clear blue sky, the smell of green chiles roasting in the fall, and how locals called New Mexico the Land of Entrapment because transplants to the state tended to stay due to the low cost of living and natives of the state tended not to leave due to lack of economic opportunity. Natalie's whole family was still there. When Ali told Natalie her mom had passed away, instead of the standard "I'm sorry," Natalie said, "That's fucking terrible" with such an incredible amount of empathy, Ali teared up. They also talked about how they both loved sitcoms (Ali's favorite was, of course, *Frasier*; Natalie's was *The Nanny*), LA's taco trucks (Natalie's favorite was Mariscos Jalisco; Ali's was La Estrella), and Julia Roberts, and how they hated karaoke, Tom Cruise, and the show *Family Feud*. They did have a spirited debate about sports—Ali had no interest and hated the loud sounds that emanated from the TV, but Natalie was obsessed with the Women's Basketball Association and the US women's national soccer team.

It kills Ali to think about having these get-to-know-you conversations all over again. Natalie was the first and only person Ali ever fell in love with, and it was a kind of love she hadn't thought was possible. She knows it sounds sappy and untrue, but she was honestly overjoyed, every day, to be with Natalie. She's convinced no one will ever be more right for her—she might find someone who ticks a few boxes, but Natalie ticked them all. No one could find that more than once in a lifetime.

* * *

"How was the meeting with Cara, then?" asks Namisa when Ali gets back to the office.

"I have a feeling she's going to decline my services," says Ali. "Which is a relief, because she would be impossible to keep on a leash."

Namisa looks up from rapid-fire typing, intrigued. "How so?"

"She told me being gay is her 'whole personality.' It seemed accurate. One of the first things she said to me was about sleeping with some woman the night before, then she spent half the lunch flirting with the waitress."

Namisa cocks an eyebrow. "Maybe you're just jealous she wasn't flirting with *you*."

Ali gives Namisa a dead stare. "*Please.* Firstly, I'm still a grieving widow, you jerk, and secondly, it was a *business* lunch, and thirdly, she's so not my type, and fourthly, she's ten years younger than me—"

Namisa cuts her off. "Methinks the lesbian doth protest too much."

5

"I just feel like if you're a man, and you write a story about a woman having rape fantasies, it needs to be really clear *why* the woman is having rape fantasies," says a female classmate in the short-story workshop Ali attends once a week after work. "Otherwise it reads like a man fantasizing about a woman fantasizing about rape, and that's pretty fucked up." The first story they're workshopping this evening was written by Gerald, a balding IT director in his forties who stinks of cigarettes and offers to give Ali a ride home every week, and every week Ali says no thank you, she'll wait for her cab.

Ali had the same feelings about Gerald's story as the classmate who just spoke, but she never would have voiced them in such a blunt way—in her feedback letter to Gerald, she simply recommended he use more interiority and more flashbacks to explain the rape fantasies. Last week Andrew, a white man who works for an organic farm yet drives a BMW, turned in a story about a young Black boy trying to decide whether to join a gang. In her feedback letter to Andrew, instead of telling him outright the story was racist as hell, Ali suggested Andrew consider making the young boy white, to avoid certain stereotypes.

At least Andrew's story had a few evocative metaphors and specific descriptions, as opposed to Gerald's, which is full of generalizations and nonsensical, useless similes—in one scene, he describes a sunset that looks "like red and yellow paint spilled across a blue tarp." Ali is rather disappointed with the entire workshop's writing quality. It's supposed to be an advanced class, and each of them had to submit a writing sample to get in, but Ali can't imagine Gerald's sample was any better than his rape-fantasy story. In all likelihood, they let in whoever applied, glad to take their money.

When Ali tries to regard her work as objectively as possible, she puts herself near the middle on the talent scale, a few clicks toward the better end. Her writing could be more lyrical and more exacting on a sentence level, but her characters feel like real people to her, and she strives to make her descriptions as specific as possible. She majored in creative writing in college and since then has taken so many writing workshops she's lost count. Occasionally she'll send a story to a few literary magazines and wait nine months to get a form rejection. Five years ago, she applied to MFA programs, and when she didn't get into any, she stopped writing for years, convinced she was a hack. But eventually life felt too meaningless, and she returned to writing her "stupid little stories," as she calls them.

She doesn't know why she feels driven to do it. She's often wondered what it must be like to not feel compelled to perfectly describe a cloud, a sunset, the ocean. To eavesdrop on people in a café and not fill in the blanks of their lives with your own imagination. To do your job for nine hours a day, five days a week (if you're lucky), and not feel aggrieved that it's taking time and energy away from your true calling.

But if writing *is* her true calling, shouldn't she have experienced some sort of success or recognition already? Is there a definitive point at which she should give up? Age forty? Her hundredth rejection from a literary magazine? A second round of rebuffs from MFA programs?

Ali hears her name and tunes back into reality: It's her turn to be workshopped, which she equally dreads and looks forward to. Her story is about a man in his eighties whose wife of sixty-odd years dies after having a stroke. In an attempt to keep his despair at bay, he establishes a routine of eating lunch on the same bench in the same park every day, and he notices a young woman who eats her lunch on a bench nearby every day, too. Eventually they befriend each other, and the man discovers the young woman is also acquainted with loss, since her mother died when she was a teenager. The story ends with the man arriving for lunch one day excited to talk to the young woman—the first time he's looked forward to anything since his wife died—but she doesn't show. They never exchanged phone numbers, so he has no way of contacting her. The young woman never comes for lunch again.

The story allows Ali to write about her grief obliquely, the way you can't look directly at a solar eclipse but can view a projection of it through a pinhole in a piece of cardboard. Ali's mother did die when she was a teenager, but that grief and her grief about Natalie are planets in different solar systems. Ali had a strained relationship with her mother, and the main emotions Ali felt when she died were guilt and relief. When Natalie died, it was pure, unadulterated, vise-gripping misery.

Ali's classmates say they like the flashbacks to when the old man was happy with his wife, but the ending is "way too bleak"—couldn't it wrap up with the old man and the young woman eating lunch together, sharing a nice moment instead? Ali squeezes her lips together, thinking these people must be living charmed lives compared to her, and thinking, for the millionth time, that she should give up this stupid hobby that is also the only thing making her life feel not stupid.

While Ali is supervising a photo shoot for a client, a call from a Los Angeles number comes through her BlackBerry. When she answers, she's greeted by a familiar croaky voice saying, "What's uuuuup."

Ali ducks around a corner and closes herself in a bathroom to dampen Shakira's "Hips Don't Lie" blasting from the speakers and the photographer yelling "YEEESSSS, I am LIVING for you!"

"Cara? I didn't think I was going to hear from you again."

"Well, I talked to those people you told me to. They all said the same thing you did." She sighs exaggeratedly. "Plus, they all said you're, like, the best of the best."

Ali decides that if she's in the bathroom, she might as well pee, and does her best to angle her stream toward the front of the toilet bowl, where it won't make as much noise. "Please, a monkey with a cell phone could do what I do."

Cara laughs. "Funny you say that. I was watching this nature show last night, and a mama monkey was teaching her kids how to floss. My mom didn't even teach me to floss! It was hard enough getting me to brush my teeth."

"I bet you were a wild kid."

"You could say I had authority issues."

Ali flushes without thinking and hopes Cara doesn't hear. "God, you're going to be one of my problem clients, aren't you? Calling me at two a.m. to bail you out of jail?"

"Oh yeah? What did I do to get myself there?"

"Hmm…It wouldn't be as banal as a DUI. Maybe public nudity? Or yelling, 'Fuck the police' at a cop?"

"Probably yelling, 'Fuck the police' at a cop *while* nude, more likely."

While washing her hands, Ali glances at herself in the mirror, and instead of wearing her usual scowl, she's genuinely smiling. "Oh God. *Have* you ever been arrested?"

"I might have shoplifted from Saks when I was a teenager."

"How very Winona of you."

"Thank you; I'll take that compliment. Winona's pretty hot for an older lady."

Ali cringes, imagines wrinkles rapidly wilting her face. "An *older* lady? I'm pretty sure she's in her early thirties."

"How old are you?"

"Around the same age as Winona." Ali turns away from the mirror.

"Well, you look younger than that."

Ali smiles. "I thought you said you never lie."

"I don't. Speaking of, there's one thing I wanna say before we make it official. I guess I'm chill with not saying anything about my sexuality, but I never want to actively lie and say I'm with a dude or whatever. Okay?"

This is what many of Ali's clients said at the beginning. But once they got a taste of fame and saw how it could be magnified by "dating" the right person, most changed their mind. "Okay."

"You promise?"

"I promise," says Ali.

Ali has been dodging calls from her dad, Gene, for weeks when he calls yet again while she's in a cab home after accompanying a client to a taping of *Jimmy Kimmel Live!* She's between the early and middle stages of a migraine—a rare one that started on the left side of her head and ice-picked its way up to her temple—which makes her want to talk to her dad even less than usual. But if she picks up, at least she won't have to keep making forced conversation with her driver, an older woman who has talked about her grandchildren to such an extent that Ali knows Miles recently turned one and was allowed to eat cake for the first time, and after his first bite he smiled bigger than he'd ever smiled before, and Jamilah is four, and she can already write her name *and* count to twenty, and she loves her little brother so much, and so on. At one point, the driver almost veered off the road to pass Ali photos of the two kids, forcing Ali to say they were "so cute" in a strained voice while gripping the handle on the roof.

"Sorry, my dad is calling," Ali says to the driver.

"You go ahead and answer, my dear! Family first!"

"Hi, Dad," Ali says, trying to sound happy to hear from him. He only started calling frequently a few months ago, when he retired from his job as a detective and seemed to remember he had a daughter.

"Oh, hi, honey," he says, his gravelly voice sounding particularly frail. "Glad I finally caught you. Especially today."

Ali isn't sure what he means. She pulls her phone away from her ear to check the date. Oh. It's September fifteenth, the day her mom died eighteen years ago, when Ali was seventeen. Ali had always thought her mom would die by suicide, but it ended up being cancer—so quotidian Ali had never seen it coming, which almost made it worse. Bizarrely, Ali's mom's death anniversary is only a few days after Natalie's. But her dad didn't remember to call her then. She presses two fingers into her throbbing left temple. "I know,

I'm sorry I haven't been able to talk. Things have been nuts at work. You remember those days, right?"

"Oh, sure. Sometimes I think I shouldn't have retired yet, particularly on days like today. The hours just kind of stretch on, you know?"

Ali wishes her dad had remarried so he would have someone other than her to talk to, to lean on. "You should call Uncle Bill," says Ali. "I bet he and Sue would be happy to have you over for a meal."

"Oh, they're real busy these days with the grandkids and all. I don't want to bother them, you know?" Grandkids again. Ali can't get away from them. "I worry I'm bothering you, too." He chuckles grimly.

Ali's teeth scrape together. "You're not bothering me, Dad." Almost every passing car has a dog in it: a white Chihuahua with an overbite sitting in its owner's lap as she drives, a pouf of orange Pomeranian curled up in a dog bed in the passenger seat, an Australian cattle dog in the back with its head out the window. If Ali didn't have to take cabs everywhere, Glen could ride with her more often. When Natalie drove, Ali and Glen would sit in the back right seat, so Glen could lie in the middle with his head on Ali's thighs on longer drives, or sit in her lap with his paws propped against the door and his head out the window on shorter ones, Ali firmly grasping his harness. If Ali ever works up her nerve to get back behind the wheel, she'll probably let Glen sit in a dog bed in the passenger seat—with a dog seat belt, of course, which she never sees anyone using. What do they think would happen to their best friend if they got in an accident? Or do other people never think this way? Must be nice. "Have you thought about getting a dog?" she asks her dad. "They keep you nice and busy, and they're great company."

"You know I'm not much of a pet person," he says. Like

children, pets require caretaking, which was never Ali's dad's forte. "Anyway, what's been going on with you? Which stars have you been schmoozing with?"

Ali knows her dad thinks her job is dumb as hell, but that's one area where she can't blame him. "Just the usual ones. I went to a screening last night for this new TV show called *Bones* with David Boreanaz. It's a crime procedural—you should watch it and tell me what they got wrong." This is Ali's dad's favorite activity, other than work: critiquing movies and TV shows like *CSI* and *Law & Order* for their detective-related mistakes. Watching those shows with his running commentary was probably the most quality time he and Ali spent together when she was young. She would memorize his corrections and parrot them back during future episodes: "You can't just wander onto a crime scene"; "Police departments don't actually have cutting-edge technology"; "Criminal profiling isn't typically used to solve murder cases." He'd be proud of her, and Ali would hope it would translate to him being around more, or asking her more questions, or helping take care of her mom, but it never did.

"I'm trying to watch less TV," her dad says. "If you're not careful, you can find yourself sitting in front of the boob tube all day."

"Well, I'm almost home, so I should get off the phone," Ali says, despite the crawling traffic on Sunset. After she hangs up, her driver gives her an accusatory look in the rearview mirror—like she's the kind of person who doesn't, in fact, put family first.

After your story is workshopped, professors say you should take a few days to let the feedback you've gotten marinate. Ali pictures the typed pages of her story submerged in a

Pyrex full of soy sauce, citrus, and garlic, the text blurring and white paper turning brown, until eventually the pages soften and become complete mush. Only at this stage is it safe to approach the story again. Ali rereads all the feedback letters and reconfirms that everyone (including the professor) thinks she should make the ending "more uplifting." She feels in her gut this is wrong, but she doesn't know what else to do. So she continues the story from the point where the young woman doesn't show up one day. The old man goes home and catastrophizes about what could have happened to her, but the next day she's there again—she just had a cold. It reminds the old man that the worst-case scenario doesn't always happen. They exchange numbers, so they can let each other know if they ever won't make it. The old man doesn't have a cell phone, so he puts the woman's number in his address book, and he realizes he can't remember the last time he wrote in it. The story ends with him regarding this new entry, and the reader is meant to infer he feels hope for the first time since the death of his wife. Ali finds herself feeling jealous of this fictional old man that *she* created.

She submits the story to ten literary journals, knowing she has a greater chance of winning the lottery, and when she's about to shut her laptop, the news announces a wildfire in the Angeles National Forest above Pasadena. It's unlikely the fire would make it to Silver Lake overnight, but she still packs a go bag with a few N95s, bottles of water, a flashlight, a change of clothes, a box of granola bars, a gallon Ziploc baggie of Glen's dry food, her well-worn copy of *Who Do You Think You Are?* by Alice Munro, a sandwich baggie full of pills and Band-Aids and a travel-size toothbrush and toothpaste, her laptop, her wallet, the gold chain necklace that holds her and Natalie's domestic-partnership bands as pendants, Natalie's Emmy for Outstanding Writing for a

Drama Series, and a map marked with evacuation routes. (Dana has promised to pick up Ali on any evacuation from the city.) Then she sets an alarm for every three hours to check the fire's progress. She starts watching *Frasier* only to discover it's a rare one where someone dies (Frasier's great-aunt), so she skips to the next one. The episode begins with Niles telling Frasier about a museum's new exhibit of "fourteenth-century Japanese netsuke figurines," and how he wants to get tickets "before the line forms." Ali chuckles, feeling her anxiety tick down like the hot engine of a car after it's been turned off.

When she wakes up to the first alarm, she's been having a dream that all of Glen's legs became paralyzed because she wasn't brushing his teeth often enough, so she puts a daily reminder in her calendar to brush his teeth at bedtime, then checks the news, which says the fire has spread into northern Pasadena. At the second alarm, she was on a beautiful beach, trying to take the perfect picture, when suddenly the waves got bigger and bigger, crashing closer and closer to her, until her whole body was submerged and a crest the height of a ten-story building loomed over her. She wakes up right before the wave breaks. The fire is now at the 134, the highway that cuts through Pasadena. In the morning, it hasn't spread any farther, but the sky is gray and the air quality is 156, which means she'll need to wear a pinchy N95 mask and keep Glen's walk short, which he never understands is for his benefit.

6

Ali spends the next day at work putting out multiple metaphorical fires: One of her clients is the face of the new hot-pink Motorola Razr, but last night was photographed at an event with a Sidekick bejeweled to match her outfit. It was the talk of the carpet, and first thing this morning, Motorola called threatening a breach of contract. Ali was able to placate the company by asking her client to change their MySpace profile picture to a mirror selfie taken with the pink Motorola Razr. Then a new client of Ali's calls her crying because every time she goes for a run, the paparazzi stalk her. Ali tells her one of the publicist golden rules: If you wear the same outfit every time you leave the house, they'll stop following you—there's no point in paparazzi getting identical photos. Then a gossip magazine writer calls and says he has a source on the record that one of Ali's clients is cheating on his girlfriend. Ali convinces the writer not to publish it, with a promise that she'll give him the imminent breakup story, plus the first story about whomever her client ends up dating next. It's all so stupid it makes Ali want to light herself on literal fire, just so she can put out a real one.

At the end of her day, Ali finally gets to do something enjoyable, even though it's technically still work. She goes over to Cara's place to see her in her own environment, because before Ali can come up with a PR strategy for Cara, she has to learn who Cara is, other than a giant lesbian. Cara says she'll make them dinner, which surprises Ali—Cara didn't seem like the cooking type.

Cara lives in Los Feliz, in one of those writers' bungalow complexes that are lined up in two rows, each house split in half to make it apartment size. When Ali approaches Cara's half bungalow, she does a double take thinking Cate Blanchett is in the window, then realizes it's a cardboard cutout and laughs. Cara answers the door holding a wooden spoon, wearing camo cargo pants and a cropped gray tank top with no bra underneath, revealing ridiculously perky breasts and a hint of nipple. Cara doesn't seem like the type to exercise, but her bare stomach is tight and toned—not with a six-pack, but with two svelte lines, one on either side of her belly button, that disappear into her cargo pants. Ali's stomach does a small somersault as she forces her eyes away from Cara's breasts and stomach and tries not to compare her thirty-five-year-old body to this twenty-five-year-old movie star's.

Cara's "What's uuup" is more drawn out than usual, her eyes floaty and slightly bloodshot, leading Ali to think Cara might be high.

"Welcome to the bachelor pad." Cara Vanna Whites an arm as Ali steps through the door, and Ali thinks that's the perfect way to describe it. On the wall facing her, three capital metal letters spell out ASS above a television, and multiple video game consoles are strewn in front of it on the carpet. Facing the television are two beat-up leather recliners, like in Joey and Chandler's apartment in *Friends*, and to the right is a vintage Ms. Pac-Man arcade game festooned in multicolored Christmas lights, clearly the apartment's pièce de résistance.

"That's how I get chicks to come home with me," says Cara when she sees Ali notice it. Ali wonders who the most recent woman Cara took home was—maybe the waitress from their lunch—and a prickly feeling crawls down Ali's back. Against her will, like her brain has been briefly hijacked, Ali imagines being the waitress: Cara's eyes fixed on her, Cara pushing her against a wall, Cara's chapped lips biting hers. But Ali guesses Cara's attention likely fades after the conquest, and it doesn't matter anyway, because Cara is her client and therefore Ali can't be interested—she wouldn't be interested even if Cara *weren't* her client. Ali must simply be reacting to Cara's charismatic star quality, which will have everyone swooning for her in *Real Love*.

"Ms. Pac-Man is also the genesis of my roommate's drag name," Cara goes on, "but he spells it p-a-c-k, in reference to fudge packing, cause he's so damn witty." She pivots toward the hallway and raises her voice. "Skylar, come say hi to my *publicist*." She enunciates the word in an ironic way and flips her hand upward. "Saying that still makes me feel fancy."

Skipping down the hallway comes a drag queen who looks just like Ms. Pac-Man: bright yellow makeup as the skin tone, a bald head with a red bow on it, a yellow dress in the shape of a circle, and red galoshes. "Hiyeeeee," he says, extending his hand, fingers down, like he might expect Ali to kiss it. Instead, Ali angles her hand upward into his and gives it a loose shake. "I'm Skylar, or I guess right now I'm Ms. Pack-Man. I'm performing at a drag show tonight."

"You look great," says Ali. "How did she become your inspiration?"

"Well, Cara and I share a love of vintage video games, as you can probably tell, and Ms. Pac-Man is my favorite. I love how she's kind of androgynous, both in the way she looks, with the bald head and circular body, and her name, with both *Ms.* and *man* in there. As a gay man who does drag, it just seemed to fit."

"That's really smart," says Ali. "Where's the show tonight?"

"The Black Cat. I'm trying to get a few more gigs. I'm trying to be an actor, too, like everyone in this town. Maybe once Miss Thing over here has taken over the world, she can get me a role."

Cara gestures around her. "Right now I'm in the same boat as you, honey. No one knows who I am."

"Trust me, that's about to change," says Ali. "Which is why I'm here."

"If you ever take on clients pro bono, call me," says Skylar, winking at Ali.

Ali laughs. "I will. How do you two know each other?"

"Best friends since junior high," says Cara. "Two peas in a weird-ass pod."

"I can give you *allll* the tea," says Skylar.

"Tea?" Ali asks.

"Skylar forgets not everyone speaks drag," says Cara.

"It means hot gossip," says Skylar.

"Well, Cara told me being gay was her whole personality, but that can't be true," says Ali. "What words would you use to describe her?"

Skylar tilts his head as he deliberates. "Ambitious, brave, bawdy, loyal, silly, open…"

"Ambitious was the first word that came to your mind?"

Skylar sticks his lips out and looks at Cara. "This bitch has been practicing her Oscars acceptance speech in the shower since before I knew her. She's for sure gonna win one someday."

Ali turns to Cara. "And *that's* why we have to be so careful about the image of you we present to the world. If you want an Oscar, you have to play the game."

"Yeah, yeah," Cara says. "Do you want a tour of the rest of the mansion?"

She leads Ali around the corner into the kitchen, where she adds spaghetti to a pot of boiling water and informs Ali they'll be having *cacio e pepe* with a fennel and arugula salad. Then they go back through the living room and turn into a short hallway that leads to a retro pink-and-green-tiled bathroom on the right and two bedrooms on the left. Cara's bedroom is decidedly more adult than the rest of the place, which Ali finds reassuring. Cara has a midcentury modern bed frame, above which hangs a framed photo of two women standing inside a convertible, and when Ali looks closer, she recognizes the baby-blue Thunderbird from *Thelma & Louise*. Geena Davis stands with both hands just below her hips and her chin tilted upward, her eyes hidden behind aviators. Susan Sarandon has one cowboy-booted foot up on the hood, and she's looking directly at the camera like *Just fucking try me*. Ali almost misses that she's casually holding a gun.

Cara gestures at the photo. "My absolute favorite movie of all time."

"Wouldn't you have been pretty young when it came out?"

"I was eleven," says Cara. "But it was my mom's favorite movie, and she didn't believe in sheltering me. A lot of stuff went over my head until I got older, and then I loved it even more. My mom and I probably watch it a few times a year."

"Wow. Not your typical mom's favorite movie."

"Yeah, but she wasn't your typical mom. She was, like, the most misandrist straight woman ever—but she wouldn't have known what misandrist meant, or misogynist, or patriarchy, or any of those other buzzwords associated with feminism. She probably wouldn't have called herself a feminist because she thought that was for 'hoity-toity' women who went to college and had white-collar jobs. She even joked she might have made me gay 'cause of all the shit she constantly talked about men." Cara pauses to affect a deep, husky voice: "'To men you're either a virgin or a whore'; 'If men got knocked up you could get an abortion at an ATM'; 'If you reject a man you have to worry he'll kill you'; 'Without men there'd be no wars'; 'Men only want kids so someone will be forced to listen to them'; et cetera."

"All true," says Ali. "She sounds amazing."

"She's my favorite person on this planet." Cara beams.

"That's so sweet. I can't imagine having felt that way about my mom."

"Really? Why not?"

Ali waves her hand in the air. "It's a long story, and tonight's about getting to know *you*." To help change the subject, Ali scans the titles on Cara's bookshelf. Again, much more adult and highbrow than Ali would have guessed. "Do you own *everything* by James Baldwin and Patricia Highsmith?"

"Hell yeah. My literary king and queen." She kisses her pointer and middle finger, then drags her fingers along their books' spines.

"You like a lot of old things," says Ali. "Classics."

"What can I say? I'm an old soul."

"That was *not* my first impression of you."

"I've got layers, mama." Cara twirls around, as if to

unwind a piece of fabric wrapped around her body. "I'll keep surprising you."

"Hi, Ali," says Nikki, a receptionist at the Hollywood walk-in clinic, a few days later. "What's bothering you today?" She says it like a barista greeting one of her regulars.

Ali knows Nikki must think she's a crazy person because she comes in every few weeks with a different ailment, but if Nikki knew how often Ali wants to come and doesn't, she'd be impressed she only sees Ali once every few weeks. "I think I'm having an allergic reaction," says Ali. "I ate a container of sliced pineapple about an hour ago, and now my throat and tongue feel really itchy and swollen, and the swelling is making it hard for me to breathe. It's been ages since I've had pineapple, and I read adults can develop food allergies out of nowhere."

Nikki rapidly types into her computer as Ali talks. "All righty, you know the drill. Take a seat and somebody will see you soon."

Ali chooses a leather chair near the front, as far as possible from the middle-aged man with a cough so wet it sounds like he's gargling pudding. Across from her, a young woman fills out paperwork while her boyfriend strokes a palm up and down her thigh. Every now and then he whispers in her ear and she giggles. Ali didn't come to the clinic as often when Natalie was alive, partly because Natalie would be able to convince her that her maladies weren't serious and partly because said maladies began to multiply after Natalie's death. There was one time when they came here for Natalie—after she almost cut her pointer finger off while chopping an onion with a brand-new (and thus razor-sharp) knife. Ali remembers Natalie kept making the nurse laugh while she was getting her stitches, but she can't remember what Natalie was saying. The young woman across from Alice looks completely healthy and unbothered, so Ali can't guess what she's here for. Maybe she and her boyfriend have been having so much sex she got a UTI. Or pregnant. Or maybe she has a heart condition or a rare autoimmune disease Ali has never heard of. Or maybe she's a hypochondriac like some would say Ali is. At that moment the young woman looks up, right into Ali's eyes, like she knows Ali's been guessing why she's here.

Ali quickly looks down and grabs a newspaper off the coffee table, scraping her teeth across her itchy tongue as she scans the headlines. The fire in the Angeles National Forest is still only 30 percent contained. Hurricane Katrina's death toll has topped one thousand, and another hurricane—Rita—is set to hit Texas in a few days. Five US troops died in Iraq following insurgent attacks. Bird flu has killed at least sixty-five people in Asia, and a public health expert at WHO warns it could kill up to 150 million people worldwide. Three Palestinian gunmen were killed following an Israeli military incursion into the West Bank.

The door to the exam rooms swings open, and a man Ali recognizes, with a wide nose and a pronounced widow's peak, calls her name. Shit. She was hoping for a new nurse, or at least one she hasn't seen recently, so she wouldn't get the usual lecture about anxiety and psychiatry.

"I saw you about a month ago, didn't I?" he asks over his shoulder as he leads her to an exam room.

"Maybe?"

"What did I see you for?"

It was for heart palpitations. "I can't remember," Ali says.

In the exam room, the man flips open Ali's chart. "It was for heart palpitations. Are you still having them?"

Ali tries to take a deep breath through her swollen throat but is only able to take a shallow, unsatisfying one. "They come and go. It's been a few days since I've had them, I think."

"If they come and go, it's likely not a problem with your actual heart. Stress and anxiety can cause symptoms like heart palpitations. In fact, stress and anxiety can cause a lot of the symptoms we've seen you for." He flips through page after page of her chart. "We've given you a psychiatry referral, haven't we?"

"I think so," Ali says, even though she knows so.

"Have you seen a psychiatrist? Or at least scheduled anything?"

"A lot of them don't take insurance," Ali says. "And the ones who do aren't accepting new patients, or have months-long lead times." She doesn't mention she only called about five psychiatrists to come to this determination. In truth, Ali doesn't want to see a psychiatrist because (a) she knows they'll make her talk about Natalie, and Ali can't stand to scratch that wound open because if she does, she might bleed to death; and (b) she knows the psychiatrist will tell her she should be on an SSRI for her anxiety, but Ali tried those in college and every single pill gave her terrible side effects. She felt like the earth's gravity had gotten stronger, like it was physically pulling her toward the ground. She remembers crawling to the kitchen to refill her water glass, not even able to make herself a piece of toast. There's no point in taking a pill that makes her feel worse than she already does. She tries to take another deep breath and fails. "Could you take a look at my throat? I'm having trouble breathing."

He closes her chart and snaps on a pair of blue rubber gloves. "Keep trying with the psychiatrists. There must be someone who takes insurance and is available. I'll have Nikki give you a printout when you leave." He takes a tongue depressor out of a glass jar. "Open."

Ali sticks out her tongue and the nurse presses it down, using a flashlight to inspect her throat. She pictures the dangling, U-shaped piece of flesh at the back waggling around as she "ahhh"s in different intonations.

"I can see some slight irritation on your tongue and the roof of your mouth, but that's very normal after eating pineapple. It's because enzymes in the fruit dissolve the protective coating of mucus in your mouth." He removes the tongue depressor and tosses it in the trash.

"So I'm not having an allergic reaction?"

"Not at all. You can eat yogurt or drink milk to relieve the sensation, or if it's really bothering you, take an antihistamine like Benadryl. It'll have a nice side effect of calming you down, too." He smiles at her knowingly. "Keep calling those psychiatrists, okay?"

7

It takes two weeks for Ali to come up with the strategy for Cara's liftoff to fame. When she finally finishes, she asks Cara to come to the office so Ali can talk her through it.

"OMG, a *binder.*" Cara inspects it as she sprawls on the white couch in front of the floor-to-ceiling windows that showcase the Hollywood Hills. "How retro! These days everything is a PowerPoint presentation." Today she's wearing a vintage Lakers jersey with her usual Calvin Klein sports bra underneath and a pair of jeans so distressed they're a few threads away from being cutoffs. Cara's unshaven, light-brown leg hair peeks through the holes, and it looks strangely soft and seductive. Ali has the bizarre urge to stroke it, but stops herself.

Ali, who's wearing a white oxford tank top over navy-blue linen pants, sits down on the other side of the couch, where she won't be tempted to touch Cara, and gestures to her jersey. "I thought you loved retro things."

"I do." Cara hugs the binder. "I love this binder so much I'm going to take it home and put it in my file cabinet."

Ali rolls her eyes. "Are you ready to move on to what's *in* the binder?"

Cara sits up very straight and folds her hands over her knees, pantomiming a professional. "Yes ma'am."

Ali turns to the binder's first page, labeled "Current Perception." "The good thing is, basically no one knows who you are, so we get to build the public's perception of you from scratch. That's way better than fighting against any preconceived notions. So who are you?" Ali flips the page. "You're the next Natalie Portman—wildly talented, smart, politically engaged—crossed with the raunchy, candid, feminist humor of Margaret Cho. No filter, no bs—"

Cara cuts her off. "Except the bullshit that I'm not gay."

Ali grits her teeth. "As we agreed, you don't have to lie about it. You just don't talk about it, or talk around it. In the media training section, I have examples of questions you're likely to be asked and responses you can give." Ali flips to the page and affects a deep male reporter voice. "You're starring in the most romantic movie of the year, so what's going on with *your* love life?"

Cara reads her part in an overly affected way, like she's a star on a midday soap opera. "Not much! Did you know filming and promoting a movie takes up almost all of your time?"

Ali changes her voice to that of a ditzy entertainment reporter on the red carpet. "What was it like working with Davi Silva, one of the world's sexiest men? You two had great chemistry on-screen, but was there any chemistry *off* camera?"

"Davi is such a great actor and I learned so much working with him. Use real-life details here." Cara goes back to her normal voice and laughs. "Should I talk about how we've both slept with the same woman? Or how he was also dating a man when he slept with that woman?" Ali knows Davi's publicist and therefore knows Davi is bisexual and favors open relationships—he basically oozes sexuality. But there's also this very wholesome side of him that loves Disneyland because he was on *The Mickey Mouse Club* as a teen, and his childhood in Canada gave him a love of knitting. For Christmas every year, he gifts his team home-made scarves, sweaters, and pot holders.

Ali cuts her eyes at Cara. "Use any real-life details *not* related to your or Davi's sexuality."

"Ohhhh, got it." Cara taps her forehead like she'll have to try hard to remember that tip.

Ali doesn't bother to put on a fun voice to ask the last question. "What do you look for in a man?"

Cara answers in a robotic monotone. "Wouldn't you rather know what I look for in a role, or a costar, or a director?"

"You get the idea," Ali says. "You can always pivot away from the question to make it about the work, or use gender-neutral language when talking about anything dating related, or fall back on the tried-and-true 'happily single and focusing on my career' answer."

Cara tosses the binder onto the coffee table and leans back, crossing her arms. "I probably could have figured all that out."

"Like I said, a monkey with a cell phone could do my job."

"Sorry, I didn't mean to—that was bitchy. I'm just in kind of a bad mood today."

"Why?"

"On my way here, I found out I didn't get this role I really wanted. Have you heard of the new movie Ilene Chaiken is producing, about ACT UP activists in the late eighties and early nineties?"

"Yeah, it's supposed to be huge."

"During the audition—I was reading for a lead role, this badass dyke who was a photographer for the movement—I kept getting in my head about how I'm supposed to be hiding my sexuality and how if I got the part I wouldn't be able to speak authentically about anything at all, so I was reading the words but my head was totally preoccupied, and of course the audition ended up being complete trash."

"Oh, Cara, I'm so sorry." Ali means it both in a general way, how you'd say "I'm sorry" to anyone who's just gotten bad news, and as a direct apology for Ali telling Cara she can't be out. Ali knows technically it's the studio and the industry at large forcing Cara into the closet, but as the enforcer, Ali feels responsible. It's always the hardest with new stars breaking onto the scene, who were happily out and then have to go back, but for some reason, it feels harder with Cara than it has with anyone else. Ali can see just how much it pains Cara to not be herself, and despite their not having spent much time together, Ali feels a strange sort of kinship with her—an easiness, like they're old friends—that makes Ali care more about Cara's feelings than her other clients'.

Cara covers her face with her hands, and Ali notices a word the size of an ant written on the outside of her pointer finger. She squints to make it out. "Bang"? When she puts two and two together, a laugh escapes her.

Cara peeks at Ali through her fingers. "Are you laughing at me, you dick?"

"Sorry, I just noticed the tattoo on your finger."

Cara pulls her hands from her face and regards the tattoo. "I got it when I was sixteen. I thought I was so clever."

Ali shrugs. "It made me laugh."

"Pretty ironic, isn't it? I'm crying about having to be closeted and you notice my super gay tattoo. Seems like the universe telling us it'll never work."

Ali knocks her shoulder against Cara's. "We'll get some tattoo concealer."

A sunbeam slashes through the window to land on Cara's impossibly accentuated cheekbones, which cut a shadowy diagonal line from the top of her ear to the corner of her lips, where she has an endearing mole that disappears into her dimple when she smiles. Cara says something but Ali misses it, lost in the mole and the cheekbones. "What?"

"If your job required you, personally, to be closeted, would you still do it?" Cara asks.

"It's not really the same as your situation. Acting is your passion; PR is definitely not mine. I do it for the paycheck and the predictability."

"It must suck ass doing a job you don't care about every day. What *is* your passion?"

Ali waves a hand in the air. "Nothing that'll get you a consistent paycheck."

"Most people can't make a living doing what they're passionate about. Fucking capitalism. So what is it?"

Ali doesn't know why it feels so embarrassing to admit. The only person in her life who knows she writes is Dana, and Ali has never let even her read a story. It just feels too intimate—like letting someone read your diary while they concurrently watch you poop. "We've gotten really off track. Let's get back to the purpose of this meeting." She picks up the binder and flips to where they left off.

"Is it…making your own soap? Beatboxing? Painting portraits of cats? Slam poetry? Bonsai?"

Ali laughs. "You got me: It's bonsai."

"That would be dope! I'd totally make you teach me."

"Anyway, if you turn to page three—"

"Nope." Cara takes the binder out of Ali's hands and tosses it across the room. "We're never going to look at that again unless you tell me what your *passion* is." She says "passion" in a French accent, *pa-syon*, while clutching her heart.

It's been a long time since someone was interested in Ali or her life. Most people in LA—even people Ali calls friends—are content to monologue at you for hours and never ask you a single question about yourself. And Dana, who used to ask Ali questions, stopped after her kids grabbed all her attention. It actually feels nice for someone to want to know things about her, but Ali is suspicious. She crosses her arms. "Why do you care?"

"I'm naturally a very curious person. And you just seem more interesting than most of the bozos who live here. All most people want to talk about is their exercise routine, their diet, or their dating life. You seem like you have more going on in there." Cara swirls a pointer finger at Ali's head.

"I do?"

Cara laughs and smacks the couch. "Come on, tell me what you love to do! Please please please please please tellllll meeeeeee."

Ali smiles. "You'll never give up, will you?"

Cara shakes her head like a toddler on a sugar high.

"All right, all right." Ali takes a breath. "I like to write stupid little short stories, okay?"

Cara tilts her head. "Why are they stupid?"

"Because. They don't accomplish anything. It's like I'm a kid, playing pretend."

Cara makes a *pshhh* noise. "You know what else is pretty stupid? Acting. Pretending to be *pretend* people. That's, like, doubly stupid." She widens her eyes and pushes out her lips to emphasize her point.

Ali laughs, and Cara laughs back, until they're both giggling in that infectious way where it's hard to stop. Cara snorts and Ali laughs harder.

"What's so funny?" Namisa stands in Ali's doorway, looking smug.

Ali wipes at her eyes, feeling weirdly upset that Namisa has interrupted their moment. "Nothing."

Cara looks up at Namisa and blinks rapidly. "Hel-*lo*." Namisa looks like Thandie Newton's twin, and today she's wearing a white crew-neck T-shirt tucked into a high-waisted black leather miniskirt with black Doc Martens.

Ali quickly interrupts with, "Cara, this is my coworker, Namisa. She's straight."

"Ohhh." Namisa points at Cara. "This is the one you're trying to keep in the closet, eh?"

Cara makes fists and squeezes them. "*And* she's British?"

Namisa gives her a wink before walking away. "Best of luck to you, Ali."

Another part of the strategy for Cara's liftoff to fame includes brand endorsements and charitable causes, which involve working with Cara's agent, Vivian Chang, and her manager, Will Goldsmith. Since agents are the money people, they set up the brand deals, but publicists need to weigh in on whether they cast the clients in a good light. Publicists handle charitable causes, but the agent needs to weigh in if donations are involved. And since managers are basically the CEOs of their clients' careers, they need to weigh in on everything.

Ali, Cara, Vivian, and Will are in a small windowless conference room at Ali's office, since it's the most central, eating salads and small-talking about what they did last night before getting down to business.

"I watched *Survivor*, obviously," says Vivian, a superfan who sends in an audition tape every year but has yet to be picked. Ali knows her through several mutual clients and thinks she's one of the few competent agents in this town. Most are white and blond, have familiar-sounding last names like Hearst or Boeing, drive Bugattis or Ferraris, and believe in conspiracy theories. Vivian, on the other hand, has first-generation Chinese immigrant parents who both worked multiple jobs, and Vivian worked her way up from the mail room after graduating from law school and deciding being a lawyer wasn't what she wanted to do.

"I just sold a few things on eBay," says Will, who's in his late forties and wearing a trucker hat that says "Extra Cheese," multiple layered and popped-collared polos, Ed Hardy jeans, and Heelys he literally skated in on. According to Cara, his main hobby is buying up all the limited-edition fashions he can and then selling them on eBay. Apparently he also sells a lot of swag his celebrity clients don't want, which strikes Ali as suspect. Other facts that strike Ali as suspect: (1) He doesn't manage any of Ali's other clients; (2) he's self-employed, instead of working for a management company; and (3) before he was a manager, he was a Realtor, and before that, he worked in human resources—professions not exactly known for requiring great skill. He's been Cara's manager since she was twelve, after he saw her in a commercial for Hot Pockets, and Ali gets the sense that Cara has outgrown him but doesn't know how to fire him.

Everyone looks to Ali to report what she did last night. In reality, she started a new short story, about a drug that's guaranteed to prevent cancer but that has to be taken every fifteen minutes. The main character's biggest fear is dying of cancer, so she thinks guaranteed prevention is worth the constant interruption to her life, but other characters would rather risk getting cancer than disrupt their daily life so severely. Ali hasn't figured out how she's going to end the story yet. "I had to catch up on emails," lies Ali. "Boring, I know."

"I finally went to go see *The 40-Year-Old Virgin* with some friends," says Cara.

The word "friends" pricks the top of Ali's scalp. She wonders if any of them were more than friends, and tries to shake the image of Cara's hand creeping up a thigh, her buttery popcorn lips caressing the delicate skin of a neck.

"'Oh, Kelly Clarkson!'" yells Will, quoting one of Steve Carell's lines from the movie, snapping Ali out of her reverie. "God, that movie is so good. I've seen it three times already."

"It was okay," all the women say at the same time, then laugh.

Vivian reaches up and tightens the hair band on her power pony, even though it already looks very tight. "Shall we get down to business and talk brand endorsements?" Vivian's Caesar salad (no croutons, no dressing, so basically a bowl of plain romaine lettuce) sits untouched in front of her. "Ever since press for *Real Love* has amped up," Vivian goes on, "I've been getting more and more endorsement requests, but none of them have seemed like quite the right fit for Cara's personality. So I want to be proactive and think about brands *we* could reach out to."

"You're sure doing this doesn't make me a total sellout?" says Cara.

"No way," says Vivian. "Everyone does it. It's a great way to seriously supplement your income, plus it's more publicity for you. A win-win."

"I like the sound of supplementing my income..." Cara still seems hesitant, though. She looks to Ali.

"I agree with Vivian," says Ali.

"Like, for real? You're not just saying that?" Cara's eyes probe Ali's, searching for the truth.

Vivian narrows her eyes at Cara and Ali in a look that says, *Why does Cara care about Ali's opinion more than mine?*

"For real," says Ali. "I can understand why it feels a little icky at first, but if we find a brand that really aligns with who you are, it could be great for your career."

"Okay." Cara nods decisively, finally on board, and takes a big bite of her Cobb salad.

Will pauses, picking tomatoes out of his caprese salad, which seems like a terrible choice if you don't like tomatoes, to loudly say, "I think it's a great idea, too."

"Let's start with the brands you genuinely love," says Vivian. "Think about what you wear, eat, drink, or otherwise use on a daily basis." She sucks the straw of her nearly empty venti chai. "Obviously, I'd endorse Starbucks." Everyone laughs.

"Well, I wake up and drink Café Bustelo, then I shower—I use Neutrogena face wash and, like, cheap-ass Suave shampoo and Dove soap. I wear Calvin Klein bras and underwear, a lot of American Apparel, and a lot of Cons."

Ali stops her, talking through a bite of Greek salad. "Ooh, Converse could be perfect. Alternative but classic at the same time."

"I was just thinking the same thing," says Vivian.

"Yeahmetoo!" Will rushes to add. A large piece of basil sticks between his front teeth.

"Calvin Klein could work as well," says Vivian, "but it's probably too big of a brand for you right now. Maybe I'll reach out to them a little further down the line, when you're more established as a legit star."

"Totally," says Ali.

"Absolutely. Yeah." Will contorts his face in effort, desperate to add value. "Maybe Neutrogena down the line, too."

"I actually don't think that's a great fit," says Ali. "I think Cara's a little too offbeat for them."

"Yeah, a little too raunchy," says Vivian.

"Yeah, you're right, you're right," says Will, trying to appear upbeat but clearly crestfallen.

"You know what else might work, though?" says Vivian. "American Apparel."

Will jumps in as Vivian says "Amer," rushing to complete the phrase at the same time so it will seem like he had the same idea. "Jinx!" he yells, but no one is fooled.

Ali could see how the feminist in Cara would hate being associated with the objectifying marketing, though. "What do you think, Cara?"

"I like their clothes, but I hate their ads. Just promise I wouldn't have to pose nude in knee-high socks while making a porno face," says Cara.

"Okay, we'll keep American Apparel as a maybe," says Vivian. "I'll reach out to Converse first, then Calvin Klein a few months after *Real Love* comes out if it skyrockets you to fame the way we're hoping. I think that's a good start. Shall we move on to charitable causes?"

Everyone assents.

"Like Vivian said before, let's start with charities you already support or think are doing good work," Ali says to Cara.

Cara grimaces. "You know what I'm gonna say."

Ali gives her a sympathetic frown. "All the gay ones?"

"Bingo." She throws her head into her hands. "God, I hate this."

"Yeah, it blows," says Will. He pushes his salad container away from him like he's finished, but he's only eaten the mozzarella.

"I actually think it's okay to have one gay one in the

mix," says Ali. "As long as it's not the first one we go public with."

"I agree," says Vivian.

"Oh, yeah. One. Just one is okay," says Will.

"Can it be the LA LGBT Center? I spent a lot of time there growing up," says Cara.

"Sure thing," says Ali. "Now let's think about a charity we could align with the release of *Real Love*. Your character is a gamer and a coder, so could we do something related to advancing the inclusion of women in tech?"

"How about the National Center for Women & Information Technology?" says Vivian.

"Perfect," says Ali.

Will picks up his silent BlackBerry and holds it to his ear before loudly saying hello. "Hey guys, I gotta take this," he whisper-yells to them before racing out of the room.

Ali gives Cara a direct-to-camera stare.

Cara laughs and holds up her hands. "I know, I know. It's just that he's been with me since the very beginning and stuck with me through some hard times. He's super loyal."

"Does he manage any of *your* clients?" Ali asks Vivian.

"Nope. Honestly, I think Cara might be his only client at this point."

"See?" Cara says. "If I fire him, he might go bankrupt or something."

"What's the last audition he got you?" says Ali. "Or even the last good idea he had?"

"Um…" Cara thinks. At least ten seconds go by.

"That's what I thought," says Ali.

8

One of Ali's least favorite parts of her job is meeting up with journalists for drinks, pretending they don't irk each other—publicists constantly bug journalists for positive coverage about their clients, and journalists mostly ignore said publicists, unless they want a comment about a recent scandal, which in turn makes the publicists ignore the journalists. Ali has a particularly intense love-hate relationship with Jason Kim, an extremely in-demand writer of celebrity cover stories for *Vanity Fair*, whom she's meeting tonight. Ali loves him because he's smart and funny and a great writer—his profiles always have an interesting angle and are full of intimacy and depth—but those attributes usually come from Jason pushing the subject to open up (Jason calls it "productive friction"), which publicists, of course, are wary of. As a gay man, he especially wants celebrities to be able to talk about their sexuality, and he rants at Ali about Hollywood keeping them in the closet. He acknowledges the problem is bigger than just publicists like her, but since he knows she's gay, too, he still prods her about it. So while Ali knows he'll write the best profile, it comes with a risk—he would never out someone outright, but he could allude to things that could add up for readers searching for clues.

"So after, like, our third interview, after I'd listened to him drone on endlessly about Kabbalah and the Atkins diet, I finally got him to open up about going to rehab," says Jason, sipping from the pink-and-white spiral straw in his Aperol spritz. They're still in the evening's small-talk portion, where Jason tells funny anecdotes about interviews he's done recently and complains about the state of journalism. "Then two weeks before the interview went to print, *Lainey Gossip* broke the rehab news. I swear, these blogs are going to put me out of a job."

"They're making our life hell, too." Ali waves at cigarette smoke wafting toward them from the back, which she worries will exacerbate the migraine that's been threatening for the last few hours. They're on yet another patio, surrounded by ivy-crawling brick. Above them, Edison bulbs are strung from the branches of a towering olive tree to the roof of the restaurant, which used to be a fire station. It's in a mostly residential section of northern Silver Lake surrounded by auto repair shops, and thus it's a rare quiet place people over thirty-five can patronize to have an actual conversation. Ali and Natalie used to come here often, and Natalie would usually get the vegetable enchiladas—the one menu item that hasn't changed over a year later. Ali turns the menu over. "I know it can be tense between publicists and journalists, but at least there's a modicum of mutual respect and ethics involved. These bloggers will kick a celebrity right in the nuts and there's nothing we can do about it."

"I know," says Jason. "They're so *cruel*, and not even in a clever way—half the time their insults barely make sense.

Did you see one of them has started calling Jennifer Aniston, who is unarguably gorgeous, 'MANiston'?"

"Ugh, what about 'ghetto tits' for Janet Jackson? Like, what does that even mean?"

"Or the 'gay midget dwarf' Tom Cruise? That's a total tautology."

"Tautology?" Ali is embarrassed she doesn't know what the word means.

"It means saying the same thing twice—midget and dwarf are synonyms, basically."

"Huh, I never knew there was a word for that. But that's why you're a writer and I'm just a dumbass publicist."

"No way, Ali. I've said it before and I'll say it again: You're much smarter and more self-aware than most people in the industry. Way more than you give yourself credit for."

"Nah."

Jason vehemently shakes his head. "Case in point?" He tilts his head toward the man at the table next to them, who, for the last several minutes, has been listing reasons he doesn't believe the moon landing really happened. "Anyway, tell me about this hot new starlet you want me to write a profile about."

"Her name is Cara Bisset, and she's in this movie called *Real Love*—"

"I've heard of it. Don't tell me." He cracks his knuckles, trying to remember, then snaps his fingers at her. "Sim love story?"

"Yup. It's Cara's breakout role, so no one has really heard of her before, but her star is going to rise *fast*. Think Natalie Portman—wildly talented, smart, politically engaged—crossed with the raunchy, candid, feminist humor of Margaret Cho."

"Is she like Margaret Cho in...other ways?" Jason purses his lips and blinks at Ali rapidly.

Ali sucks the straw of her nearly empty seltzer and lime, which she drank instead of alcohol for fear of the ever-looming migraine. "Let's not go down that road, Jason."

He drops his chin onto his fist in an exaggerated *Thinker* pose. "Let me guess. Asking about her romantic life is off-limits."

"Isn't that a little expected? Especially from a male journalist?"

He crosses his arms. "You're right. Let's not go down that road. I guess I just don't know what's supposed to incentivize me to write about her. Especially if no one even knows who she is right now."

"That's all about to change, though. After *Real Love* comes out and flies to the top of the box office, every journalist is going to be *desperate* for a piece of Cara. I'm telling you right now: She's going to be a huge star. Oscars, plural. You'll agree with me after you watch this screener." Ali slides a DVD case across the table. "I'd watch this ASAP. I wanted to give you first dibs on her profile, because I truly think you'd write the best one—"

Jason fans his face with his hand like he's hot. "Ah, resorting to flattery?"

Ali looks him in the eyes. "You know I mean it. But if you want to look a gift horse in the mouth, there are plenty of other journalists who'd jump at the chance to write the very first profile of a superstar."

He sighs exaggeratedly. "Fine. I'll try to watch the screener soon."

Ali clicks her tongue. "The sooner the better."

*   *   *

While Ali is at work, writing a press release about a launch party for a client's new fragrance, she gets a text from Cara:

Did you read the short story in The New Yorker this week?

Um, yes. Did YOU?

Yeah. Now that I know your big short story secret, I figured I should read a few.

Warmth suffuses Ali's chest as she imagines Cara reading the story because she wants to better understand Ali. So what did you think?

Cara responds with Randy Jackson's *American Idol* catchphrase: That's gonna be a no from me, dawg.

Lol I usually feel the same way about New Yorker stories. There's a deadness to them.

Cara's text comes through right after Ali's; they must have sent them at almost the same instant. Felt kind of like... dead.

The warmth in Ali's chest intensifies. Ha! You owe me a coke. If you want, I'll bring you a book or two of alive stories the next time I see you.

Tiiiiight.

"Ali! Can you come in here?" says Victoria as Ali walks by her office.

Ali reverses course and sticks her head in the door. "What's up?" Victoria is almost finished with a page from her most recent adult coloring book, called *Fuck This Shit*. Each page has a "funny" curse-laden phrase in the center, surrounded by mandala-esque geometric designs. The current page says, "Go fuck yourself with a cactus," and Victoria has colored it using myriad shades of green. A bowl of pastel-colored milk sits at her elbow, which means she must have had Froot Loops for breakfast.

"I just got off the phone with the *Real Love* people, and they had an interesting proposition for you."

Ali steps farther into Victoria's office and raises her eyebrows.

"How would you feel about going on Cara's world promotional tour? One month, thirteen cities, the usual deal."

Ali puts a hand on her hip. "To babysit her?"

"Also to stay in five-star hotels in amazing cities like Paris, Tokyo, and Berlin."

A carousel of images flits through Ali's head: a croissant and an espresso from a bustling sidewalk café with a striped red-white-and-blue awning; a tree powdered with cherry blossoms over a placid lake with a red torii gate near the shore; a cold beer in Ali's hand while she wanders the side streets of Kreuzberg, the smell of currywurst in the air. Ali's chest balloons in excitement before she remembers that the cities she's visited with Natalie will trigger painful memories, and the cities she hasn't visited with Natalie—now they'll never be able to. The balloon pops and shrivels. "It's not like you get to spend any actual *time* in the cities on a promo tour."

"I wouldn't know. What I *do* know is they're offering us a buttload of money for you to do this. Enough for you to get a *biiiig* bonus."

Ali narrows her eyes. "How big?"

"Like, a quarter of your salary."

"Whoa." Ali sinks down into a floral-printed chair across from Victoria's desk. "They must be really worried about Cara."

"One of them said it's like 'trying to keep a lid on a very gay volcano.'" Victoria laughs.

Ali shakes her head. "I feel like this could be setting me up for failure."

"Listen, you do your best, and we get paid either way."

Ali leans back and drums her fingers on her knee. "Who would handle my clients in my absence?"

"Namisa can take the A-listers, and we'll give the rest to Hailee and Ilana."

Ali scoffs. "Ilana? She can't even get a coffee order right."

"Maybe I could help out, then."

Ali tries to formulate a diplomatic response.

"Never mind. Your face just said that's a bad idea. But we'll figure something out! You should really think about this, Ali."

"I will," she says.

Over the weekend, Dana accompanies Ali and Glen on a walk in Elysian Park, which Natalie used to do most Saturdays. For months after Natalie died, Ali avoided going there, before she realized avoiding all the activities she used to do with Natalie resulted in her never leaving the house except for work or work events. Ali loves walking Glen in the park because she doesn't have to worry about drivers abruptly backing out of driveways or barely hitting the brakes at stop signs. Granted, coyotes populate the park, and gigantic off-leash dogs like huskies and mastiffs charge at Glen full speed, making Ali's hand dart to the pepper spray until the dog simply sniffs Glen's butt or lowers itself into a playful pose. But in general, Ali's anxiety is at least two levels lower than when she walks Glen on the street.

They're there about an hour before the sun sets, when it's cooler and less crowded. The temperatures have finally dropped slightly, from the high eighties to the low eighties, and the fire in the Angeles National Forest has been mostly contained, so the air is back to its usual semitoxic quality and smells not of burning trees but of tantalizing grilled meat from the barbecues below, where the beats of salsa music bump up against the repeated "Für Elise" jingle of an ice cream truck.

"It's *gorgeous* out," says Dana, which is what Angelenos say to each other at least once a day from October to June. (From July to September, they say, "It's *so hot* out.")

"*Gorgeous,*" agrees Ali. She raises her arms to let the breeze lick her pits and takes a deep breath, enjoying the menthol-y smell of the eucalyptus trees that tower over the trail, their peeling bark revealing watercolor-esque stripes of copper, sage, and periwinkle.

Glen seems to agree, too, bounding down the trail with his ears bouncing and his half-black, half-white mohawk waving in the wind.

"It's so nice to be away from the kids," says Dana. "Cayenne has acid reflux, and all she does is scream-cry. Even now, my ears are ringing. And Arlo *bit* me the other day because he didn't want to pick up his toys." She pulls back the sleeve of her shirt to reveal a jagged arch of red, crusty marks on her forearm.

"Jesus, Dana. Is that, like, normal behavior for a kid?"

"That's exactly what I googled after it happened, and apparently it is." She throws her hands in the air.

Glen darts off the path, sniffing voraciously until a buck-toothed gopher pops its head out of a hole in the ground. Glen stands statue still, his front paw pointed at the gopher and his tail vibrating, until he dives snout-first into the hole. He comes up empty, as always, and proceeds to frantically dig, dirt whipping behind him. There are so many gophers in Elysian Park, Ali probably spends half of every walk standing still while Glen hunts them, but she doesn't mind. It's a hell of a lot better than having a biting child.

"Anyway, tell me about your nonkid life," says Dana.

Ali tells her about Cara and *Real Love* and the promo-tour offer.

"Let me guess. You're telling yourself all the reasons you *shouldn't* go?"

"Listen, promo tours are like *Groundhog Day*—you watch your client give the same interview over and over, and it doesn't even matter that you're in a different city each time because you're only there for, like, twenty-four hours. Plus you know I don't love flying. Plus it seems like Cara is a real time bomb."

As Ali was talking, Dana's phone dinged with a text, and she pulled it out of her pocket to read it. "Fucking Christ on a motherfucking cracker!" She stops and looks up at the sky, releasing a noise between a sigh and a snarl, then looks back at her phone.

"What?" Ali dreads whatever kid disaster has struck this time.

Dana answers while rapidly typing. "Arlo bit the kid he's having a playdate with, and now the mom wants me to come pick him up. I'm going to call José." She brings the phone to her ear and mouths, "Sorry" before turning away.

Ali mouths "It's okay," even though this is probably the 437,894th conversation to be interrupted by Dana's kids. She feels like a jerk to be jealous of them, but she misses the days when she had Dana's uninterrupted attention, when the connection between them felt strong as duct tape. They've been friends since birth, because their moms were best friends, too—Ali's mom always called Dana's mom her "rock." In Ali's childhood photo books, there are pictures of her and Dana lying on hand-stitched quilts as googly-eyed infants, running naked through the spray of the hose in the backyard as toddlers, trick-or-treating in complementary costumes like Little Red Riding Hood and a wolf as elementary schoolers, beaming with their brand-new driver's licenses in high school. Like sisters.

The night Ali's mom died, Dana brought over homemade blueberry muffins (Ali's favorite), *The Muppet Movie* (their favorite since childhood), and a box full of 365 notecards, each with one memory of Ali's mom per day of the following year, like the time Ali's mom let them skip school and drove them to the water park, or the time she made the most disgusting chili ever (Ali's mom was a notoriously bad cook), or the time she caught them Yahoo! searching for penises on the family computer when the internet was brand new. Each year on the anniversary of Ali's mom's death, without fail, they would get together to eat blueberry muffins, watch *The Muppet Movie*, and share memories. The first year they didn't get together was right after Dana had Arlo, when she was barely sleeping or functioning. The next year, Arlo had a stomach flu, and the year after that he had a terrible ear infection. And then there was Cayenne. Ali knew she couldn't blame Dana's kids for needing their mom, but sometimes it did feel like Ali had lost not only her mother and her partner, but also her best friend.

"You're *always* working," Dana says into the phone, her voice slightly raised. José is a developer for Google and if he's awake, he's working, according to Dana, who is now essentially a stay-at-home mom who used to work at a gallery and who intermittently paints vaguely genital-esque abstracts that look like a cross between Georgia O'Keeffe and Jackson Pollock. *Dismembered testes caught in a lint trap* is how Ali unkindly describes Dana's work in her head.

"Thank you," Dana says in a very *un*thankful manner before turning back to Ali. "José is going to pick him up."

"Oh good," says Ali, and they start walking again.

Dana shakes her head, as if to clear out the cobwebs. "What were we talking about?"

"I think you were about to try to convince me to go on tour with Cara."

"Right!" She claps her hands. "Here are some reasons you *should* go. Your eyeballs will see new things and you'll interact with new people and yes, newness is scary, but it's also a chance to break out of a rut. I'd say you could use that, especially after this past year."

As they've walked, a steady stream of couples have passed by: a tired-looking man and woman with a newborn strapped to the woman's chest, two men and a Frenchie all in matching red bandannas, an extremely fit shirtless man and sports-bra'd woman running together. As each couple passes, Ali wonders which person from each couple will die first, and how. The woman with a newborn strikes Ali as a teacher—she'll die in a school shooting five years from now. One of the bandannaed men will die of a heart attack in his sixties. The extremely fit shirtless man will fatally crash his motorcycle in the next three months. "Being in a different country won't make me forget Natalie died, Dana. I'll just be in Paris or Tokyo, missing Natalie there instead of here."

"I know. But you might not miss her as much, because you'll be distracted and won't constantly be doing things you used to do with her." Dana gestures around them as if to say, *Case in point.*

The trail curves and downtown reveals itself to their right, the sun nestling between towering buildings and tinting the clouds a peachy pink. Admittedly, it's a view Ali has seen hundreds of times, but each time the view changes slightly: what's blooming or not blooming, the sky's color, the clouds' shapes. Tonight, spotlit in the foreground, is a cloud that looks like the Kool-Aid Man, one leg raised like he's about to kick through a wall and say, "Oh yeah!" In the ads, kids are in a boring situation, like math class, before the Kool-Aid Man busts in and shakes things up. Ali can't help but wonder if the cloud has conspired with Dana to reinforce the idea that Ali needs to break out of her routine. "I'll think about it."

A perk of birth control is that Ali only gets her period once every three months, but when it comes, it comes with a vengeance. It's also the biggest trigger for her migraines. During her last few periods, she was struck by ten-day migraines that rendered her barely functional. On the first day she takes an inactive pill, she feels a sense of impending doom, like she's rounding a corner in a haunted house.

When her period starts, it's as bad as she feared. The migraine is present in full force as soon as she opens her eyes, assaulting all her senses: She can barely tolerate light, sounds, tastes, or smells. She wishes she could become a sea cucumber, lazily swaying on the pitch-black, deadly quiet ocean floor. Instead, she closes all the blinds in her apartment and writhes around in bed and nibbles on saltines and swallows as much naproxen as is allowed and bemoans, for the millionth time, that she can't see a neurologist until February and crawls to the microwave to warm her heating pad before laying it over her eyes. Dana texts to ask if there's anything she can do, and Ali says other than replacing her head with a nondefective one, no. Near the middle of the ten-day abyss, she has to cancel a meeting with Cara, and since Ali never cancels meetings, she explains it's due to a decimating migraine.

Yo that SUCKS BALLS, Cara writes back. My mom used to get really bad ones so I know a few things that can help. What's ur address? I'll bring u some remedies.

Ali has had to cancel meetings with clients due to migraines before, but they always just write back, "Feel better!" Ali notes how Cara doesn't ask *if* there's anything she can do but simply says she's coming to help, which makes her offer hard to refuse. Still, Ali does: Thanks so much for offering, but you don't have to do that!

What are you using for relief rn?

Naproxen, a dark room, and feeling sorry for myself

Lol so u don't have a migraine head wrap, an essential oil stick, or anything herbal?

No, but I'll really be fine

Remember when I wouldn't give up until you told me your passion? I won't stop texting till you give me your address

Ali debates whether to give in.

Address plz

Address plz

Address plz

Ali laughs for the first time in days and sends her address. Normally she would never let a client she barely knows do a favor for her, but Cara was insistent, and Ali is desperate. An hour later, the doorbell rings, sending Glen into a barking fit that spikes Ali's migraine. Ali hoped Cara might just leave the stuff outside her door, but when she peeks through the blinds, Cara is standing there, waiting.

Ali looks down at her threadbare gray tank top with a tomato soup stain on it from last night. Her black sweatpants are covered in Glen's white fur, but she tells herself Cara isn't the type to care and cracks the door. Bright sunlight needles her eyes. She puts a hand over them and blinks rapidly, black splotches obscuring her vision. Glen sticks his snout into the door's crack and sniffs repeatedly, growling.

"Sorry," says Cara, who's mostly obscured by the splotches. "I don't know if this is super weird or not, but I know this bomb Thai massage that, like, *always* got rid of my mom's migraines. Would you wanna fuck with that?"

The black spots dissipate enough that Ali can see Cara. She's wearing a holey white T-shirt, loose knee-length cut-off jean shorts, and beat-up black Converse. Her hair looks cleaner and softer than usual. Ali is extremely tempted to take Cara up on her offer, but it doesn't seem appropriate, letting a client rub her body. "No, that's okay," Ali says, even though it feels like her brain and eyeballs are about to explode.

Cara must sense her hesitation. "You look like you're in a lot of pain, man. Let me help you out. Seriously." She takes a step forward like she's going to come inside whether Ali lets her or not, so Ali moves aside. Glen continues growling until Cara kneels down and lets him sniff her hand, then scratches under his chin and behind his ears.

"Wow, your place is Hilary SWANK," says Cara, taking in the floor-to-ceiling windows in the living room that over-look a row of palm trees Ali calls "her girls" and the framed Kandinsky *Open Green* print above a brown leather sectional sofa that sits on a geometric Bauhaus Moroccan rug. She turns to the kitchen and her jaw drops further at the Carrara marble countertops and blue hexagon backsplash tiles and shiny silver appliances. After Natalie died, Ali had to move out of their two-bedroom apartment and, in a fit of melancholy, got rid of all their existing furniture, replacing it with items she could previously never bring herself to spend money on. She put the furniture in an exorbitantly expensive one-bedroom apartment in the Silver Lake hills. Life, she saw now, was not only short but also unbelievably cruel, and she might as well spend a portion of the money she had been judiciously saving since she was a teenager to live in a solacing environment while she was still here.

"It's usually cleaner." Ali looks around, feeling self-conscious about the floors that haven't been vacuumed in a week and the crumbs on the counter.

"What are you talking about? It's fucking immaculate." Cara opens the freezer to put a slouchy object made of purple fabric inside. "This is a cold head wrap." She searches for a place where it will fit. "And this"—she gestures to the freezer's contents, which include towering stacks of labeled Pyrex containers and Tetris-esque grids of frozen meals and drawers crammed full of frozen fruit and vegetables—"is a hoarder's freezer."

Ali laughs, despite the pain zapping her brain. "I wasn't allowed to throw food away as a kid. I guess it stuck with me." She rearranges the frozen meals until there's a few inches of space to insert the head wrap. "Plus I like to be prepared, just in case."

"Of what? A nuclear apocalypse?" Cara is still staring, open-mouthed, at the freezer.

Ali shuts the door. "Something like that."

"What's all this?" Cara taps her foot against the multi-gallon glass jugs of water stacked up next to the fridge.

"Drinking water," says Ali.

"What's wrong with tap water?"

"My friend who's an environmental lawyer said there's jet fuel and all kinds of other nasty stuff in it."

"Huh. Why don't you get those blue plastic jugs everyone else gets?"

"Plastic can cause cancer."

Cara shakes her head and grins. "You're a little neurotic, aren't you?"

Ali rolls her eyes good-naturedly, even though it hurts. "Just a little."

"Anyway." Cara pulls a glass vial out of her bag. "This is a magic migraine stick with therapeutic-grade peppermint, spearmint, and lavender essential oils." She sits down on the couch and taps the spot beside her. Glen jumps up to occupy the spot and they both laugh. Ali scoots him over and sits next to Cara. "Face me." Cara opens the migraine stick and rolls it on Ali's temples. After a few seconds, Ali feels an extremely pleasant tingling sensation and smells the mint and lavender. Cara uses two fingers to massage firm circles where she rolled the oil. Ali closes her eyes and a satisfied groan escapes her.

"This is so wildly unprofessional of me," Ali says. Between a publicist and a celebrity client, there usually *is* some blurring of the line between personal and professional, but it's never the publicist's personal life that's revealed, it's always the client's—generally due to some moment of crisis. Ali has had to comfort crying clients through breakups, peel drunk or drug-addled others off bathroom floors, bail them out of jail, deliver their stool samples to various labs, pick up and deliver their Plan B, shuttle their dead pets to the vet for cremation, and so much more. But in these situations, it's always Ali helping clients—never the other way around. Partly because it's Ali's job to help her clients, partly because Ali is so private they would never know she needed help, and partly because most celebrities are so self-centered it would never even *occur* to them to help. Many of them don't even know Natalie died.

Cara is clearly different. The current situation is such a ludicrous role reversal that Ali thinks she might be in some kind of alternate reality. Maybe one she likes—it *is* kind of nice being the one taken care of for a change. So nice that Ali feels tears sting her eyes, but she uses all her willpower to banish the liquid back into the ducts where they belong. She knows she should tell Cara to stop, but the massage genuinely seems to be helping—if the migraine was a ten when Cara arrived, it's now an eight. Plus, it just feels so exquisite to be touched.

"I won't tell if you don't," says Cara, still massaging Ali's temples. "Is that too much pressure?"

"No, it's perfect," Ali murmurs, self-conscious about her breath since she can't remember if she brushed her teeth this morning. Cara's breath, which wafts warmly against Ali's face, smells slightly fruity and sour, like she ate a plum recently. It's not unpleasant. Ali opens her eyes just slightly. In her sight line, Cara's shirt is slashed over her chest, revealing her gray Calvin Klein sports bra, the swell of her breasts above it, and the dark, inviting line between them. Ali quickly closes her eyes again.

"Growing up, we had a neighbor in our apartment complex who was a Thai massage therapist. She taught me this—she called it pulling out the bad wind—to help my mom's migraines." Cara moves from the temples to other parts of Ali's face, tracing deep lines with her thumbs along Ali's hairline, through the middle of her forehead, above and below her eyebrows, and below her cheekbones, to the space between Ali's two jawbones, where she again uses two fingers to massage in circles. "Do you mind if I leave a red mark on your forehead?" she asks.

Ali has been so distracted by the sublime feeling of the massage that she can barely speak. She has no idea what Cara is asking. "You can do whatever you want if it'll get rid of this headache," Ali says.

"This is called the indicator. How red it is shows how bad your headache is." Cara proceeds to use her thumb and pointer finger to repeatedly pinch and pull away the skin between Ali's eyebrows. It hurts, but Ali doesn't care. "Wow, it's really red. You must be in a fuckton of pain."

"This is helping," says Ali.

Cara turns Ali around and rubs the back of her head, neck, and shoulders. "Girl, you are *extremely* tight." She wiggles her thumb over a knot between Ali's shoulder blades.

"That's what she said," mumbles Ali, and they both laugh.

"Really, though, it feels like you have cherries lodged in your muscles."

"Yeah, I've been told I carry a lot of tension…physically and mentally," Ali says.

When Cara digs into certain spots in Ali's neck or back, Ali feels it in different areas of her head, and she has to stop herself from saying "Yes" every two seconds. At some point, tears once again sting her eyes, but this time she can't stop them. They leak from the corners of her eyes in pure gratitude. Ali has no idea how much time has passed when Cara squeezes her shoulders in a way that suggests she's done and asks, "How do you feel?"

Ali opens her eyes, feeling like a bear emerging from hibernation. She searches her body for the pain that was there not even an hour ago, but she can't locate it. "That's bizarre," she says. "I think my headache is gone."

Cara makes a fist and pulls her elbow down in a victorious gesture.

"I don't understand how that's possible," Ali says. "I had that migraine for a *week*. I could kiss your feet."

"You know what you *could* do to thank me?"

Ali has no idea what she's going to say. "What?"

Cara grins. "You could come on promo tour with me!"

"Oh," says Ali. "I haven't decided yet." Next to her, Glen growls and yips in his sleep, his paws twitching like he's running. Ali hasn't been away from him for a single night since Natalie died, and she doesn't like the thought of it. What if he thought she'd died, too?

Cara bounces on her butt like a toddler. "Come on, it'll be so fun!"

"*Fun* is a word you'll never use to describe a promo tour after you've done one."

"At least I'll get to leave this stupid-ass country for the first time in my life."

Ali pets Glen, trying to calm him through his bad dream. "You've never been outside the US?"

"Naw, man. I grew up with a single mom in the Valley. We shared a studio and lived off instant ramen. I guess I had a little money when I was filming *Overruled*, but I gave a lot of it to my mom so she could pay off her credit card debt. Currently I can barely afford my rent, but they're going to put me up in five-star hotels all over the world. It's bananas."

"What city are you most excited to see?"

"I know it's cliché, but probably Paris. I fucking love croissants."

"Paris is my favorite city," says Ali. "Or it used to be…" Before Natalie died and stained all of Ali's beautiful Paris memories with grief. "It's where my partner and I got engaged," Ali says, before she realizes she's said it out loud.

"Oh, are you…?"

"I was. In a domestic partnership."

"Oh," says Cara. "Split up?"

Ali imagines telling Cara Natalie is dead, and the ensuing sympathy and awkwardness, and instead says yes, wishing it were true—at least it would mean Natalie was still alive, and there was a chance they could be together again.

"Sorry," Cara says. "Or congratulations? I know for some people, breaking up is, like, a good thing."

Ali shakes her head. "Not a good thing. But let's not talk about it." Her stomach gurgles and groans, alerting her that she's hungry for the first time in days, now that the migraine has abated. "Are you hungry?"

"Hell yeah," says Cara. "All I've had today are some fruit snacks."

Ali laughs. "What adult eats fruit snacks as a meal?"

Cara shrugs. "They have vitamins in them."

"Still, I don't think they qualify as *food*," says Ali. "Should we get delivery?"

"Girl." Cara gives her a chastising stare. "You could live for *weeks* off all that shit in your freezer. You shouldn't be allowed to bring any new food into this place until you've cleared some out." She struts over to the freezer and opens it, leaning over to inspect the contents.

"You sound like my parents," says Ali.

Cara reads from the labeled Pyrex containers on the second shelf. "Lasagna, vegetarian chili, chickpea curry, spicy marinara sauce, Persian noodle soup...Ooh! Chicken pho. That sounds really good." She looks at Ali for approval.

Ali's throat constricts. "Not chicken pho," she croaks, and tries to swallow down the feeling. Chicken pho was all she could eat for months after Natalie died, plus barely sweetened cinnamon oatmeal and sleeves and sleeves of saltines with mugs of mint tea in between. Now the thought of any of those foods (minus saltines, due to their plainness) sends nausea careening through her body. "What about Persian noodle soup?" Ali gets up from the couch, which makes Glen pop up from his dead sleep to follow her.

Cara frowns. "What's that?"

"It's sort of like Persian minestrone, but the base is made from herbs and greens instead of tomatoes. It's really good."

"Okay, I'm sold. With homemade chocolate chip cookies for dessert?"

"Sure." Ali smiles at Cara's childlike excitement.

Cara pulls two Pyrexes from the freezer like she's playing a game of Jenga, careful not to dislodge the containers above or below the ones she wants. "You made all this stuff from scratch?"

"I did." Ali turns the faucet to hot and places the Pyrex of soup upside down underneath the stream of water. Glen sits right beside her, his ears raised in hopeful anticipation of a treat. "Only because you're the cutest patootie," Ali whispers. She opens the fridge to give him a cigar-size piece of dried chicken breast that he chomps between his teeth before trotting to the living area to eat it over the Bauhaus rug, which he believes is his personal napkin.

"So you like to cook, then?"

"I wouldn't say I like to, but I had to learn when I was little."

"Why? Were you on one of those kids' cooking competition shows?"

Ali laughs. "No, I just had to take care of my mom a lot. She...wasn't well."

"In what way?"

Ali jiggles the Pyrex and feels the frozen block of soup release from the edges. "You ask kind of invasive questions, you know that?"

Cara tuts her tongue. "Only because you're so vague

about your personal life! Trying to find out anything about you is like pulling teeth."

"I'm your publicist. You're not supposed to know anything about my personal life."

"Well, I'm a different type of client. To work well with you, I have to know who you are. We have to establish a rapport." Cara says the word gutturally, like she's French. "Plus, like I said before, I'm curious about you. You seem like you've had an interesting life."

Ali blasts a puff of air out of her nose. "That's one word for it." She removes the lid from the Pyrex and shakes the container over a pot until the block of soup squelches free and thunks into it.

"Why don't you just use the microwave?"

Ali gives Cara a look like it should be obvious.

"Oh." Cara makes a half-amused, half-sympathetic face. "The radiation?"

"Bingo." Ali lights a burner and puts the pot down.

Cara boosts herself onto the counter and sits there, swinging her legs. "So why *are* you such a hard nut to crack?"

Ali adjusts the soup to be more directly over the whirring blue flame. "When I tell people about my life, it makes them uncomfortable."

Cara crosses her arms. "Try me."

Ali opens her mouth, then closes it. Her chin shakes.

"Dude, I just gave you a massage for, like, an hour, and we're about to eat your frozen hoarder food. I think at this point it's safe to say we're becoming friends. And I don't know if you know this, but friends usually talk about their lives and shit."

Ali can't fathom why a young, hilariously hip person like Cara would want to be friends with an old fuddy-duddy like her.

"So go on, tell me about your life!" Cara says, giving Ali a gentle shove.

"Okay, okay." Ali takes a deep breath. "My mom was bipolar. It was really rough. Then she died from leukemia when I was seventeen."

"That's really fucking horrible, but I'm not uncomfortable. What else?"

Ali prods at the soup with a wooden spoon, trying to release a chickpea near the bottom. Her heart thuds so forcefully she wonders if Cara can hear it. "My partner and I didn't split up. She died last year." Her throat tightens, making her voice high and trembly. "She was crossing the street, in a crosswalk, and got hit by a car." She squeezes her eyes shut, refusing to replay the disjointed movie she's watched a million times in her head by now of Natalie's death.

"Jesus Christ. Your mom *and* your partner? That's a really raw deal."

Somehow Ali manages not to cry. "Yeah. Because of all that, you could say I have some issues with anxiety."

"That's fucking understandable. Anything else?"

Ali blows out a stream of air and pushes her palms into the countertop's edge—a pose that seems to say, *This one is a real doozy.* She chases a smile from her mouth, setting it in a serious line. "My dad is a member of the mob."

"Holy fuck, are you serious?"

Ali looks at Cara and bursts into laughter. "That was the only one I was lying about, I swear."

"You jerk!" Cara picks up the wooden spoon and whacks Ali on the arm with it.

"Ow!" Ali runs into the living room and Cara runs after her, slapping her all over with the wooden spoon.

"I'll stop if you come on promo tour." Cara wallops Ali's thigh.

"Glen, help!" Ali yells, and Glen barks at Cara while jumping on his hind legs to try to steal the spoon. Ali curls into a child's pose and Glen jumps on her back to protect her, growling at Cara fiercely.

Cara holds out the spoon to him and they play tug-of-war, Glen's sharp nails digging into Ali's back.

"Uncle, uncle!" Ali screeches.

"I don't believe those were the magic words," taunts Cara. She pulls the spoon harder, which makes Glen's nails dig into Ali's back deeper.

"Fucking fine, I'll come on promo tour!"

Cara releases the spoon and Glen hops off Ali's back, victorious. "You mean it?"

Ali snatches the spoon away from Glen before he can chew it to pieces and replaces it with a rawhide. She said she'd go to get Glen (and Cara) off her back, but now it feels right. Maybe she *does* need to Kool-Aid Man her life. "Sure."

"You swear on Glen's adorable spotted ear?" Cara pets it with one finger.

Ali laughs. "I swear on Glen's adorable spotted ear."

10

That night Ali dreams she's walking Glen in a nondescript suburban neighborhood when she looks up and sees a blazing plane falling through the sky. It's headed right toward them, but Ali just stands there, frozen. Glen barks, the sound anguished and high pitched, and strains against his harness, but Ali holds his leash tight and keeps her eyes on the plane. When it's right above them, Ali feels a strong breeze against her face and squeezes her eyes shut. Then she jolts awake. The clock says it's 3:03 a.m. Glen is sleeping safely next to her, her little spoon, and lightly snoring. She wraps her arms around him and tries to fall back asleep, but by 3:45 she concedes to putting on *Frasier*. It's the episode where Marty starts dating Sherry, the brash bartender from McGinty's whom Frasier and Niles can't stand. It's especially funny to Ali that the writers named her Sherry, since Frasier and Niles love sherry, the fortified wine. When Sherry comes over for the first time, she jokingly asks which room is hers, then says she thinks humor is like medicine. "Guess we're in the placebo group," Niles says to Frasier. Before the episode ends, Ali falls asleep, waking briefly to shut the laptop screen when she hears the "Tossed Salads and Scrambled Eggs" outro music.

In the morning, Ali is tempted to back out of her promise to Cara, but when she arrives at work, Victoria says how glad she is that Ali agreed to the promo tour. Cara must have told the studio immediately. Ali is actually glad Cara has forced her into a corner, because when left to her own devices, she almost always chickens out.

In the afternoon, Ali texts Jason Kim: I'm guessing you haven't watched the screener yet, because otherwise you would have told me you'd write the profile.

She gives him an hour, and when he doesn't reply, she texts again. Five other journalists have said they'd love to write it, but I'm stalling because you're the one I want…

He immediately texts back, as Ali knew he would. Which journalists?

Ali sends their names. Technically two of them are maybes, but Jason doesn't need to know that.

Ah, the B-list profile writers

The one Krista wrote about Paris was pretty well-received

Oh come on, it read like it was straight-up copied and pasted from the press release. There was no productive friction at all. I could have done way better

That's exactly what you'll say after you read the profile of Cara you didn't write

FINE, I'll watch the screener!

Watch it tonight. I have to give the other journalists an answer tomorrow

In the morning, Ali texts Jason with the ace up her sleeve: Matt Tyrnauer said he's interested in writing the profile. Matt Tyrnauer is Jason's journalist nemesis.

Ok ok I'm literally watching the screener right now

Two hours later, he texts again: Ok you were right. Cara Bisset is EVERYTHING. Shall we schedule the interview for next week?

Ali immediately calls Cara to talk strategy. "If he's suspicious we're keeping your sexuality under wraps, we'll have to give him something else that feels like insider info," says Ali while on a walk with Glen. As he thoroughly investigates a smell, Ali watches a mockingbird repeatedly dive-bomb a raven perched on a telephone wire across the street. The raven is, of course, much bigger, and Ali is surprised the mockingbird isn't more scared of it. But the raven seems to just sit there and take it. "Do you have any skeletons in your closet?" Ali asks Cara.

Bloops and bleeps come through the phone like Cara is playing a video game. "If it was up to me, I wouldn't have any."

"You know what I mean. If you were a much more private person, what would you not want to talk about in an interview?" When the mockingbird flies, white patches in the middles of its wings and outer tail become visible, turning it from a plain gray bird to a stunner.

"I got a nose job when I was seventeen. When I was cast for *Overruled*, it came with the *suggestion* I get one."

Ali tries to remember Cara's nose but can't, and realizes this is probably the exact purpose of nose jobs. "Suggestion from whom?"

"I don't know, exactly. The information was passed on to me by my agent. Probably the studio?" A bloop comes through the phone, like the sound of an air bubble rising through water. "At the time I was like, *Of course, I'll do anything*, but now it makes me really mad and I regret it. I permanently *changed my face*, you know? That's fucked up."

"It really is. But you're willing to talk about it?"

"Yeah, I don't care."

Glen is finally ready to move on from whatever smell kept him occupied for the past minute or so, but now Ali needs to know how this mockingbird-vs.-raven battle will end. "It's good you don't know who exactly made the request—when you talk to Jason about it, keep it that way. Don't say the studio, or implicate anyone specific. And you have to make Jason feel like he pulled the information out of you, not like you freely volunteered it. We can even play it like you're disobeying me by revealing it."

"Gotcha."

Ali looks up at the telephone wire—now only the mockingbird is perched there, so the raven must have flown away. She wishes she had just an ounce of that mockingbird's bravery.

"Hi there," says the receptionist at the twenty-four-hour animal hospital in Glendale, where they're almost as familiar with Ali as the people at the walk-in clinic in Hollywood. In Ali's defense, the people at the emergency vet are mainly familiar with her because it's where she brought Glen after he was attacked by an off-leash husky—it almost tore off Glen's right front leg, and he needed surgery and multiple checkups. But she *has* brought him here for a few other maladies: a not-so-serious eye infection, diarrhea that looked like it had worms in it that turned out to be pieces of white rice, the time he ate berries fallen from a palm tree Ali worried were poisonous but turned out to be acai berries, and a rash that went away after a few days. Today she's brought him for another skin issue—he has an unknown allergy (probably environmental, because she's done food allergy testing and avoids every item on the list) that sporadically covers his skin in pus-filled bumps that eventually burst and crust before subsiding. The allergy is currently flaring, his whole body riddled with bumps, and an orange-size cluster of them are shockingly red and bleeding, so Ali is concerned they're infected. His primary vet can't see him for over two weeks, as usual, which is why she's brought him to the animal hospital after work.

"All right, honey, take a seat, but it'll probably be a few hours because there are animals here with much more serious issues," says the receptionist, a hint of judgment in her tone.

Ali and Glen sit down near the water cooler, a few chairs away from a red-haired woman holding a corgi with a curving line of staples down its entire back that barely hold together the swollen skin. Ali gives the woman a sympathetic pout and asks, "Was your dog attacked?"

The woman nods. Light freckles dapple her face and arms. "A pit bull at the dog park. Shook her like you'd shake a martini in a tumbler."

On Ali's lap, Glen is currently shaking almost that hard, as he does every time they come to the animal hospital since his attack. "God, I'm so sorry," Ali says. "My dog has been attacked, too. Nearly lost his right front leg, but he's okay now. Will she fully heal?"

"They think so. At least physically, but I'm not sure about emotionally. This is the second time she's been mauled." The woman leans down to pet the corgi, which doesn't react—her brown eyes appear vacant and hopeless.

"Oh my God, the poor thing." On walks with Glen, as Ali's heart speeds up before every semihidden driveway they pass, she tells herself the likelihood of him being attacked again is slim, but she knows this logic is flawed. It's what she told herself after her mom died: She had filled her disaster quotient, and nothing that terrible would ever happen to her again. But disaster knows no order or fairness; it's capricious and strikes when it pleases, so you always have to be ready.

"Minnie?" calls a nurse from the hallway that leads to the exam rooms.

"That's us," the woman says to Ali. She stands and coaxes the corgi to do the same. The dog gives her a look like *Life is meaningless and filled with an endless amount of pain* before standing reluctantly and slowly waddling away.

Ali hugs Glen, inhaling his Dorito-y smell, and whispers that he's a very good boy and she's so sorry for bringing him back to a place that makes him so nervous, but she's concerned about his bleeding bumps, and she hopes her concern is valid and not a manifestation of her hypochondria, but often it's impossible to tell. On the TV mounted on the wall, *House Hunters* is on, and the husband wants to live in the country, but the wife wants to live closer to town. Ali tries to focus on the different yet nearly identical houses, but against her will, her mind wanders to the day Glen was attacked.

They were on a familiar route, one they had walked dozens of times, when they approached an unfenced yard with an unleashed husky that must have weighed over a hundred pounds. Its owner was nowhere in sight. Ali pulled Glen away, but the husky was too fast—it sprinted toward them and locked its jaws around Glen's leg before Ali could even blink. She can still hear the surprised scream that escaped Glen before he kicked into fight mode and viciously battled back. Ali unsuccessfully tried to pull them apart until the owner appeared and stuck his finger up the husky's butt to release her jaws. He claimed it was the first time she'd ever attacked another dog, but in hindsight, Ali recognized the only way he'd know about the finger-in-butt trick was if an attack had happened before.

A neighbor across the street who had witnessed the whole thing drove Ali to the animal hospital, then sat with her in the waiting room for hours until a vet came out and told them Glen would be okay. He would need surgery, and his front leg might not ever regain function, but he would survive. When Ali went into the exam room to see him, he looked at her with the same vacant, hopeless eyes as the corgi.

The attack happened three months after Natalie died. Glen's physical recovery took over a month (upon which Ali was relieved to discover his front leg functioned fine), but his emotional recovery took about four months. For the first few weeks he refused to go on walks at all and would only pee and poop in the backyard, then he'd go out to the patch of grass on the street, then he'd do a short loop around the block. Then they added another block, then another and another, until eventually he was doing full walks again. Sometimes he still gets spooked and sits down, refusing to move. But most days he trots along happily, or so it seems—maybe he puts on a brave face but his mind is a rat's nest of what-ifs just like Ali's.

The receptionist changes the TV from HGTV to MSNBC, where they're breaking the news that Schwarzenegger just vetoed the gay marriage bill. Ali isn't surprised, but it still stings. She and Natalie were together for twelve years and had a domestic partnership, but Ali still couldn't call Natalie her wife, the word that felt the most correct. If all Ali's closeted clients were out, would it significantly change LGBT acceptance? Would it have made Schwarzenegger sign the bill instead of veto it? Maybe. Actually, probably. The thought sends a guilty shudder down Ali's spine. Dozens of openly gay celebrities would force the public and the government to see that gay marriage isn't a niche issue, that it affects even the world's biggest, most beloved stars. Even if the culture isn't "ready" for dozens of celebrities to come out, if they came out anyway, they would force the culture to be more accepting. Such is the usual pattern of change. Ali sighs, resigned. It's not like there's anything she can personally do about it.

Hours pass. More animals with more serious issues come in: an orange tabby cat hit by a car, a schnauzer vomiting blood, a hairless cat with unexplained paralysis of the legs, a golden retriever who ate a whole bar of dark chocolate, a French bulldog stung by a swarm of wasps. Ali could sit there all day and Glen might never be seen. After hour three, she tells the receptionist she's going to leave, since she now realizes Glen's issue is not as pressing as the rest. Back at home, she gives him a bath with his antiseptic shampoo and dabs the bumps with hydrogen peroxide. The next day, the bumps have stopped bleeding and are much less red. After a few days, they're gone entirely.

"So, do you feel like you're on the brink of stardom?" Jason Kim asks Cara as his opening question. Ali, Jason, and Cara are sitting on yet another restaurant patio, drinking coffees (Ali's is decaf) and waiting for their various brunch items: an easy-to-eat omelet for Ali, the market hash for Jason, and a BLT with a sunny-side-up egg for Cara. Today it's seventy-two and sunny—the end of October has finally brought cooler temperatures, and Ali doesn't even mind that her seat isn't underneath the umbrella's shade. A yellow angel's trumpet tree hangs over the wooden fence to the side of her, and Ali contemplates what a delightful job it must be to name flowers, because they *do* look like angels' trumpets.

"Not really," says Cara. "No one knows who I am right now, which Ali keeps telling me I should enjoy while I can—"

Jason interjects. "Try to forget she's here."

"Okay." Cara holds up a menu to block Ali's face. "But yeah, I think it'll hit me once the movie is out, or, like, when paparazzi chase me down the street."

"You say that like you're looking forward to it," Jason says.

"I kind of am," says Cara.

Two men in muscle tanks and backward hats are sitting at the table next to them, and their entire conversation has been about their daily workout routine and meals. "It's all about combining proteins, dude," says the man with bigger muscles. "Beans *and* meat, not one or the other."

"For a lot of actors, there's this tension between the acting part and the fame part," says Jason. "But it seems like you might embrace it?"

"It might be uncool to admit, but I very much fuck with Miss Fame," says Cara. "I've wanted it ever since I was young. Growing up, my mom worked for this cleaning company that specialized in celebrity homes, mostly actors. And sometimes she'd bring me with her, and I would run around these mansions, wishing they were mine. So the way I thought I could improve my situation—living in a nasty-ass studio in the Valley with my mom—was to become an actor. Then I'd have fame and money. Even more than fame, I'm looking forward to the money part."

A bee lands on the rim of Jason's cup of orange juice, and he waves it away. "How are you doing financially right now?

I know for a lot of actors, even after they get their first big break, they can still barely pay their bills."

"Yeah, that's me right now. I feel like a lot of actors are embarrassed to admit it, but I'm not. I'll talk about anything."

The server (a man, luckily, so Cara won't be tempted to flirt with him) drops off their food, and they pause their conversation.

Once he's walked away, Jason raises his eyebrows at Cara. "You'll talk about anything, huh?" He swivels his head toward Ali, waiting to see if she'll object, and Ali gives Cara a fake warning look, hoping Cara knows this is the moment to drop the nose-job story.

"If it was up to *me*, I'd talk about anything." Cara takes a bite of her BLT. Yellow yolk runs down her chin and she wipes it, then licks her finger. "But I'm learning that's not the Hollywood way."

Jason slowly unfolds his napkin and places it on his lap. "Have you been told not to talk about certain things?"

Cara glances at Ali and juts her chin defiantly. "Yes." Her steely eyes send a bolt of fear through Ali's stomach—is Cara about to reveal not the red herring, but the *real* secret?

Jason's mouth twitches at the edges before he presses his lips together. Ali can tell he's using all his willpower to withhold his excitement—he's like a fisherman who's felt a tug on his line and is doing everything he can not to spook the fish. "Would you *prefer* to talk about those things?"

Cara takes another sizable bite of her sandwich and chews thoughtfully. She's the only one eating. "Yes," she says, not looking at Ali.

"But she's smart enough to know that keeping quiet is best for her career," says Ali, her voice shaking with uncertainty over whether she's fake-protesting or really protesting.

"I've seen the way it wrecks actors to be forced into silence," Jason says to Cara. "It turns them into a dry husk."

Cara tsks her tongue. "You don't need to convince me," she says to Jason. "I've already decided I'm going to tell you."

Ali swears she sees Jason's pupils dilate. "Cara, don't do this." Ali's heart vibrates against her chest like a speed bag being pummeled by expert fists.

Jason stays quiet, his eyes glinting, muscles tensed in anticipation.

Cara takes a deep breath and looks down, spreading her hands out on the table. "When I was cast for *Overruled*, it came with the *suggestion* that I get a nose job."

Relief floods Ali's body to the point that she feels like she's floating. Cara really *is* a phenomenal actor.

Jason shakes his head like he didn't hear her right. "Wait, *what?*"

"I was seventeen and it was my first big job, so I said yes," Cara continues.

Jason's excitement deflates, leaving his body slack. He glares at Ali. "Do you really think I'm stupid enough to buy this bullshit?"

Ali finally takes a bite of her omelet, which is now lukewarm. "Do you want to hear about the nose job or not?"

Ali sees Jason perform the internal calculation about whether he can storm out and not write the story or whether he should take the scrap they've thrown him, knowing they'll give it to another journalist if he turns it down. He grits his teeth. "Fine. Tell me about the nose job."

11

"Before you do the talk show circuit, we need to come up with your funny anecdote," says Ali a few days later. They're in her office, armed with iced lattes and donuts from the place around the corner.

"Oh Christ," says Cara, chewing her strawberry glazed, sprinkles falling onto her *Ren & Stimpy* T-shirt.

"They can usually be slotted into five categories." Ali lists them on her fingers. "One, a funny childhood story, usually about getting in trouble. Two, a funny encounter with another celebrity—bonus points if it's about having a crush on said celebrity, but obviously we'll want to steer clear of this for you. Three, an everything-goes-wrong story that usually entails traveling. Missed flights, lost luggage, stuff like that. Four, a really embarrassing story that's best if it involves bodily functions. And five, being pulled over by a cop at the worst possible time. Combining elements from different categories, or adding drunkenness to *any* category, makes for the strongest possible anecdote."

"Wow, you've really distilled this to a science, huh?"

Ali mimes pushing glasses up her nose and talks in a stuffy accent. "The anatomy of the anecdote, if you will."

Cara laughs and gives Ali a fist bump.

"Examples of recent celebrity anecdotes include when an actress met Martin Scorsese for the first time. Unbeknownst to her, her dress was unzipped and her thong was out the entire time, so that's a classic number two–number four combo. Another actor told a story about getting into a bar fight with a fan in Dublin, which is number three plus being drunk. You get the idea?"

"Absolutely." Cara makes a bored face and sucks the straw of her almost-empty latte. It makes the classic bong-like sound, and she keeps sucking the straw even after the liquid is gone, for comedic effect.

Ali waits for her to finish. "Is there anything you can think of off the top of your head?"

"I have a sickening one—I guess you could classify it as a funny childhood story? But it would kinda let the lesbian cat out of the bag."

"What is it? Maybe there's a way for us to leave that part out."

Cara clears her throat and pats her chest like she's getting ready to tell a lengthy tale. "When I was in high school, after I came out, this guy kept saying really fucked-up, rapey shit to me about how after he put *his* dick in me, I wouldn't be gay anymore, and I told my mom—not because I expected her to do anything, but because I was just venting—and she actually went over to this guy's house, knocked on his door, and his dad answered, so my mom told his dad she would Lorena Bobbitt his son if he didn't stop threatening to rape me. Badass, right? So the dad, of course, thought the sun shone out of his son's ass and didn't believe my mom, so he called the cops, they showed up, my mom and the dad both told their sides of the story, and the cops ended up filing a restraining order against the kid! He never bothered me again."

"Wow, your mom sounds so cool. We could leave out the part about him harassing you because you're gay—he could just be doing it because he's an asshole."

"But me being gay is kind of, like, central to the whole story. My mom wasn't just defending me, she was defending my sexuality. That's why it meant so much to me."

"Okay, we'll find something else. What about a funny encounter with another celebrity?"

"One night I was making out with ████████ in the bathroom, and then—oh. Whoops. Guess we can't use that one."

Ali drops her head into her hands and pulls at her hair.

Cara leans back and crosses her arms. "What anecdote would *you* tell, if you were going on these stupid-ass shows?"

"I honestly don't know if I have one."

"Come on, there has to be something."

Ali scans her memory, and a laugh escapes her.

Cara perks up. "What?"

Ali waves her off and takes a big bite of chocolate cake donut, so her mouth is too full to answer.

Cara smacks her arm. "Come on, you know how this goes. I'll never stop pestering you till you tell me."

Ali takes a sip of latte to wash down the donut and giggles, covering her mouth with her hand. "I did poop my pants once."

"Seriously? Or are you fucking with me again à la *Dad is in the mob*?"

"No, seriously. I have IBS—"

Cara laughs and smacks her thigh. "Of course you do!"

"What do you mean *of course*?"

"Girl. Everyone I know with extreme anxiety has IBS."

"You think I have *extreme* anxiety?"

"Says the woman who refuses to use a microwave and gets her water shipped in special glass bottles."

"Okay, whatever. Do you want to know the story of how I pooped my pants or not?"

"There's nothing I want more."

"Okay. So every now and then I get these really intense bouts of diarrhea, usually after eating too much fatty food or when I'm stressed or upset, and one day, a few weeks after my partner died, I was walking Glen and the cramps hit and I was like *Oh fucking no*. We were probably forty minutes from the house, and it was a completely residential area so there was no restaurant or store I could stop in to use the bathroom, and I held it and held it and held it—and I don't think you understand how difficult that was; it was probably one of the hardest things I've ever done—until finally a few blocks from my apartment it just came out. I remember thinking, your partner is dead and now you've pooped your pants—things truly can't get any worse. I was wearing shorts and it dripped down both my legs and all over my sneakers, and thank baby Jesus I didn't see anyone up until I got to the walkway that leads to my apartment, but then, of course, my *male model* neighbor was leaving his apartment, and he was about to say hi to me when he noticed I was covered in shit. And I could see him trying to decide whether to acknowledge it or not, like to ask if I was okay, and I said in this really low, Darth Vader voice, 'Just walk away,' and he did. My only consolation was that soon after that I moved, so I never had to see him again."

Cara slow claps. "Okay, pants-pooping anecdote!"

Ali shakes her head, trying to remind herself she's in her office, working. "I can't believe I just told that story to a client." First Ali let Cara massage her, and now this? Her unprofessionalism is escalating. Publicist Ali hopes it won't go any further, but regular Ali kind of hopes it does, because she's having more fun than she's had in a year. It feels nice to open up to someone, to laugh and get a brief respite from the omnipresent doom. "Have you ever pooped *your* pants?"

"No, never."

"You must have some bodily function story."

"One time when I was really drunk, I puked on this girl's vulva as I was going down on her."

"Yet another story you can't tell." Ali breaks off a piece of bear claw. "I guess you were right when you told me being gay is your whole personality."

Cara pushes out her lips. "I *did* tell you."

Out the window, a palm tree sparkles in the wind. "Should we just make something up?"

Cara breaks off another piece of bear claw. "Fuck it, I'm already lying about my sexuality."

Ali picks up a blank notebook and pen and writes "THE BEST ANECDOTE OF ALL TIME" across the top of a page. "Okay, where do we start?"

"How about…my twenty-first birthday? I feel like that's a night shit could go down."

"Perfect. What did you actually do that night?"

"Went to a drag show."

Ali tilts her head in consideration. "Let's actually use that, so it's rooted in the truth. And so many straight women go to drag shows now, we don't have to worry it'll make you seem gay. What celebrity could you see there? Someone really unexpected. Like…Bill Murray but not Bill Murray."

Cara snaps her fingers. "Steve Buscemi!"

Ali lets out a loud, singular *ha!* "Oh my God, that's *perfect*. When you hear his name, you automatically laugh."

"But I don't think I should see him inside, in case he's never been to a drag show. We're standing outside after the show, shooting the shit with this drag queen, and we see him standing outside the bar next door..."

Ali picks up where Cara leaves off. "And he's the drag queen's favorite actor, so she's trying to work up the courage to say hi—"

"Wait, what's the drag queen's name? I feel like it could be a great place to get a laugh."

"Hmmmm. What's a funny word?"

"Dongle?"

"Kerfuffle?"

"Meatball?"

Ali points at Cara. "Ooh, I like the idea of something food based, but meatball isn't quite it. What about...poutine?"

Cara claps. "Yes, poutine!"

"You know how some queens create a phrase with the first and second name, like Avery Goodlay? What could we do with poutine?"

Cara places her chin on her fist as she thinks, then she shoots off the couch. "Poutine Anya Tits!"

Ali screeches a laugh and stamps her feet. She truly can't remember the last time she felt so utterly silly. It feels like being a kid again, back before the world went to shit. She even feels physically lighter, like she'll float off the couch at any moment. "I don't think you can say tits on TV, though... Poutine Anya Bazongas?"

Now Cara screeches and falls sideways onto the couch in a giggle fit. "Yeeeeeees!"

Namisa sticks her head in the doorway. "What on earth is going on? Every time Cara's here it sounds like you two have taken laughing gas."

Ali wipes her eyes. "We're coming up with Cara's late-night anecdote."

"Well, it sounds like a bloody winner."

"We're getting there," says Ali.

Namisa nabs a jelly donut, then backs out of the room. "As you were."

"Love you, Namisa." Cara blows her a kiss, and Ali tries not to let it spoil the moment they're having.

"So," says Ali. "Poutine Anya Bazongas"—she pauses to giggle silently—"is trying to work up the courage to say hi to Steve Buscemi when he gets into a car..."

Cara keeps going. "And a delivery guy has just parked his Vespa to bring someone a pizza, but he left the Vespa running, so Poutine Anya Bazongas hops on and for some reason I jump into the sidecar..."

"And you two proceed on a mad chase through West Hollywood trying to catch Steve Buscemi, during which Poutine's wig flies off her head and her size-ten stilettos fall off her feet..."

Cara claps in excitement. "And after running a red light we get pulled over by a cop, and I'm so nauseous from being whipped around in the sidecar, I puke all over myself the second he walks up."

"But luckily the cop lets you both off with a warning, and you two return the Vespa..."

"And when Poutine explains it was to chase down Steve Buscemi, it turns out the delivery guy loves him, too, and the night ends with Poutine getting the delivery guy's number. And as far as I know, they're still together?"

Ali puts a hand to her heart. "Absolute perfection. I have chills."

They fist-bump and fall back onto the couch, lolling

their heads and sprawling out their arms—the way the story built and built, excitement mounting as each of them played off the other until the satisfying, full-circle finale—it feels a little...postcoital? For a millisecond, Ali wonders if they'd have the same kind of electric chemistry in bed. Then she banishes the thought from her mind.

Cara turns toward her. "Is that what it's like to write a short story?"

Ali huffs. "I wish. It's not nearly as fun, because you have to do it alone. Which reminds me, I brought you these." She rifles around in her tote bag and presents Cara with two books: *Who Do You Think You Are?* by Alice Munro and Amy Bloom's *Come to Me.* "They're basically my bibles."

Cara hugs the books to her chest. "Well, then. I'll worship them."

Warmth suffuses Ali's chest. She still doesn't understand why Cara cares so much about her interests, and wonders whether it's specific to Ali or if Cara is this curious about everyone. Either way, it makes Ali feel special.

12

Everything they've been preparing for is about to hit like a tornado. Ali scans her planner, noting all the important dates:

Monday, October 31: Cara on *Jimmy Kimmel Live!*

Tuesday, November 1: Cara's *Vanity Fair* cover story hits shelves

Wednesday, November 2: Daylong press junket at the Four Seasons in Beverly Hills

Thursday, November 3: *Real Love*'s LA premiere at Grauman's Chinese Theatre in Hollywood

Friday, November 4: *Real Love*'s US release

Friday, November 11: *Real Love*'s French release

November 11–December 11: World promo tour, including stops in Paris, London, Berlin, Copenhagen, Venice, Seoul, Tokyo, Sydney, Dubai, Cape Town, Rio de Janeiro, Buenos Aires, and Mexico City.

* * *

First up is Cara's debut on *Jimmy Kimmel Live!* Ali is, of course, always extremely anxious when her clients give interviews in front of a live audience, but she's even more anxious about this one since Cara is such a loose cannon. Ali's bowels are also a loose cannon in the hours leading up to the interview, even though the pre-interview went well and Cara mostly knows what to expect. What most viewers don't realize about late-night show interviews is that it's been decided beforehand what the host and the guest will talk about. A few days before the appearance, a producer from the show will call the guest and discuss several anecdotes the guest could use. Then the producer and the host choose the most funny and/or interesting anecdotes and create an order for the on-air conversation. Then, when the guest arrives on the day of their appearance, the producer comes to their dressing room and gives them the final details.

Ali, Cara, and Will are all sitting in Cara's dressing room waiting for the producer to arrive. Today Will is wearing a trucker hat that says, "Girls Gone Wild Film Crew," and he's eating a box of Nerds candy, tilting his head back, dumping them in, and then crunching them open-mouthed. Cara paces around the room, practicing the order of her Poutine story. Ali goes to the bathroom again, and when she comes out, the producer is there to inform them the conversation will go as follows: Cara will give a brief description of *Real Love*, then talk about how she got into acting with the anecdote about accompanying her mom on cleaning jobs, then tell the twenty-first-birthday anecdote.

"Totally doable," says Ali after the producer leaves, putting her hands on Cara's shoulders to stop her from pacing. "You've got this."

"Yeah, says the person who's blown up the bathroom like ten times since we got here," says Cara. "What if I accidentally say something gay?"

"Your subconscious knows not to, so you don't even need to keep it in your conscious mind. Just try to be yourself. You're a very charming, likable person."

"A very gay, very charming, likable person," says Cara.

"Do you want some melatonin?" Will asks Cara through a mouthful of Nerds. "Might help you calm down."

"Melatonin helps people *sleep*," says Ali. "We don't want her to pass out during the interview."

"If all else fails, just imagine Jimmy Kimmel naked!" Will laughs. "In that outfit, he'll probably be doing the same to you."

"God, I knew I shouldn't have worn this." Cara pulls at the hem of the one-shoulder minidress her stylist convinced her to wear, saying it was important to emphasize her sex appeal in her initial appearances so men would go see *Real Love.* To accompany the minidress, the stylist chose six-inch heels and an eye so smoky it could set off an alarm. Cara doesn't look like herself at all, and Ali had to have a conversation with the stylist about bringing more options next time and how it was possible for Cara to look sexy but also like herself: perhaps a miniskirt paired with Cons and a vintage T-shirt, or some cleavage peeking out from an oversize blazer, or a mesh top with a sports bra underneath, etc. Ali found it quite easy to imagine all the specifically Cara ways she could look sexy.

"Davi's going on," says Will, pointing to the TV, and they all turn their attention to it.

Davi is the first guest, since he currently has a lot more star power than Cara. He wears a checkered suit that he jokes is too tight since he didn't try it on beforehand, and then he bungles the description for *Real Love* in a very endearing way before talking about his *Mickey Mouse Club* audition, where he burped and farted at the same time—he calls it a furp—and somehow still got the job, and how his sister is his best friend and they live together, cooking and doing face masks and competitively knitting. He ends with a not-great Ace Ventura impression that's even funnier due to its lack of likeness. Ali imagines Davi's publicist in the dressing room next door pumping his arm in victory, because Davi always manages to come across as sexy, relatable, sensitive, and hilarious all at the same time.

Then it's Cara's turn, and Ali feels like a nervous mother hen as she gently pushes her out the door.

"She's the up-and-coming star of the most romantic movie of the year. Please welcome Cara Bisset!" says Jimmy on the TV.

Ali grips the arms of her chair as Cara teeters out in her six-inch heels. Just as she steps onto the platform where Jimmy's desk is, she trips—at first just lunging forward but seeming to catch herself, but then she goes all the way down to her knees. The audience collectively gasps and Ali's heart rockets into her throat. Jimmy and Davi bolt out of their seats to help Cara up, then help her sit down in the chair closest to Jimmy's desk. Davi moves onto the couch beside the chair, squeezing Cara's shoulder in a reassuring way. "It's okay, it's okay," he mouths to her before they cut him out of frame.

"Are you all right?" Jimmy asks as he takes his spot behind his desk.

"Laugh it off, laugh it off," Ali coaches from the dressing room.

Cara laughs and covers her face with her hands, then says, "Oh yeah, that's totally how I've always imagined the grand entrance of my first-ever appearance on a late-night show would go!" The audience laughs.

Ali's heart drops back into her chest.

"I'm just not used to wearing these damn things." Cara raises her foot to show off the six-inch heel.

Ali can barely hear Cara over the Nerds crunching between Will's teeth. She asks him to take a break and he pouts.

"What kind of footwear do you usually wear?" asks Jimmy.

"Converse sneakers!" Cara says, and Ali hopes this will tie the knot on the Converse brand endorsement deal Vivian has been negotiating. Maybe they could even use the clip of Cara tripping as part of the promotional material. "With jeans and a hoodie."

"That sounds comfy," says Jimmy. "I wish I was wearing that right now."

"Should we both go change?" Cara stands halfway up like she's about to leave, and the audience laughs. Cara sits back down, pulling at the hem of her minidress. "Just kidding. Kind of."

"Should we get to why you're here? The movie *Real Love* that comes out in two days? That you're starring in alongside this hunk?" Jimmy gestures to Davi, and Davi winks at him. "I mean, the reviews are insane, there's Oscar buzz…This is your first big movie, right?"

Cara nods.

"Pretty exciting stuff! Are you enjoying it?"

Cara makes a serious face. "Can I be honest with you, Jimmy? I hate it." She quickly breaks, and the audience laughs. "Gotcha. Of course I'm enjoying it!"

"Do you want to tell everyone what *Real Love* is about?

Davi tried to describe it for us, but he did a really terrible job." The audience laughs, and Davi grimaces comically.

"Sure," says Cara, glancing around at the different cameras. "Where do I look? Can I make it any more obvious I've never done this before?" Again, the audience laughs. It's loving this babe-in-the-woods routine.

"Just look at me," says Jimmy. "Tell *me* what the movie's about."

"Well, Jimmy, it takes place in the future, and it's about this female gamer—that's me—who's really into simulation games, like SimCity and stuff like that, and in one of these games, she decides to design the perfect guy, since all the real-life dudes suck, and she ends up falling for him so hard that she enters the simulation to try to be with him."

"What a premise! Are men really that bad? That you ladies would enter a simulation to be with a *fake* man?"

Cara laughs, but Ali sees fear flash through her eyes, because they're getting close to the verboten topic. Thankfully, Cara regains her footing quickly. "Absolutely. Men are the worst." She smiles a winning smile, and the audience heartily laughs, thinking she's joking. Win-win!

"What about Davi?" asks Jimmy. "He can't be the worst, can he?"

Cara and Davi make mischievous faces at each other. "Ehhhhhh," says Cara. "No, I'm kidding. Davi is probably as close as you can get to the perfect guy." The audience "awwww"s, and Davi puts a hand to his heart, then Cara playfully pushes his shoulder. To anyone who doesn't know Cara is a lesbian, it looks like they're flirting, and Ali feels an irrational cloud of jealousy flare.

"Am I sensing some chemistry here?" says Jimmy. "Did the on-screen romance travel off-screen?" The audience "oooooh"s, titillated. Publicist Ali knows speculation about whether two costars are dating is box-office gold (see *Mr. & Mrs. Smith* and *The Notebook*), but regular Ali has the urge to punch the TV.

Cara turns a grimace into a forced smile. "Sorry to disappoint, but no, we're totally just costars and friends." She nervously shakes her leg—and it looks like she's lying about their relationship.

Davi nods and looks down, making it look like he's lying, too. "It's the truth." The audience loudly boos.

"What a shame," says Jimmy. "You two would make a severely good-looking couple. Wouldn't they?" he asks the audience, which cheers wildly. Ali can already see the clip circulating on YouTube the next day.

"This is perfect," says Will. "Opening weekend is gonna be *big*. Here we come, blockbuster!"

"Yeah," says Ali. "Perfect."

The rest of the interview flies by—they talk about how Cara got into acting and her first big break in a Hot Pockets commercial, and then it's over. They don't even have time for the twenty-first-birthday anecdote Ali and Cara worked so hard on.

When Cara reenters the dressing room, Will gives her a resounding high five, then picks her up, slings her over his back, and carries her around the room like a trophy. "Best interview ever, best interview ever!" he chants.

"Was it really okay?" Cara asks Ali after Will sets her down.

"It was great." Ali forces a smile. "Really. A publicist's dream."

"I didn't get to tell the Poutine story, though!" Cara pouts. "It was so good."

"It doesn't matter," says Ali. "The stuff with you and Davi will play way better than that."

"Really?"

"Really."

And it does. The next day, just as Ali predicted, the clip of Cara and Davi denying their relationship goes viral—the same day the *Vanity Fair* cover story comes out with the headline "The *Real Love* Star Is the Real Deal." The clip plus the profile mean everyone in the country suddenly knows who Cara is. Ali was wildly nervous about what Jason would say in the profile, and although the bulk of it isn't incriminating, toward the end, Jason writes:

> "Throughout the interview, it seems as if Cara is holding back, and she admits there are topics her team has suggested she keep to herself. You can feel the dimming effect this has on her, and it's a shame, because she's clearly a star who could shine even brighter if allowed to do so."

This last line hits Ali in the gut, because she knows it's true, and in that moment, she hates her job and herself. For the millionth time, she plays out the scenario of quitting and starting her own agency, and for the millionth time, she backs away from the idea entirely.

Ali worries how much people will read into that line about Cara holding back, but luckily, thanks to the symbiosis between the clip and the cover story, it doesn't read as Cara being closeted but as her hiding her relationship with Davi. Ali scours the celebrity gossip blogs for any indication that someone might suspect Cara, but they all seem to think she's fucking Davi.

* * *

www.HollywoodsWorstNightmare.com

DAVI SEXXXSI SILVA AND HIS NEW FLAV-WHORE OF THE WEEK

Davi Sexxxsi Silva has a new flav-whore every week, and why shouldn't he? He's just so sexxxsi. This week it's his co-star literally no one had ever heard of before today, **Cara Bisset**, from the new movie *Real Love*. During an interview on **Jimmy Kimmel Live!**, they claim they've never bumped uglies, but look HOw the flav-whore's leg shakes, and look HOw Davi looks down at his dick like he's remembering her sucking it! Pretty sure we can still see some jizz on her face. Turns out all you gotta do to get your name out there is suck some sexxxsi dick! She sucked it so hard she made the cover of *Vanity Fair*! The article says, "There are topics her team has suggested she keep to herself," and we have a feeling we know juuust what "topics" they're referring to: Davi's dick and balls, in Cara's mouth! Hope she knows she's just the flav-whore of the week, though.

Ali and Cara are in Starbucks for a debrief. Cara points at the photo of her and Davi accompanying the blog post, with a crude doodle of a penis—presumably Davi's—ejaculating dots of white jizz onto her face. "Guess I've finally made it," she says, referencing how almost every female celebrity on *Hollywood's Worst Nightmare* has had jizz drawn onto her face. People sitting nearby keep glancing at Cara, and someone even snaps a covert picture of her with their flip phone. Ali thinks about how this is probably one of the last times Cara will be able to exist in public with any amount of anonymity.

"The other way to know you've made it?" says Ali. "When every gossip blog calls you a synonym for slut." *Fame Ho* calls Cara a "knockoff ho bag," *Pop Vulture* calls her an "overflowing cum dumpster," *CeleBrutal* calls her a "blowjob biotch"—it goes on like that for a while. Ali shakes her head and slams her laptop closed. "Meanwhile, Davi is just sexy."

"I wish people knew who I was because of the movie and how good I am in it," says Cara.

"They will," says Ali. "The good thing about this new internet age is that a story can run the news cycle in forty-eight hours and then something else replaces it. By the time the movie comes out on Friday, this will be old news."

"I hope so," says Cara.

While Ali is shopping in Whole Foods that evening, her dad calls for the third time that week, which is excessive, even for him, so Ali picks up in case something is wrong.

"Hi, Dad, is everything okay?"

"I just wanted to let you know I found some real cheap plane tickets for Thanksgiving, in case you wanted to come home."

"Have I not told you yet? I'm actually going to be abroad during Thanksgiving this year. I'm going on a worldwide promo tour with one of my clients." Ali is relieved to have an excuse—she hates the obligation of going home for holidays, and resents that her dad makes her feel guilty about it as an adult when he missed holidays because of work all the time while she was growing up. Ali much preferred spending holidays with Natalie's parents, two sisters, and countless aunts and uncles and cousins. Everyone at least pretended to be happy. It made it easier not to think about Ali's mom—both her absence and the holidays she'd ruined:

The Thanksgiving she was supposed to host but abandoned when she got overwhelmed, peeling out of the driveway ten minutes before everyone was supposed to arrive. The Christmas Eve her mom took Ali shopping and went on such a manic spree she maxed out all her credit cards, then started stuffing her pockets with jewelry and perfume. They were caught by Macy's security and would have been arrested if Ali's dad hadn't worked for the police department. He made Ali's mom return all the gifts, so there were no presents for Christmas the next day. Ali has dozens more stories like that.

"A worldwide tour! Sounds nice," says Ali's dad with a tinge of jealousy, which annoys Ali, because there's nothing stopping him from traveling the world himself—he just refuses, either because he hates spending money or because he's scared to be out of his comfort zone, or he actually just doesn't want to, which Ali has a hard time believing. "I'm perfectly happy right where I am," he always says, but to Ali, it reeks of protesting too much. The only country he's visited other than the United States is Canada, since their town is only an hour's drive from the border, and the first time he flew on a plane was to visit Ali in Los Angeles. She tried over the years to convince him to take a trip abroad with her and Natalie, but he always said the same thing: "I'm perfectly happy right where I am."

"Who's the client you're going with?" he asks.

Ali pushes her cart by the strawberries, their sweet scent wafting. She peers into the cartons—the berries look incredibly fresh and firm, but every year strawberries are at the top of the "dirty dozen" list of fruits and vegetables with the most pesticide residue, so Ali never buys them, even though they were her favorite growing up. Most fruits are full of pesticide, except for melons, pineapple, and papaya, so those are the ones she usually buys. "No one you'd know," she says to her dad. "A young actress just starting out."

"Is she a total diva bitch?" he asks, used to Ali complaining about her clients.

"No, she's actually kind of great." Ali steps around the woman in yoga pants and a sports bra who must have squeezed every avocado on the display to grab two of her own. "Really funny, like, she cracks me up all the time, and really interesting, and genuine, and she's just...different than most clients. Different than most *people*. It's really easy to talk to her."

"Sounds like she might be more than a client," her dad says.

"I guess we are becoming friends."

"Not more than friends?" In many ways, Ali's dad wasn't a perfect parent, but one thing he did get right was accepting Ali right away when she came out to him at twenty-three. He looked up at the ceiling and said, "Well, Mary, you owe me twenty bucks." To Ali he said, "I always had a feeling, and I think it's A-OK."

"Dad!" Ali's cheeks heat up. "No!"

"Okay, well, don't be like me and stay a widow the rest of your life. Gets goddamn lonely."

This makes Ali feel guilty she doesn't visit more, even though she knows she isn't a replacement for a romantic partner. Her parents were high school sweethearts; neither had dated anyone else seriously before, so they were each other's first love. Maybe this is why, even after all these years, her dad has never even *tried* to meet someone new. So stubborn and stuck in his ways. It would ease the mental burden on her to know he had someone else in his life. But every time Ali asks him about it, he says some version of "I'm perfectly happy on my own."

"You know, there's something you could do about this loneliness," Ali says. "It's called dating."

"Ali, I know every single person in this town."

Ali moves on to the meat department, where she grabs a package of free-range, organic, hormone-free, antibiotic-free, non-GMO, 100 percent grass-fed sirloin. She tries not to buy chicken, due to the high bacteria levels, and she never buys ground meat, because who knows what could be hiding in that. "If I were you, I'd move. You're retired—it's not like there's anything keeping you there anymore."

"What about my family? I think that's a reason to stay here, even if you don't."

He says it lightly, but Ali still feels it like a jab. Part of her wants to fire an equally accusatory statement back, about how he always cared more about his job than he did about Ali or her mom, or how Ali didn't exactly feel tethered to a place filled with difficult memories.

Ali's mom's bipolar symptoms began to appear after Ali's birth, when Ali's mom was in her early twenties—she thought it was postpartum depression, but when the highs and lows didn't stop after a few years, she went to a doctor and was officially diagnosed. Whenever she was going through a depressive episode, Ali's dad would ask Ali to stay home from school and look after her mom, since he could never miss work due to the life-and-death nature of it. Ali probably missed a whole third of each school year. Whenever she *did* go, she'd be too worried about her mom to focus. Would she have slit her wrists or swallowed a bottle of pills or left the car on in the garage, the way she always threatened to? Or would she simply be passed out in bed with her soaps on TV? If Ali was lucky, she'd be on an upswing, blasting Fleetwood Mac ("Dreams" was her favorite) and dancing in the living room completely naked. But the upswings never lasted more than a few days, and they were invariably followed by plunging drops. That was Ali's whole life: up and down and up and down like a roller coaster she had never asked to ride, and Ali, of course, hated roller coasters. When Ali left for college and finally got some distance from her family, she could see how messed up the dynamic had made her, and she started going to therapy. The therapist said her high levels of anxiety stemmed from her mother and never knowing what to expect, which was a huge revelation—Ali had always thought she'd just been born anxious. The therapist also said Ali's dad forced her into a parent role at far too young an age, which was a form of emotional abuse and neglect. Ali thought those words seemed a bit extreme, but she does have lingering anger toward her dad. The two of them have never talked about it, of course, which is the Midwestern way, so it just stays all bottled up in Ali's body, filling her with dread at the thought of seeing him. But instead of saying this, she settles on diffusing the tension. "Yeah, North Dakota is crawling with good publicist jobs."

"Well, if you won't come home, maybe I'll come to you. What about Christmas? Will you be back from your trip then?"

Ali's heart speeds up and her stomach drops. Whenever she thinks about seeing her dad hypothetically, it seems like a nice idea, but whenever it edges toward reality, it seems like a terrible one, mainly because of all the aforementioned childhood trauma. But also because when her dad comes to visit her, he's out of his comfort zone and full of judgy comments about how expensive and inconvenient everything is. She *will* be back from the promo tour by Christmas but says, "I'm not sure, I'll have to check the schedule."

"Let me know," he says. "It sure would be nice to see you."

13

Wednesday: the daylong press junket for *Real Love* at the Four Seasons in Beverly Hills. As usual, Ali is extremely anxious about how it will go, but by the evening, Cara has nailed all thirty-one interviews so far, staying on message and energetically expressing her enthusiasm for the film in a way that appears candid, fun, and fresh. The journalists mostly behaved as well, with only one asking the verboten question about her romantic life, to which Cara replied, "I've been working so much, my pubes might as well be tumbleweeds," which got a stunned laugh from the journalist and no follow-up questions. At 4:45, Cara is down to her last interview for the day, and Ali has a migraine as painful as *Crossroads* and *Glitter* combined, but at least she's now unconcerned about Cara bombing her interviews, so she rubs her temples as she vaguely listens to Cara give the same answers she's already given thirty-one times.

I totally think we could be living in a simulation.
How much more far-fetched is that than God?

Davi loved to mess with me on set. He'd come into my trailer every day when I wasn't there and drop king-size candy bars in my toilet, so I kept having to ask maintenance to unclog it, and every now and then he'd fill my water bottle with vodka, so every day for weeks I'd be taking these really cautious first sips, and of course, whenever it had been long enough that I'd forget and just start gulping, it was vodka. I got him back, though—during a love scene, I wore pasties with his mom's face on them. He never pranked me again after that!

Hana was such an empathetic director. If you feel safe, you can act a lot better, which is like duh squared, but I only realized that recently.

My ex once said I was the most stubborn person she'd ever known—

At the word *she*, Ali snaps to attention. Of course, it had to be a filmed interview in which Cara made a big gay slip. Cara realizes what she's said and sits there positively frozen, her mouth hanging open, before looking at Ali with widened what-the-fuck-do-I-do eyes. The journalist notices Cara looking at Ali, and in an attempt not to draw attention to it, Ali blinks calmly, trying to telegraph to Cara she should just breeze past it, but instead Cara backpedals: "And um, by *ex*, I mean an ex-friend. You know how when you stop being friends with someone it can feel like a breakup?"

Ali looks at her watch—it's been nine minutes out of the ten allotted for the interview, which is close enough. She claps her hands and stands up, sending a throbbing bolt of agony through her skull. "Okay, I think we've got it, yeah?

Thanks so much, everyone!" She approaches the journalist, a blonde woman with horsey teeth. She started at *E! News* a few months ago, so Ali doesn't know her well enough to know whether she'll agree to cut the offending part or not. "I think we can cut the last question, yeah? Cara has been in interviews all day, and she's so tired, and you know how your brain just stops working at a certain point?"

"Sure," the woman says, a black sesame seed lodged between her two supersize front teeth. Her face and tone are completely unreadable, and Ali can't tell if she's saying it in an agreeable way or in a *Sure, when pigs fly* way.

But if Ali belabors the point any more, it'll be as obvious as a straight woman saying she watches *The L Word* for "the great writing." She falls back on one of the golden rules of PR: When in doubt, bribe. "I'm not sure if you know, but Sarah Jessica Parker is one of my clients, and we're looking for a journalist to do a feature on her next month to promote *The Family Stone.* I think you'd be a great fit. Would you be interested?"

"Oh. Why do you think I'd be a great fit?" Again, the woman says it in a flat way, and Ali can't tell if she's trying to call her out on the bribe or genuinely asking.

"You asked great questions," Ali says, even though her questions were the same as all thirty journalists' before her. "You seem really perceptive." Ali's head feels like the inside of a pinball machine, with a steel ball ricocheting against every nook and cranny.

"Huh, no one's ever said that to me before."

Ali can't believe this woman. She pulls a card from her bag and thrusts it at her. "Call me if you're interested in the piece on SJP," she says, with absolutely no idea whether the woman is going to take her up on it or whether she'll publish the video with a title like "Cara Bisset Reveals All About *Real Love...and* Her Ex-Girlfriend."

Thursday: the LA premiere at Grauman's Chinese Theatre in Hollywood. Cara wears a pink Paul Smith suit (with no shirt underneath and stilettos) that the photographers go wild for, and Ali can't help but stare as Cara strikes pose after confident pose, her cheekbones glinting in the cameras' flash, her lipsticked mouth slightly, seductively open, the inverted parentheses of her cleavage peeking through the blazer's deep V. The goofy person in ridiculous athleisure outfits seems far away from this stunning, sophisticated model. Ali decides to stay and watch the movie, which she rarely does, and is surprised by how rapt she is—she leans forward in her seat the whole two hours, like a kid who sits on the floor while watching TV because they want to get as close as possible to the magic of it all.

All of Cara's qualities that have charmed Ali in real life are not only evident but enhanced on-screen—her disarming openness, her silly wisdom, her protective irony, her subversive bawdiness...It's all there in her on-screen character, Alessa, a woman virtually no man would be able to handle—so she creates one who can handle her instead. Preferring this unreality to reality, Alessa enters the simulation so she can live more truthfully. The tagline for the movie is "Real love in a fake world," and Ali delights in how brilliantly oxymoronic it is. Cara nails that tone. When Ali was doing media training with her, Cara said, "The movie is a pretty apt metaphor for straight women—Alessa creates the perfect man because one literally doesn't exist. Most straight women hate men and most straight men hate women, but they're still inexplicably attracted to each other. Heterosexuality is so flawed, and Alessa understands it'll probably never work in reality. That's really fucking heartbreaking! I obviously can't say any of that to the press, but that's how I was able to find my way into the character." When you watch the movie through this lens, Cara's role becomes even more powerful. She has that *presence*, that Meryl Streep/Julia Roberts je ne sais quoi where in every scene, both the character's motivation and the opposite of that motivation are present in her face and her voice and her body. As the credits roll, Ali feels in her bones that Cara will win an Oscar—either for this movie or another one soon to come.

Everyone else seems to think so, too, because at the after-party at the Roosevelt Hotel pool, there's practically a receiving line to speak to Cara. Ali hangs out nearby, trying to quell the feeling of wanting Cara all to herself, nabbing hors d'oeuvres and champagne flutes from circling servers dressed as sims, admiring the David Hockney painting on the bottom of the pool—a multitude of curved blue lines shaped like elbow macaroni that, when taken together, look like waves—and briefly catching up with other clients and industry people. Everyone outside Hollywood assumes after-parties are the epitome of fun, but for Ali, they're just after-hours work. She'd much rather be at home in her pajamas, where "Hollaback Girl" by Gwen Stefani is not blasting and strobe-like flashes from cameras aren't threatening to give her a migraine and groups of women with duck lips aren't screeching about their Jimmy Choos.

After about an hour, the crowd around Cara finally abates. She seems simultaneously elated and exhausted as she plops down next to Ali on a bench. "Brad Pitt told me my performance was *luminous*."

"I'd have to agree," says Ali. "It was pretty impressive."

In the course of one evening, Cara has gone from her unknown newbie client to a star.

"Why are you staring at me like that? Do I have food on my face?"

"Honestly, I think I'm a little starstruck."

Cara, who is on her umpteenth glass of champagne, pushes Ali so hard she falls sideways on the bench. "Get outa here."

Ali sits up and brushes her hair out of her face. "I mean it. Now I get why you've been practicing your Oscars acceptance speech since you were a kid. You're gonna need it soon."

For the first time since Ali met her, Cara blushes. She covers her face with her hands. "Staaaaaaaahp!"

"Okay." Ali sips her champagne and pointedly surveys the space, avoiding Cara's eyes. A straight couple vigorously makes out a few benches away from them, Jack Black strikes a comically seductive pose on a chaise longue while someone takes his picture, and a shirtless Davi cannonballs into the pool.

Cara nudges Ali's shoulder with her own. "Actually no, don't stop."

Ali laughs. "You know you're talented as hell."

Cara twirls the stem of her champagne glass between her thumb and pointer finger. "Some days I definitely think so. Others I'm not so sure."

Ali points in Cara's face. "Don't pretend to be modest; it doesn't suit you."

"I'm being real! You must know what I'm talking about—it's true for all artists. When you're writing your stories, some days aren't you like, *I'm the shit*, and other days, aren't you like, *I'm a* piece *of shit*?"

Ali sticks out her bottom lip. "I'd say I spend most of my days in the piece-of-shit category."

"Really?"

"I've never been published or gotten into an MFA program or anything, so I must be a hack." Ali slurps her drink as if to emphasize her point.

"Please. I bet you're a regular Patricia Highsmith. You should let me read your stuff!"

"No way." Ali shakes her head vehemently. "I've never even let my best friend read my stories."

Cara grabs another champagne flute from a passing sim. "That's probably your problem—you don't put yourself out there enough. If you let me read one of your stories, I bet it'd get published in the *New Yorker*. And it would be their first time running a story that didn't suck hairy, poop-smeared ass!"

Ali screeches a shocked laugh, and Cara laughs back until they're mired in one of their giggle fits.

Cara wipes a finger under her eye. "You know I'll never give this up. I'll wear you down."

Ali waves her hand toward the virtual reality station, where people wearing VR headsets swivel their heads and wave their arms, walking back and forth "in" the setting of *Real Love*. "You better go put on a headset, cause that's the only way you'll be reading a story of mine."

The opening bars of "We Belong Together" by Mariah Carey emanate from the DJ booth. Natalie was a hard-core Mariah Carey fan, to the point where she would call out sick from work on days Mariah released a new album so she could simply listen to it over and over. What would Natalie have thought of *The Emancipation of Mimi*, which came out seven months after her death? Ali guesses Natalie's favorite would have been "Shake It Off," but she'll never know for sure, a fact that sits in her stomach like a cold brick.

"Oh shit, this is my SONG!" Cara yells, jumping up. She grabs Ali's hand and pulls her toward the music, but Ali throws her weight in the opposite direction.

"I don't really dance."

Cara rolls her eyes and pulls harder, muscling Ali into the area where people are dancing. Ali stands there, obstinate, as Cara swings her hips from side to side and snaps her fingers in a purposefully hokey way. When Mariah sings, "What I wouldn't give to have you lying by my side," Cara points at Ali and locks eyes with her in a half-joking, half-serious way, and a lightning bolt strikes Ali's stomach. Somehow she's not thinking about Natalie anymore. Cara throws her hands around Ali's neck and smiles her goofy smile and Ali lets her body fall into rhythm with Cara's. Sometimes when two people dance, there are those initial awkward seconds where their hips don't match up and they have to figure out who's going to follow whom, but this doesn't happen with Ali and Cara—they instinctively choose the same pattern of *left right left left, right left right right*. Up close, Ali can smell Cara's perfume, a mix of cardamom and lemon zest that makes Ali think of muffins, and a bizarre little movie starts to play in her head: she and Cara in pajamas in Ali's sunlight-soaked kitchen, Cara pouring batter into a muffin tin as Ali hugs her from behind and kisses the curve where her back meets her neck. Ali shakes her head—she's only had a glass and a half of champagne, but she hasn't eaten much, so it must be going to her head.

When Mariah gets to the chorus, Cara slinks down Ali's body until she's in a spread-legged squat, and at "we belong together," she grabs Ali's hands and pulls them toward her so forcefully, Ali loses her balance and falls right on top of her.

But it almost feels choreographed as Cara laughs and rolls Ali onto her back in a wrestling-esque maneuver, then straddles her and places Ali's hands on her hips. Ali feels like she and Cara are the only two people on earth, and she forgets to worry about whether anyone is watching. Cara gyrates to the beat, bopping Ali's nose to the line "I only think of you" and biting her bottom lip, again in that half-joking, half-serious way. Ali truly can't tell whether Cara is doing a bit or flirting with her, but her body doesn't know the difference and responds with a hot flash between her legs.

A different kind of flash illuminates the air for a split second—a camera flash—and Ali can't believe she's been so careless. Her panicked publicist brain takes over as she sits up and yells at Cara to get off her before marching away to try to find the person who took the picture. An hour later, she's had no luck. She tells herself maybe someone was taking a picture of something else, or if the picture *was* of her and Cara, maybe the person who took it has no shady intentions and simply wanted it for themselves. All she can do at this point is cross her fingers and hope.

Friday: *Real Love*'s US release. On opening night, it makes $18 million, securing the number one spot at the box office. Ali credits the massive popularity of the YA book series *Real Love* is based on, Davi's star power, Cara's breakout performance, the dating rumors about the two of them, and the fact that they're not competing with any other huge titles. (The number two spot is *Chicken Little*, and number three is *Jarhead*. In two weeks, *Harry Potter and the Goblet of Fire* will come out, and it will definitely unseat *Real Love*.) Still, it's a huge feat to get the number one spot at the box office for even one day.

Ali texts Cara: !!!!!!!!!!!!!!!!!!!!

I know. I'm kind of freaking out but also kind of can't believe it

To be earnest for a sec: I'm really proud of you. You deserve it!

Ew earnestness. Jk, thank u, that really means a lot coming from u

What are you doing to celebrate??

My mom and I are in the McDonald's drive-thru getting hot fudge sundaes. It's what we've done to celebrate ever since I was little. She just told the cashier I'm starring in the #1 movie in the country & he said he didn't know who I was, but he gave me extra fudge anyway lol

I hope you know that's prob the last time that will happen

What? Getting extra fudge?

No, someone not knowing who you are

I'm ready for it!!

Just remember that when you're out in public from now on. People are watching

On Saturday, *Real Love* makes $20 million, and on Sunday, it makes $14 million, bringing its opening weekend grand total to $52 million—still the top spot.

Everyone is riding high when the dominoes start falling. First, it turns out there's not only a photo from the "We Belong Together" dance, but also a video of Cara grinding on top of Ali, complete with a zoom-in on Cara biting her bottom lip and Ali making a completely embarrassing face like she's in ecstasy. It's on all the gossip blogs and on YouTube and has over a hundred thousand views (which is officially the threshold for going viral) and three thousand comments. It was posted by someone with the username dildo_swaggins, with the comment "Just gonna leave this here..."

Ali clicks on dildo_swaggins's profile, where it says she's a movie blogger, which must be why she was invited to the after-party. Ali finds her on Facebook and sends her a message asking if she'd be interested in an exclusive interview with Cara in exchange for deleting the video, but she never writes back. Every time Victoria pops her head into Ali's office, Ali pretends to be on an important call to avert a scolding. She hopes the video will lose steam, but after ten journalists ask her for a comment, she says, "Cara was just joking around and having fun. As her publicist, I can very confidently say we are *not* dating."

The day after, *E! News* releases its video interview with Cara from the press junket, and it shows not only Cara's pronoun slip but Ali cutting in and saying, "Okay, I think we've got it, yeah?" The journalist is careful in the copy accompanying the video not to draw any conclusions about the gaffe, but the gossip blogs go ahead and do that for them:

www.EatGossipAndDie.com

IS CARA BISSET A HO FOR BOTH MEN AND WOMEN?!

Last week, **Cara Bi-sset** (see what we did there?) made her internet debut for denying sucking **Davi Silva**'s sweet schlong (even though we all know she did!), and this week it seems she's moved on to carpet munching. Nom nom nom. First, she **grinded all up on her publicist** at a party and today she referenced an ex-GIRLFRIEND in an *E! News* interview. Remember Cara's *Vanity Fair* interview that said, "there are topics her team has suggested she keep to herself"? Now we're thinking that refers to Cara being such a horny slutbag she'll fuck anything that moves! Does Davi know? Is the dirty whore cheating on him? JUSTICE 4 DAVI!!!!!!

14

"We have to do something to dispel these rumors," says Ali. They're sitting in the American Airlines Admirals Club, waiting for their flight to Paris, the tour's first stop.

"I'm not changing my mind about lying," Cara says through a mouthful of chips.

Ali doesn't know how anyone eats before flying. She herself has been on and off the toilet all day with anxious diarrhea. The thought of taking a plane flown by highly trained pilots makes her *slightly* less nervous than the thought of driving a car herself, but it's still pretty high on the list of activities she'd prefer never to do. She's already taken her first Ativan and will take the second one right before takeoff. If there's bad turbulence, which there usually is on transatlantic flights, she'll take another. "You don't have to lie, but maybe you and Davi could get dinner in Paris, and we'll tip off a paparazzo or two, and Davi could put his arm around you, or you could hold hands, or kiss his cheek, or do something else that *suggests* you're more than friends without having to say anything."

Cara licks her fingers. "Won't it be pretty obvious if we do that right after all these rumors about my sexuality?"

Ali waves her hand in the air. "You'd be surprised what people will fall for when they want to."

Their boarding announcement comes through the intercom. "Let me think about it," says Cara. Ali takes that as her cue to run to the bathroom one last time.

Ali and Cara are in business class, sitting next to each other—Ali in the window seat, Cara in the aisle. On the plane, Ali begins her sanitization ritual, which consists of putting on a face mask and plastic gloves, then cleaning every surface in her area with Lysol wipes—the tray table, the remote, the video screen, the overhead buttons for light and air, the window shade, even the wall. Finally, she covers her seat with a blanket from home and takes her second Ativan.

Cara watches Ali do all this with a half-amused, half-concerned expression. "Remember when I said you were a little neurotic? I'm going to update that to *extremely* neurotic."

"That's probably fair." Ali sits down, but keeps her mask on as people board, huffing or coughing or talking loudly to their companions.

"I'm guessing flying isn't, like, your favorite activity?"

"It's pretty low on the list. What about you? Doesn't faze you a bit?"

A man with a backpack slung over his shoulder stomps by, and the backpack hits Cara in the face, but the man doesn't notice. Cara leans away from the aisle. "Not the flying part."

"What part, then?" Ali studies the people who stream by on their way to coach: a lanky man with greasy glasses and a greasy Pizza Hut box to match, a raccoon-eyed woman with a baby strapped to her chest whose diaper smells like it needs to be changed, a platinum-blonde girl with a heavily made-up face wearing what has to be the most uncomfortable plane outfit ever: a sequined T-shirt, leather pants, and stilettos.

"I have claustrophobia, so when I sit in coach, things can get a little dicey, especially if I don't have an aisle seat, but this is chill."

"Wow, you're actually afraid of something. What else triggers it?"

Cara lists them on her fingers. "The car wash, elevators, small rooms with closed doors, closets, both literal and figurative." She gives Ali a pointed look.

"Are you saying being closeted as an actor triggers your claustrophobia?"

"Yeah, it's about being physically *or* emotionally trapped. And I feel pretty fucking emotionally trapped not being able to express who I am." She gazes out the window, her lichen irises looking especially on the gray side. Tiny red lightning bolts shoot through the whites of her eyes.

"Jesus, Cara, I'm sorry. I knew you didn't like it, but I didn't know it was triggering an actual *phobia*. That makes me feel terrible. Forget what I said about those photos with Davi."

Cara's eyes shimmer and she wipes at them like they're itchy. "I know you aren't personally responsible. You're just trying to help me succeed within a homophobic industry that's ironically full of homos."

Ali laughs. "I'm complicit, though. I could counsel my clients to come out."

Cara sticks out her lips. "Girl, if you counseled all your clients to come out, you probably wouldn't *have* any clients."

* * *

Thanks to the Ativan and a vodka soda, Ali falls asleep shortly after takeoff, but she wakes up a few hours later when a man a couple of aisles back starts coughing. She peers out the window and decides they must be flying over the Midwest, due to the green circles in various stages of completion: some semicircles, some with quarters missing like a pie chart, a few Pac-Mans. Ali googled it once and found out the green circles are fields filled with crops like corn or soybeans or wheat. On the screen in front of her, Ali taps the map to see where they are: Kansas.

It's then that she notices her laptop isn't on her tray table—she was trying to work before she fell asleep—but on Cara's, and Cara is attentively squinting at the screen.

"Is that my laptop?" Ali asks, just to make sure.

Cara nods distractedly, deep into whatever she's reading.

In the aisle next to them, two kids—probably around three and five—sit by themselves, watching Pixar movies (*Finding Nemo* for the three-year-old, *Monsters, Inc.* for the five-year-old) while snacking on avocado-and-cucumber sushi rolls. Ali can't imagine sitting in business class, much less eating sushi, at such a young age. Her first airplane ride was when she went to college, and she tried sushi sometime her freshman year. It wasn't until her late twenties that she first rode in business class, when she was high enough on the publicist ladder to accompany clients on trips.

"And what are you *doing* with my laptop?" Ali asks Cara.

"Reading one of your stories."

"Good one." Ali leans over to see what Cara is actually looking at, and to her horror, it's a Word doc in Times

New Roman font, double spaced. She recognizes a sentence from "Lunch Date," her story about the old man and the girl who start meeting up for lunch, and her stomach lurches before she snaps the laptop's lid closed and snatches it, holding it against her chest protectively. "That is, like, the hugest, most uncool invasion of privacy *ever.*" Ali has been enjoying Cara's curiosity about her, but this is too far—Ali feels violated.

Cara smiles mischievously. "Don't you want to know what I thought, though?"

Ali shudders, her heartbeat reverberating through her whole body. "No. It's not funny or cute, Cara. It's upsetting." Ali slams the laptop down onto her tray table.

Cara's face pales. "Oh. I'm sorry. You're right, I totally should have asked. Please don't be mad at me while we're trapped on a twelve-hour flight together. I'll never do something like that again, I promise."

Cara legitimately looks terrified, and Ali feels herself soften. "Okay."

"You really don't want me to tell you how much I liked it?"

Ali pushes out her lips. "I guess that's the least you could do." Her stomach gurgles with heat and acid, and she covers her face with her hands.

"It was so fucking good, Ali."

Ali peeks through her fingers. "Really?"

Cara pulls Ali's hands away from her face and holds them in hers. She gives them a soft squeeze and looks at Ali with complete openness. "Really."

Ali swears she feels a crack burst open in her chest. Cold air whooshes in, taking her breath away. She looks down, away from Cara's eyes. "You're just saying that to be nice."

Cara withdraws her hands from Ali's. "Don't do that. You *know* I wouldn't lie."

"You're right. I'm sorry. It's just weirdly hard to accept praise, you know?"

"Nope, I'm a total ho for praise."

Ali laughs. The gap between the seat in front of her and the wall reveals that the person sitting in front of Ali—a middle-aged woman who kind of looks like Oprah—is watching *Boys Don't Cry*, and it's the scene where Brandon (Hilary Swank's character) and Lana (Chloë Sevigny's character) are on a date. Ali wonders what Oprah's look-alike is thinking. Did she choose the movie knowing what it was about? Is she part of the LGBT community herself? Or does she have a kid who is? Or is she simply an open lady?

"If I say more, will you accept it?"

"I'll try," Ali says, still peeking at *Boys Don't Cry* through the gap. Brandon and Lana are standing in front of a vintage blue car, but when they lean in to kiss, the movie abruptly cuts to the next scene, censored for in-flight entertainment—yet another reason Ali can't counsel Cara to come out.

"I loved all the characters, but I loved the old dude's dead wife the most, and that's impressive because usually dead people in fictionalized stuff are so unspecific, but this lady felt three-motherfucking-D. The part where the old dude is remembering how his wife used to trick him into thinking she was about to tell him something bad by saying, 'I have to tell you something' or 'Ugh, I just remembered—' in this annoyed voice, and when he'd say, 'What?' she'd say, 'I love you!' And she would do it infrequently enough that he'd usually forget and fall for the trick? Man, I loved that. It felt so real."

"Natalie used to do that," Ali says to Cara. Growing

up with parents who didn't say, "I love you" before bed or before leaving the house, Ali had never imagined she could be with someone who would say it multiple times a day, unexpectedly—while they were walking Glen or sitting on the couch watching TV or brushing their teeth or even in the middle of the night. And the amount of times Natalie professed it never cheapened it—it always felt 100 percent genuine. Ali truly never tired of hearing it. She thinks it will be impossible to find a second person on earth who could love her so wholeheartedly, and vice versa.

"I figured the story was sort of a way for you to deal with your grief," says Cara.

"Yeah, you could say that."

"The line about the weak smile, like a tea bag that's already been used once and barely colors the water? Get outa here!" Cara smacks Ali's arm.

Ali snickers. Being told you've written a great simile might be better than sex.

"Can I give you one suggestion without you thinking it'll invalidate all the good stuff I just said?"

Ali nods.

"The ending felt a bit too wrapped-up-with-a-bow-on-it to me. Like, I kind of wanted the girl to never come back."

Ali juts her chin forward. "Are you serious?"

"What, too bleak?"

"No, that was my original ending!" Ali slaps her tray table. "All the people in my workshop said it was too depressing."

"Fuck those stupidheads."

Out of nowhere, the plane jerks down so violently Ali's butt almost leaves the seat. She grasps the armrest as the fasten-seatbelt symbol dings and flashes. "Flight attendants, please be seated," says the pilot in a hurried, terse voice. Ali hates taciturn pilots who won't give passengers the slightest detail about what's happening, because it makes her worry the plane is about to crash. She glares out the window, which usually helps to calm her, but the sun is setting in a thin orange line along the darkening horizon and it's difficult to tell where they are in relation to the ground. The plane shudders again and Ali grabs her cup of water before it tumbles over. Holding it isn't much better—Ali can't tell if her hand is violently shaking or if it's the plane.

"Hey, nervous Nellie, it's okay," says Cara.

Ali squeezes her eyes shut and shakes her head vehemently. Whenever she would get like this while flying, Natalie used to sing her a song called "Turbulence Is Normal" to the tune of "Everyday" by Buddy Holly. "Every day, turbulence is normal. It's just the plane and the sky having a little quarrel." Ali can't remember any verses after this, though, and it makes her want to scream and cry and break dishware because Natalie isn't here—because the longer she's gone, the more Ali will forget.

"Honey, you've gotta breathe," says Cara, taking Ali's hand. "Exhale through your mouth."

Ali obeys.

"Okay, now close your mouth and inhale through your nose for four seconds." Cara taps Ali's hand for each second. The plane shakes like it's a wet dog trying to get dry, and Ali's breath catches. "It's okay, keep breathing. Good. Hold it for seven seconds. Now exhale through your mouth for eight seconds. Good. Again."

Cara repeats the breathing instructions while also massaging the hand she's holding, squeezing the pressure point in the flap between Ali's thumb and pointer finger, then using the insides of her pointer and middle fingers to squeeze and quickly slide from the bottom to the top of all Ali's fingers, a snapping sound issuing each time. After a few minutes, the breathing and the hand massage have helped the turbulence to feel somewhat normal, and while Ali would have preferred Natalie's song, she's grateful another form of comfort was offered to her.

15

When they land, it's 9:00 a.m. Paris time. They're stay-ing at the Ritz in the First Arrondissement, neither the hotel nor the neighborhood Ali would have chosen—the hotel is too fancy and the neighborhood too touristy. When Ali and Natalie took their trip to Paris to celebrate their tenth anniversary, they rented an apartment from a friend of a friend, which they preferred over staying at a hotel, so they could cook some meals at home and feel more like locals. The apartment was a lovely mix of old farmhouse decor and modern touches, and it was in the Seventh Arrondisse-ment, above a flower shop and across the street from a bakery where elementary schoolers would swarm for midday crois-sants and adults would stop for baguettes on their way home from work.

Ali's favorite activities while traveling are taking long walks through neighborhoods, so she can really get to know them, and visiting smaller, less touristy art museums. So for Ali, she and Natalie walked all over the narrow cobble-stone streets of the Marais with its pastel buildings, up the charming hills of Montmartre, past stone houses covered in ivy with window boxes full of flowers and quaint shutters, and almost the entire length of Rue du Bac, with its small shops and cafés. For museums, they went to the Rodin sculpture museum, where they giggled at the sculpture of all the butts pressed together, and the Musée Marmottan Monet, where they admired all the Impressionist paintings.

Natalie's favorite traveling activity was strolling through parks and gardens, because she was such a flower freak. So for Natalie, they visited the Tuileries Garden, with its orderly rows of trees and sculpted shrubbery, and the Parc des Buttes Chaumont, with its towering quarry cliffs, and they took a day trip to Giverny, where Monet's house was and where he painted his famous *Water Lilies*. It ended up being like Disney World for flowers, just absolutely mobbed with tourists, so they didn't stay long—neither of them wanted to battle crowds. The only time they saw the Eiffel Tower was from a cab at night, all lit up.

On their second-to-last day there, before Ali woke up, Natalie snuck off to a fancy patisserie near the Sixth Arrondissement that made Ali's favorite croissant, the Ispahan, composed of rose, raspberry, and lychee, and surprised Ali with it when she woke up. After a few delicious bites, Ali's teeth hit something hard, and she spit out a glob containing shiny metal—a ring. The band was white gold, with a large aqua chalcedony stone on the bottom surrounded by a hand-notched halo. On the top, a smaller faceted moonstone was surrounded by melted white gold circles. By the look on Natalie's face, Ali understood it was an engagement ring. (Both Ali and Natalie thought diamonds were the greatest marketing scam of all time, and Ali much preferred the chalcedony—her favorite gemstone—and moonstone.) The ring had been made by one of their close friends, who was a metalworker. "Yes, yes, yes," Ali had said before Natalie even had the chance to formally ask. Even though this was well before gay marriage was legal, they could still have a commitment ceremony and file for domestic partnership.

There wasn't even a microscopic amount of doubt when Ali said yes—she was sure she wanted to spend her life with Natalie. Because Natalie was the first and only person Ali had ever been in love with. Because Natalie would always walk to the grocery store when Ali had a craving. Because Natalie always took Glen on his morning walk so Ali could sleep in. Because Natalie let Glen choose where he wanted to go on walks, and cooked Glen his food, and let Glen share her pillow at night. Because Natalie talked constantly through every TV show and movie about the quality of the writing, and when Ali watched something by herself, she missed the commentary. Because Natalie told Ali she loved her countless times a day. Because Natalie had terrible road rage but was self-aware enough about it to turn it into a joke. Because when Ali was having a panic attack, Natalie would blast Donna Summer and they would dance until it went away.

Because they agreed about all the Big Stuff: Neither was religious (Natalie had been raised Catholic and realized it was all a sham in college, after which she became a staunch atheist; Ali had been raised areligious but defined herself as 99 percent atheist and 1 percent agnostic); neither cared about owning a home—not that they could even afford it, but like diamonds, they both thought it seemed like a total scam; neither wanted kids (Ali was too afraid of a calamity happening to a child, and Natalie was too career driven); they agreed about keeping separate finances so they'd never have to judge each other for their spending (Natalie loved to shop, whereas Ali rarely bought anything for herself); and they both thought humor was the most important element of a relationship, Natalie with her in-your-face meanness, like she was constantly performing at a roast, and Ali with her more subtle, dry wit—anyone other than Natalie and their closest friends had a hard time telling when Ali was joking.

Because they almost never fought. Ali couldn't take any more conflict after a childhood with a bipolar mother, and Natalie's parents had "fought like *Jerry Springer* guests" and she'd vowed to never be like that in a relationship. (Natalie had a lot of anger, but luckily, it was never directed at Ali but instead at Los Angeles drivers, her boss, people who didn't pick up their dog's poop, bigots on the internet, and AT&T customer service representatives.) In Ali and Natalie's twelve years together, neither had ever yelled at the other, and they never bickered about the trivial topics other couples seemed to—who did more chores or who was right about some completely unimportant fact. The rare times they did have calm disagreements, those disagreements tended to be about how Natalie thought Ali needed to go back to therapy for her anxiety (Ali had stopped after college) or how Ali thought Natalie worked too much. Re: therapy, Ali would usually placate Natalie by finding a therapist who had a long wait time for new patients, and when her appointment came months later, she would tell Natalie it hadn't been a good fit—which tended to be true, since when you're resistant to the very idea of therapy, most therapists end up not being a good fit. Re: Natalie working too much, Natalie usually acknowledged she did put in a lot of hours per week, but she told Ali it was different because while Ali didn't care about her job, Natalie was incredibly passionate about hers—writing for TV had been her life's dream, and she'd had to work hard to make that dream a reality.

It was interesting the two had such similar opinions, because personalitywise, they were basically opposites. Ali was passive and Natalie was aggressive, Ali was an introvert and Natalie was an extrovert, Ali was the planner and Natalie was sporadic, Ali was patient and Natalie was impatient, Ali was a realist and Natalie was a dreamer, Ali was fearful and Natalie was brave. Her courage was hands down what Ali missed most about Natalie. Yes, Ali suffered from an anxiety disorder when Natalie was alive, but it was much more manageable thanks to how safe and calm Natalie made Ali feel—she was the most effective antianxiety treatment Ali knew of, and she wishes there were a pill that could replicate Natalie's effects.

Ali tries to push aside all the reasons she misses Natalie as she checks into the splashy Ritz with its marble columns and velvet drapes and gold chandeliers. Her plan for the day is to hide in her hotel room and sleep until the premiere this evening, which is nearby in the Second Arrondissement. She only has to last a day. The *Real Love* group will fly out early tomorrow morning, and then Ali will be free of this city and its painful reminders.

But as Ali is making her way to her room, Cara links her arm through Ali's and says, "Where should we get breakfast? McDonald's?" She says "McDonald's" in a French accent, pinkie out.

Ali gently pulls her arm out of Cara's. "I'll be eating breakfast in my room, then sleeping until the premiere."

"What?" Disappointment hangs on Cara's face. "It's my first time out of the US and you're going to make me explore Paris all by my little naive self?"

"I'm too tired. Do you know how exhausting it is to fly when you spend every single second thinking the plane is going to crash?"

Cara looks at Ali skeptically, then softens her tone. "Are you sure you're not just trying to avoid certain memories?"

"No," Ali snaps, slamming her hotel door in Cara's face.

After a shower—through the entirety of which Ali sobs and curses the weak water pressure—she calls the restaurant to order room service breakfast, but no one picks up, so she calls the front desk and is informed the restaurant is only open for dinner. Ali considers trying to sleep through the trombone-esque noises of her hollow stomach, but it's been over eleven hours since she had a meal. She's so hungry she feels like she might puke, and she remembers when Glen used to vomit neon-yellow foamy bile on his morning walks after they first adopted him. When they took him to the vet, she told them he was simply overly hungry, so they started feeding him before his walks instead of after, and the puking miraculously stopped. Now Ali misses not only Natalie but also Glen, and she cries again, picturing him curled up like a croissant with his sad eyes at the dog sitter's house. After a few minutes, the craving for an actual croissant is strong enough that she shoves a pair of sunglasses on her face and leaves the hotel.

Outside, Cara is tilting her head at a printed map of Paris, turning it this way and that.

"You're already lost?" Ali says.

"I have the world's worst sense of direction," she says. "My instinct is always the opposite of what's correct."

"Where are you trying to go?"

Cara bites her front teeth over her bottom lip. "The Eiffel Tower," she says, her voice lilting upward in embarrassment.

"Seriously?"

"I don't know where else to go! I thought you were

gonna be my tour guide. Why aren't you asleep in your room, anyway?"

"There's no room service," Ali says. "So I'm going to grab something to eat."

"Can I come?" Cara perks up like a dog told it can come on a walk. "Or would you rather be alone?"

Ali reluctantly waves Cara along. Cara smiles beatifically and starts skipping after her. The cafés they pass are full of tourists wearing New Balance sneakers and fanny packs, pointing at menus with pictures of the food, saying words in an American accent like "croy-sant" and "expresso." "I should have known we wouldn't be able to find a decent meal in the First Arrondissement," says Ali. "We're not far from the Marais."

"The what?"

"The gayborhood."

Cara jumps and yips. "See! I told you I needed you as my tour guide." Then her face goes somber. "Are you sure you're up for it?"

Ali nods, once. "I can't avoid Paris forever. I love it too much." As the words leave her mouth, church bells chime, and a crisp breeze blows free the yellow-red leaves of an oak tree they're passing under. Two French schoolkids run out of a bakery sword-fighting with baguettes. Ali feels her heart buoy back into place. As they walk, Cara keeps screeching and grabbing Ali's arm and pointing to the neon-green "Pharmacie" signs and madeleines cooling in the windows of boulangeries and corner bistros with red awnings and rattan chairs, exclaiming, "OMG, that's SO French."

Every single corner bistro they pass is jam-packed with locals, and Ali wonders if they're all that good or if French people just love the vibe. Every other person they pass is smoking and effortlessly stylish. Ali can't believe she was going to hide in her hotel room all day. She would have missed the sweet-smelling steam from a crepe stall, a street musician playing Prelude in C Major on a harp, the rev of a scooter rounding a corner, the delicious dirty-sock smell of fromageries, the rhythmic sound of cars driving over cobblestones, and all the unique Parisian doors that are like works of art. Ali even delights in the smell of urine, due to the French habit of *pipi sauvage* (otherwise known as open-air peeing).

When the streets become narrow and cobblestoned and the buildings fade to pale pastels and the windows of boutiques feature more and more fashionable clothes, Ali knows they're in the Marais. They wander up and down a few streets before finding the place she's looking for: Les Philosophes, a classic French sidewalk café that's always bustling. Ali uses her high school French to order a slice of quiche and salad for herself, cheesy scrambled eggs and salad for Cara, two café au laits (Ali doesn't remember how to say decaf, plus she feels like she could use the caffeine), and an extra bread basket, which she remembers comes with a croissant.

"Look at you, Frenchie!" Cara says.

Ali makes a smug face and brushes imaginary dirt from her shoulders.

"Did you come to this restaurant with your partner?"

Ali says yes and tries to remember the details—they came for lunch, and they got a pureed vegetable soup and a gigantic salad covered in prosciutto and melon and melty goat cheese on toast. Since they had gotten engaged the day before, she remembers they talked about gay marriage and whether it would ever become legal in the States. At that time, it was only legal in the Netherlands, and they granted themselves a quick fantasy in which they moved to Amsterdam, biking along the canals with Glen in a basket between the handlebars, smoking joints in coffee shops (though marijuana tended to make Ali anxious), and eating warm, gooey *stroopwafels* from adorable stands on the street. Instead, they ended up having a simple commitment ceremony in Los Angeles in their backyard. They wouldn't have wanted an extravagant wedding anyway, but still—it would have been nice to have the option.

Cara's voice snaps Ali back to the present moment. "What was her name?"

Ali's throat tightens. "Natalie."

"Would you tell me about her, or would that make you too sad?"

Ali considers this. Maybe, to be here without being devastated, she needs to stop fighting the urge to remember Natalie and instead give in to it. "Paris was her second-favorite city, behind Mexico City, because that's where her mom's family was from, and she used to visit every year. Her biggest obsessions were Julia Roberts movies, Mariah Carey, and plants. When we'd take Glen on walks, she would literally high-five bunches of bougainvillea, and wiggle her pointer finger in morning glories like she was tickling them, and pinch succulents the way a grandma might pinch their grandkid's cheek. She didn't have a favorite flower because she could never choose. Whenever she was in a bad mood, she'd watch Mariah Carey music videos until she felt better. And she must have rewatched *Pretty Woman* at least twenty times. She loved to tell people how it was originally called *3,000*, for the money Vivian gets for spending the week with Edward, and how it ended with them not getting together, but with Edward going back to New York and Vivian and Kit going to Disneyland for the day to spend Edward's money. Everyone assumed the screenwriter was pissed about the fairy-tale ending, but he said he was just happy to finally sell a script and be working. 'At least selling out means you're selling,' Natalie would say. She moved to LA because she wanted to get into screenwriting and TV writing and we met that same year, when we were both twenty-three. She was the first person I fell in love with. The first woman I'd been with, too—the only woman I thought I'd *ever* be with."

At the table next to them, a woman wearing a trench coat and leather loafers who looks like she's in her fifties sits by herself, drinking a carafe of white wine (though Ali and Cara are eating breakfast, it's past noon). The woman isn't reading a book or looking at her phone. She's just people-watching in a very content manner. Ali wonders if this woman lost her spouse, too, years ago now, and has reached a state of comfort with her aloneness. The thought that Ali could ever reach such a state sends bolts of disbelief and protest through her body.

Cara widens her eyes. "Natalie was your *first*? At twenty-three?"

"Yeah, I had literally no idea before meeting her, but in hindsight, it was completely obvious I had been a lesbian my entire life."

"Why do you think you didn't figure it out sooner?"

Because publicists like me were forcing celebrities to lie about their sexuality, and you can't be what you can't see, Ali thinks, but she knows if she says this to Cara she'll look like the biggest hypocrite on earth. Which she is. "I was just trying to do what everyone seemed to be doing."

Ali thinks back to her childhood. The thumbtacked pictures of John Cusack and Rob Lowe above Ali's bed, the same bed where she and a female friend invented a game called "nap time" in which they pretended to be asleep while they rolled around and pressed their groins together. They pretended to be asleep because it wasn't something they could possibly want when they were conscious. When they heard Ali's mom coming up the stairs, they would spring apart like a bomb had gone off.

Sleepovers with female friends where they watched movies about the girl always getting the guy and sighed as they ate whole packages of Oreos. One night, they decided to play a game of strip poker, and she had never wanted to win a game so badly but couldn't really pinpoint why. When most of them were down to their bras and underwear, everyone else agreed it was time to call it quits, but Ali wanted to keep playing. She still remembers the uncomfortable, judgmental looks on their faces when they laughed and told her she was gross.

The UCLA campus was full of people who wore Doc Martens and had dyed pink hair and facial piercings and kissed people of the same gender in furtive corners at parties. But the women who kissed people who looked like Ali generally had short, slicked-back hair and wore oversize flannel shirts and walked around like there was an apple stuck between their legs. Ali had no desire to kiss this type of lesbian, so she assumed she wasn't a lesbian herself.

"I didn't know lesbians could be people like you or me," says Ali.

Cara cocks her head. "Do you think that could have something to do with public figures like me being forced to stay in the closet? By publicists like you?"

Ali pulls her face back like she's been slapped, even though it's exactly what she was just thinking. "Wow, ouch."

"I'm just saying, it's trash you didn't have any gay role models, so wouldn't it be nice for kids these days to have some?"

"They do have some."

"Yeah, a *few*. Nowhere near the amount of actual gay celebrities."

Ali releases a weary sigh. Even though it's true, she doesn't know if she can bear to hear it right now. "Are you really picking a fight with me while we're talking about my dead partner?"

Cara presses her lips together, chastised. "Sorry. You're right."

The food arrives, and Ali and Cara both immediately rip off a huge piece of croissant and stuff it into their mouths, making faces of ecstasy.

Ali takes a sip of her café au lait and swallows her bite of croissant. "When did you come out, anyway? As soon as you shot out of your mom's vagina?"

Cara laughs. "Yeah, pretty much. I officially came out in high school, but I had known since I was a little kid."

"What about your love life? I assume you have a bit more dating history than I do."

Cara talks through a mouthful of eggs. "My mom calls me a love junkie because I'm, like, always in a relationship. It's actually pretty weird I'm single right now. Sometimes I feel like I'm dating you." She says it with a hint of a laugh, but her eyes are genuine, probing. Like she's just confessed something and wants Ali to respond in kind.

Ali's stomach swooshes and she looks away from Cara's eyes, laughing like it was fully a joke and changing the subject as fast as possible. "Who's your most significant ex?"

"That would be Maurene. She wrote *Refrain*, the indie movie I was in before this. We were only together for nine months and I've been in way longer relationships, but with her, it was somehow more intense. Maybe because she was older."

Ali's stomach swooshes again. "How much older?"

"Eight years."

"Wow. Is the age difference why you broke up?"

Cara shakes her head. "She left me for another woman. I was pretty motherfucking heartbroken for a while. Maybe I still am. I haven't dated anyone for real since."

Ali raises her café au lait and extends it across the table. "To being heartbroken and single in Paris."

Cara knocks her mug against Ali's, and the woman sitting next to them interjects, unapologetic about her eavesdropping. "I say, to being single and open to possibilities in Paris." She winks and holds her wineglass out to them, and they humor her, tapping their drinks against hers with a hollow clink.

16

They make time for a quick sighting of the Eiffel Tower (which Ali finds surprisingly arresting up close, even though it's swarming with tourists) before they have to get back to the hotel for Cara's styling, hair, and makeup. Luckily, Cara's stylist brought plenty of good options this time around, and after a bit of back and forth, they settle on a black Chanel shorts suit with a mostly unbuttoned sheer blouse underneath. To offset the elegance of Chanel, they grunge up the look with black lace-up boots, a choppy wet-hair look, and a smudged smoky eye. While Cara gets her hair and makeup done, which will take at least three hours, Ali does her own: a tight, high ponytail so her hair won't get in the way, tinted moisturizer, mascara, blush, and a swipe of lipstick. In between, she answers last-minute premiere ticket and party invitation requests on her laptop. Ali wears a plain Paul Smith jumpsuit in black—the color all celebrity publicists generally wear at events—to be as inconspicuous as possible.

The premiere is at the Grand Rex, the biggest movie

theater in Paris, with an art deco facade modeled after Radio City Music Hall. As soon as Cara hits the red carpet, camera bulbs flash like strobe lights and all the photographers yell in their French accents, "Look at me!" "Over the shoulder!" "Over here, Cara!" Cara is clearly overwhelmed, looking in every direction, turning this way and that. "Remember," Ali says, standing beside Cara just out of the frame. "Hold one pose for five full seconds. Then move down, strike a different pose, move down, strike another one, until you're at the end." Cara nods, puts a hand on her hip, and juts out her chin. She holds the pose as instructed, then moves along.

After the photographers, there's the press line: video first, then print, then online. Ali wants Cara to talk to E! first since it's the biggest outlet, but the interviewer is still talking to Davi. Ali catches her eye and points to Cara, and the interviewer gives her a quick nod, so Ali holds Cara back until Davi moves on. The interviewer asks Cara the same questions every interviewer asks every time: "Are you excited?" "Who are you wearing?" "What did you do to get ready?" "What was it like working with Davi Silva?" and "Did you have a good time on set?" Cara will have to answer these questions dozens of times before the night is over, and Ali wants her answers to be most fresh for the biggest outlets, like *Vogue* France and *Vanity Fair* France. Only one female interviewer from one of the smaller outlets asks Cara about the rumors surrounding Cara's dating life, to which Cara replies, "Should we just pile on and say *we're* dating?" and this charms her enough for her to leave it alone.

Finally, they reach the end of the carpet. During the premiere, the *Real Love* promo tour group, which consists of Ali, Cara, Davi, Hana Itō (the director), Rosa Espinoza (the writer), Kevin Johnson (the producer), and Brandon Jones (the studio publicist), eats dinner at a restaurant nearby. For many of them, it's only their second meal of the day, and they're all a little grumpy after the red-eye flight. Hana and Rosa complain about the racist questions they were asked on the red carpet (an interviewer called Hana Chinese when she's Japanese; another interviewer asked Rosa if there was any good Mexican food in Paris), Kevin complains about an actor dropping out of the next film he's producing due to the lagging schedule, and while Davi is in the bathroom, Brandon complains about having had to track down a B_{12} shot for Davi earlier that day.

They're all so exhausted that they only stay at the after-party for an hour. But once Ali's head is on her very fluffy Ritz pillow, she's so overtired she can't fall asleep. She rummages through her suitcase until she finds the season 5 *Frasier* DVDs she brought for this exact purpose. In the season's first episode, Frasier meets an attractive woman at an airport bar, and when she says she's going to Acapulco, he says that's where he's going, too. On the plane, he confesses he followed her, and the woman immediately requests a seat change, and Ali feels inordinately proud of this fictional woman—if Ali had been in her position, she probably would have just sat there and squirmed the whole flight so as not to be rude to a creepy stalker.

Just as Ali is drifting to sleep, a knock on the door jolts her awake. Ali's heart pounds forcefully with thoughts of thieves and murderers and rapists before she remembers she not only closed the hinged bar lock but also wedged her trusty rubber doorstop underneath the door, as she does whenever she travels. But what if it doesn't work this time? She tiptoes to the eyehole and peeks through it, holding her breath, but it's just Cara. Ali pulls out the doorstop and swings the lock open.

"I thought I heard *Frasier*!" says Cara, who's staying in

the room next door. She's wearing sweatpants and a vintage sweatshirt that says "Beaver Canoe" on it. "You can't sleep, either?"

"Nope. It's driving me nuts."

"Could I…come in and watch with you? Sitcoms put me to sleep like that." Cara snaps her fingers.

The thought of Cara falling asleep in Ali's bed makes Ali's stomach somersault. But the possibility is also strangely comforting. Between helping Ali with her migraine and quieting her panic attack on the plane, Cara has proven she can be a calming presence. Maybe it would actually help Ali sleep. She really needs it. And sleep is all they would do, of course. Ali opens the door wider and waves Cara in, then peeks out into the hallway to make sure no one saw. Even though they're not doing anything wrong. Unusual, maybe, for a publicist and their client to share a bed on tour. But not wrong.

Cara dives into the bed like she's diving into a pool. "How are you watching it? I couldn't find it on TV."

"I brought the DVDs," Ali says. "Have you ever watched *Frasier*, or is it too old for you?" Ali positions the laptop between them.

"I've watched it, but I'm more of a *Seinfeld* ho."

Ali fluffs her pillows. "Sometimes that show makes me too uncomfortable."

"That's the point. It's, like, the original cringe comedy."

"I don't watch sitcoms to cringe, I watch them to calm down. One *Frasier* is the equivalent of two Ativans and a hot toddy."

"Thank God you brought those DVDs, then. Otherwise you might have developed a dependency problem on this trip."

Outside, the alien sound of a siren blares by, reminding

Ali she's in Paris with a low note followed by a high note on repeat instead of the drawn-out, sliding wail of American sirens. "What do *you* do to fall asleep?"

"What do you mean, what do I do?"

"How do you wind down?"

"I guess I...don't? I just get in bed, turn off the light, close my eyes, and fall the fuck asleep."

"How long does it take you? To fall asleep?"

"Like, a minute? Maybe five, tops."

"I didn't know that was actually possible. That's, like, a superpower." Ali had thought difficulty sleeping was the human condition. Her mom either slept constantly when she was depressed or was up all night when she was manic, and her dad had a habit of waking up at 3:00 a.m. and making coffee whenever he was working a case he couldn't solve. Natalie had insomnia, the kind that would wake her up at around five in the morning, and she could never get back to sleep—it was why she always took Glen for his morning walks. And Ali, of course, had the kind of insomnia that made it difficult to fall asleep. Once Ali and Natalie could afford it, they rented two-bedroom apartments so they could sleep separately, since between their opposite insomnias, they were barely getting any rest. They only shared a bed on vacation—a king—and even then they still tended to sleep poorly.

"If you're such a champion sleeper, why can't you tonight?" Ali asks.

"Jet lag? Excitement? Who knows. Let's see if your *Frasier* drug does the trick."

Ali hits play to resume the show. Cara cackles at a few jokes, then, as advertised, passes out before five minutes have gone by, her fingers twitching like Glen's paws when he's recently fallen asleep. Ali wishes she could siphon some of Cara's brain chemistry into her own mind. She tells herself Cara slumbering blissfully in her bed might have that effect—it will give her a good example to replicate. She closes her laptop and moves it to the floor, then mirrors the position Cara is in: on her side, facing Ali, her hands tucked under her chin. Ali breathes in and out when Cara does, and after a few minutes, the air moves easily in and out of her chest. Her heartbeat slows, her muscles loosen, and her eyelids droop.

The next time Ali opens her eyes, light floods the blackout curtain's edges. She's on her other side, and Cara is pressed up against her back, Cara's warm breath wafting on her neck. Cara's arm is also draped over her hip. Normally Ali is aware of all her movements during the night, but she has no memory of how she ended up as Cara's little spoon. Cara sighs and scooches even closer to Ali, her arm wrapping around Ali's stomach, her lips grazing Ali's neck. A power surge shoots through Ali's body. Cara must not be awake, Ali thinks. But then Cara's fingers move against Ali's bare stomach, just below her belly button. At first, Ali assumes Cara's fingers are simply twitching, but then she realizes the rhythm is more regular. Like she's gently strumming a guitar. The tip of Cara's nose caresses the curve of Ali's neck, her breath tickling ever so slightly, and goose bumps prickle Ali's arms. Cara's groin presses into Ali's butt, and almost involuntarily, Ali pushes back, another surge shooting through her. Then the alarm blares and they both spring apart. Ali fumbles to turn off the alarm and takes a few deep breaths before turning toward Cara, hoping her cheeks aren't bright red.

Cara rubs her eyes like she's just waking up and smiles at Ali in a mischievous way that could mean she's acknowledging what almost happened or could mean nothing, since Cara's smiles are frequently mischievous. She stretches her arms above her head and yawns. "Man, I slept like the dead, d-e-d. What about you?"

"Surprisingly, me too," says Ali. "I think you're an even better drug than *Frasier*."

"I *have* been told I'm habit forming," says Cara.

Ali rolls her eyes. "We have to be at the train station in two hours. We should get ready."

In the Chunnel on their way to London, Ali and Cara don't have seats next to each other—the whole entourage is scattered throughout the train—so Ali spends the trip alternating between catastrophizing about a tunnel fire and replaying the scene from the morning. Cara's lips and nose brushing Ali's neck. Cara's fingers strumming her bare stomach. Cara's groin pressing into her butt. What did it all mean? To Ali, it seems most likely that Cara was in a barely conscious state, the way men can wake up with an erection without it meaning they're actively turned on. In this scenario, if Ali asks Cara whether she was awake, Cara won't know what she's talking about, and Ali would have to die of embarrassment. Even if Cara *was* awake, it might not mean she has feelings for Ali—Cara the lothario might have simply gotten desperate, and Ali was the closest warm body. It's hardest to imagine Cara was making a move on Ali because she has feelings for her.

Sure, Cara calls herself an old soul with her love of James Baldwin and Patricia Highsmith and *Thelma & Louise* and vintage video games, but that doesn't mean she's interested in someone with actual wrinkles and so much emotional baggage it could fill ten U-Hauls. And sure, they have fun together coming up with fake stories about drag queens and dancing to Mariah Carey, but Cara is so gregarious she could have fun with Dick Cheney—hell, she could probably sit alone in a room and make herself laugh for hours. And yes, Cara does seem especially interested in getting to know Ali, forcing her to open up about her life and her passion for writing, but she might just be a naturally inquisitive person. And while Cara does seem to like taking care of Ali, she might nurture everyone in her life the same way.

What about the question Ali has refused to ask herself until now: How does *she* feel about *Cara*? When she woke up and Cara was spooning her, she didn't feel uncomfortable or wriggle away; she liked it and wanted it to continue. It's strange, because the thought of touching or being touched by someone other than Natalie made Ali recoil until very recently. But she didn't recoil from Cara. It feels wrong to have liked it. Natalie only died a year ago. Or, Natalie died over 365 endless days ago. A year feels like both a few blinks and an ineffably long span of time. Could Ali actually be ready for...something? Not a relationship, but something? It would probably be best to start with a kiss from a stranger. No feelings. But Ali has always found it hard to be physical with someone without feelings. Like trying to drive a car without gas.

Does Ali have feelings for Cara? Cara makes her laugh like no one else, giddy giggle fits and deep belly laughs that feel like an abdominal exercise, and laughter has always been the most important component of Ali's relationships. Since meeting Cara, Ali has talked about herself more than she has in years, and she's found she doesn't hate it as much as she thought she did. She only hated other people's reactions. Nothing makes Cara uncomfortable, and she listens in a way even Ali's closest friends don't—Dana distracted by her children, some having fallen away after Natalie's death because they never knew what to say, others who could monologue through an entire two-hour brunch without real-izing Ali hasn't spoken a word about herself. Most amazingly, Cara makes Ali want to be braver—to fight back against the homophobic Hollywood system, to believe in her writing, to believe the world is not wholly a dangerous place. When Ali is with Cara, she feels the closest approximation to happiness and hope since before Natalie died. She feels like there's finally a point to getting through each day. And the point is Cara.

Jesus fucking Christ. She didn't realize it all went this deep. By the time she gets off the train, she's worked herself into such a tizzy that she has a level-ten migraine and has to skip the scheduled pub crawl with the *Real Love* cast plus ten lucky fans. Instead, she orders a bowl of mulligatawny to be sent to her room, takes a naproxen, and counts the days until her neurologist appointment (over three months).

17

Ali wakes in the early morning to an email from an unknown sender with no subject line. The body of the email says, "Give me something better if you do not want these photos in the news." Ali's stomach drops as she clicks the attachments. It's photos of two women kissing, and Ali doesn't even have to zoom in to know. It's Cara, of course, making out with one of the lucky fans who won the pub crawl. They're in a dark alley—at least it's not a public bar where everyone could see them—but the photos are still plenty incriminating. In one shot, Cara grabs the woman's shapely ass as they laugh into each other's mouths. In another, she licks the woman's neck like it's an ice cream cone. Ali flashes back to Cara nuzzling her neck in bed yesterday and feels incredibly stupid.

She squeezes her laptop so hard her hands shake before storming out of her room and slamming her fist against Cara's door.

Cara's head peeks out. "What's up?" She shields her eyes from the hallway's bright light. She's wearing a white hotel robe, which could suggest she threw it on because she slept naked—maybe next to the lucky fan. "I have a Lindsay Lohan–level hangover."

Ali holds her laptop in front of Cara's face, a picture from the paparazzo still up. Her hands are shaking. Yesterday she almost admitted to herself she had feelings for Cara, and now this. It feels like using the heel of a dirty boot to crush the fragile body of a baby bird who can't even fly yet.

"Shit." Cara fully opens her door, revealing an empty, disheveled bed to which she retreats, curling into the fetal position.

"What the fuck were you thinking?"

Cara wraps her arms around her knees and rocks back and forth. "Clearly I wasn't. I don't even remember that, or how I got back to the hotel. I must have blacked out."

Ali puts her laptop down on the bedside table. "Promo tour is not the goddamn time to be getting blackout drunk, Cara. Do you know how fucked this makes both you *and* me? I should have known I couldn't let you out of my sight. You're like a *child*."

Cara pulls back her face, stung.

"And just when I was starting to think—"

Cara sits up and runs a hand through her greasy hair. "What?"

"Nothing."

She tilts her head and narrows her eyes at Ali. "Are you mad as my publicist, or as yourself?"

Ali scoffs. "As your publicist, of course."

"Really?" Cara crosses her arms. "Are we going to keep pretending yesterday morning didn't happen?"

Ali's heart speeds up. "So you *were* awake?"

Cara makes a confused face. "Yeah, weren't you?"

"Yeah. I just wasn't sure if…"

Cara stands up and takes the few steps to close the distance between them, her nose almost touching Ali's.

Ali swears she can feel electric currents radiating from Cara's body, and her heart thumps like an earthquake shaking the entire building.

"I only kissed that girl last night because I couldn't kiss you." Cara strokes a thumb across Ali's cheek, then slides her hand to the back of Ali's neck and pulls her in, softly pressing her slightly chapped lips against Ali's before tilting her head and opening her mouth. Cara's tongue brushes against hers and Ali's vagina gulps like it's been dying of thirst for the past year and has finally taken a big, satisfying drink. Ali actually gasps at the sensation, which makes Cara smile into the kiss before she pulls back and asks Ali with her eyes: *We're really doing this?* But Ali can't stand being separated from Cara's mouth—she pulls Cara back in and surprises herself by taking control, backing Cara up against the door, digging her fingers into her hips, and choreographing the kiss with different rhythms and pressures. Her mouth feels like it's in a kaleidoscope, getting lost in the changing dimensions of it. A fleeting feeling of guilt rises in her chest as she remembers how Natalie used to be the one to drive their kisses. It's enthralling to be in control now, deciding the speed and anticipating the twists and turns. In this moment, she feels like she could drive not only a kiss but a car or a bus or even a plane.

A loud knock shakes the door, and they both jump. "Housekeeping!"

"No thank you!" Ali yells back before they both collapse against the door, giggling.

Once their laughter has petered out, Cara takes Ali's hand and threads their fingers together. "So."

"So," says Ali.

Cara raises her eyebrows and pushes Ali's shoulder with her free hand. "Say something!"

"What, you wanna be total lesbians and dissect the meaning of the kiss we just had?"

"Obviously!"

Ali's laptop dings with another email from the paparazzo, and she crawls over to read it out loud. "If you do not reply within one hour, I will leak them."

Cara's face goes serious. "What do we do?"

Ali crawls back to Cara and leans against the door. "Well, we either let him leak them or we give him something better."

Cara grimaces. "Like what?"

"Photos of you and Davi. At this point I think you two would have to be kissing to get the other ones thrown out. But it's completely up to you, Cara. After what you told me on the plane, I don't want to push you one way or the other."

Cara tuts her tongue. "This is really funny timing. I ran into ███████████, of all people, last night during the pub crawl."

"Oh yeah, I heard he's here filming the new Coen brothers movie."

"I had been drinking for a while when I saw him, so I was more on my say-whatever-I'm-thinking bullshit than I otherwise would have been—"

"Sober, you're already the most candid person I know, so I can't imagine the geyser of truth you become when drunk."

"Let's just say I let him know I was feeling pretty trash about the whole hiding-my-identity thing. And what he said really hit home for me. He said, 'Everyone who matters knows the truth—my family, my friends, my colleagues, and most of the media. The only people who don't know are the general public. The Midwest masses who wouldn't watch my movies if they knew I was a ho-mo-sexual. And who cares about them?'"

"Gay kids who need role models make up the general public, too. Isn't that what you said at breakfast in Paris?"

Cara scoffs. "I'm a little gagged that you, my publicist, are playing coming-out devil's advocate right now."

"You've fought me every step into the closet so far. Did one conversation change your mind?"

"It's easy to fight you when you're the bad guy basically giving me no choice, telling me I have to do this if I want to be successful. Has that part changed? Do you really think I could have the same career trajectory if I came out right now?"

Ali bangs the back of her head against the door. "The truth is, I have no idea. No emerging actor in a blockbuster movie has come out at the beginning of their career, so we don't know what the effect would be. Everyone says it would hurt your career, and that *is* the more likely outcome, but no one knows for sure. This exact moment might be when things are changing enough to do it."

"Yeah, those odds don't sound great, honey."

"So what do you want to do?"

Cara presses her thumbs into her temples. "I don't think I can make this kind of life-altering decision with this hangover in the next hour, so I guess by default, we take the fake-ass pictures with Davi. Isn't it funny the day we finally kiss is the day I start bearding?"

Ali knows she's the one who initially told Cara she had to be in the closet, and Ali knows it's the best choice for Cara's career, but now that they're finally going through with the ruse, Ali's stomach sinks. "Yeah, hilarious."

* * *

Ali and Cara bang on Davi's door for a full thirty seconds before he opens it.

"Good God, man! What?" He's wearing just Calvin Klein boxer briefs with a pronounced bulge and is scratching his eight-pack.

"Can we come in?" says Ali. "We have a proposition for you."

"Uhhhhhh." He glances behind him, and Ali sees two naked bodies, both with beautiful orbed butts, sprawled over his king bed.

"Oh my God, seriously?" says Ali. "You have two minutes to get them out of here."

The door closes and Ali stands there with her arms crossed, shaking her head. "That must have been some pub crawl last night."

"Londoners can really drink," says Cara. "We were just trying to keep up and show the contest winners a good time."

"Well, mission accomplished."

"Please don't be mad at me. Pleeeeeease." Cara sticks out her bottom lip and makes puppy-dog eyes.

Before Ali can answer, Davi's door opens and a gorgeous man and woman slink out, smiling sheepishly at Ali and Cara.

Ali holds her arm up to stop them and looks at Davi. "At least tell me they signed NDAs."

He picks up a short stack of paper from the bedside table and winks at her. "Always."

Ali puts down her arm and lets the man and woman pass. "That reminds me," Ali says to Cara. "We need to find the girl from last night and get her to sign one, too, since I'm guessing you didn't remember?"

Cara makes a guilty face. "That is probably correct."

"So I'm not the only one who got some last night?" Davi high-fives Cara as she and Ali walk into the room. "Noice."

"That's kind of what we're here about." Ali sits on the leather couch across from the bed, where a jock strap is partially wedged between the cushions. "A paparazzo got pictures of Cara kissing one of the girls, and he's threatening to leak them unless I give him something better."

"Aha." Davi reclines on the bed and holds his hands behind his head. "So you're here to ask if I'll beard for Cara?"

"If you'll beard for *each other*," Ali says. "I'd say it could benefit you, too." Ali gestures to the jock strap.

"I know how to keep my freaky shit on lock, though." Davi gestures to the NDAs.

"You know those probably aren't enforceable, though."

Davi's face drops. "What? Why not?"

"Did your team not go over this with you? A contract has to provide value for the person signing it, and sex can't be that value."

"Why not? Sex with me is pretty damn valuable, if I do say so myself." Davi pops his pecs to illustrate his point.

"A court would likely disagree. The value in an NDA is usually money, but it's against the law to pay for sex, so."

"So why do we even bother with presex NDAs, then?"

"Because your average person doesn't know this, so it scares them into keeping quiet. But if anyone asked a lawyer to look at these NDAs, they'd say what I'm saying."

Davi sits up straighter. "So I'm not actually protected? Anyone I've ever slept with could come forward at basically any time?"

"Yup."

"Fuuuuck, man." He runs his hands through his hair. "If that's true, then it would actually be a pretty bad idea for me and Cara to beard. Because if I hooked up with someone, they'd think I was cheating on her. And if I told them we weren't actually together, the NDA doesn't protect that information."

"In that case, you could probably pay the signee in exchange for their silence about you and Cara not actually being together. But not the sex."

"I don't know, man. I really don't like lying. When I was a kid and I would lie to my mom, I'd break out in a literal rash, like my body was allergic to it. And it wouldn't go away until I confessed."

Ali hadn't foreseen Davi being so resistant to the idea. To her, it seemed like an obvious win-win. "You saw how crazy people went for that clip of you and Cara on *Jimmy Kimmel*. The public would be overjoyed to find out you two are together. You'd be all over *People*, *E! News*, and the gossip websites. Then even more people would go see *Real Love*, which means more money for you, which means more money for your next movie…Do I need to go on?"

"Eh, I've got plenty of money."

Clearly Ali needs to switch tactics. "If you won't do it for yourself, will you do it for Cara? She's just starting out. She has an amazing career ahead of her. But not if these photos leak." No one would think it, because Davi is so ridiculously good looking, but he's actually a good person who cares about other people. "Put yourself in her shoes."

He looks at Cara, and her face crumples. "I don't want to beard, either, Davi." Her voice warbles, and a single tear cascades down her cheek. "I was dead set against it, actually. But I don't know what other choice I have. Acting is all I've ever wanted to do. I hate that my sexuality could make it impossible to do what I love."

"Fuck, man." Davi wrenches a hand over his face, and when he removes it, his eyes are glassy. "Fine. But not for too long, okay?"

Ali nods. "Just long enough to get through this."

Ali emails the paparazzo and promises something very good is on the way, then checks with Brandon, *Real Love*'s studio publicist, about whether he's okay with it, to which he replies, "Duh squared!" and mimes flicking individual bills off a stack of money. Then Ali schedules an emergency Skype with Cara's agent and manager, Vivian and Will.

Ali isn't even fully finished asking the question before Vivian says, "*Absolutely* they should beard." Agents are typically down for anything that would make their client (and therefore themselves) more money. "After the Jimmy Kimmel video made the rounds, I was dying to suggest it, but I was afraid Cara would fire me. Glad you're on board, girl."

"Only because I was forced into a homophobic corner," says Cara, who's sitting next to Ali at the desk in her hotel room.

"Cara, are you sure this is what you want, hon?" says Will, who appears to be wearing just one popped-collar polo today. There also appears to be genuine concern on his face. "I know it feels like you have to do this, but you don't. I'll stand by you even if the photos of you and that girl come out, and we'll find a way to keep you working. Anyone who doesn't want to hire you? I'll call them out for being homophobic." He bangs his fist against his desk, fired up. "Maybe we could even sue them!" Another fist bang. "And I'll write an op-ed for the *New York Times* about how we need to change this closeted culture." Fist bang. "And I'll organize a rally!" Fist bang. His face contorts with emotion. "You're like a daughter to me after all these years, and I want to support you with everything I have."

Ali is taken aback. She never would have thought that Will, of all people, would be so passionate about doing the right thing. Now she feels like a complete jerk. "Will's right, of course," Ali says to Cara. "You don't *have* to do this. We all have your back whatever you decide." Ali turns back to the screen. "Right?"

"Right," says Vivian. But her face says she'd drop Cara as a client as soon as she stopped making money. "It's important to be realistic, though. I wouldn't be doing my job if I told Cara things would be totally fine after coming out."

"Are you saying I'm not doing my job?" says Will.

"Guys, let me spare you a fight," says Cara. "Will, I truly appreciate how willing you are to stand up for me, but sadly, I do think coming out right now would tank my career. It's trash, but it is what it is. I put myself in this position through my own mistake. Now I'm going to do what I need to do. I don't feel one hundred percent about it, but I wouldn't feel one hundred percent about coming out, either. I can always come out later."

"Great," says Vivian. "I have another meeting in ten, so let's discuss the details of the photo op. For first kiss photos, a beach vacation is normally the setting, but obviously it's November, and you're all in London."

"What if they just kissed on the red carpet at the premiere tonight?" says Will. "Everyone would lose. Their. Minds."

Victoria and Ali trade a *Will-is-so-stupid* look. "But we need to give the paparazzo something exclusive," says Victoria.

"Plus, I think we want it to feel more organic than that," says Ali. "Like a pap just happened to catch a genuine moment between them and they weren't aware of it. Right, Cara?"

"Um, sure? I didn't know we were going to get so granular about the details. I thought Davi and I would just, like, walk down any street and kiss each other."

Ali, Vivian, and Will heartily laugh. "If only," says Ali. "Our jobs would be so much easier if that were the case."

"How about a dinner date?" says Vivian. "What are the hot London restaurants to see and be seen at?"

"That doesn't seem very on brand for Cara and Davi," says Ali. "I think we're going for the 'Stars—they're just like us!' vibe. That's what the public is really loving right now. The thrill that they're peeking at seemingly unguarded, everyday moments."

"What, like getting sandwiches at Pret?" jokes Will.

"That's actually perfect," says Ali.

"Does it matter that most people in the US don't know what Pret is?" asks Vivian.

"No, I think it gives it a nice London flavor," says Ali. "What do you think, Cara?"

"Whatever you masterminds say."

"Okay, great," says Ali. "I'll check with Davi and his team and get back to you."

18

Davi's agent says Davi did a Subway sandwich ad last year, so Pret would be a conflict of interest. Ali brainstorms a few other options and sends them to both teams, and everyone's favorite is Maison Bertaux, London's oldest patisserie, on Greek Street in Soho. It's an unassuming place with a cramped, charmingly cluttered interior—bric-a-brac like cutout butterflies, old teapots, and postcards adorn all the walls and surfaces. It feels a bit like the kitchen of a loving grandmother who's in the early stages of hoarding but who also makes utterly delicious pastries. Perfect for Cara and Davi to seem like down-to-earth celebrities who eat carbs, just like us. (In reality, Davi hasn't touched bread in a decade—he barely even lets himself *look* at it—which is how he says he maintains his eight-pack.)

Ali emails the paparazzo to be there at 1:00 p.m., and he'll see Cara and Davi sitting at the royal-blue tables and chairs outside. Ali tells Cara and Davi to order what they'd actually order at a patisserie if calories didn't exist, so Cara orders a *pain au chocolat* and, after much hand-wringing,

Davi orders a coffee éclair, and they split a pot of Earl Grey tea. Ali seats them at an end table, farthest away from other customers, and scoots the chairs as close together as possible, facing the street, so they can cozy up against each other. They're both wearing scarves and sweaters and wool peacoats, and Cara is wearing minimal makeup to make the photo seem as unstaged as possible. "Lots of smiling, lots of laughing—but not too much, try not to look manic—lots of touching, a few kisses here and there, lots of gazing into each other's eyes, and absolutely no looking in the paparazzo's direction," Ali says before standing far enough away that she won't be in the shots.

Davi allows himself one real bite of the éclair, at which point his eyes roll back into his head like he's in pure ecstasy, and the rest he chews and covertly spits into a napkin. Cara, of course, hams it up by *Lady and the Tramp*-ing the éclair with Davi and licking cream from his upper lip, but she acquiesces to one serious kiss, Davi's hand splayed lovingly across her cheek. Ali reminds herself it's fake as jealousy churns in the pit of her stomach and she remembers the feeling of Cara's slightly chapped lips on hers. Something that absolutely should not happen again, but she absolutely wants it to. Underneath the jealousy, there are deeper, scarier feelings that Ali fights against acknowledging: Dread. Despair. For Cara and herself and the potential romance between them. Because with this photo op, there's no going back to the truth.

The paparazzo is very happy with the photos, and he gives Ali the CF card that stores the images of Cara and the girl from last night. Since he's the only one with these photos of Cara and Davi, he'll be able to sell them to the highest bidder for a relatively life-changing amount.

Ali has just a few hours of free time before that evening's

premiere, time she would have spent with Cara, but Cara has to get a mani-pedi and a wax for her eyebrows and legs—the kind of primping she would normally never do at home, but these details matter now that she's a superstar dating another superstar.

Ali spends her time strolling through Soho's messy grid of streets and alleyways, some swanky, some grubby, passing colorful, charming pubs, fish-and-chips shops emanating the tantalizing smell of fried food and malt vinegar, grand theaters, and fashionable shops housed in brick Georgian or Tudor-style buildings. She had forgotten how anxious London makes her as a pedestrian, with cars coming from the opposite direction Americans would expect at crosswalks. And even though there are road markings that say, "Look right" or "Look left," Ali still can't get the hang of it and almost gets hit by multiple black cabs and once by a red double-decker bus, which huffs a gray cloud of noxious diesel fumes right into her face. When she's about to have a heart attack, she thankfully hits pedestrianized Carnaby Street with its flashy art installations, many of which are Christmas themed as the holiday approaches: a giant snowman surrounded by snowflakes, bright green holly leaves, a plethora of twinkling stars. But then it's the crowds, instead of the cars, making her anxious. By 4:30 p.m., the pubs are absolutely packed with red-faced, snaggletoothed Brits spilling onto the sidewalks with their frothy glass mugs of hoppy-smelling beer.

Ali decides she'll keep walking to Hyde Park, which takes her through quieter Mayfair with its elegant Georgian townhouses, exclusive hotels, gourmet restaurants, and high-end fashion boutiques. Then she hits the park, a true country-esque respite in the middle of the city with rows of trees boasting an array of goldenrod, auburn, russet, crimson, maroon, and sepia leaves. They smell toasted and musky-sweet, not yet rotten. Unleashed dogs run through the grass, barking and yipping and growling at each other, and Ali feels a sharp stab of missing Glen. She hopes he's eating. Usually for the first few days of any work trip, he'll go on a hunger strike brought on by separation anxiety, which always makes her feel terrible. And this time she'll be gone for a whole month. She tries to send him a telepathic message that she loves him and misses him and promises she'll be back, eventually.

Back at the hotel, Ali already has an email from the editor of *Us Weekly*, who bought the pictures of Cara and Davi. The latest issue comes out in two days, and they're scrapping what they originally planned for the cover and replacing it with the Cara-and-Davi news. Ali gives them quotes from a "witness" at Maison Bertaux, an anonymous "close friend," an "unnamed source," and a "fan." Two days later, the magazine hits stands. *Us Weekly* chose a picture of Cara and Davi gazing into each other's eyes for the cover, with the kiss photos inside.

Us Weekly

ARE REAL LOVE STARS IN LOVE FOR REAL?

EXCLUSIVE NEW KISS PHOTOS PROVE THE ROMANCE IS REAL

Turns out we were right to spot sparks between *Real Love* co-stars Davi Silva and Cara Bisset during their appearance on *Jimmy Kimmel Live!* The two have been spotted kissing at a bakery in London on their promotional tour. "They really seemed to be enjoying each other's company," said a witness at the bakery. "They were smiling, laughing, cuddling, gazing into each other's eyes, and KISSING! They seemed very comfortable with each other and very close—like people who have been dating for a while." According to a close friend, "Sparks started flying while filming *Real Love*, but they didn't want to ruin their working relationship, so they held off." What professionals! "Once filming ended, they gave in and started dating, at first casually, but it's recently gotten serious. They are head over heels!" We've yet to receive any confirmation from the pair themselves, but another source says, "They're both very private people, and I don't know if they'll ever be willing to talk about their relationship publicly. I think that shows the extent to which they value it. They both deeply care about each other and are very happy." Their fans seem very happy, too. "You can just tell watching the movie that there's this great chemistry between them," says one fan. "I'm glad to know it's real! Not only are they both smoking hot, but they also seem like great people." We agree! Is it too soon to call them Cavi?

Within hours, the internet is aflame with headlines like "Breathe If Your Favorite New Couple Is Cavi" or "I Would Enter a Simulation for Them." One or two gossip blogs are suspicious ("I spy a fauxmance with my little eye"), but most people swallow it hook, line, and sinker. The photo of Cara licking cappuccino foam from Davi's upper lip even becomes a meme, with Cara as "me" and Davi as "a spoonful of peanut butter" or Davi as "me" and Cara as "my dog when I return from running a 5-minute errand." Victoria emails

Ali: "The studio says to keep up the good work :)." But Ali doesn't feel good about it. In fact, she feels miserable—more than she usually does when feeding fake stories to the press, because this time her client is someone she truly cares about. Sure, bearding will be great for Cara's career, but it won't be great for her mental health or her real love life, which Ali could have been a part of until now.

"Well, I guess we pulled it off," Ali says on the flight to Berlin.

"Yaaaaaay," Cara says sarcastically.

"You got like twenty K new followers on Facebook and MySpace," Ali says. "In *one* day."

"How many do you think I would've gotten if the photos of me and that girl were released?"

"Not twenty K, that's for sure. Davi is a *massive* international star. Attaching yourself to him is like steroids for your publicity. And name recognition is seriously half the battle in this business—now everyone in the world knows who you are."

"It's wild one photo can do that."

"Now you know why everyone does it." Ali peers out the window at the glittering English Channel. The flight has been oddly smooth so far, and Ali almost wishes turbulence would shake the plane so Cara would take her hand. But no matter how incessantly she's been replaying their kiss, she needs to stop thinking like a teenage girl with a crush and start thinking like Cara's publicist. Plus, her doomsday brain has already started tabulating the reasons a relationship with Cara wouldn't work: Cara isn't old enough for a serious relationship. Cara might not be interested in being with Ali, period. Maybe she just wants to have fun on the promo tour, but when they get home and other women are around, Cara will drop Ali like it's hot, as Snoop Dogg and Pharrell say.

Ali probably isn't even ready to be in a relationship again—her grief and PTSD are all tangled up in this new desire. She already worries Cara will die anytime they're not together—she could be hit by a car coming from the unexpected opposite direction while crossing a London street, she could slip and fall in the shower, she could choke on a too-big bite of food, she could find a stage IV lump in her breast, she could be stabbed by a robber, she could plummet to her death in a faulty elevator...They could both die on this plane right now and never get the chance to kiss again. The thought makes Ali want to grab Cara's face and make out with her fervidly.

As if Cara has read her mind, she whispers, "Are we ever gonna talk about the *other* kiss?"

"The one with you and your lucky fan?" Ali whispers back.

Cara rolls her eyes before squaring them on Ali, batting her eyelashes exaggeratedly. "You know which one."

"I think, as nice as it was—"

"'Nice'? That's the word you're gonna use to describe the kiss that absolutely flooded my basement?"

Ali's cheeks kindle and her clit practically jumps out of her jeans. "Really?"

"Um, yeah." Cara leans toward her and bites her lip. "You didn't think it was hot as hell?"

"I did, but you and I both know it's a bad idea for so many reasons."

Cara widens her eyes, playing dumb. "Like what?"

"There's the whole me-being-your-publicist thing. And now that you're bearding with Davi, we have to be super careful."

"We can be careful in each other's hotel rooms."

A flight attendant pushes a rattling drink cart past them.

"I think you're just horny, and I'm the only person you can hook up with without anyone finding out." It comes out sounding like a dig against Cara, but in Ali's head, she meant it against herself. As the older, nonfamous one, she feels wildly insecure about her desirability.

Cara's face goes somber. "Why would you say that? Haven't I made it totally obvious how much I like you?"

"You could have anyone. Why me, a neurotic widow who's a decade older than you?"

"Okay, firstly, I find your neuroticism really fucking cute, and I like being the one who comforts you. Secondly, everyone has a past with some traumatic shit they haven't really gotten over. And thirdly, didn't I tell you I have a thing for older women? Girls my age are like a blank, boring-ass page."

"Meanwhile, I'm like a diary entry from hell."

Cara laughs, then abruptly stops. "Wait, do you not like *me*? And you're flipping it and saying I must not like you, so you don't have to say it?"

"No, I *do* like you—"

Cara uses a whiny voice to imitate Ali from a few seconds ago. "Why, though?"

The sound of crinkling plastic bags fills the plane as people eat their snacks. "You told me, so I guess it's only fair for me to tell you, huh?"

Cara sits up straight and places her crossed hands on her knee expectantly.

The plane shudders, and Ali grabs Cara's hand, then remembers they're in public and lets go. "I love laughing with you, and I love how brave you are. When I'm with you, I feel braver. I also feel…happy. And for a while I truly thought I would never feel that again."

"Let me get this straight. I make you happy, an emotion

you weren't sure you'd ever feel again, and you think we should *stop* kissing?"

A woman sitting one row up empties a package of oyster crackers into a cup of tomato juice like it's soup. "It's terrifying to feel happy again," says Ali. "It could be taken away any second."

"Would you rather be lonely with a false sense of safety?"

Natalie used to love posing would-you-rather questions involving two equally terrible situations: Would you rather be forced to listen to twenty-four hours of sports noises (Ali was constantly asking Natalie to turn down the volume, with the yelling commentators and blaring horns) or twenty-four hours of Nickelback (Ali's least favorite musical group)? If you could only watch one TV show for the rest of your life, would you rather watch *House Hunters* or *Family Feud*? This seems like one of Natalie's impossible questions: Would you rather be happy and terrified or lonely and seemingly safe? "I don't know," says Ali, and she truly doesn't.

After the plane has hit the runway and everyone has turned on their phones, reading texts and emails, Cara grabs Ali's arm. "Holy shit."

"What?"

"Vivian emailed saying the casting director for the next *Star Wars* movie wants me to audition for a motherfucking *lead role*."

Ali blinks rapidly. "What?"

"I know. I would've thought it'd be years before I was asked to audition for a huge franchise like *Star Wars*, and even then, like, a small supporting role. Why do you think they want me?"

Ali shakes her head at the line of impatient people who already clog the aisle, waiting for the door to open. "Number one, because you're talented as hell. Number two, because

Real Love is slaying at the box office. And number three, honestly? Probably because you and Davi are slaying the internet."

"Whoa. So this is why people beard."

"Yup. You wouldn't think it would affect casting decisions, and yet…I've seen it happen time and time again."

"I truly had no idea." Cara shakes her head, her eyes wide and ravenous. "Honey, I'll beard for life if it keeps going like this!"

19

In Berlin, they stage a Cavi photo op at the Christmas market in Gendarmenmarkt, where a sea of white, star-topped tents nestle between the former French Protestant church on one side of the square and the former Prussian Lutheran church on the other. They go at night, when all the buildings are lit from below and all the lights are twinkling, so it feels especially cozy. Ali chose the Christmas market to project a wholesome image of Cara and Davi and to show their relationship progressing: Shopping for gifts for each other's family means things are getting serious. Since it's thirty-six degrees Fahrenheit here, Cara dons a knitted hat with a big pom-pom and Davi chooses a bomber hat, and they both wear puffer jackets and fur-lined winter boots. The paparazzo captures them drinking steaming mulled wine from custom Christmas mugs shaped like boots, eating roasted bratwurst (in one photo, Davi lovingly wipes mustard from Cara's lip with a thumb), kissing in front of the big Christmas tree, and purchasing presents: Davi buys Cara's mom an entire porcelain Christmas village, and Cara gets his parents homemade sheepskin slippers. (In actuality, they both chose the gifts for their own parents, and will give them to their own parents.) Every photo is of something Ali wants to do with Cara, and she counts the torturous minutes until the paparazzo gets all the shots he needs and leaves. Thankfully, right after he does, Davi goes to meet up with a German friend, so Ali and Cara can finally be alone and enjoy the market together.

The moment it's just Ali and Cara, the place finally comes alive for Ali, like someone flipped a switch in her from spectator to participant. Her senses drink it in: the smell of cinnamon and clove in the mulled wine; the foreign sounds of a multitude of different languages—not just the upside-down English of German, but also slushy Russian and guttural French and birdsong Vietnamese and the repeated *sh* sounds of Farsi and ones Ali can't even guess; the adorable German wooden toys that reflect every profession a person could have (she finds a detective holding a magnifying glass and a notepad and buys it for her dad); the sweet, toasted smell of candied nuts; the intricate handmade beeswax candles shaped like corncobs and Christmas trees and pine cones; the array of nutcrackers with their hunched shoulders and long furry beards and humorous chompy teeth...The market is incredibly charming, and almost fools Ali into thinking she enjoys Christmastime. For some reason, Europeans' fondness for Christmas seems less creepy than Americans'. Perhaps because they separate it from religion more than Americans? Because Europeans politicize it less? Ali and Cara ponder this while they eat fresh-baked hand bread filled with gooey cheese and mushrooms. A camera flashes nearby, and for a second Ali thinks she's the one in a photo op, but it's just someone taking a picture of the giant Christmas tree. It's both funny and sad to Ali that Cara and Davi's fake relationship is mirroring Cara and Ali's real one: The day Ali and Cara kissed, Cara and Davi did, too. When Ali and Cara had a delightful time at the Christmas market, she and Davi did, too. The more Ali thinks about it, the more it's not funny at all—just crushingly sad. All these light-filled moments with Cara under a dark cloak of secrecy.

The cloak is starting to weigh on Ali.

At the TV show appearance the next day, fans flood the sidewalk with "Cavi4Eva" and "Cara + Davi = Real Love" posters, and the host bombards Cara and Davi with questions (*When did you start dating? Are you in love? What's it like dating a costar?*), but they say they prefer to keep their relationship private, and the audience loudly boos. *Real Love* holds steady in the number one slot at the US box office, and Cara shows Ali her inbox full of emails from Vivian with offers to audition for roles in the next Tarantino, Sofia Coppola, and Cameron Crowe movies.

Ali hasn't gotten a good night's sleep since Paris, when Cara lulled her into the deepest slumber simply with her presence, and part of Ali wants to invite Cara to bed just for the rest, but she knows that's a slippery slope—since the kiss, she's insisted they stay in their own rooms.

That night in Berlin, as she's watching her third *Frasier* and the clock ticks past midnight, the phone in her room rings, sending her shooting out of bed.

"Hello?" Ali says suspiciously, her heart beating in her ears.

"Are you awake?"

Upon hearing Cara's voice, Ali collapses on the bed and lets out a breath. "Jesus, you scared the shit out of me."

"Sorry, it's not like I can text you since we're in *Europe* and all. Guess what's on TV?"

"What?"

"Guess!"

"This should be fun. *Face/Off*?"

"Nope."

"*Sleepless in Seattle*?"

"Nope."

"*Law & Order: SVU*?"

"Nope."

"Okay, I give up."

"*Thelma & Louise*! Dubbed in German, of course."

"What channel?"

"Thirty-two."

Ali reaches for the remote, turning on the TV before punching in the channel. It's the scene where Thelma sashays into a diner in the morning with her hair frizzed out around her head and her jean shirt unbuttoned below her breasts and a goofy smile—it looks a lot like Cara's trademark grin, actually. The voice actors have a low, serious-sounding tone—or the German language might just make them sound this way—and it makes the scene even more comedic.

"Is this after she's slept with J.D.?" Ali asks.

"Yup. Louise asked what happened to her hair and Thelma said, 'Nothin'. Got messed up.'" Cara cracks up at her reenactment.

"Do you know this movie line for line?"

"Pretty much. Louise just said Thelma seems like she's crazy or on drugs. Then Thelma said J.D. came back, and she finally understands what all the fuss is about now. That could be us tomorrow morning, girl. All sexed up and blissed out."

Ali flashes back to Cara's lips, Cara's tongue. "Stop."

"Are you a top or a bottom? I had assumed you were a bottom until you took charge and pushed me up against that door."

"Come on, no one is simply a top or a bottom. At least it didn't work that way with me and Natalie. But as you know, she's my only frame of reference."

"That's wild. I can't imagine staying with the first woman I slept with."

"How many women *have* you slept with?"

Cara scoffs. "That's such a hetero question. It's all based on penetration with a penis. With lesbian sex, you can't delineate that easily."

"I guess that's true. Have you ever slept with a man, or are you a gold star?"

There's a long pause. "It's kind of complicated," Cara says, her voice tight. "But technically, yeah, I'm a gold star."

"What do you mean, technically?"

"I'll tell you some other time." Cara clears her throat. "What about you? Were you a virgin until you met Natalie, or did you give the D a whirl?"

Ali laughs. "I gave it way more whirls than I should have. I puked every single time after I slept with a man, but I just kept doing it, hoping it might get better at some point. What's that saying? 'The definition of insanity is doing the same thing over and over again, but expecting different results'?"

"Christ, Ali. That's really sad. Sounds like you should be making up for lost time by coming to my room."

"Nice try."

"SIGH. Guess I'll be over here, alone, thinking about you."

* * *

Ali and Dana almost never go more than a few days without talking or texting, even if it's just about something inane like their newest bodily ailment (a weird muscular twitch on the side of Ali's knee; a stabbing pain in Dana's colon) or an update about someone they went to high school with (Facebook photos of the ugly baby who belongs to the couple who have been together since sophomore year). Even if they're not substantial, these little updates help Ali feel like they're still connected.

While Ali's been in Europe, they've been emailing back and forth. Ali's latest message is about her two favorite things in Berlin: (1) the little traffic light man, with his hat and nose and power-walk stride; and (2) the ubiquitous seeded-brown-bread triangle sandwiches with cheese, cucumber, lettuce, and herbed mayo. When Ali ends the email with P.S. Cara and I might have kissed, Dana replies immediately: GET ON SKYPE RIGHT NOW.

Ali plugs in her webcam and clips it to the top of her laptop screen, then waits for Skype to load. When Dana appears on video she is, of course, breastfeeding Cayenne. Arlo is in the background scribbling on the wall with a red crayon.

"Dana, did you know Arlo is—"

"I know." Dana waves a hand toward him dismissively. "It's easier to clean it later than to stop him from doing it."

"So what's going on with you?"

"No. Uh-uh. We're talking about you kissing a movie star." Dana points at Ali and her arm blurs as the video lags, then briefly pixelates before coming back into focus. "You didn't tell me you liked her!"

"I didn't know I did. I mean, I knew, but I didn't even admit it to *myself* until we were in Paris, which is pretty weird since Paris is, you know—"

"Yeah, I know." Dana switches Cayenne from her right to her left boob. "I need details. Who initiated it?"

"Cara."

"That makes sense."

"Why?"

"A, because you're still, like, grieving. And B, because I don't think you've ever made a move on someone in your entire life."

"Okay, harsh, but probably true."

Arlo moves to a new, blank wall with his crayon. Dana says something, but Ali can't make it out as the audio lags, then skips, the video pixelating again.

"What?" says Ali.

Dana comes back into focus. "How was the kiss?" she says loudly, overenunciating.

"It was good." Ali grimaces and covers her face with her hands. "Really good."

"Why do you look like you're confessing to a crime?"

"Because it feels wrong to like someone, to kiss someone, after Natalie."

"It's not wrong, Ali. It's part of moving on with your life, which has to happen at some point."

"A big part of me truly thought it wouldn't."

"That's the magical thing about time. It can change how you feel."

Ali leans her head against her hand. "I have no idea how I feel."

"Do you want to kiss her again?"

Arlo continues covering the wall with crayon, and Ali spots shapes in the scribbles like one would in the clouds: a dragon, a feather, Jesus. "I shouldn't. The studio hired me to keep her in the closet, and instead I'm kissing her!"

"I didn't ask if you *should* kiss her again. I asked if you wanted to."

Ali grimaces again.

"I'll take that as a yes."

"I shouldn't," Ali repeats.

Dana rolls her eyes. "Life is short. You know that better than anyone. If you want to kiss her, just do it. You're actually, like, the *best* person to be kissing her. Since you're her publicist, you know how important it is for it to stay a secret. Plus, if she's kissing you, she probably won't be kissing anyone with looser lips."

Ali tilts her head. "That's a surprisingly good point."

A crayon flies into frame and bounces off Cayenne's head, and she blinks in confusion before starting to scream. "Goddammit, Arlo! How many times have I told you not to throw things at your sister? Ali, I better go. The next time we talk, I want to hear about another kiss."

Ali deflates as the screen goes black. She wishes they could have debriefed for longer—not being able to talk about Cara has felt like trying to keep a lid on a geyser, and this was the shortest spurt ever. She feels like a high schooler with a crush who wants to say Cara's name as much as possible, who could go on and on about all the reasons she likes Cara, how she's worried Cara doesn't like her as much as she likes Cara, and how she can't stop thinking about what might or might not happen next.

20

Ali loses track of which day it is and what city they're in. She's heard Cara give the same answers to the same questions so many times she's truly starting to wonder if *she's* in a simulation. Ali survives on children's chewable multi-vitamins, naproxen, Ativan, the *Best American Short Stories* anthology from last year, photos of Glen emailed by his dog sitter, and hotel club sandwiches. Cara sends the *Star Wars* team a virtual audition video, and shortly after, they tell her she's progressed to round two and ask for another.

Halfway through the tour, they arrive in Tokyo, where they're staying for a few days to give everyone a small break. Ali was prepared for her anxiety to skyrocket—everything she's ever heard about Tokyo was about how crowded and frenetic it was—but to her surprise, she finds most parts of the city quiet and tranquil. Their luxury hotel in the financial district is also the quietest hotel Ali has ever stayed at, hands down. She could probably win an award as the world's lightest sleeper, so she barely sleeps in most hotels, due to the slamming doors and the street noise and the people in

adjacent rooms blaring their TVs or partying or yelling at
their screaming kids. But in her Tokyo hotel room, all Ali
can hear is the sound of her own breathing, and she spends a
blissful night earplug-free. She credits this to the rule that all
guests must remove their shoes upon entry to the hotel, the
tatami mats lining all the floors, the soundproof windows,
the doors with antislam hinges, cleaners who don't begin
until the afternoon, and the very conscientious and hospita-
ble hotel staff. They truly seem to care about guests having a
perfect-as-possible stay.

Ali finds this is true of Japanese people in general:
They care about people other than themselves, which
is a novel concept for most Americans. Hana, *Real Love*'s
director, tells her it's because Japanese people live according to collectivism, the practice of giving a group priority
over each individual. Due to collectivism, there's hardly
any crime: All the bikes lined up next to the subway station
are unlocked, women run through dark parks at 11:00 p.m.,
and literally *no one* litters. Ali wonders how this is possible, because there are barely any public trash cans—they
were removed after they were used as vessels for sarin
gas attacks in the nineties. (And yet, Ali thinks, America
refuses to pass gun control laws even with mounting mass
shootings.) Ali squints into dark corners of alleys, under
bridges, and along riverbanks, but never finds a single
piece of litter—Hana says most people carry it home. Also
thanks to collectivism, when someone is sick, they wear a
face mask to protect others from catching their germs, and
the rates of homelessness are extremely low. But Hana says
it's not only collectivism that motivates much of Japanese
people's behavior—it's also shame. They don't want to dis-
honor themselves or their families, so they behave accord-
ingly, which seems to Ali like a more fraught idea than

collectivism, but as a tourist, she can't believe how utopian their society seems, at least on the surface.

On their last night there, after a long day of press, everyone wants to do karaoke, which Ali regards as the lowest depth of misery. But when she tries to go back to the hotel instead of joining them, they physically restrain her and drag her to a corny place full of themed rooms like Heaven, with crystals underneath a glass floor and modern white decor; Candy, with bright rainbow-colored sweets encased in glass on the table and the walls; and the Aqua Suite, a room with a rectangular hot tub from which you can sing.

"That sounds super unhygienic," says Ali, but everyone else agrees it sounds super fun and they book it, plus unlimited drinks.

"I can't understand the appeal of a bunch of drunk people who can't sing being crammed into a room, yelling along to subpar songs," Ali says to Cara as they follow the hostess to their suite.

"I think it's about release," says Cara. "Which you could use a little more of." She raises her eyebrows.

Businessmen in suits with loosened ties stumble the halls slurping sake, and the Beatles emanate from multiple rooms. The Aqua Suite isn't as impressive as it looked in the photos: The hot tub is basically a glorified bathtub. In front of it, there's a bench and table for those not in the water. Ali slides onto the bench and leans over to sniff the steaming water—it smells like a wet dog. Almost immediately, a waitress brings in a tray with a bottle of sake, seven shot glasses, and seven Sapporos. Along with Ali, Cara, and Davi, the director, Hana Itō, the writer, Rosa Espinoza, the producer, Kevin Johnson, and the studio publicist, Brandon Jones, are all in the room. Although they've been traveling together since the start of the press tour, there hasn't been much time for socializing, so Ali doesn't know anyone particularly well (other than Cara, of course). She's nervous at the idea of being forced to get drunk and sing, and also the idea that they might sniff out what's going on between her and Cara, who's just sat down next to her so close their thighs are practically overlapping, at which Brandon raises an eyebrow. Ali gives Cara a pointed look and scoots down the bench.

Davi pours everyone sake shots, then holds his up and yells "*Kanpai!*" before knocking it back in one swig. Everyone follows suit, including Ali, because *when in Tokyo*. The last time she had sake was in college and she remembers it tasted like rubbing alcohol, but this sake is slightly sweet and nutty and Ali doesn't mind it. By the time she's looked back at Davi, he's stripped down to his boxer briefs and is stepping into the hot tub. His body is truly a sight to behold, and Ali can understand why he's currently *People* magazine's "Sexiest Man Alive." His abs almost braid like a loaf of challah, which is ironic, considering his zero-carb diet. Even without the abs, his stop sign–shaped face with piercing eyes and pouty lips could win awards. Ali has to admit he and Cara would make an extremely good-looking couple, and it's no wonder fans have gone bananas for them.

Like he's reading her mind, Brandon says, "Nice job getting them on board with Cavi, by the way. The studio is *elated*." Brandon is gay, too, but unlike Ali, he actually has PR career ambitions in addition to personal wealth ambitions, and therefore has no qualms about keeping celebrities closeted—he would cover up a client committing murder if it meant he'd reach the top. "Cliffside Malibu mansion," he sings whenever making a morally questionable publicist decision.

"Thanks," says Ali. She feels like she's just been

complimented for her ability to sell knockoff watches out of a trench coat.

Davi gets the night started by singing "I'm Too Sexy" by Right Said Fred, a fitting song for him. While singing, Davi drips water down his abs, humps the faucet, and wets his hair, throwing his head back like a swimsuit model, spraying water all over the room. By the end, everyone is damp and laughing and loose, including Ali, who takes a second shot of sake when it's handed to her. Next, Rosa slinks around the room to "Criminal" by Fiona Apple, who she says is the best lyricist of all time. Ali hasn't heard the song in years, but she still remembers every word and surprises herself by singing along.

"I think you're enjoying this," says Cara, poking Ali in the ribs.

Ali swats her hand away. "It's not *terrible*."

Then Kevin, who's normally so robotic Ali has found herself looking for a barcode on his neck, launches into a passionate, full-throated rendition of "Say It Ain't So" by Weezer. He thrashes around so much that by the end, his face is bright red and he can barely breathe. Everyone takes another shot.

Hana perfectly mimes the piano to Vanessa Carlton's "A Thousand Miles," and Brandon *American Idol*s "I Will Always Love You" by Whitney Houston, after which they all give him a standing ovation. Then Cara sings the opening lines of "I Want to Know What Love Is" by Foreigner. Her voice is terribly off-key but she leans into it, turning it into a schtick by singing earnestly into the microphone. She keeps gazing at Ali throughout the song, and Ali isn't sure whether it means something. But when Cara gives Ali a staring-through-your-soul *look* as she belts out, "In my life, there's been heartache and pain. I don't know if

I can face it again," Ali knows she's referencing their conversation from the plane to Germany. Cara is singing as if she's Ali, scared to love again but still wanting to. At the chorus, Cara drops to her knees and beseeches the sky as she belts out the completely off-key words. Ali laughs, but then her chest swells and her eyes sting and she can't believe it, but a cheesy eighties song is making her realize she *does* want to know what love is again. She wants Cara to show her.

When the song ends, Brandon gives Ali another questioning look, but she tells herself everyone is too drunk to fully realize what just happened. She stumbles out and runs to the bathroom, a group of giggling women who smell like jasmine exiting as Ali enters. She leans over to check the stalls for feet, and sighs in relief when there are none. In the mirror, she blinks back happy-but-terrified tears. She turns on the faucet and bends over to splash cool water on her face. When she straightens up, the mirror reflects Cara standing next to her. They make eye contact, and Ali doesn't even bother drying her dripping skin before turning to Cara and placing her hands on either side of her face, leaning in to kiss her softly but definitively. They take a moment to linger on each other's lips, the gravity of what's happening traveling between them, before they tilt their heads and brush their sake-coated tongues. Ali's stomach whooshes like a flock of birds taking flight. Cara's hands slip under Ali's shirt and her arms wrap tightly around Ali's warm back as Ali's thumbs stroke Cara's cheeks. Their tongues sweep more widely through each other's mouths before they pull back, each catching the other's lip between her own. Ali doesn't know whether they've been kissing for one minute or five when the door opens and they spring apart, but luckily it's just a middle-aged woman who doesn't even glance at them before shutting herself in a stall and letting out a motorcycle-esque fart that echoes through the toilet bowl. Ali and Cara snicker.

"Let's get out of here," Ali whispers.

Cara cocks her head. "How do you think that would look, publicist of mine?"

Ali frowns. "You're right. I guess we have to go back, at least for a bit. You go first. I'll follow in a minute."

Cara gives her a quick goodbye peck and Ali leans forward, trying to delay the moment of separation until she's on her tiptoes and Cara is out the door. Ali props it open to watch Cara glide away, and feels a tug on her heart—and her clit. Back in the karaoke suite, Brandon is singing "Emotions" by Mariah Carey, and he even does the trademark high notes at the end, pressing a finger to his ear in an imitation of the queen herself. The song is yet another reminder of Natalie that colors the bathroom kiss with sadness and guilt, but Ali's desire is strong enough to overcome it this time. Maybe it's just the convivial atmosphere of the karaoke bar or the sake shots, but for the very first time, it occurs to Ali that Natalie would want her to be happy, which would include her meeting someone new. It's almost like Natalie's spirit, if it still exists somewhere, somehow, has dropped this idea into Ali's brain, telling her it's okay. Ali's eyes well up. There are, of course, other reasons she and Cara shouldn't be together, but maybe, just for tonight, in celebration of this newfound peace, she'll forget them.

She forces herself not to look at Cara constantly, and tearing her eyes away is like ripping Band-Aids off her irises. She's so distracted, she doesn't notice everyone has been badgering her to sing until they're all chanting her name. If she gives in and does it, maybe they'll all be so satisfied they'll agree to leave, and then Ali and Cara can get back to what they started.

Ali gulps down another shot of sake and, before thinking about it too much, selects an all-time favorite, "Shoop" by Salt-N-Pepa, which happens to be apropos for her current state. (Except for the "What's my weakness? Men!" part, of course.) As the song begins, everyone in the room cheers, and Ali feels strangely calm, like she's having an out-of-body experience. When she raps the first line, the voice that emanates from the speakers doesn't sound like hers—it sounds bold, confident. She struts around the room, letting it all out, and at the line about licking a lollipop, Ali stops herself from pantomiming on Cara and instead chooses Brandon, trailing her tongue from his jawline up to his eye.

"Who is she?!" yells Brandon, clapping and whooping.

By the chorus, Ali is feeling encouraged enough that she breaks into the dance routine from the video, complete with bending over and popping her butt, falling to her knees and spreading them, and swiveling her hips in circles. Whenever she allows herself to glance at Cara, Cara's mouth is hanging open, her eyes heavy with hunger.

By the second chorus, everyone is on their feet, singing along so loud Ali can't hear herself anymore. The noise fills up all the space in her brain and she forgets herself—it's an incredibly pleasant sensation, similar to that of meditation. As an attempted antidote to her anxiety, she once read a book about Buddhism, and she remembers its philosophy that there is no unchanging, permanent self—we are each merely a speck that makes up a greater whole. It's here, in the hot tub karaoke room, everyone screaming along to the same song, voices becoming indistinguishable from each other, that Ali feels this connection to the greater whole. Ali laughs, to think she's having a near-religious experience because of an activity she previously despised.

She marks the song's end by cannonballing into the hot

tub, unbothered by how disgusting it is and that she's wearing her favorite jumpsuit. She lies there in the scalding water feeling utterly emptied out, like she just punched someone in the face, or had an orgasm, or took a really satisfying poop.

Cara leans over the edge and smirks. "Do we have ourselves a karaoke convert?"

"I see what you mean now about release," Ali says.

It then occurs to Ali, miserably, that karaoke would be a great photo op for Cavi. When she floats the idea to the group, they all enthusiastically agree, especially Malibu-mansion Brandon. Ali flips through the song book, trying to decide which one would be best, opticswise. "Ain't No Mountain High Enough" by Marvin Gaye and Tammi Terrell? Too earnest. "Crazy for You" by Madonna? Not fun enough. Then she sees it: "Crazy in Love" by Beyoncé, which strikes the perfect tone.

Cara and Davi ham it up like a couple of actors and everyone goes into paparazzi mode capturing it all: them staring deeply into each other's eyes, Cara doing her best to imitate Beyoncé's signature booty-bouncing uh-oh dance, Cara and Davi making crazy eyes at each other while they sing the chorus, Davi rapping Jay-Z's verse, Davi naked with a post-photo-sesh black bar over his crotch to the "got me sprung and I don't care who sees" line. Ali sends the best ones to the online editors at People.com and UsMagazine .com, yet again feeling jealous and sad. No one knows the truth about Cara singing "I Want to Know What Love Is" to her, about the kiss in the bathroom, about any of it. All these hidden moments pile up under the cloak of secrecy, making Ali feel even heavier.

After the photo shoot, everyone agrees it's time to call it a night. They pop into the closest store and buy dry clothes: a sweatshirt that says, "How depressing," a T-shirt that says,

"No bitch yes freedom," and sweatpants that say, "Fart sexy style" on the butt. Then they stop for a quick bowl of ramen at a hole-in-the-wall place and everyone agrees, unsurprisingly, that it's the best ramen they've ever had. Back at the hotel, Ali and Cara make a show of wishing everyone good night and going into their separate rooms, but Cara gives Ali a simultaneously sexy and hilarious wink that Ali knows means she'll be over in a few.

21

While waiting for Cara, Ali tries her best not to freak out and think about all the reasons they shouldn't do what they're about to do. She takes a quick chlorine-removing shower, brushes her teeth and gargles with mouthwash, turns off the overhead lights and turns on a bedside lamp, throws all the clothes strewn around the room into her suitcase, and debates what to put on—real clothes or pajamas or just a bra and underwear or a hotel robe? She settles on pajamas: a white T-shirt with no bra underneath (which is kind of sexy, right?) and supersoft black sleep shorts and black cotton briefs, which qualify as nice underwear for Ali, since they don't have any rips or stains like most of her underwear.

And then she doesn't have time to think about or do anything else because three soft knocks come through the door. She opens it as her stomach does an intense somersault, and there's Cara, wearing a white T-shirt with no bra underneath and light blue men's boxers. They both crack up at their similar outfit choices, which Ali is grateful for since it diffuses any potential awkwardness, then she grabs Cara's arm and pulls her into the room before anyone can spot her standing there. Ali locks the door, and the loud click seems to announce the situation's finality: YOU ARE ABOUT TO HAVE SEX WITH CARA BISSET. Her stomach does another somersault as she turns around and regards Cara, her hair also wet from a shower, her lichen eyes with pupils enlarged either from the room's dimness or from desire, her trademark goofy grin and the mole that disappears into her dimple, the dark circles of her nipples pushing against the fabric of her white T-shirt.

Cara's eyes are on Ali's nipples, too. "Great lesbian minds, huh?" Cara bites her lip and takes a step toward Ali, which is all it takes to close the distance between them. She leans forward and touches her nose to Ali's cheek, blowing a warm puff of air that makes all the hairs on Ali's arms stand up. She trails her nose across Ali's cheek to her earlobe, which she tenderly bites before continuing to ever so slowly trail her nose down Ali's neck to her collarbone. She traces the length of it, pausing to nuzzle the dip in the center between the bones, before trading her nose for the softness of her lips and crawling back up. In the spot below the angle of Ali's jaw, Cara pauses to flick her warm, wet tongue against Ali's skin and Ali gasps, a bolt of eagerness shooting through her. Cara gives her one more lick before she lightly drags her lips across Ali's jaw. When she reaches Ali's mouth, Ali expects to finally be kissed, but Cara continues grazing her lips and nose all around the perimeter of Ali's mouth, driving her wild. When Ali purses her lips, trying to make contact, Cara pulls back.

"Uh-uh-uhhhh," she sings chastisingly.

"Fuck that." Ali grabs Cara's hips and swiftly switches their positions so Cara is backed up against the door.

"Ooh, pushy!" Cara says, before Ali covers her smiling

mouth with her own. While their kiss at the karaoke bar was sweet and slow and emotional, this is deep and fast and hungry, Ali's body taking over from her mind. Her tongue probes, her teeth bite, her lips smack. She sinks her fingers into the soft flesh surrounding Cara's hips, then pushes her own hips into Cara. Cara responds with a surprised exhalation and pushes back before grabbing Ali's ass with both hands to pull her closer. Ali feels a floodgate release. Their raised nipples brush through their thin T-shirts, and Ali keeps one hand on Cara's hip while bringing the other to Cara's breast, over the fabric, cupping the round, perfect heft of it before tracing circles with her thumb, getting closer and closer to Cara's nipple but not actually touching it before widening the circles again. She does this a few times before finally grazing Cara's nipple, then lightly pinching it while sucking on Cara's tongue. At this, Cara moans, not quietly. It occurs to Ali they should get away from the door, in case a coworker walks by and hears. She's very impressed with herself for having this coherent thought while her brain feels like it's drowning in desire.

She reluctantly backs away from the door and takes Cara's hand, leading her to the bed and laying her down before crawling on top of her.

"So you're a top." Cara's eyes glint as she scoots toward the pillows. "I would *not* have called that."

"I don't know what or who I am right now," Ali says, and she doesn't, because Ali, Cara's publicist, would never be this irresponsible. Ali, the anxious self-doubter, would worry she doesn't have the sexual prowess to carry it off. Ali, Natalie's partner, would let *Natalie* lead *her* to the bed and lay her down. Ali, the grieving widow who hasn't seen the point in living for the last year, suddenly sees it.

She leans down and licks Cara's upper lip, then kisses it

gently before biting it. As they tilt their heads and open their mouths to feel the magic of each other's tongues, Ali grinds down onto Cara, matching the rhythm of the kisses to the rhythm of her hips. Cara reaches up and strokes Ali's breasts over her T-shirt to the same rhythm. Like karaoke, this is a form of meditation—everything feels so good Ali can't think about anything other than the sensations. She kisses her way down Cara's neck, then gives her nipples additional over-the-T-shirt attention, nuzzling and biting and licking until the fabric is wet, before she pulls the shirt up and over Cara's head. Cara follows suit and removes Ali's.

They both take a minute to take each other in, smiling in hungry appreciation, before Cara swiftly sits up and takes a breast in her mouth, swirling her tongue around Ali's nipple and growling. Ali doesn't know what possesses her—she's normally never this forward—but she grabs Cara's hand from her other breast and brings it to her mouth, delivering a lick from the base to the tip of her pointer finger, then her middle finger. Cara looks at her with heavy-lidded eyes, and Ali holds eye contact as she takes both fingers fully in her mouth. Cara mumbles a few profanities and lets herself fall back on the pillows. Ali slides her tongue up and down a few times, until Cara's fingers are good and wet. Then she ushers Cara's hand down the length of her body, watching Cara's pupils dilate and her mouth fall more and more open, before she pulls her shorts and underwear away and guides Cara in.

Cara's eyes roll back in her head. "Jesus, you're an *ocean*."

Ali exhales an "Mmmmmm" and leans forward, easing the tension from the band of her shorts and underwear on Cara's hand, until her breasts graze Cara's, hard nipples against soft, warm skin. They both groan. As Ali moves, their breasts continue to slide over each other, adding another pleasurable sensation to the mix. Risking overload,

Ali reaches under the band of Cara's boxers but stays on top of her underwear, using two spread fingers to tease her. The cotton material is nearly soaked through already.

"Please," Cara whispers.

Ali laughs into Cara's neck.

"Please, Ali, please," Cara says, desperately now, and Ali gives in, plunging her hand past the underwear band. She gets lost in a panoply of sensations: the warm, slick velvet surrounding her own fingers; Cara's fingers gliding across Ali like a figure skater, doing figure eights and salchows and triple loops. Their movements don't mimic but complement and speak to each other. It's like they're reading each other's minds—at a certain point Ali can't tell her body from Cara's: They are one rocking, writhing mass.

The shorts and underwear are getting in the way. "Wait," Ali says, and in one swift motion, she pulls down Cara's, then steps off the bed to remove her own. She stands there for a second, strangely uninhibited, drinking in Cara's mussed hair and eager eyes and flushed cheeks and red-bitten lips and her perfect handfuls of breasts and the svelte line on either side of her abdomen and the speech-bubble shaped birthmark coming out of her belly button that Cara has joked about tattooing with "I'm hungry!" and her straight hips and the expansive European triangle of hair between her gangly legs and her callous-covered feet with uneven toes.

"Come back before I die," says Cara, and Ali laughs and crawls back up her body, straddling her and reaching a hand down to resume what they had been doing, but Cara stops her. "I want to feel you on me." Cara takes hold of Ali's hips and pulls her down onto just the right spot.

"Fuck," they both say at the same time.

Ali's warm wetness encompasses Cara and Cara's warm wetness encompasses Ali and she can't believe there are people with vulvas who haven't tried this. It's like the world's best slip n' slide. Ali's hips grind away and Cara's arch up to meet her until Cara's body tenses and her breathing gets short and hard and her fingers dig into the dips of Ali's hips and she jerks forward and yells, "Jesus Christ on the cross!"

"What?" Ali falls on top of her, giggling. "Did you just say…"

Cara is laughing, too, her chest and stomach quaking. "I swear I've never said that during sex. I have *no* idea where it came from."

Ali falls to the side of Cara. "I guess you were moved by the spirit…of my pussy."

"Let's see what you say when *you* come." Cara sits up on her elbow and snakes her hand between Ali's legs.

Ali sighs happily, closing her eyes and getting back into the groove. Cara starts with slow up-and-down strokes, like she's lazily strumming a guitar to tune it before playing the actual song. Waves of pleasure reverberate through Ali's body, releasing low noises from her throat. She feels like she could luxuriate in the feeling for hours, but eventually her body becomes impatient for more. Cara adds speed and pressure, using a consistent rhythm to bring Ali closer and closer.

"This feels so good, but I just need to—" Ali sits up and swings her leg over Cara, then brings Cara's hand back.

"Okay, you big toppy top," says Cara.

"Shut up." Ali smiles as she rocks her hips and bears down on Cara. This was always the position that did it for her, but the placement or movement of Cara's hand isn't working. In essence, Cara isn't touching her the way Natalie used to, and Ali doesn't know how to ask for it—she can't remember the specifics; she just knows it felt different. Then Ali is thinking of Natalie, her hair always dyed an unnatural shade like purple or pink or blue and her deep brown eyes and how she would release a litany of curse words as she came and how afterward she craved a salty, crunchy snack like potato chips or Cheetos. Ali's eyes sting, and even though she wills it not to happen with every ounce of her being, tears escape and roll dramatically down her cheeks.

Ali covers her face with her hands. "I'm sorry."

Cara's hand stills. "Ali, what's happening?"

Ali climbs off Cara and lies on her back, staring at the ceiling. "It's probably the last thing you want to hear."

Cara brushes a tear from Ali's cheek with her thumb. "You were thinking of Natalie?"

"I'm sorry."

"Stop apologizing. It's totally okay. What made you start thinking of her? Do you know?"

Ali shakes her head in a lie.

"It's probably just because I'm the first person you've been with since her. That's bound to be a little…jarring."

"You're probably right." Ali stops herself from saying sorry again, and turns to look at Cara. "I want you to know I was really, really enjoying myself until the memories butted in."

Cara strokes her cheek. "Glad to hear it, but I feel bad you didn't finish. Do you want to try something else?"

Ali shakes her head. "I think the moment has passed. But I want to try again soon, okay?"

"Okay." Cara kisses her gently and clicks off the lamp. Ali rolls onto her side and pulls Cara's arm around her, trying to shake the feeling that she's ruined everything, that she's damaged goods and will never be fit for anyone ever again. In the morning, Cara will either already be gone or act stilted and distant before going back to her room, and later she'll tell Ali they made a mistake and should just stay friends, and once they get back to LA, Ali will stop being Cara's publicist and they won't see each other for months, until Ali runs into her at a restaurant in Silver Lake where Cara will be sitting across from a young model, and Ali will resign herself to her widowhood, never dating again.

But in the morning, Ali wakes up to Cara spooning her, stroking the dip in her hip and nuzzling the back of her neck—not the absence or awkwardness she expected. For a second, Ali panics her alarm didn't go off and they've overslept, but then she remembers she didn't set an alarm because their flight isn't until the afternoon, and it's one of those rare days where they don't have to rush out the door. She relaxes into Cara's touch.

"I thought for sure you'd be gone by now." Ali pushes her butt back into Cara.

"What do you mean, gone?" Cara rubs a palm over one cheek.

"Like, escaped to your own room, to never be naked with me again."

Cara laughs, shooting air from her nose onto Ali's neck. "Oh my God, Ali, you're such a catastrophizer." She squeezes the butt cheek she was rubbing. "I was actually thinking we could pick up where we left off."

Contentment radiates over Ali like hot sunlight. "Yes, please."

Cara crawls her hand over Ali's hip and tickles her fingertips along the insides of Ali's thighs, through her triangle of curly hair, around her belly button, and between the undulations of her breasts. As she ghosts a finger over Ali's nipple, Cara lightly bites her neck and Ali moans, arching her back. Cara rewards her with a full pinch to the nipple and a lick from her clavicle to her ear before trailing her hand back down to Ali's hip, butt, and thighs. She makes this up-and-down journey a few times, Ali's excitement mounting with each repetition, until Ali can't take it anymore and slings her top leg over Cara's, opening herself up. Cara keeps teasing her, dancing her fingers all around the area Ali most wants her to touch until Ali literally drips onto Cara's thigh, at which point Cara growls deeply and plunges a finger between Ali's warm slickness. They both gasp.

They stay like this for a while, Cara's fingers blissfully sliding up and down before Ali says, "Wait," and sits up on her knees, prompting Cara to do the same, still behind Ali. This way, Ali has leverage and can press down on Cara's hand while Cara presses into Ali's backside. Tingly waves of pleasure reverberate through her body. The feeling swells and swells and Ali follows it until it bursts open and releases a weight she didn't know was so heavy. Without it, her body feels amazingly light and ethereal.

"Christ on the cross," Ali says, reaching back to pull a handful of Cara's hair.

Cara laughs into Ali's neck and smacks her butt.

Ali immediately feels the need for another, and brings back Cara's hand, to which Cara enthusiastically says "Oh, OK!" and bites Ali's neck. It only takes a few seconds, but this one is even deeper and more assured than the first. Like taking a second bite of a delicious dish and confirming its sublimity. Ali feels positively scooped out, like she's light enough to float toward the ceiling.

She only gives herself a second to recover before reaching behind her and touching Cara, who's already most of the way there and finishes in probably a minute flat. They fall back onto the mattress, breathing heavily. The outside world once again enters Ali's perception: Past the windows, she can barely hear horns honking and a jackhammer pounding the pavement. The back of Ali's head pulses sharply—a migraine warning. She chugs water and tries to relax the muscles in her face, jaw, neck, and shoulders. But her phone keeps buzzing with email notifications, all the online press coverage of Cara and Davi's content from last night. "We're Crazy in Love with Cavi at Karaoke"; "Uh-oh! Cara Bisset Can't Dance Like Beyoncé." With each headline, Ali's agitation builds until it becomes agony. It's like the magical, transformative night between the two of them never even happened. She wants to squeeze her eyes shut and plug her ears against all the lies she helps to propagate—she never wants to leave this room that safely contains her and Cara and their current feelings. They seem delicate, capable of being disturbed by the smallest change, like a sleeping baby or an egg poaching in barely boiling water or a monarch butterfly emerging from a chrysalis, its wings crumpled and wet and not yet ready for flight.

22

Being physically separated from Cara becomes harder and harder. As Cara answers questions at press events, Ali imagines Cara's mouth enveloping hers, Cara's breasts grazing hers, Cara's hips jutting against hers, one hand squeezing Ali's ass and the other moving between her legs. They get careless—holding hands on the street in Australia, kissing in elevators in Dubai, plunging their hands down each other's pants in bathroom stalls in South Africa. Ali learns Cara likes her hair pulled and her butt slapped, that she yells about Christ/Jesus/God *every* time she comes, that afterward she craves sweets and will order chocolate cake and ice cream sundaes and pudding from room service. Ali learns that she herself likes being called "angel" in and out of bed (it starts off as a joke but quickly turns into a real term of endearment), that she can come ten times in a row, that she can fall asleep in seconds when Cara is spooning her.

Ali also learns Cara gets really mean when she's hungry, that she dreams about her childhood cat most nights, that her favorite activity on a rare day off is to go to McDonald's and order all their country-specific items and sit there for hours people-watching, that she's a whiz at learning new languages and masters a few phrases even if they're only in a country for one day, that she shrugs and says, "Planes be like that" whenever a flight is delayed (which is often), that her favorite way to kill time is to play hot hands, that as a native Angeleno she hates being cold more than anything.

Eventually, Ali learns not only who Cara is but who she was: Cara tells her about how she grew up so broke she ate ketchup-and-mustard sandwiches and got a single pair of socks most Christmases; how her mom once stole a ring from ███████, the TV chef (who she said was the meanest to the cleaners), to pawn so she could pay for Cara's acting classes; how Cara was so unpopular in high school that a group of girls left a signed note in her locker telling her to kill herself and she seriously considered it for a few days; how she was insecure about not going to college so would puzzle her way through books by Plato and Proust; how after seeing herself on TV for the first time, she developed an eating disorder she still struggles with; how she was raped by the director of *Overruled* but didn't tell anyone about it for years, not even her mom, because her mom would have made her tell someone and she was too afraid of getting blacklisted and never working again.

"Whenever I read about him in the news it takes me right back," Cara says. They're in Buenos Aires, in Cara's hotel room, late at night. She's just read the news that *Overruled*'s director, Dan Perry, will direct a buzzy new dramedy on HBO. She's pushed her laptop away from her and sits at the head of the bed, her hands wrapped around her knees, rocking back and forth. "I hate that it still affects me this much. Like, I just want to be over it, you know?"

Ali rubs a hand across Cara's back, surprised to find this

heavy pain and trauma buried underneath Cara's silly, buoy-ant surface. But sickeningly, most of the women Ali knows, including many of her clients, have been sexually assaulted or raped—she knows she's one of the lucky few who haven't. Dana was assaulted by her closest male friend in college, and Ali has seen how it still affects her. "Most of the people I know who have been assaulted say there's no such thing as ever being fully over it," says Ali. "That there are times it lies dormant and times it rears its head, and all you can hope for is longer dormant periods. But it will always be with you. Just like grief. Sorry, I know that's probably not what you want to hear, and it's not like I'm an expert. I've never been through something like this. I just know a lot of people who have."

"Man, that's bleak. But I guess it makes sense. It took me five whole years just to be able to say the word rape, to understand that's what happened to me. So I'm probably still like...in the infancy of processing it."

"Can I ask when it happened? You don't have to tell me anything if you don't want to."

Cara stops rocking. "No, I think I should. If you want to really know me, you have to know this, you know?"

"I understand." And Ali knows that at some point, if things with Cara keep progressing, she'll have to really talk about her mom and Natalie—until she does, Cara won't truly know her. But Ali has been waiting for the right time, when something contextual like this might come up and force Ali to talk about it, instead of just bringing it up out of the blue.

Cara takes a drink of water and pushes her hair behind her ears, steeling herself. "It happened when I was eighteen, at the wrap party for the first season of *Overruled*. I drank more than I ever had, and blacked out. The next day, I kept getting these little flashes of memory about Dan." Cara's voice wavers, and she audibly swallows. "Him pulling my underwear down, thrusting into me, saying, 'Good girl.' But, like, the faintest, fastest flashes—I thought I was imagining it. Because I had never wanted to have sex with a man, and I didn't think Dan would have...done that, because he was like a father figure to me. He helped me try to understand those books by Plato, and he'd take me to Dodgers games, and my mom and I even spent Thanksgiving at his house with his wife and fucking kids. So after a few days went by, I asked him. Like, did something happen between us the night of the wrap party? And he said yeah, you don't remember? And I said no, not really. And I asked if he was sure I had wanted to. And he got mad then, and said I had begged him for it, and that's when I knew he was lying. But I still didn't know if it was actually rape. I didn't know it counts if you're blackout drunk, because you can't say no, you know? I figured it was my fault I got so wasted. And I didn't know it counts if it's someone you're really close to. Because all we were ever told about rape growing up is that it happens with a stranger. Like, a hateful, evil man. Deranged, even. In an alley, at night. That a weapon will probably be involved. It will be terrifying and you will know what to call it. You will report it to the police immediately and the man will be apprehended. End of story. I didn't know someone who claims to love you like a daughter could...could rape you." Cara's voice squeaks toward the end, and she puts a hand over her eyes as her face contorts and she starts to cry.

Fury strikes a match in Ali's chest. She'd like to hunt this man down and kill him with her bare hands. "God, Cara. That's atrocious. Just horrifying. I'm so sorry."

Cara shakily inhales as tears spill from her eyes, rolling down her cheeks and collecting at her chin before dripping onto the white duvet. Her whole body convulses as the tears keep coming.

Ali hands her the tissue box from the bedside table, then rubs her back and waits until she's ready to keep talking.

Cara wipes a tissue across her chin. "It wasn't until another actress told me she was raped by Dan, five years later, that I finally believed it had happened to me. At first I felt super stunned, then super validated: He had done it to someone else. It hadn't been an isolated incident; some version of it had probably happened tons of times. I wasn't overreacting. I hadn't made it up. I wasn't crazy. And in a weird way, I was glad it had happened to her, too—I know that sounds super fucked up, but I just don't know if I ever would have been able to truly acknowledge it without that confirmation."

"I think that's actually super common," says Ali. "A lot of other people have told me they only processed their assault or rape when they learned it happened to someone else. It's a really unfortunate but understandable phenomenon."

"Yeah. So then I was like, *Okay, I was raped*. I finally told my mom. And she convinced me to tell Will. And he was so great about it. Just believed me instantly and didn't tell me taking action could ruin my career—he was ready to burn everything down. I honestly think that's why I've stayed with him, even though I know I could get, like, a 'better' manager now. So anyway, we filed a criminal complaint, and the LAPD referred my complaint to the DA, but they wouldn't prosecute. That ruined my life for like a full year. I was just so angry he would get away with it, you know? I'm still angry. I tried to convince the other woman to file a complaint, but she wouldn't, and I tried to find other women it had happened to, but no one would talk. Meanwhile, he's just living his life, still working, not affected at all. And every time I see him or hear about him or hear about any kind of sexual assault, I lose it. And I don't know how *not* to, you know? I really wish I did."

"I know," Ali says. "It's infuriating that these men always seem to be able to walk away. I've helped other clients file criminal complaints, too, and they never go anywhere. So we just have this whisper list, basically, of men we try our damnedest not to work with. Guess I'll add Dan to it."

"Pretty fucked society we live in, huh?"

"Yup." Ali reaches for Cara's hand and strokes Cara's "bang" tattoo on her pointer finger. "Wait. Is this why you said it was complicated when I asked if you were a gold star?"

Cara nods. "I know people think it's, like, a totally innocuous question. But for me, it's pretty loaded."

"God, I'm sorry. That was so stupid of me." Ali smacks her palm against her forehead. "I know all about loaded questions." She affects a dopey voice. 'Are you close with your parents?' 'What are you doing for Mother's Day?' 'Do you have a significant other?' People ask questions like nothing traumatic has ever happened to anyone."

"True *that*," says Cara.

Ali lifts Cara's hand and kisses it. "I'm really sorry this happened to you, Cara. It's not okay, and I think it's okay for you to feel not okay about it. I'm here anytime you want to talk."

"Thanks." Cara leans over and puts her head in Ali's lap, and Ali runs her fingers through Cara's brittle, split-ended hair. "I do feel a little better."

"Well, I'm glad I could return the favor," says Ali. It was nice to be the person providing comfort for once. It reminds Ali that she doesn't have to feel like such a burden. Even if Cara's mom and partner didn't die, she still has deep trauma of her own, like any human does—even if they're a seemingly carefree superstar. Ali has peeked underneath the surface now, and she feels closer to Cara than ever before.

A few days later, in Rio de Janeiro, it's Ali's turn to peel off some layers when she wakes up in the middle of the night crying after having a particularly vivid dream about her mom teaching her how to fly through the sky like a bird, telling her she doesn't have to be afraid.

"When my mom was manic, being with her could feel magical like that," Ali tells Cara. "One time she called my school and told them I was sick and drove me to Canada, where we swam in a limestone lake with turquoise water that looked like it belonged in the Caribbean. Another time we stayed at an all-you-can-eat buffet for the entire day, eating plate after plate of food. Once she took me to a pet store and bought me three puppies. Then, when she swung down into depression, she returned them all. That was the thing about the good times—they never lasted. So I could never just enjoy them; I was always waiting for the other shoe to drop. Braced for impact, you know? I think that's why I have such bad anxiety."

"That makes total sense," says Cara. They're lying on their sides, facing each other, and Cara reaches out to stroke Ali's wet cheek with a thumb. "It sounds like a really nerve-racking childhood."

"Yeah. Because for every good memory with her, I have five bad ones. When she wouldn't get out of bed and there was no food in the house, so I'd just eat spoonfuls of mayonnaise because it was the most filling condiment we had. How I could never have friends over because she was too unpredictable. When she'd be in the hospital for weeks at a time. When it was my birthday, or my big game, or my recital, and she wouldn't show up. When I found her in the garage with the car running. When I found her covered in puke with all the pills emptied from her bottles...You get the idea."

Cara tuts her tongue. "Damn, Ali. That's really heavy. I'm so sorry you were dealing with all that when you were just a kid."

Ali turns over and lies on her back so she won't have to look at Cara during what she says next. "I know this sounds terrible, but when she died, I felt...free. For the first time in my life. Like, obviously I also felt ravaged with grief, but also free."

Cara takes Ali's hand and squeezes it.

"Does that make me a horrible person? Because I still feel guilty about it."

"No, it doesn't make you a horrible person. It makes you human. I think anyone would have felt that way."

"Ugh, being a human is the worst." The door of the adjacent room slams, and a rowdy group of people enter. Bass-thumping music turns on. It's 2:00 a.m., and Ali desperately wishes she were back in the blissfully quiet hotel room in Tokyo.

Cara calls the front desk and complains, and shortly after, they hear the neighbors' phone ring. The music is turned down to where Ali can still hear it but at least it isn't thumping. "Hey, where was your dad during all the hard times with your mom?" Cara asks. "You didn't mention him."

Ali scoffs. "Working. Always. He was a detective, so I know his job was important, but I also think he used it as an excuse a lot of the time. To not deal with what was happening. You could say I have some anger toward him about it."

"That's pretty understandable." A loud thump comes through the wall. "Has he ever apologized?"

"No. We've never talked about it."

"Oh. So he doesn't even know you're angry?"

"Maybe not, but I feel like he should. Like, he knows he wasn't there." Another thump comes through the wall, then another, until it's rhythmic.

"I find expecting people—especially men—to read your mind usually leads to disappointment. Have you ever thought about talking to him about it?"

"Of course, but you know I'm not the most confrontational person."

When the thumping doesn't stop, Cara gets out of bed and pounds on the wall with the side of her fist until it does. "It doesn't have to be confrontational; it can just be talking about your feelings."

Ali laughs. "You're clearly not from the Midwest. We don't do that."

Cara gets back in bed and snuggles up against Ali. "Well, you should. I feel like a heartfelt apology could be really healing for you. You've already lost your mom and your partner. Don't you want to have the best relationship possible with the family you have left?"

This hits Ali in the gut. She's never thought about it like that—like her relationship with her dad is a precious commodity she should work to maintain. "I'll think about it."

23

After visiting thirteen cities in the span of thirty days, they're back home, with perfect December weather: high sixties and full sun, camellias boasting their exquisite blooms, aloe plants brandishing their fiery torches, and California holly berries making LA feel festive. When Ali picks up Glen from his dog sitter, he jumps on her so ferociously she's covered in scratches for more than a week, but she's so overjoyed to see him she doesn't care.

Ali receives her gigantic bonus check for a promo tour well done, and she'd love to take things easy at work for a while, but winter is always a busy time, as campaigns for Oscar votes heat up approaching the ceremony. This year, Ali has several clients in the running for best and supporting actor and actress. Cara has been nominated for best actress, but she's no longer Ali's client, since Ali was only contracted to work for her until the end of the promotional tour. Ali has conflicted feelings about this. On the one hand, they can now date without Ali feeling like she's doing something ethically wrong. (The agency doesn't have a set rule against dating clients, but obviously it's highly discouraged.) They'll still have to be careful not to out Cara, but at least one of Ali's biggest worries is off the table. But on the other hand, now that Ali isn't Cara's publicist, Ali can't help Cara lobby for Oscar votes, which is a shame because Ali truly thinks Cara gave the best performance out of all the contending actresses.

Ali spends her days doing additional media training with her clients about creating the best narrative to win (which usually includes aligning with an archetype like the underdog or the hero and reflecting values that appeal to voters), organizing press junkets and panels for her clients, accompanying them to lavish dinners and parties to make sure they seem as likable as possible, and securing press coverage like daytime talk show and late-night TV appearances, magazine articles, blog posts, video content, radio shows, and podcasts, which Ali never would have thought would become so popular—"podcast" was the *New Oxford American Dictionary*'s 2005 word of the year.

These are all things Cara is also busy with once they're back from promo tour, even though she's already spent the past few months talking about *Real Love* nonstop. Cara also goes in for her third *Star Wars* audition, and she amiably agrees to a selfie and/or an autograph every time a fan recognizes her in the wild, which has been happening more and more often, and Vivian sends her on countless other auditions for big, buzzy projects in between all the Oscars obligations. Thanks to Cara's efforts, it's looking like she's a real contender for the Oscar—even the blogs who were slut-shaming her a few short weeks ago seem to agree:

www.FameHo.com

CARA BISSET IS NO LONGER A KNOCKOFF HO BAG—SHE'S NOW A HAWT FENDI SPY BAG

So. We previously thought **Cara Bisset** was a total knockoff ho bag, but then we met her at a *Real Love* FYC screening party, and we regret to inform you that she's actually a super talented actress and she was so freaking nice and funny and we're kind of obsessed with her now. She took a million selfies with us and took shots with us and even challenged one of us to a dance-off (we'll call it a tie, okay?!). She and **Davi Silva** were so fucking cute, too. They still refuse to talk about their relationship but it's so obvious from the way they joke around and look at each other that they're totally in love. We even heard they're spending Christmas together this year and meeting each other's family for the first time! OMG, do you think he'll propose?? Regardless, we know who's getting our vote for best actress this year—not that we have an actual Academy vote lol, but if we did, it would def go to Cara Bisset!

Part of Ali was afraid that once she and Cara were back home, the spell of being abroad and removed from their daily reality would break and Cara would want to stop seeing her, but one rare nonevent night, while they're eating delivery Indian food and watching a rerun of *Seinfeld* (the one where Elaine pretends to live in the janitor's closet of a nearby building so she'll be in the delivery zone of her favorite Chinese place),

Cara turns to Ali and says, "You're not bumping lovelies with anyone else, right?"

Ali swallows her bite of chana masala and laughs. "No, I'm not." Her heart beats faster before she asks, "Are you?"

"Well, yeah, I'm sleeping with tons of other people. I just wanted to make sure *you* weren't," Cara says in an exaggeratedly ironic tone.

Ali rolls her eyes. "Do you remember how blatantly you were flirting with the waitress the first time I met you? While talking about sleeping with a different woman the night before?"

Cara grins through a bite of chicken tikka. "That's what I do when a really pretty person makes me nervous. It's, like, lesbian peacocking."

"You thought I was pretty?"

Cara shakes her hands at the sky like she's beseeching God. "Are you *ever* going to truly believe I like you?"

Ali gives Cara a grimace. "I asked Natalie if she was sure she loved me, like, every day."

Cara shakes her head. "Is it because you felt unloved as a kid and all that?"

"Bingo." Glen, who's sitting between them, barks at the sound of a jingly dog leash outside. "You are the cutest angel baby on earth, but no barking," Ali says, bopping him on his cold, wet nose.

"Well, I'm literally asking you to be my girlfriend," Cara says. "That should make you pretty confident about my feelings for you."

Ali widens her eyes. "Your *girlfriend*?" She didn't expect this at all—in fact, she's been expecting Cara to call things off any day now. And if Cara didn't call it off and if they did get serious enough at some point, Ali assumed *she'd* have to bring up being exclusive. She never would have thought the decade-younger, easygoing, hotter person would ask *her*. It feels like a huge dose of happy adrenaline being injected into her veins. Ali gophers her front teeth over her bottom lip. "Okay."

"Okay, you believe I like you? Or okay, you'll be my girlfriend?"

"Both." Ali leans over Glen to kiss Cara, her head swimming with the surreality of the moment. She is Cara Bisset's girlfriend. Well, at least in private. Her heart sinks when she remembers. She tries not to let it ruin the moment, tells herself it's enough. But keeping the relationship secret has been bothering Ali more and more, and she's been thinking about talking to Cara about the possibility of coming out.

The irony of Ali having been the one to initially insist on Cara's closetedness isn't lost on her. In the past, whenever she counseled celebrities to keep their sexuality hidden, it was easy because it didn't affect her. Now that she's inside the cover-up, it seems downright cruel—like depriving a human being of food or water. Part of the joy of being with someone is declaring it and sharing it, and while they can do this with their closest friends and family, it just doesn't feel the same. Ali wants the world to know Cara is hers—she wants to accompany her to red-carpet events not as a publicist but as a partner, she wants to hold Cara's hand across the table in restaurants, she wants Cara to be able to be herself and talk about their relationship in interviews. Soon she'll tell Cara it might be time for her to publicly come out—it's what Cara has wanted since the beginning, and it'll be such a relief for her. They can plan out the perfect time and way to do it, and the studio might not be happy, but at least Ali and Cara will be. The only hitch would be Cara getting the *Star Wars* role, but Ali thinks that's as long a shot as a golf ball landing on the moon.

When they open their eyes after the kiss, Cara looks down at Ali's chest, where her V-neck shirt has fallen open to reveal the swell of her breasts. "Hmmm." She hooks a pointer finger in the V of Ali's shirt and pulls it farther away from Ali's body. "Hmmmmmmmm. What's going on down here?"

Ali giggles.

Cara extends her finger and runs it down the valley between Ali's breasts, then over the tops of them, brushing a nipple. Ali's skin goose bumps as they kiss again, deeper this time. Kissing Cara feels so deeply blissful, it should be a controlled substance. Ali still can't believe she can kiss Cara anytime she wants—well, anytime she wants when they're alone.

Ali crawls over Glen to straddle Cara, and he lets out a loud, petulant sigh, knowing they won't be paying attention to him for a while. They laugh, and Cara slides her hand under Ali's shirt as they keep kissing, Ali grinding on Cara and grabbing fistfuls of her hair while Cara squeezes Ali's ass with her other hand. Cara lifts Ali's shirt over her head and holds her palms up to Ali's breasts, letting her nipples slide up and down. Then Ali whips off Cara's shirt and lets their breasts dance against each other. They're both breathing heavily at this point, and Cara dives a hand down Ali's pants, past her underwear and straight to the good stuff.

"Hel-lo, girlfriend of mine," Cara says. At hearing the word *girlfriend*, Ali feels any remaining bodily fluids rush down to greet Cara's hand.

Cara notices and growls the word again, biting Ali's neck. "My girrrrrlfriend."

Ali loves the possession of it, the youthfulness of it, especially after a year of feeling like she belonged to no one and was at the end of her life.

Cara says the word a few more times, and that's all it takes to send Ali over the edge, three times in quick succession. Once she's regained her breath, Ali slides down to the floor and pulls off Cara's pants and underwear in one fell swoop, then authoritatively pushes Cara's legs open, which elicits a gasp from Cara that drives Ali wild. She hitches her hands underneath Cara's knees and they lock eyes, desire smoldering between them, as Ali lowers her head. She watches Cara the whole time, as Cara bites her bottom lip, as her jaw falls open, as her cheeks grow more and more flushed, as her head falls back, her perfect collarbones straining against her skin, and as she yells, "In Jesus's name, amen!"

Cara cups Ali's cheek in her hand. "Thank you, girlfriend."

"You're welcome, girlfriend," says Ali.

In a moment of especially bad timing, Ali's phone lights up with a call from her dad. She's planning on letting it go to voicemail when Cara says, "You should get that. He's called you, like, five times already this week."

Ali pushes out her bottom lip and shakes her head.

"Come on. It won't be that bad." Cara presses the answer button, then hands the phone to Ali.

"Hi, Dad." Ali glares at Cara while holding her arm over her breasts, like her dad might be able to see her.

"Hey, jet-setter!" he says. "Are you back from your trip?"

"Yup, just the other day," Ali says, though it was probably a week ago now.

"Well, how was it?"

Ali pictures her and Cara naked in a multitude of hotel rooms. "It was fine. Mostly flights and press junkets and trying to eat a vegetable once every few days."

"You didn't get to have any fun?"

Cara must be able to hear him, because she pokes Ali's boob with her foot.

A laugh escapes her.

"What's funny?" her dad says.

"Sorry," Ali says. "My…friend is here and she's being annoying."

"Which friend?"

"You don't know all my friends, Dad."

"Is it that client of yours, the one you were on tour with?"

Cara pokes Ali's boob with her foot again and Ali swats it away.

"What makes you say that?"

"Just a feeling. The last time we talked, it sounded like—"

Ali cuts him off before he can say something embarrassing that Cara might hear. "How are *you* doing? What's new?"

"Well, remember how I had asked you about visiting for Christmas?"

Ali's stomach drops. "Yeah?"

"You were gone for so long on your trip and I know you were probably too busy to reply to my emails, but I figured it would be easier if I came to you, and one day I found a really good deal on a flight, so I went ahead and snatched it up."

Her heart speeds up. "What? You're coming to LA?"

Hurt seeps through her dad's end of the phone. "Don't sound so excited."

Ali feels the usual combination of guilt and anger. "No, it's great—just a surprise. What are your dates?"

"December twenty-third through the thirtieth."

Jesus Christ, a whole week? "You know I'll be working a lot of that time."

"Don't worry, I'm staying in a hotel nearby so I can keep

myself busy when you're busy. Just sitting in the sunshine will be great. Yesterday we got seven inches of snow!"

Goose bumps prickle Ali's skin just at the thought of it. "I don't miss that."

"You always hated the cold. Seems like you ended up in the right place. It'll be nice to see what your life is like there now. It's been so long."

Ali imagines his judgy comments about her expensive apartment and furniture. *How much did this leather couch set you back? I'm afraid to eat off a table this fancy.* He always makes it seem like Ali never comes home because she's a snob who thinks North Dakota is too far beneath her now, when in reality, going home gives Ali PTSD. "When's the last time you were here? Five years ago?"

"I think it was more like seven."

Details from that visit flit through Ali's mind: her dad making vaguely racist comments to service workers, complaining about the heat, complaining about the cost of food and beverages and activities, complaining about the traffic, complaining about how far away they had to park, complaining about the number of homeless people. Her chest tightens as she thinks about going through it all again. "I have to go, Dad, but I guess I'll be seeing you sooner rather than later." She tries to keep her voice upbeat.

"Looking forward to it!" he says, and Ali hangs up before she has to say, "Me too."

She throws her head into her hands and squeezes her fists around handfuls of hair. "I can't believe he booked a trip here without asking me."

Cara rubs her back. "It won't be that bad."

Ali raises her head to scowl at Cara. "You've never met my dad."

"Will I?"

"Oh." Ali didn't think they were quite at that stage yet. She isn't sure if she feels ready to introduce him to someone who isn't Natalie. She thinks about how the three of them finally reached a comfortable place in the years preceding Natalie's death—Ali could go to the bathroom while the three of them were out to dinner and not worry about leaving them alone; Natalie got her dad into the WNBA, and they would watch games while Ali read or wrote; when they all went on walks with Glen, Natalie would point out each and every plant to her dad, tell him its formal name and its common name, and give him fun facts about each one, and he genuinely seemed to enjoy it. Ali probably hasn't been alone with her dad in over eight years. She can't decide if the thought of being alone with him is worse or better than the thought of introducing him to Cara. "Would you even *want* to meet him?" Ali asks Cara reluctantly.

"For sure! Dads love me. Moms, not so much."

"Well, lucky for you…"

"Yeah. Is Christmas a shitty time for you two?"

"It would be less shitty if I didn't have to see him. He just…reminds me of everything from my childhood, you know? It makes me feel even more anxious than usual." Ali can already feel her body going into panic mode: her heart racing, her breathing strangled, her head swimmy.

Cara gets down on the floor and wraps Ali in a warm hug. "Would it help if we all spent Christmas together? Me and my mom, you and your dad, Skylar and Dana and her fam?"

Ali's body revolts at the thought of creating new holiday traditions that don't involve Natalie and her family. The elaborate nativity scenes Natalie's dad would set up in their front yard. The bacalao *navideño* and pozole and tamales and buñuelos Natalie's mom and aunts would cook. The dozens of poinsettias covering every surface of the house.

Natalie sneaking from her childhood bedroom down to the foldout couch in the basement where Ali slept—not because Natalie's parents were homophobic, but because they wanted to treat Ali just like they would treat a male partner, which meant no "funny business" in the house. Ali's chest feels like it's being torn open—never again will she get to experience these holiday traditions. If she refuses to create new ones, what will she do? Spend every Christmas alone, or just with her dad? Perhaps a big Christmas with Cara and her people *is* a good idea.

"U-Haul alert!" Ali tries to joke. "We just made it official tonight and now you want to spend Christmas together with all our people?"

"Listen, I love U-Hauling. Why not jump the fuck in?"

"Because. What if the water is way too cold, or there's a shark, or the waves are too intense? If you wade in, you know what to expect." But maybe Cara is right. Maybe Ali needs to force herself past the discomfort of creating a life without Natalie, and quickly, like cannonballing into a cold pool just to get it over with.

"Angel, no one *ever* knows what to expect. Your life is a pretty good example of that."

24

Ali spends the time before her dad comes fending off almost daily migraines, dealing with the DUI of a high-profile client, doing more Oscars work, seeing *Brokeback Mountain* in theaters twice and bawling both times (Ali has always loved the Annie Proulx short story it's based on), wondering if the movie's success means Hollywood is moving toward more gay acceptance and what that could mean for Cara and Ali's closeted clients, and reading lines with Cara for her *fourth Star Wars* audition, this time with her potential costar Ewan McGregor to test their chemistry, which makes Ali worry Cara might actually get the role. When Ali and Cara read lines, Cara's talent is undeniable—it fills up the whole room, and Ali knows the casting director must feel it, too. Of course Ali wants Cara to get the role, hypothetically, but realistically, she's worried it will make it even harder for them to be together.

The narrative Ali created is that Ali and Cara became "gal pals" while on tour, and since Cara and Davi are dating, Davi introduced Ali to his "best buddy" Tyson (in actuality,

Davi's nonexclusive lover for years), and Ali and Tyson began dating. The four are frequently seen out on double dates, which allows them to spend time with the people they're actually dating while upholding the heterosexual illusion.

You'd be surprised how much two women can get away with under the guise of being friends—Ali and Cara go out to meals, the movies, concerts, sports games, etc., and as long as they don't sit on each other's faces, no one is any the wiser. (Honestly, they probably *could* sit on each other's faces, and the gossip mags would write a headline like "Gal Pals Chat About Their Boyfriends While Practicing New Yoga Poses.") They even spend a romantic weekend in Malibu, and the media simply calls it a "girls' getaway." Every time Ali reads a headline about them being just friends, it feels like taking a cheese grater to her heart. Once, she even rips a magazine to shreds. But she doesn't want to rain on Cara's fame parade, so she keeps her mouth shut. Almost every time Ali and Cara leave the house now, multiple people recognize Cara and ask for a selfie and/or an autograph, which Cara always seems genuinely delighted by.

"You're never just the slightest bit bothered at the constant interruption?" Ali asks Cara one day after the fifth fan approaches her while they're out getting coffee.

"No way, it's totally touching," says Cara.

Ali crosses her arms. "If it was me, I'd get annoyed."

"Well, good thing you're not the movie star!" says Cara, bumping Ali's hip with her own before collecting their free coffees from the barista who recognized her earlier.

Ali and Cara's friendship isn't the only fiction Ali has been cooking up. While she was on promo tour, seeing and hearing and smelling and tasting so many new things, she felt an overwhelming urge to write more earnestly and frequently than by taking a short-story workshop once every few months, so she decided to apply to another round of MFA programs. She's narrowed it down to about fifteen, all fully funded and in places she could stand to live. She stops herself from asking whether Cara could stand to live in any of those places because (a) Ali probably won't get in anywhere anyway; (b) who knows if she and Cara will still be together by the time she'd have to move—a thought that makes her heart violently constrict; and (c) even if she does get into a program *and* she and Cara are still together, Cara likely won't be able to come—she'll have to be in LA for meetings and auditions, or elsewhere for filming. Every school has different requirements and deadlines, and Ali has an unwieldy Excel spreadsheet that tracks all the criteria.

For her writing sample, she uses "Lunch Date." After much deliberation, she reverts to the original, more depressing ending, since Cara told her it was better. The main item Ali is missing from the applications is the personal statement, which is supposed to explain "your purpose in pursuing graduate study, any research you wish to pursue, and your future vocational goals." Ali has no idea how to answer. She wants to pursue graduate study because she wants to write in a more serious way, but she doesn't know the *purpose* behind being able to write more seriously. She reads to escape her reality, and sometimes she thinks she writes for the same reason, but her stories usually mimic her life in their darkness, so she isn't really escaping her reality; she's just transposing it. Why, when she can make up any scenario on earth—the sweetest love story, the happiest ending—does she always choose catastrophe and sadness? She supposes she wants the stories to seem realistic, and that's what's realistic to her. "Nobody who had a happy childhood wants to be a writer," someone said in one of her workshops, and she remembers it struck a chord.

As a kid, she started keeping a diary to catalog her mom's behavior, to try to make sense of it. At first, she was rigorous about describing what had really happened, but eventually she'd make up happier scenarios. Instead of "Mom wouldn't get out of bed all day and there was no food in the fridge. When I told her I was hungry, she just rolled over," it became "Mom and Dad took me to Pizza Hut and we got ten whole pizzas! All the other kids were so jealous and I got so full I puked!" But whenever she went back and read these happy lies, they seemed so boring. So she decided to keep lying, but instead of making situations happier, she started making them worse, so her real life would seem better by comparison. Instead of "Mom wouldn't get out of bed all day and there was no food in the fridge. When I told her I was hungry, she just rolled over," it became "Mom wouldn't get out of bed all day and there was no food in the fridge. When I told her I was hungry, she told me to eat the cat. So I did—I got a steak knife from the kitchen, slit its throat, and ate its raw flesh. It didn't taste good, but at least I wasn't hungry anymore."

Yeah, her day had been bad, but at least she hadn't had to eat her cat. As Ali got older, writing worst-case scenarios became an outlet for her anxiety. A therapist in college once told her that worrying gives you the illusion of control—if you anticipate bad things happening, you think you can prevent them. So is writing just another form of worrying, giving her the illusion of control? While she's writing, she does feel pretty powerful, creating a world where she's in charge, where people think and act and say what she wants them to, where events play out the way she sees fit. In real life, she feels pretty fucking powerless, with a job that forces her to hypocritically counsel clients to stay in the closet, a secret relationship, a driving phobia, and a body and mind that are at the mercy of her migraines and anxiety. So she writes to control a fictional world because she has no control in the real one? Wow. She can't believe she never saw it before. But she's not sure if this deeply psychological answer is what MFA programs are looking for. She closes the blank Word document and tells herself she'll figure out exactly what to say later.

Ali is at work, writing a press release about a client's new ethically sourced, cruelty-free, nonsynthetic makeup line when Cara calls her.

"You're not going to believe this," Cara says as a greeting.

Ali can't tell if her tone is foreboding or exciting. "What?"

"I got the motherfucking *Star Wars* role!" She screams for a few solid seconds and it's so loud Ali has to pull the phone away from her ear.

The first emotion Ali feels upon hearing the news is dread, and she realizes she's been hoping Cara *wouldn't* get the role because it'll make it that much harder for her to come out. But Ali manages to say in the most upbeat tone possible, "Oh my God, that's amazing!" Thankfully Cara can't see her flat face or sunken body language.

"I am gooped and gagged and gobsmacked! I've been sitting in my car literally screaming. I was so sure I wasn't going to get it, you know?"

"I know," Ali says, and stops herself from saying *Me too*. "If they're willing to cast such a green actor, it just goes to show you how undeniable your talent is."

"Are you sure it was my talent? Or was it more like my relationship with Davi?"

"Talent is *always* the first consideration. A buzzworthy

relationship is like the cherry on top. It might get you an audition, but it'll never get you the role."

"Do you think I'm ready for this? Everything is happening so fast."

"Where's all this insecurity coming from? You sound like me!"

"It's just pretty fucking weird when all your dreams start to come true."

Ali laughs. "You got the role because you deserve it—you wouldn't have gotten it if you weren't ready."

"Thanks, angel. You're the best."

Ali cringes. "I'm really happy for you," she says, and tries to will herself to feel it.

25

The day Ali's dad arrives, it's not just raining but pouring, which is so rare she takes it as an omen that the visit is doomed.

"Getting the rental car took an hour and forty-five minutes, then the drive took about the same," he says exasperatedly when he arrives wet-shirted at her doorstep. "And I didn't pack a raincoat because you said it never rains!"

"I said it *almost* never rains." Ali gives him a quick hug, marveling at how he still smells exactly like their house when she was growing up: part mustiness from the constantly flooding basement and part artificial "fresh laundry" from the room spray Ali's mom used in lieu of cleaning. She ushers him inside, and when Glen inevitably barks at him, she rushes to the fridge to get his treats.

"And you wonder why I don't have a dog!" he says.

Ali rolls her eyes into the refrigerator, then hands her dad the bag of chicken-apple bark. "Give him a few of these and he'll quiet right down."

"These look fancy." He squints at the ingredients.

"Restaurant-grade chicken breast certified for human consumption by the USDA, apples from Washington, potato starch, and mint and parsley grown in the USA. Hell, I might as well have one myself." He pops one into his mouth and chews thoughtfully.

Ali laughs. "How is it?"

"Could use salt." He instructs Glen to sit and gives him one.

"Are you hungry? I have human food."

"I wouldn't turn down some cheese and crackers." He sits down at the table and runs his hand over the wood like he's about to ask how much it "set her back."

Before he can, Ali says, "You look good, Dad. Are you doing anything different?" She last saw him over a year ago, when he came to Albuquerque for Natalie's funeral, but he somehow looks younger now than he did then—his head is still bald on top and his goatee is still gray and he's still wearing the same square wire-framed glasses he's worn his whole life, but his skin looks smoother, his eyes brighter, his body leaner and more muscular. Despite how much he complains about retirement, it might be good for him.

"I joined a gym because there's nothing else to do, and I've gotten into cooking because my doctor says I need to watch my sodium intake." He harrumphs.

Ali grabs a smoked cheddar from the cheese drawer, which she bought specifically for her dad because she remembered it was his favorite, and slices thick pieces. "What about your skin? Are you using an anti-aging cream or something?"

"You know Shirley Donaldson, who lives at the end of the street and is always hawking that Avon stuff? She was diagnosed with ovarian cancer a few months back, so I bought a jar of moisturizer just to be nice. Figured I shouldn't let it go to waste." He shrugs. "You know who else has cancer? Bruce. Stage four lung cancer, probably from all those cigarettes."

Bruce was her dad's boss at the precinct. "That's terrible." Ali brings the cheese to the table with a box of organic Triscuits.

"I've been to three funerals this month." He places a piece of cheese on a cracker. "Alan Mack had a stroke, Dan Carey had his third heart attack, and Jean Olson's breast cancer came back after she thought she beat it two years ago." He shakes his head and bites into the cheese and cracker. "At least it gives me something to do." At this he chuckles.

"Jesus, Dad. You've always been so blasé about death. Even at Mom's funeral, you didn't cry."

"Hey, *c'est la vie* until it isn't." He pops the other half of the cheese and cracker into his mouth, as if to punctuate his thought.

Ali scoffs. "I wish I could feel that way."

"Why don't you?" he asks, like he genuinely has no idea.

"Because my mom *and* my partner died, Dad. That kind of thing can give you a complex."

He waves his hand in the air. "You've had a death complex since you were a kid, even before anyone died."

"What do you mean?"

"You never wanted to go to school because you were afraid something was going to happen to Mom."

Ali blinks rapidly, like there's something stuck in her eye. "Because she was constantly threatening—and trying—to kill herself! And I never *wanted* to miss school—you would *tell* me to stay home with her."

"I would tell you you could, because it seemed like you wanted to."

Ali crosses her arms against her walloping heart. "No, I wanted to go to school like a normal kid, Dad."

He holds his hands up, palms out. "I'm sorry if I misread the situation."

Ali can't decipher if he's telling the truth—if he really thought she wanted to stay home from school all those times—or if he's revising history to make himself feel better. She wants to ask him so much more: Does he think she *wanted* to learn how to cook when she was six years old? That she *wanted* to scrub the toilets? That she *wanted* to fight with her mom about taking her medication every day? That she *wanted* to comfort her mom when she talked about not wanting to live? She remembers what Cara said about how she should share her feelings with her dad so they can move past the past. This conversation has certainly given her an opening. And she knows she's much less likely to bring it up later, out of the blue. Her heartbeat feels like it's shaking the whole apartment as she says, "Do you know how hard it was on me, feeling like I was dealing with Mom alone? That I could never count on you for help?"

He scowls. "I know I worked a lot, but I needed that job to support you and your mother. I did the best I could, Al. Let's leave it at that."

"No, Dad. I think we need to talk about this. Get it all out in the open."

"Why? The past is the past; we can't change it."

"You're right, we can't change the past, but we can change our perception of it. Our understanding of it. So I'm asking you: Do you know how hard it was on me, feeling like I was dealing with Mom alone?"

He tuts his tongue and looks out the window, where a dog walker is being pulled along by a churning sea of pups, thanks to a brief break in the rain. "Wow, there must be at least ten dogs there!" Glen barks at the jangling of all their leashes.

Ali tries to hold her voice steady, tries to hold back her tears. "Dad, look at me."

He reluctantly shifts his eyes back to her. Behind his thick glasses, his eyes look shiny, and his bottom lip wobbles.

Oh, fuck it, Ali thinks, and she lets herself cry, hot tears waterfalling down her face.

He follows suit, taking off his glasses and holding a hand over his eyes. "Of course I know it was hard on you, Ali. I hate that I didn't—that I *couldn't*—do better for you. But if you want me to be completely honest, I was barely holding it together myself. There are things you never knew about, concerning your mother. That I protected you from. At least I did that."

Curiosity thrums in Ali's stomach. "What kinds of things?"

He wipes his eyes and puts his glasses back on. "I promised myself I would never tell you. It's not the kind of stuff a child should know about their parent."

"I think I have to know, Dad. In order to forgive you and move on."

"To *forgive* me?"

"Yeah. I've been pretty angry with you, all these years." Upon saying it, Ali practically feels the anger rush out of her body via her mouth, like a cloud of toxic cigarette smoke. "It's why I barely come home or call. Did you not know?"

His mouth twists like he's in physical pain. "I had a sneaking suspicion, but I told myself you were just really busy."

"Please tell me, Dad. Please."

He sighs shakily and looks down at the table. "When she'd go manic and disappear, there were usually drugs involved, as well as…other men. She'd blame the men on the drugs, saying she hadn't been in her right mind, but I think she knew what she was doing. She said I never let her have any fun. Probably because I was trying to keep her sane and keep my job and keep money in our bank account and keep you from knowing how bad things actually were. Once, when I was trying to convince her to take her medication, she came after me with a baseball bat. And I know you think I was always working, but there were plenty of times I had to call out or leave to deal with some crisis involving your mother, and my boss would try to be understanding, but then he'd suggest a leave of absence or a 'less demanding position,' like I didn't have a family to support. I had to open a bank account your mother didn't even know about because she was so financially reckless. And I'm not sure if you remember the time she disappeared for a week, and I found her in Florida? She'd intended to leave us. For good. And I convinced her to come back, for your sake…but maybe that wasn't the right thing to do. I loved your mother, but I was also very angry at her. Because of that, I'd spend a lot of time at work, avoiding her. And now you're angry at me. I'm so sorry, Ali. I did the best I could, but I know it wasn't even close to good enough."

"I had no idea that other stuff was going on," says Ali. She thought she was taking the brunt of the pain her mother inflicted, but it was like an iceberg—there was a whole unwieldy mass under the surface she couldn't see. The cloud of anger Ali exhaled from her body now feels like it's dispersing, wafting out the cracks between the door and the walls and mixing with the air outside. It's incredible that an emotion you've carried around for decades can vanish just like that. It almost seems like a magic trick.

He raises his eyes to look at her and asks, feebly, "Can you forgive me?"

Ali reaches across the table and takes his dry, warm hand. "I think I can, now." She swears she even feels the knot at the back of her skull, where her migraines usually start, begin to loosen.

For the first time in a long time, Ali finds she can enjoy her dad's company. She takes him to the Huntington botanical gardens, her favorite Italian place on Silver Lake Boulevard, the Getty, her favorite dumpling place in Glendale, and El Matador Beach in Malibu. She learns he can now bench-press 135 pounds; that he knows how to cook omelets, roasted chicken, and a perfectly seared steak; that he watched *Real Love* and thought it was "pretty good"; that he renovated the downstairs bathroom all by himself; that there's a woman from the gym he's kind of been seeing.

"She's a widow, too," he says. They're sitting outside Ali's favorite taco place in Echo Park; a slight sunburn is reddening his nose. "Her husband died a few years ago after a major heart attack. And her sister has schizophrenia, so we have a lot in common."

"That's great, Dad. I'm really happy for you."

"Really?" He shifts around in his chair uncomfortably and takes a sip of his blue horchata. "It isn't upsetting for you?"

Ali swallows her bite of chicken *tinga* taco. "No way; I've always wished you would find someone after Mom died. It took you long enough!"

"I dated here and there, but it was never anything worth telling you about. Wendy is the first person who feels serious enough to mention."

"I'm glad you told me." Ali pats his arm.

"What about you?" He bites into his fourth taco, a mole poblano. "Is there anything you want to tell me? I've seen you smiling and giggling at your phone these past few days. Don't forget I'm a detective." He raises his eyebrows expectantly.

Ali sighs theatrically. "*Fine.* She's that actress I went on tour with, the one you keep asking about."

Her dad claps. "From the first time you mentioned her, I knew."

"I haven't told everyone about us yet, partly because it feels too soon after Natalie…"

"Trust me, honey." He covers Ali's hand with his own and blinks a few times in quick succession, his eyes going glassy behind his wire frames. "A year or ten years or even twenty years makes no difference. Some days I still miss your mother like I saw her yesterday, and other days I can barely remember her face. Grief changes, but it's always there. Being with someone else will never change that."

Ali's entire body stiffens in refusal. "I don't like thinking of the days when I'll barely be able to remember Natalie's face. I don't want to get to that point."

Her dad squeezes her hand before letting go. "I know. It's terrible. All I can say is…grief and joy can sit right beside each other, sometimes. And you might as well give yourself more opportunities for the joy to sit down."

A few days after the talk with her dad, Ali decides it *is* a good idea to spend Christmas with Cara and Ali's people—it's time to move on and create new traditions. Ali tells Dana and her family to arrive at one and she tells everyone else three, so when Dana arrives first at 3:15, it's perfect.

"Sorry I'm late." Dana blusters in with a snotty-nosed Cayenne on her hip, and when she sees the other guests aren't there yet, she smacks Ali's arm. "I thought you did the hour-earlier trick?"

"I did the *two-hours-earlier* trick today," Ali says as Arlo chases Glen down the hall.

"Damn you!" Dana shakes her head at Ali before handing her a wooden serving bowl that, in typical Dana style, isn't covered. Ali peers inside and sees one of Dana's ubiquitous "greens and grains" salads. José hands over homemade cranberry kombucha and a vegan blueberry-ginger kuchen, a German cake Dana's mom used to make every Christmas.

Glen emerges from the hallway with his ears down and

Arlo's hands clamped around his tail. "Arlo, let go," says Dana. "That's not a nice way to touch a doggy."

Dana and Ali's dad hug hello. "How many years has it been?" he says. "I can't believe you have two kids!" He bops Cayenne's nose, and she smiles at him. "Feels like yesterday you and Ali were making rock soup and playing with your Barbies in the cardboard house your mothers made." He squeezes Dana's shoulder. "I wish they were here today. At least they have each other, wherever they are now. I like to think about the two of them in heaven, gossiping about the neighbors and secretly smoking their menthol cigarettes, and dyeing each other's hair with those boxes from the drugstore."

Dana swipes a finger under a weepy eye. "I wish they were here, too. I'm glad at least you are."

Ali's dad squats down to say hello to Arlo, who's hugging Dana's leg. "Hi there, Arlo. I'm Ali's dad."

"You're old!" Arlo yells.

"Sorry," Dana says to Ali's dad, and musses Arlo's hair reprimandingly. "You're supposed to say, 'Nice to meet you.'"

"It's okay. I am old," Ali's dad says to Arlo. "Do you want to guess my age?"

Arlo smiles mischievously. "Ten!"

"That's the highest number he knows," Dana says, and Ali's dad laughs. Ali wonders if her dad is secretly sad she's not having kids—if he was looking forward to being a grandparent. He never asked Ali and Natalie about grandkids, unlike some pestering parents, but when Ali told him, unprompted, that she and Natalie didn't want kids after they had been together a few years, he simply said, "Good choice. You'll get a lot more sleep!"

"Do you want to open a present?" Ali says to Arlo. He immediately lets go of Glen's tail and follows Ali to the Christmas tree. She hands him his present and he rips it open, then frowns at the package inside: geometric wooden blocks painted vibrant colors that Ali got at the Christmas market in Berlin. "You can make patterns with them, or stack them...," says Ali, but Arlo continues to frown.

Dana pokes his shoulder. "Say thank you."

"Thank you," Arlo mumbles while staring at the floor.

Dana scowls. "I swear, all that's fun to him is destroying things or hurting people or animals."

"You can build a tower with the blocks, and then knock it down?" Ali suggests to Arlo.

His eyes light up and he nods like a bobblehead. Ali pulls apart the packaging and dumps the blocks onto the rug.

Cara and her mom and Skylar arrive then, all wearing ugly Christmas sweaters: Cara's has a screen-printed vintage picture of fruitcake; her mom's is covered in green garlands and ornaments; Skylar's says, "Santa's favorite HO." It's the first time Ali has seen Skylar without his Ms. Pack-Man makeup, and Ali takes in his short afro, button nose, and shy smile. Cara's mom is the one who looks done up like a drag queen, with foundation shellacked over her skin, visible contouring lines, overdrawn cherry-colored lips, and fake eyelashes so long they brush Ali's face when Cara's mom pulls her into a tight hug and tells Ali in a gruff but amiable voice to call her Deb. "So you're my baby's girlfriend *and* her publicist," she says. "Does that mean you're responsible for all the success she's having?"

"I *was* her publicist," Ali says. "And I think Cara's success is mostly due to her natural talent and charm."

"She got it from me," Deb says, shimmying her shoulders and pushing out her lips. "I wanted to be a star, too—a singer. I had a real nice voice before I ruined it with all those cigarettes. Oh well. Now Cara is living my dreams. I couldn't be prouder of her!"

When Cara approaches Ali, they hesitate, unsure whether to kiss hello. Deb pushes them toward each other and says, "Go on, girls, there's no paparazzi here!"

They give each other a quick peck before Cara passes Ali a tray of rolls she made herself. Skylar hands over a sweet potato pie, and Deb presents a massive Tupperware of "my famous ambrosia salad," a twelve-pack of Budweiser, and an Entenmann's coffee cake.

Deb and Ali's dad say hello, and she pulls him into a hug, heartily slapping his back. "What do you think of this Christmas weather?" She gestures out the window to where it's sunny and sixty-five degrees. The line of palm trees sparkle in the breeze. "Do you miss the snow?"

"Not one damn bit," he says, and they both laugh. "How long have you lived here?" he asks.

"Since I ran away from home at sweet sixteen," she says. "I never looked back!"

"Where was home?"

"A one-room, decrepit shack housing eight people in Bumfuck, Georgia," she says. "What about you?"

"A barley farm about ten minutes away from where I live now in North Dakota."

Deb widens her makeup-laden eyes. "I can't imagine staying where I grew up!"

Ali's dad shrugs. "And I can't imagine leaving."

"Even with all this sunshine and lack of snow?" Deb teases, elbowing him.

"Well, I think I'll just visit more often," says Ali's dad, looking at Ali hopefully, and Ali smiles, finding she doesn't mind the thought of that now. Not at all.

Cara and Ali's dad hug next. "I watched *Real Love*

recently," he says. "You were very good in it! You remind me of Julia Roberts, you know? She has that star quality, but she's also so likable, so seemingly down-to-earth."

Cara puts her hand to her heart. "Oh my God, thank you. I will absolutely take that compliment." She turns to Ali. "Ali, I love your dad."

Ali smiles, relief sweeping through her body. "Those are exactly the qualities I tried to emphasize as her publicist, Dad."

He points at Ali. "Smart girl."

"Ali told me you were a detective," Cara says to Ali's dad. "I'm dying to know which movie or TV show you think actually got it right." And there's Cara, charming Ali's dad right back. Things are almost going *too* well.

Her dad's eyes light up. "Hands down, *The Wire* on HBO. I looked it up, and the guy who wrote it was a police reporter for over a decade. He really knows his stuff."

Ali feels it's finally safe to go to the kitchen and try to fit all the food in the fridge. When she returns, she finds Cara helping Arlo build a tower, Deb and her dad having a spirited conversation about *Law & Order: SVU*, and Skylar and José talking about how they both know the same drag queen named Raja. Dana is nursing Cayenne in the corner, a rare blanket over her chest, probably for the parents' sake. Ali plops down next to her.

"This is nice." Dana gestures around them.

"Kind of weird, though, right?"

Cayenne burps from under the blanket. "I will say, I never thought I'd be spending Christmas with you and your new *girlfriend* this year," says Dana.

"I know." Ali grimace-smiles. "We're moving kind of fast."

"I remember the first time I met Natalie, the way you

looked at her. Full-on vulnerability. You look at Cara like that, but I can see fear at the edges of your eyes now."

"It's pretty terrifying, feeling these feelings again."

Arlo kicks the tower he and Cara just built, squealing in delight when the pieces scatter. Cara gives him a high five. "Does Cara want kids?" Dana asks.

Ali tilts her head. She doesn't know the answer to this question, and it sends a tremor through her stomach. "I actually have no idea. My guess would be no, but she's young, so maybe she doesn't know yet." *I'm in a relationship with someone who is too young to know for sure whether she wants kids or not*, Ali thinks. At times, she completely forgets about Cara's age. Then she's reminded by a bright neon flare like this. "I thought *I* wanted kids when I was twenty-five. Isn't that, like, unimaginable?"

"No, because I remember when you said you did. It wasn't until you and Natalie had been together for a few years that you became sure you didn't. I never knew if she influenced your opinion or if it was a decision you came to on your own."

"Probably a bit of both."

"Maybe if Cara wants them, you'll change your mind," Dana says, a hopeful glint in her eye.

Ali laughs. "Sorry, Dana, but that's a hard no."

Dana tuts her tongue. "Well then, you better find out where Cara stands before things get even more serious."

For dinner, Ali made a short rib stew that simmered in the slow cooker for eight hours (plus a vegan stew for Dana and fam), and Ali's dad showed off his newly acquired cooking skills by making homemade macaroni and cheese. Ali loads up a side plate with ambrosia to try to curry favor with Deb, even though Cara tells her she doesn't have to eat it.

When they sit down, Ali's dad raises a glass. "Merry Christmas, everyone."

"Or as we say in our house…," says Deb, looking at Cara.

"It's Christmas," they say in a womp-womp tone with an exaggerated shrug.

Ali's dad laughs. "Why do you say that? Doesn't feel very festive."

"We've just always kind of hated Christmas." Deb crinkles her nose. "All those expectations like expensive presents, the picture-perfect family…We never had that."

Ali's muscles loosen—someone's finally willing to admit it! "You know what? I've always hated Christmas, too."

Ali's dad stiffens. "Don't say that, Ali." Ali thought after their no-holds-barred conversation the other day that it would be easier to get her dad to open up and be more honest, but she's found old habits die hard, and his initial instinct is still to pretend like everything is fine.

"Come on, Dad. You know it was usually hell with whatever was going on with Mom. Then it was hell when she was gone."

He wrings his hands, clearly uncomfortable with Ali airing their business.

"It's certainly terrible after you've lost someone," says Dana, and José reaches over to hold her hand.

"No tea no shade, but I think deep down *everyone* hates Christmas. As a black, gay drag queen with a traditional-ass family, I know *I* do."

"I guess you all have a point." Ali's dad's face softens. "It does kind of feel like…going through the motions."

"Feels better once you admit it, doesn't it?" says Ali.

He nods sheepishly.

"Say it with me, everyone!" yells Deb.

"It's Christmas," they chorus with a shrug.

After that, any trace of awkwardness leaves the room. When they finish eating, they play Taboo, and Deb and Ali's dad win despite not being able to use any shared references. Deb insists they celebrate by taking shots, and Ali's dad gets tipsier than she's ever seen him. He lets Skylar "beat his face for the gods" (a drag expression Skylar teaches them that means doing makeup extraordinarily well) and allows Cara to create a Facebook account for him. He updates his status to: "The hot take is I hate Christmas but I love my family and new friends," which makes everyone "awwwwwwwww."

Ali agrees—it's a much nicer Christmas than she expected to have, but at the same time, she misses Natalie so much it hurts like a full-body flu. Last Christmas was only a few months after losing Natalie, and Ali refused to celebrate, spending all day indulging her sadness by watching tearjerkers like *Beaches*, *Ghost*, and *Steel Magnolias*, one of Natalie's favorites. When dinnertime rolled around, she got drive-through McDonald's chicken nuggets and fries. This day is certainly better than that one.

She reminds herself that Natalie would want her to be happy, not miserable, as she remembers the first Christmas she went home to Albuquerque with Natalie. It was the first time in her life Ali experienced a noncalamitous Christmas. Sure, Natalie's parents fought constantly, but it was all about the stupidest stuff like the best route to the store or which movie to watch or how to load the dishwasher. The biggest upset of Christmas Day was when the dog ate a cake they had left to cool in the back room, and the second biggest was when Natalie's aunt made a vaguely homophobic comment.

Otherwise, they all just opened presents and ate food and watched NBA games and made small talk.

Ali thinks about what her dad said about grief and joy, and feels them sitting on either side of her. It's like when it's freezing outside and you're sitting next to a fire—one side of you is blazing hot and the other is frigid, and there's no way to marry the two extreme sensations, so you just feel them both at the same time.

When everyone leaves around midnight, Cara stays.

"So was it a good idea?" she asks. "U-Hauling our people to a combo anti-Christmas?"

"The best," Ali says. She piles leftovers into the fridge while Cara loads the dishwasher.

"Do you think your dad liked me?"

"I think he *loved* you," Ali says, and she stops herself from blurting, *I think I love you, too.* Huh. She knew her feelings for Cara were getting intense, but she didn't know they were on *that* level. She probably just had too much to drink and is feeling mushy about how well the day went. Then she remembers Dana's warning to find out where Cara stands on kids before their relationship gets more serious. She can't love someone whose opinion about children she doesn't even know. "Arlo seemed to love you, too." Ali tries to keep her voice light and casual. "It made me wonder about whether you want kids."

"Hell no," says Cara, and relief flows through Ali's veins. "I want to be the fun aunt for my friends' kids who lets them eat a whole gallon of ice cream and doesn't give a fuck."

Ali wedges a tinfoil-wrapped slice of pie on top of a carton of eggs. "Are you sure?"

Cara stops loading the dishwasher, a soapy plate in her hand. "Ah, shit. Do you want kids? Is that why you're asking?"

"No, no, I really don't want kids," Ali says. "I was asking because I hoped you didn't, either."

"Well, good." Cara puts the plate in the dishwasher, then comes over to Ali and wraps her hands around her waist. "Now let's hope we don't get accidentally pregnant." She presses her hips into Ali's.

Ali laughs. "It's okay, I'm on birth control."

"Good, cause I fucking hate condoms, man." Cara affects a deep bro voice. "It just doesn't feel as good if I know I'm not potentially knocking a chick up."

Ali laughs harder. "Personally, I *love* the feeling of jizz dripping down my legs when I get up to go to the bathroom."

"Ew!" Cara smacks Ali's arm. "Does that really happen?"

"Yeah, I wish I didn't know that."

"Well, you'll have to make up for it by having as much sex with women as possible." Cara squeezes Ali's hips, then runs her hands up the sides of Ali's body. When her hands reach Ali's armpits, she bends her knees and, to Ali's surprise, lifts her off the floor and places her on the kitchen counter. "Starting now."

Ali runs a hand over Cara's surprisingly shapely shoulder and desire ripples through her. "Holy shit, you picked me up."

Cara kisses a bicep. "The benefits of being forced to work out with a personal trainer six days a week, now that I'm gonna be in a *Star Wars* movie."

Ali smiles as her stomach sinks, wishing Cara's career advancement didn't feel in direct opposition to their relationship. As if to demonstrate her strength again, Cara faces away from the counter and places her palms on the edge. She lifts herself up and all the muscles in her arms become taut, her tendons straining against her skin. When her butt hits the countertop, Ali swings her leg over Cara's lap and straddles her.

"My intergalactic hero." Ali threads her fingers through the hair at the nape of Cara's neck to pull her head back and kiss her. As their tongues extend and brush and swirl and retreat, Ali thinks Cara really *does* feel like a kind of superhero to her: Cara makes her feel less afraid, and makes her happy, which felt impossible a short while ago, and when their bodies are together the way they are now, Ali feels almost delirious. They stay like this for a few minutes, Ali's hips pressing down and Cara's fingers sinking into Ali's ass and hips until they move to slide Ali's T-shirt over her head and unclasp her bra. When she's sitting in Cara's lap, Ali's breasts are level with Cara's nose, and Cara takes the opportunity to bury her face between the swells, taking a deep, blissful breath like she's happened upon a utopian field of sweet-smelling flowers. She raises her hands and presses the sides of Ali's breasts inward so they embrace her cheeks, then abruptly lets go, making them jiggle. Ali laughs as she slowly raises and lowers her legs so her nipples graze all the features of Cara's face—up and down the swoop of her nose, across the prominent bones of her cheeks, along her parted, hungry lips. When Ali's nipple reaches the middle of Cara's lips, Cara parts them further to lick and suck and bite.

"I want you in my mouth." Cara looks up into Ali's eyes.

A surge so powerful it could cause a blackout shoots through Ali. She looks down at her sleep shorts and puzzles over how she's going to get them off while on the counter, her knees already throbbing from pressing into the countertop. Aha: Against the wall is the knife block with the scissors at the bottom. She grabs the scissors and opens them up, then slices through the top band of her shorts and underwear over her right leg.

Ali places Cara's hands on either side of the cut fabric. "Rip," she instructs her.

Cara's eyes widen in excitement, and she does what she's told. She has to put some muscle behind it, but eventually the cotton tears apart, the noise resounding through the room. They repeat the process with the left leg, and Ali realizes it might not have been quicker than taking off her shorts the normal way, but the rough, animalistic nature of it has definitely made them both more excited.

Ali leans over and snags the dish towel from the stove's handle, folding it over twice before placing it under Cara's head. Then she crawls up Cara's body and arranges her knees on either side of Cara's head, so they also receive the towel's cushioning. Cara grasps Ali's hips and pulls them down and Ali gasps as she's met with a long, warm, upward lick. She clutches the cabinet handles for balance and leverage but otherwise stays still, letting Cara set the pace: She starts with slow, luxurious licks up and down, then adds coaxing circles at the top, then flicks and kisses until Ali's hips shoot forward. After that, they move rhythmically, bringing Ali closer. She feels so connected to Cara that the words *I love you* almost tumble out of her mouth again, but she presses her lips closed, trapping them. It's funny—sex in the kitchen should feel risqué and hot, and it does, but after the day they spent together, it also feels deep and serious. It feels like—well, it feels like making love.

27

The next morning, they're driving to breakfast on Santa Monica Boulevard in East Hollywood when a pedestrian—a man wearing one Timberland boot and a dirty puffy coat with no shirt underneath—emerges from behind a parked car and crosses the street even though there's no crosswalk and traffic is coming right at him. Cara hits the brakes with a few feet to spare, but when Ali turns her head toward the red convertible in the lane beside them, the woman is staring down at her phone. Ali doesn't see the man get hit, but she hears the screeching of tires and the thud of impact before she squeezes her eyes shut, presses her hands over her ears, and starts rocking back and forth.

Ali hears Cara click on the emergency lights and open her door. High-pitched wailing, presumably from the woman who hit the man. A flash of Natalie's body in the street, one of her legs splayed out to the side like a rag doll's. Cara's voice saying, "Hey, man, are you okay?" Another voice—a man's—but the words are indistinguishable. Horns angrily honking, probably people wondering what the holdup is. A faraway siren.

A hand on her shoulder makes Ali jump.

"Ali, angel, are you okay?" asks Cara.

"Is he alive?" Ali croaks.

"Yes, he's going to be okay," Cara says. "Looks like he has a broken leg and will need stitches, but nothing life threatening."

Ali's whole body shakes, including her jaw, which chatters like she's freezing.

"Did this trigger some PTSD?" Cara rubs Ali's back.

Ali nods.

"Okay, just let me give my statement to the police and then we'll go home. Can you make it a few minutes?"

Ali nods.

Ali has known that for her and Cara to feel real, she'll have to tell Cara everything about what happened when Natalie died. Not because Cara wants to know, but because Ali wants to tell her. Because as Cara said when telling Ali about her rape, to know her is to know the worst thing that ever happened to her. She's been waiting for the "right" time to bring it up, if there ever is such a time, and this seems to have forced it.

Back home, after Ali has taken a thirty-minute hot shower and drunk a chamomile tea and eaten a piece of toast, she begins. It was a Thursday. September 9. A rare night when Natalie wasn't working late and Ali wasn't at an event, so they cooked. Cold peanut noodles, because it had been a hot day. They ate on the couch while watching TV, which was how they always ate dinner. That night they were watching *The Wire*, Natalie's favorite show at the time.

After the show, there was a commercial for Oreos that made Ali intensely crave them. Plus an ice-cold glass of milk to dunk them in. She was like a pregnant woman—when she had a craving she had to satisfy it. She vocalized this desire for Oreos to Natalie, knowing there was a chance Natalie would offer to walk to the grocery store, as she frequently did when Ali had a craving. And of course, Natalie said she'd walk to the grocery store, because they were out of trash bags anyway. She gave Ali a kiss and they said I love you, as they did every time one of them left the apartment.

That night, Ali forgot to check what time Natalie left, which she usually did when Natalie ran errands or walked Glen without her, because the thing was, Ali *always* worried about Natalie dying. They had multiple LA friends who had been hit by cars while walking or running in crosswalks (they'd all lived, but still) and knew others who had gotten into bad accidents while driving. By timing Natalie's absences, Ali could know when to expect her back—or when to start worrying. The grocery store was only a few blocks away, probably a five-minute walk each way, plus five minutes in the store, so fifteen minutes total. Twenty if there was a long checkout line or if she ran into an acquaintance or if she had to wait at multiple red lights.

A major four-way intersection between their apartment and the grocery store was particularly dangerous due to drivers running red lights—Ali and Natalie frequently got back from solo dog walks or errands and recounted how they had almost been hit at this intersection. Whenever it happened and they were together, Natalie would yell, "What the fuck?" as loud as she could at the car, or if it was within reaching distance, she would slap her hand against the car to make her point. Ali chastised her whenever she did this, telling her a man was liable to get out of his car and shoot her, but Natalie couldn't help herself. She liked to joke about walking with a baby stroller and pushing it into the crosswalk a few feet ahead of her, so when people almost hit it, they'd be scared straight. But Ali told her LA drivers probably wouldn't care even if they hit a baby.

Since Ali hadn't checked the time when Natalie left, she didn't know exactly when to start worrying, so she probably waited a few more minutes than she usually would have, which of course she couldn't stop thinking about in the days and weeks and months after—how if she had texted Natalie sooner, maybe she could have prevented what happened. She knew it was completely illogical, but her brain still went there. Regardless, when it felt like Natalie had been gone for twenty minutes or so, Ali texted her.

Everything okay?

When she didn't reply after a few minutes, Ali texted her again.

Hello?

When she didn't reply, Ali called her and it went to voicemail. Ali's heart was beating pretty fast at that point, but Natalie frequently took longer than expected, so even when Ali would call her and she wouldn't pick up, she'd arrive a few minutes later. Ali waited probably three minutes, then called again. It went to voicemail. She waited a few more minutes, during which she stood up and looked out the windows, even though the main street wasn't visible from their apartment, then called again. Voicemail. At this point, she was barely breathing.

Maybe Natalie had run into a neighbor, and they were LA-monologuing at her. Maybe the person in front of her at the grocery store had had an issue with their credit card or with the price of an item and she'd had to wait. Maybe her mom had called, and she was pacing around outside, talking to her. Ali decided she'd just walk toward the grocery store and she hoped she'd run into Natalie before she reached the four-way intersection. She debated whether to bring Glen, but since dogs weren't allowed in the grocery store and she might have to go in to look for Natalie, she settled on leaving him at home. She begrudgingly put on a bra and nicer loungewear than what she had been wearing, grabbed her purse, and told Glen she'd be right back.

She dashed down the walkway between apartment buildings, and when she reached the main street, she narrowed her eyes toward the grocery store, trying to make out the shape of Natalie's body. At the main intersection, multiple cars were honking, and she told herself maybe there had been a car crash or maybe there was construction going on, but deep down she knew. She started running, wishing she had put on better shoes than flip-flops. It was still humid out, and sweat beaded above her lip and between her breasts.

As she got closer, she saw a black SUV idling in the middle of the intersection with its emergency lights on and a crowd of about ten people making a circle around something. Her stomach dropped then, and she ran faster, saying, "No no no no no" out loud. When she reached the crowd of people, she pushed through them and immediately saw the blue-and-white-striped tank top Natalie had been wearing when she left, except around her abdomen it was red with blood. One of her legs was splayed out to the side. Her head was facing away from Ali, so Ali couldn't tell if she was conscious. Ali took in all these details in less than a second, then screamed or wailed or a combination of both and turned away from Natalie in horror. Whenever she thinks back to this moment, she feels ashamed she turned away, but she was just so afraid.

A man asked Ali if she knew the woman who had been

hit. She told him she was her partner and asked if Natalie was okay. The man said they had already called an ambulance, as if that answered her question, then told her the person who did it had driven away. Ali didn't care about that; she cared if Natalie was alive. She didn't want to look and had to look. She turned around and said Natalie's name, asked if she could hear her. Natalie didn't move. She took tentative steps toward Natalie, avoiding the rivulet of blood snaking down the pavement, then stepped over her so Ali could see her face. It looked surprisingly placid, and Ali didn't know whether to take this as a good or bad sign. She squatted down and forced herself to quickly press her fingers against Natalie's warm neck. There was a pulse, and Ali finally cried because she thought everything would be okay. She told Natalie she loved her and asked her to please hang on.

The ambulance arrived, even though Ali had no memory of hearing sirens approach. The paramedics pushed her away and Ali couldn't see everything they were doing, but she remembers one pressed his pointer finger into Natalie's forehead, then yelled that they had to move. Ali told the pointer finger guy she was Natalie's partner and asked to come in the ambulance. He told her she could go in the second one—the one without Natalie in it.

The closest hospital was Hollywood Presbyterian, about a seven-minute drive away. Ali kept asking the EMTs she was riding with to tell her honestly whether they thought Natalie would be okay or not, and they kept insisting they didn't know but that the doctors would do everything they could. It made Ali irrationally angry that they wouldn't tell her anything specific, and she imagined strangling one of them—the man with the goatee and gauges in his ears, because he was the most aloof—until he would give her his honest opinion. But of course, Ali just sat there.

At the hospital, they told her to wait in the reception area. She wasn't sure if she had to fill out any paperwork, but she couldn't imagine remembering dates and names and numbers, so she sat in a chair and tried to focus on the details of people around her. A young girl with red-rimmed eyes and a missing front tooth lay with her head in her mother's lap, and the mother gently stroked the girl's hair with long fake nails. It made Ali want her mother—well, not *hers*, she had never been very comforting even when she was alive, but a mother type. Ali thought about texting Dana, but she'd just ask questions, and Ali didn't have any answers. The one she wanted was Natalie.

Ali was thinking about whom she'd ask to watch Glen while she stayed at the hospital with Natalie after she woke up when a doctor and a balding man in schlubby pleated khakis approached Ali and asked her to come with them to a private room off the reception area. Their faces were completely unreadable. The private room seemed like a place you'd need if you were going to tell someone their partner had died, but Ali had felt Natalie's pulse under her fingers and she loved Natalie more than anyone in the world had ever loved their partner, so she told herself that they were just updating her on Natalie's condition. Still, Ali felt like she was going to faint or poop or puke or leave her body entirely.

When they got to the private room, the doctor ushered Ali into a chair and sat on the coffee table in front of her. He stared at her feet for a few seconds before looking up into Ali's eyes. Her throat spasmed so violently she coughed.

"I'm so sorry," he said. "There was internal bleeding—"

"No." Ali squeezed her eyes shut and plugged her ears and shook her head violently back and forth. You can think the worst thing in your life has already happened to you, like your mom being bipolar and then your mom dying, but this pain was almost inconceivable.

"Would you like to see her? To say goodbye?" the doctor asked.

Ali said no again and kept shaking her head back and forth. She absolutely did not want to see Natalie. If she saw her, it would be real, and it couldn't be real.

The man in the schlubby khakis put his hand on Ali's shoulder. "I know this is very hard," he said.

She snapped her shoulder away from him. "Who the fuck are you?"

"Your social worker," he said.

"No," she said for the millionth time. She couldn't deal with this bumbling *man* on top of everything. "Could I have someone else?" she asked the doctor. "Like a woman? Or a gay person, at least?"

"I am gay," the man said quietly, and Ali looked at him again, scanning his body for clues. She didn't find anything, and she supposed people wouldn't know she was gay just by looking at her, either.

He asked Ali if she wanted a priest and she said no.

He asked Ali if she wanted Natalie's belongings, and she wanted to say no again, but knew logistically she would probably need Natalie's credit cards, to cancel them (this thought made her shudder in refusal), and her cell phone. Ali said yes, but not the clothes. She didn't want to see the blood. He brought her Natalie's purple canvas tote bag, with the eggplant pin that said "no thank you" and the fruit cart pin that said "100% fresh fruit," and a plastic bag that contained trash bags, two green bananas, a bag of sour cream and onion chips, a quart of 2 percent milk, and the Oreos Ali had asked for: the reason Natalie was dead. Ali flinched and turned away.

He asked if Ali was ready to talk to the police about whoever had hit Natalie and Ali said no.

He asked if there was anyone Ali could call to come pick her up and stay with her for the night, but Ali couldn't imagine herself telling Dana, or anyone, the truth of what had happened, so she said no.

He drove Ali home in a rusty blue Volvo that seemed like it was from the early nineties, and when he turned the key in the ignition, "Believe" by Cher blasted from the speakers. There was her clue, Ali supposed. He reached his arm out to turn the music down, but Ali stopped him. The whole drive, they didn't speak, simply listened to the song and felt it vibrate through the car's seats, and Ali didn't see how she could believe in any life after this love.

When she got home, Glen did what he always did when one showed up but the other didn't—he sat in front of the door, waiting for Natalie. Their dinner plates were still on the coffee table in front of the couch, and at the sight of the congealed noodles, Ali leaned over and puked. She had had an extreme phobia of vomit since she was a child—when her mom or dad had a stomach flu or food poisoning, she would go sleep in the car so she wouldn't have to hear it, and whenever people vomit in movies or TV shows, she still closes her eyes and plugs her ears and hums. After the events of that night, though, it was a bit of a relief. To this day, Ali still can't eat peanut noodles or Oreos. Glen stayed in front of the door all night, even after Ali had taken four half-milligram Ativans and gone to bed. She barely slept despite the drugs.

On Glen's walk the next morning, he glued his nose to the ground like he always did when one of them had recently left. He pulled Ali, choking himself on his harness, to the exact spot where Natalie had been hit and pointed his paw at it like he did when he smelled a gopher in a hole. Ali tried to pull him past the spot, but he sat down, refusing to move. The walk sign disappeared and cars honked and Ali wanted to scream at them, "THIS WAS WHERE MY PART-NER WAS HIT AND KILLED BY A CAR NOT EVEN TWENTY-FOUR HOURS AGO," but instead she picked Glen up and carried him back to the apartment that didn't feel the slightest bit like home anymore.

Then she finally called Dana. Luckily/terribly, since Dana's mom had died not too long before, she knew what to do. She even went and identified Natalie since Ali refused to do it. It was hands down the biggest favor anyone had ever done for Ali, and she was thankful there was at least some-one in her life who could be there for her in this way. Dana sat next to Ali and held her hand while Ali called Natalie's parents and her own dad and while she talked to the police. They told Ali eyewitnesses had seen a silver Prius hit Natalie and drive away, but no one had gotten the license plate. Ali almost laughed, because every single person in Los Angeles drives a silver Prius. It was better Ali didn't know, to be hon-est, so she couldn't obsess over it.

What she did obsess about were the Oreos and the pre-cise moment Natalie had died. Had Ali imagined Natalie's pulse thrumming against her fingers because she was so des-perate to believe Natalie was still with her? Had it happened on impact? Or a few minutes after? Or while Ali was standing there looking at her? Or in the ambulance on the way to the hospital? Or in the OR? When Ali got the death certificate, it said the time of death was 10:23, but she had no idea what time anything had occurred—not when Natalie had left for the grocery store, not when Ali had left to find her, not when the ambulance had arrived, not when they'd arrived at the hospital. Nothing. Eventually Ali told herself it had hap-pened in the OR, so Natalie would have heard Ali say she loved her while she was lying in the crosswalk. Ali knew it was extremely clichéd to think she was to blame because of the Oreos, imagining scenarios in which she had never asked for them or had gone for them herself, but she still indulged in this line of thinking and sometimes still does.

Ali hasn't let herself relive Natalie's death so fully in a long time, and in the days after she tells Cara everything, Ali's grief swallows her back up like a great whale. She's left barely alive in the pitch black of its cavernous belly, tossed this way and that with no orientation or control. It feels nearly as bad as right after Natalie died—it's almost like she's died a second time. But now at least Ali isn't alone in her grief—she has Cara, to hold her and listen to her and make her laugh and make her soup and watch *Frasier* with her, reminding Ali that not everything is horrendous and there is reason to hope.

28

Once the whale has spit Ali out, she feels like the second-to-last barrier to moving forward with Cara has come down. The final one is Cara coming out and going public with their relationship. Now that Ali and Cara have gotten so serious, every headline about Cara and Davi feels like a slap in the face. Cara is the best thing in Ali's life, and she wants to shout it from the rooftops, but there's a suffocating hand clamped over her mouth. The worst part is, Ali knows it's her own hand: She put the idea about bearding with Davi in Cara's head, and she carried it out, knowing it would make the movie and Cara more successful. How can Ali begrudge Cara that? Is Ali simply being too selfish? Why should her feelings trump Cara's career? But she can't help the way she feels, and she feels like if she sees one more Cavi news item, she'll explode into pieces so small she'll disappear.

Ali loves being a lesbian—it's a core component of her personality. Probably the core-est. Like the fiery, metallic ball at the very center of the earth, holding it all together. For most of her young life, she was a stranger and a mystery to herself. She felt so incredibly lost, with no idea why. When she came out at twenty-three, everything finally made sense. She felt like she met herself for the first time. Being forced to hide that now would be like extinguishing the fiery metallic ball, leaving her cold and lifeless.

Ali decides to bring up the coming-out issue while they're at dinner at a buzzy new Italian restaurant in Silver Lake. The place is filled with gay hipsters in purposefully mismatched outfits like Carhartt pants with a silk blouse or Adidas track pants with leather loafers—the kind of stuff Cara wears—but then there are a few people who look like Westsiders, women with waist-length wavy blonde hair and lip injections and foundation-blanketed faces and men who must spend most of their time at the gym.

"I'd love to be able to lean across this table and kiss you right now," Ali says.

"I know." Cara pouts and extends her foot under the table to slide it up Ali's calf instead.

"What if I could?"

"What are you talking about?" Cara says, her voice still playful, her foot still sliding up and down Ali's calf.

"What if…" Ali takes a deep breath and lowers her voice. "What if you came out?"

Cara's leg stops moving. She lets out an incredulous laugh. "What?"

"I know I'm the one who told you to stay in the closet and orchestrated everything with Davi, so I get that this is wildly hypocritical…but I've been having a really hard time with our relationship having to be a secret. It makes me feel invisible and imprisoned and icky, like I'm back in the closet with all that shame. I know this is the first time I'm voicing it, so it might come as a surprise to you, but I've been wrestling with these feelings for a while now. I haven't said anything before because I know it's unfair for me to ask, but I'm at a point where I have to. Would you ever consider coming out?"

Cara's mouth hangs open. "Is this really happening right now?"

Ali grimaces. "I know. How the tables have turned, huh?"

"You can say that again." Cara shakes her head. "Why? Why are you asking me to do this now, after you spent months convincing me *not* coming out was the right choice?"

"Because I love you." Ali didn't know she was going to say it. She plows on before waiting to see if Cara will say it back. "And it's too painful for me to keep that love a secret."

"But you're the one who told me coming out was career suicide. Do you not believe that anymore?"

"I don't know. I admit it's hard for me to see things objectively. But you just got cast in a *Star Wars* movie. Your career is doing well enough now that maybe you could take the leap."

Cara scoffs. "Yeah, a leap off a cliff. You *really* don't think *Star Wars* would recast me if I came out right now?" She narrows her eyes at Ali. "Be honest. Answer as my publicist and not my girlfriend."

A young woman with one side of her otherwise breast-length hair buzzed approaches their table and fully fails to read the vibe. "I'm so sorry to interrupt, but are you Cara Bisset?" she says.

Cara smiles her new movie star smile, the tension from a few seconds ago melting away from her face. "That's what I've been told."

Ali huffs quietly, annoyed that their time together is constantly being interrupted by fans and that Cara never seems to care—in fact, she still seems overjoyed every single time someone recognizes her. Since Ali met her, Cara has never made a secret of wanting to be famous, but it's no longer just something she talks about—now it's reality. The issue is, Ali wasn't prepared for how it would feel to watch Cara's fame play out with fan after fan, how much Cara would lap it up and not tire of it even as time went on. This trait is Cara's only unattractive quality to Ali—it makes Cara seem like all of Ali's other narcissistic, insecure clients who are constantly looking for validation, even though most of the time, Cara seems neither narcissistic nor insecure. Ali worries Cara's craving for fame, and Ali's distaste for it, will become a bigger issue the bigger a star Cara becomes. Plus, Cara's celebrity is dependent on her staying closeted, which is the other big issue—the two essentially go hand in hand.

The woman laughs. "Oh my God, I just had to come tell you, you were so incredible in *Real Love*. I'm an actress—well, I'm *trying* to be—and I found so much inspiration in all the choices you made. Do you have, like, any advice for someone starting out?"

A sad look clouds Cara's face. "There's something great about being unknown and naive and full of yearning. Once you've quote unquote made it, it can be easy to feel disillusioned about all the bullshit surrounding the acting. So cherish the spot you're in right now. It's special in its own way."

"Wow, that's such great advice," the woman says, her voice so upbeat she's obviously faking her enthusiasm—she was probably hoping for Cara's agent's phone number and not a nostalgic life lesson. "Before I let you get back to your dinner, in case I haven't already totally annoyed you, could I get a picture with you?" She takes her digital camera out of her purse expectantly.

"Absolutely." Cara stands up. "Do I have any food in my teeth?" She exaggeratedly pulls her lips back from her teeth.

This is what she asks every fan before they take a photo together, to make herself seem human and relatable, which she actually was, before the last few weeks. Now it seems like more of an act than genuine traits Cara possesses.

The woman laughs like every fan laughs. "No, you're perfect." She glances at Ali for the first time. "Actually, could you?" She holds out her camera.

"Sure." Ali makes a show of standing up.

Cara wraps a hand around the woman's waist and they lean their heads together, Cara with her lazy, cocksure smile and the woman absolutely beaming.

Ali takes a few purposefully uncentered or blurry photos, feeling petty but annoyed enough to still do it. It was obvious she and Cara were in the middle of a serious discussion, and this woman still felt entitled to bother them.

"Got a bunch of good ones." Ali hands the camera back to the woman.

"Thank you *so* much," the woman says to Cara. She holds her hand over her heart. "I can't wait to see you in whatever's next."

Cara gives her a wink before she scampers away. When the woman gets back to her table, she goes through the photos on the camera and frowns.

Ali and Cara sit back down. "You love that," Ali says accusingly.

Cara holds her hands up, palms out. "It's part of the deal."

"Do you have to say yes every single time, though? We were in the middle of an important conversation."

"You're the one who told me I have to exude likability. That if I say no, people will bad-mouth me online, and then there goes my reputation."

Ali takes a drink of wine. "I said that as your publicist. Now I'm your"—Ali pauses to lower her voice—"*girlfriend*, and it's grating, constantly being interrupted by your fans."

"Yeah, the whole publicist-versus-girlfriend thing is getting a bit tricky, isn't it?" Cara shakes her head. "I asked you, before that woman interrupted us, what you would say as my publicist about coming out right now. Not my girlfriend; my publicist."

Pain pricks the right side of Ali's head, near her temple, and she wonders if it's just one of those ephemeral flashes or if it will develop into a full-blown migraine. "I don't know, Cara. It could go either way."

Cara leans back and crosses her arms. "Which way would you say is more likely?"

Ali stares down at the white tablecloth. There's a pink stain, probably from marinara sauce, in the shape of a heart.

"That's what I thought. So you're essentially asking me to sacrifice my career for our relationship. That's pretty fucking unfair."

"I thought you might be excited at the thought of coming out. It's what you've wanted ever since I met you."

Cara shakes her head. "Not ever since, *when*. It's what I wanted when I met you, when I was naive and had no idea how things work. If I had come out then, *Real Love* probably wouldn't have done nearly as well, and I wouldn't have been cast in this *Star Wars* movie, and come to think of it, we probably wouldn't even be together because you wouldn't have been sent on tour to keep me in the closet."

Ali winces at the thought of not having Cara in her life these last few months. Without her, it would have been more bleakness and drudgery and depression. The server sets down their entrees—mushroom risotto for Ali and pasta

Bolognese for Cara—but Ali's appetite has disappeared. She waits until the server has stepped away, then says, "So coming out is a definite no for you?"

"At least right now, yeah. Let's wait and see how things are after the *Star Wars* movie."

Ali shakes her head. She can't believe this Cara is the same Cara who called lying about one's sexuality "morally sketchy" at their first lunch. How did they get from there to here? Did fame really twist Cara's perception and personality so effectively that her moral compass is now oriented in a completely different direction? "After the *Star Wars* movie, there'll be another opportunity you can't say no to that might be compromised by the truth. I've seen this play out a million times, Cara. I just never knew what it was like from the inside, how terrible and suffocating it was."

"How big of an issue is this for you? If I don't come out, will we be okay?"

"I don't know," Ali says, and she truly doesn't.

For the next few weeks, they try to work around the coming-out issue, but it's like trying to work around an unending crevasse. New pictures of Cara and Davi looking coupley pop up online every few days: Cara and Davi getting coffee, Cara and Davi hiking in Runyon, Cara and Davi kissing in a car, Cara and Davi eating dinner at a romantic restaurant, Cara and Davi holding hands on the beach in Malibu. Ali goes to a college friend's wedding, and since they can't risk covert pictures being taken and posted, she has to go alone. The situation really comes to a head when Cara gives an interview in *Vogue* and talks about her and Davi's relationship for the first time:

VOGUE

"I'VE NEVER BEEN IN LOVE LIKE THIS"

Throughout the interview, Bisset radiates intense "in love" energy, but when I ask her about her relationship with Silva, at first she gives her standard answer: "We prefer to keep our private life private." The more we talk, though, the more he keeps coming up, until she finally can't seem to hold it in anymore: "I've never been in love like this. Like, I'm giddy, but it also feels like a really grounded, adult relationship. It's the first time I've truly seen a future with someone. We bare our souls to each other, laugh ourselves silly, and have dynamite chemistry. I didn't know it was possible to find a relationship this complete." No wonder the chemistry in *Real Love* felt so real, huh?

Cara warns Ali about the interview before it comes out, says the interviewer "bullied" her into talking about it, downplays how much she said. But the day the magazine hits stands, Ali reads the whole piece, and by the end, her hands are shaking in rage.

"I told you I want you to come out, and instead you cement your relationship with Davi?" Ali slaps the magazine down on the coffee table. They're at her apartment, sitting on opposite ends of the couch, the evening news muted on TV. Glen lies on the floor, his front legs tucked under him and his ears pulled down in his "sad pose"—he hates when people fight.

"It's not like I *wanted* to say anything! I told you she was bullying me hard-core."

"It didn't read like that. It read like you happily divulged everything."

"Of course she made it read like that! It doesn't look good for her to admit she practically forced me."

The subtitles on TV (Ali keeps these on even when the TV isn't muted) mention Bush has officially won a second term, after a delay due to Democrats challenging Ohio's electoral college votes. "Your new publicist never stepped in?"

"She was on her BlackBerry replying to emails the whole time. I tried to make eye contact with her to let her know I was uncomfortable, but she didn't even notice. Kind of made me wish you were still my publicist. This new one really sucks."

"Clearly." Now the subtitles mention Nelson Mandela admitting his son died of AIDS at age fifty-four.

"I'm sorry, okay? Can't you forgive me because everything I said in that interview was obviously about you?" Cara crawls to Ali on the other side of the couch while smiling dopily, like she's sure this pardons her. "I meant it, you know. When I said I've never been in love like this." She swallows and holds a hand against Ali's cheek. "I love you, Ali."

Ali turns away. She's been driving herself crazy wondering why Cara hadn't said it yet and wondering when she would, if ever, but upon finally hearing it, Ali doesn't feel the elation and reassurance and love she expected to feel. Instead, she feels hollow, because it reinforces the secrecy of their relationship. Even though Cara told Ali the article was about her, the letters on the page spell *Davi*. "Saying it in this context ruins it, Cara. Can't you see that? The first time you said you were in love with 'me'"—Ali makes air quotes around the word—"the world thought you were talking about Davi. That's not sweet; it's painful. Your fake relationship with him has been paralleling our real one this whole time, from our first kiss to now, and every time I see a new picture or read a new article, it makes me feel completely erased. Like *our* relationship is the fake one. And this interview was, like, the ultimate erasure, which basically makes it official that you're not coming out." Ali shakes her head and looks at the TV, where the subtitles mention an investigation into allegations of prisoner abuse at Guantánamo Bay. "I don't know if I can live like this anymore."

Cara reaches for her. "Ali, what are you saying?"

"I don't know. Let's get some sleep and talk tomorrow."

"Get some sleep...together? Or do you want me to go?"

Since Ali and Natalie almost never fought, Ali feels unequipped to navigate this kind of tumult. She feels like a child lost in the woods. "I think you should go. I need some time alone."

"Okay." Cara bites her lip as her eyes begin to glisten. "Good night, then," she says, squeezing Ali's hand before turning to leave.

"Good night," Ali says, and when she closes the front door, she collapses against it. She can't believe the relationship that essentially brought her back to life is now tearing her apart. It all seemed to happen so fast, too. It was such a surprise when Cara said no to coming out. But Ali only has herself to blame—maybe this is karma giving her what she deserves.

It's a catch-22: She doesn't want to break up with Cara, but she can't stay with her under the current circumstances. Is Ali even willing or ready to be alone again? To grieve not only Natalie but the small green bud of this new relationship? To wake up crying with no one to cheer her up or talk to her? To dread the weekends because there's no work to distract her from her sorrowful solitude? To eat dinner alone on a tray table in front of the TV? To go to bed with no one to kiss good night, except Glen?

This is what she does later that night, having made no decision about what to do.

29

It occurs to Ali that it might be helpful to talk to the partner of one of her closeted clients—one of the rare ones who isn't also famous, to see how they cope with the situation. Ali wants to hear it's possible to have a long, healthy relationship despite the public not knowing about it. , an A-list actress in her early forties with two Academy Awards (who funnily enough is the person Ali saw kiss her partner backstage at that red carpet event all those years ago), gives Ali permission to talk to Cathy, her partner of twelve years, who's a producer (they met on set in the nineties).

Ali meets Cathy at her and ████████'s gated Beverly Hills estate, in the expansive backyard next to the pool, where they can talk candidly. Cathy pours them iced tea as various employees flit about trimming roses, washing the windows of the Cape Cod–style mansion, carrying hampers of laundry and bags of groceries, and sweeping the tennis court across the way.

"Thanks for talking to me," Ali says. "I can't get too specific, but I've recently become involved with someone who can't be out, and I just wanted to talk to someone who knows what that's like. See if you have any tips for how to make it work."

Cathy laughs a deep, raspy laugh. She has short textured blonde hair somewhere between a pixie cut and a bob, kind of like Ellen DeGeneres's, and a wide face with a square jaw and bulbous nose, and she's wearing knee-length mesh basketball shorts and a Lakers sweatshirt. She's definitely the more masculine-presenting one in the couple. "I sure as hell don't know," she says.

Ali squeezes a lemon wedge into her iced tea and laughs back, thinking Cathy's joking. "Oh, come on."

"No, really! I have no frickin' idea, because I wouldn't say my relationship with ██████████ *does* work. So my tip would be to get out of the relationship you're in ASAP. Before it becomes any more serious. Because things are never going to change, no matter how many times she promises you they eventually will."

Ali is confused. She thought ██████████ and Cathy were completely happy. "By things changing, you mean her coming out?"

Cathy points finger guns at Ali. "Righto."

"Oh." Ali takes a sip of iced tea. It's deliciously strong, and she reminds herself not to drink more than half a glass, or else she'll get terrible anxiety. Once, she had an iced tea so strong she had to call out of work the next day. "So that's, like, an issue for you two?"

"Hon, it's *the* issue. The number one thing we fight about. The reason we're in couples therapy. Every frickin' year she tells me she's going to come out next year, then, when next year rolls around, surprise, surprise, she doesn't. She's been telling me this since our first frickin' date. I guess I'm the stupid sucker for believing her every time."

Ali's heart sinks. She drinks some more iced tea, measuring her swallows. A small part of her wants to believe Cara would come out sooner rather than later. But the larger part of Ali pictures her future with Cara year after closeted year, fight after fight, until they're both wrinkled with regrets. "So obviously, you've made it clear to her that you want her to come out."

"Obviously. I was willing to be patient when we first got together, but now that it's been twelve frickin' years, my patience is about gone, man. I've given her a year deadline—she's gotta come out by January first, 2007. If she doesn't, I'm gone." Cathy smacks her palms together, then sends one flying off like an airplane.

"Really? You'd throw away twelve years?"

"*She's* the one who'd be throwing them away," Cathy snarls, spitting out a piece of mint from her tea.

Ali takes one final gulp of her iced tea, savoring it, because she's now at the halfway mark. "It's really that bad? I got the impression that basically everyone except the general public knows you're together. So it's not like you two are even *that* closeted."

"Sure, all of Hollywood and all our family and friends know we're together. But she still can't pose for a picture with me on the red carpet. She still can't thank me when she wins an award. She still can't talk about me in interviews. And we still can't kiss in public. It all still stings, and it all adds up. Death by a thousand frickin' cuts, ya know?"

Ali can already feel the caffeine twisting her intestines and walloping her heart and jittering her eyeballs. Or maybe it's just this conversation, which is not going the way Ali had hoped. She had thought Cathy would say something like "You get used to it" or "Everyone who matters knows" or "The love we have for each other makes up for it." Not this absolutely demoralizing tirade. "You don't worry you're being selfish?" Ali asks. "Don't you think her career would suffer, at least a little?"

"The woman has two frickin' Academy Awards. I think she'd be okay."

Now that Ali has told herself she can't have any more iced tea, her tongue feels impossibly dry. One more sip couldn't make a difference, could it? Impulsively, Ali reaches for the glass and takes one more drink, holding it on her tongue for a few seconds before swallowing. "What do you think it is, for you? The reason you can't just let it go and let her stay in the closet?"

"I just hate secrets. They destroy everything. My mother gave a baby up for adoption when she was a teenager, and that secret destroyed her until the kid found her and she had to tell me and my siblings and my dad. Suddenly she was like this new, happy person. And I can see how keeping this secret destroys ███████████, even if she won't admit it. She might have two Oscars, but she doesn't have inner frickin' peace. No one with a secret is actually okay. No one."

Ali tells Dana she needs to talk, so they go on a hike. Instead of their usual Elysian Park trail, they switch things up and take the Bill Eckert Trail in Griffith Park, another one of Ali's favorites. It starts near the creepy abandoned zoo and then heads north, wending its way through the middle of the park.

"So what's up?" asks Dana, huffing as they begin the steep ascent. She has Cayenne strapped to her chest, who was supposed to be with José's parents, but they canceled at the last minute because José's mom took a fall and sprained her ankle. Right now Cayenne is burbling happily, but Ali knows it's only a matter of time until she starts screaming.

"Things with Cara aren't going so great," says Ali, also huffing to keep up with Glen, who's trotting along excitedly with no apparent difficulty, pulling at his leash.

"Oh no," says Dana. "Is it the coming-out issue?"

"Yeah. I just can't seem to get over it, no matter how hard I try."

"Why? Like, what's the sticking point?" As if on cue, Cayenne starts fussing. Dana grabs the pacifier clipped to Cayenne's shirt and sticks it in her mouth. For two seconds she seems appeased, but then she spits the pacifier out and starts crying in earnest. They're nearing the lookout point with the wooden bench that faces Glendale and the San Gabriel Mountains. "She's probably hungry," says Dana. "Do you mind if we sit?"

"Sure," Ali says, trying not to show her frustration. Glen reaches the end of his leash, then turns around and gives Ali an annoyed look, like *What's the holdup?*

Dana sits, takes out her boob, and tries to guide it into Cayenne's screaming mouth, but Cayenne dodges this way and that. "You *know* you're hungry," Dana says to her. "Stop resisting!"

Ali turns behind them, taking in the view of Bee Rock, a steep outcropping named for its hive-like shape, and the surrounding hills. Thanks to some recent winter rain, they look especially verdant—the grass near the bench is so bright, it almost appears neon. A mockingbird in the tree next to the bench competes with Cayenne's cries, whistling one repeated note almost like the beeping of a smoke detector, before it switches to three descending notes, like *figaro figaro figaro.*

Finally, Cayenne relents and accepts the nipple. "Phew," Dana says. "What were we talking about?"

"You asked me why I can't get over Cara not coming out."

"And?"

"It just makes me feel really invisible. Both in the relationship and to myself. You know how huge coming out was for me. I hate having to hide what I feel is the most intrinsic part of myself."

"I know what you mean. Back in the day, when José was first able to pass as cis, that was kind of an issue for me. Strangers finally called him sir, friends stopped slipping with his pronouns, and everyone who didn't know us before assumed we were just a normal straight couple. And understandably, he didn't want me to tell anyone we weren't. But I hated the way that felt—like my LGBT identity was being erased, because before José, I had always dated women, and when I started dating José, he was a woman, too. And you know I've always completely supported him and his transition, and I was happy for him, that the world was finally seeing him the way he wanted, but I was also sad for me, you know? It felt like going back in the closet in some ways."

A group of hikers approach the bench Dana and Ali are sitting on, then veer away when they see Dana's boob. "I remember you talking about that at the time," says Ali. "Did you ever bring it up with him?"

"I think I said something about it feeling 'weird' to be perceived as being in a straight cis relationship. But I didn't tell him how it made me feel sort of erased. That just felt like it wasn't okay to admit to him, as a trans person. Like hey, I know you're so happy you can pass as cis now, but it actually kind of sucks for me? How selfish."

"I worry I'm being selfish, too. Like, if she came out, she'd be risking sacrificing her career for me."

"I think that's why coming out has to be her decision." Cayenne stops suckling and smiles. "There, that's better, isn't it?" Dana baby-talks to her, and lifts her up to give her a kiss. While Dana is smooching away, Cayenne abruptly projectile-spits up all over Dana's face. Some even gets in her mouth. Ali jumps back, but Dana just laughs and spits out the spit-up. The sour smell spreads through the air as Dana digs a thin blanket out of her backpack to wipe up the mess.

Ali truly doesn't know why anyone would *choose* to become a parent. She waits until Dana and Cayenne are cleaned up and they're back on the trail before asking, "How did things resolve with you and José? Did you just eventually stop feeling that way?"

"Once the new thrill of passing wore off, I think he got more comfortable being open about who he was. Like, obviously he wasn't going to tell a complete stranger that he's trans, but he told everyone at his new job, and he told new friends and acquaintances, so it didn't feel so much like we were hiding anymore. And at a certain point, I just had to stop caring so much about how strangers perceived me. Like, so what if a barista at a coffee shop doesn't know I'm part of the LGBT community? *I* know who I am."

"No, I definitely need all baristas to know I'm gay."

Dana laughs. "I'd just give it some time, Ali. You might feel differently about it in a few weeks or months. Or maybe you won't, and then you'll know for sure. Or maybe Cara will decide to come out sooner rather than later. Who knows!"

Ali groans. "So you're telling me to keep living in purgatory?"

Dana grimaces. "That's really how it feels?"

"Yes."

"Okay, how about this old trick?" Dana turns to the side and puts two hands behind her back. "Number one means you break up with Cara. Number two means you stay with her despite her not coming out. Pick a hand."

Ali briefly debates, then points at Dana's left arm.

Dana pulls her left hand in front of her, revealing one pointer finger held up. "So that's break up. How do you feel?"

Ali's heart wrenches in protest. Her throat tightens. "Devastated."

"Well, there you have it," says Dana.

"Wait. Pretend I picked the other hand," says Ali.

Dana reveals her right hand, making the peace sign. "You stay with her despite her not coming out. How do you feel now?"

Once again, Ali's heart wrenches in protest. Her throat tightens. "Also devastated."

"Well, shit, Al. I don't know what to tell you."

30

Cara suggests a weekend trip to Palm Springs so they can get away from it all. They arrive late Saturday morning and stay at the newly opened Parker, a sprawling five-star resort, which truly does feel like a getaway with its labyrinth of pathways and lush landscaping. The hotel was designed by Jonathan Adler, so it's full of colorful kitschy touches that make the place feel a bit like your rich, eccentric gay uncle's estate. In the lobby, there's a vintage light-up sign that says "DRUGS" in an old-timey drugstore font, a knight in shining armor, a zebra-patterned rug, and a mantel covered in a rainbow of interestingly shaped glass vases. In the lounge, an entire wall is covered in macramé owls. The hallways are carpeted in a hexagonal print supposedly inspired by *The Shining*.

After checking in, they relax by the palm tree–lined pool that overlooks undulations of dry, dusty hills. There's not a cloud in the sky, and it's seventy degrees—hot in the sun, but cool in the shade. Cara sits in the sun and rereads James Baldwin's *Go Tell It on the Mountain*, and Ali sits in the shade of an umbrella and reads *Magic for Beginners*, a recent short-story collection by Kelly Link that's making Ali feel very insecure about her own ambitions as a writer. A month ago, she completed her MFA applications and sent them in. Now she has to apprehensively wait to hear back until March, oscillating between hopefulness and despair multiple times a day.

Across the pool, two women—one in board shorts and a sports bra, the other in a black bikini—sit on one chaise. The one in the bikini sits between the sprawled legs of the one in board shorts, resting her head against the woman's sports-bra'd chest. They stroke each other's arms and kiss and apply sunscreen to each other's bodies. Ali wants to say something to Cara like *Could be us*, but she keeps her mouth shut. Both women are wearing sunglasses, but Ali keeps feeling like the woman in the bikini is watching her and Cara. Probably trying to figure out if Cara is who she thinks she is. After an hour or so, Bikini gets up and presumably goes to the bathroom, and on her way back, she stops next to Cara's chaise.

"Sorry to interrupt," she says, and Ali thinks, *So much for getting away from it all*. "Are you Cara Bisset?" Bikini has chin-length red hair and pale skin covered in freckles, but her shoulders are violently red with sunburn.

"Who, me?" Cara says, jokingly looking around.

Bikini laughs. "You were so amazing in *Real Love*. The best performance of the year, hands down."

Cara fans her face. "You wouldn't happen to be an Oscar voter, would you?" The Golden Globes were last week, and Cara lost to Hilary Swank for *Million Dollar Baby*, which has made her even more determined to win the Oscar.

Bikini laughs again. "No, but one of my friends is, and he already said he's voting for you."

"Oh, amazing. Are you…in the industry?" Cara asks.

"Oh no, not at all." Bikini waves her hands dismissively. "What I do is much more boring."

"What do you do?" Cara manages to sound genuinely interested, and Ali privately rolls her eyes.

"I'm in publicity. Like I said, not very exciting."

"Oh! That's what she does." Cara gestures at Ali.

Ali begrudgingly looks up from her book. "Yup."

The woman grimaces. "Sorry I said it was boring! That's just what I think."

"No, it's definitely not my idea of a great time, either," Ali says. *Neither is this*, she wants to add.

"Wait, I think I recognize you, too." Bikini claps. "Are you the person in the tabloids who's always with Cara on those…double dates?" She says "double dates" with a whiff of irony, like she's putting the phrase in air quotes.

Cara nervously glances at Ali, also clocking the intonation.

"That's me," says Ali. "The gal pal." It falls out of her mouth before she can stop herself. She didn't mean for it to sound ironic—she was just quoting what the tabloids always call her—but it does.

Bikini laughs a knowing laugh. "I *thought* I got a vibe about you two!" she says, slapping her thigh.

Cara widens her eyes at Ali.

"Oh, sorry if that sounded, um—I didn't mean—we *are* just friends," Ali says.

"Don't worry, I won't tell anyone," Bikini says. "It's just nice to know I'm not crazy!"

"We really are just friends, though." Cara's eyes brim with panic.

"Okay," Bikini says. Her freckled cheeks are almost as red as her shoulders. "Sorry. I didn't mean to—regardless,

I won't say anything, even if there's nothing to say anything about." She skirts away and bumps into a chair. It makes a loud metallic scrape. "Have a good rest of your weekend!"

They watch as Bikini practically runs back across the pool. This time, she sits down on the bottom half of the chaise, facing away from Ali and Cara. The two women exchange a few words, then Board Shorts smiles. She seems to look at Ali and Cara from underneath her sunglasses, then quickly looks away. "Shit," says Cara. "Shit shit shit. Why on earth did you say that?"

"I'm sorry, it just came out," says Ali. "We probably shouldn't draw any more attention to it by visibly fighting in front of her."

"Then let's go to the room," says Cara.

Ali follows a few paces behind as Cara power walks to the room. Once inside, Cara angrily tugs all the curtains closed until the room is dark as night. Then she turns around and asks Ali, with her arms crossed, "Did you say that on purpose?"

Ali perches on the edge of the bed. "What, the thing about me being the gal pal? Of course not. It just kind of fell out of my mouth. And I definitely didn't mean for it to sound so sarcastic."

Cara narrows her eyes at Ali. "You're sure? Because it seems like, since I won't come out on my own, maybe you want someone else to do it for me."

A sharp pain stabs Ali's chest. It feels like it goes right through the center of her heart. "You really think I would do that?"

"I don't know." Cara peeks through the blinds like she's afraid someone is watching them. "I really don't know anymore."

Ali feels like she doesn't know who either of them is

right now, like all their months of getting to know the deeper people inside have suddenly vanished in a time warp. "If you truly think I'm that type of person, you should probably just break up with me right now," Ali says, her voice shaking. It's a dare she hopes Cara doesn't take—Ali doesn't want this to be over, but if Cara really believes Ali would out her, Ali doesn't see how they could move forward.

Cara's mouth becomes a thin line. "Is that what you want?"

"Of course not!" says Ali. "But I don't know why you would stay with me if you truly think I would out you."

"I don't, I don't." Cara rushes to the bed and sits next to Ali, taking her hands in hers.

Ali leaves her hands limp inside Cara's "Then why did you ask if I said it on purpose, if you knew I didn't?"

"I don't know." Cara releases Ali's hands and throws herself back onto the bed. "I just wanted to make sure. I was mad and looking for someone to blame." She takes a deep breath. "The Oscars are in a month, basically, and I've been doing everything I possibly can to win. I've been running myself ragged doing all these events and answering the same inane questions for the trillionth time and posing for the trillionth selfie...I just don't want it all to be for nothing. Being outed would completely ruin my chances."

"I know how hard you've worked and how much you want to win," says Ali. "I would never do anything to jeopardize that. I'm sorry I had a slip of the tongue, but that was all it was. And I really don't think that woman will say anything. I think she's just a lesbian who was excited at the idea of us being lesbians, too." Ali takes Cara's hand and squeezes it.

"Yeah, it sucks we couldn't tell her the truth. It would be nice to bond with fans that way. Maybe next year..." Cara tugs Ali's hand until Ali falls onto the bed next to her, and they kiss, but it doesn't feel zippy like it usually does, because Ali keeps thinking about what Cathy said, about ███████████ always promising to come out next year and then never doing it. Dread sinks into the pit of Ali's stomach.

"Are you hungry?" Cara asks when they pull back from the kiss.

"Yeah, that Norma's place looked cute," says Ali, referring to the orange-hued patio restaurant on-site at Parker where she saw everyone eating eggs Benedict earlier.

Cara bites her lip. "What about room service?"

"Why? It's so nice out."

"Room service is so indulgent, though."

Ali props herself up on an elbow. "Are you worried about that woman seeing us?"

"No." Cara covers her face with her hands. "Maybe."

"Oh my God, seriously? I won't touch you at all, I promise. We'll behave like good gal pals."

Cara writhes around. "I just won't be able to enjoy myself or my food worrying about her or other people watching."

"Cara, there's always someone who might be watching. That's the case every time we leave the house."

"It just feels different when I know there's a woman out there who knows I'm gay."

Ali huffs. "So are we going to get room service all weekend?"

"I don't know! Can we just get it for this meal?" Cara touches her nose to Ali's. "Pleeeeease? I know it's pathetic. Please just humor me."

"Okay, fine."

They look at a menu, and Cara orders a spicy shrimp quesadilla. Ali orders fish tacos. When someone knocks on the door and yells, "Room service!" Cara gives Ali a worried—almost sickened—look.

"What?" Ali asks.

"What if that woman paid the hotel staff to give her extra info? What if this room service person is like...here to spy?"

Ali laughs. "Are you being serious?"

"I don't know. I just feel totally freaked out right now! Remember those articles a while back, before Brad and Angie made it official, about how they booked a room here and it must have meant they were together? Someone at this hotel clearly talks to the press."

Another knock at the door, another room service announcement. "Cara, there's no way anyone here could prove we aren't just two friends staying in the same room."

"Could you just...go where they can't see you while they bring the food in?"

Another knock, this time louder and longer. Cara, in a full panic, flings open the closet door and pushes Ali into it. "A little on the nose, don't you think?" Ali says as Cara closes the door. Ali's heart wallops in indignation.

She hears the main door open. Cara apologizes for the wait and turns on the lights, which stripe Ali's body in white, due to the angled slats on the outside of the closet door. Ali can't believe she's a thirty-five-year-old *out* lesbian who is still, somehow, hiding in a literal closet. She feels rage and frustration and helplessness and betrayal and loneliness and shame and grief, because in this moment, she truly, for once and for all, knows her relationship with Cara is over. There is no moving forward from this. The room service table rolls in and the employee asks where to put it. Cara says next to the table—her voice is warm and unbothered, like she didn't just push her girlfriend into a closet moments ago. The metal covers clang as the employee removes them. Cara says everything looks great and thanks him. The main door clicks closed. Ali waits, like a child in time-out, for Cara to tell her she can exit.

When Cara swings the closet door open, she takes one look at Ali's face and says, "This isn't going to work, is it?"

"No, it isn't." Ali steps out of the closet and sits on the bed, and Cara sits next to her. They're both already crying intensely, their bodies heaving, breaths shaking, noses sniffling.

"I'm sorry," says Cara.

"Me too," says Ali.

Cara buries her face in Ali's lap. "This is the fucking worst. No one should have to choose between their career and their person."

"I know," Ali says. "I can't believe I've been playing a part in this for years. I feel so disgusted, now that I know the terrible toll it takes."

"Can we stay friends?" Cara says, turning to look up at Ali. "I don't want to lose you completely."

Tears drip from Ali's chin onto Cara's face, blending with hers. Ali gently wipes the drops from Cara's cheeks, and Cara puts her hand over Ali's, interlacing their fingers. They both squeeze so hard their fingers turn white. "I think that'll be too hard for both of us."

"Can I at least kiss you right now?"

Ali nods, and Cara sits up to give her a slow, sad, passionate kiss that makes Ali want to take it all back, but then they'd be right back at the same impasse.

31

In the month following the breakup, Ali gets a migraine so excruciating she ends up at urgent care for three shots in the butt: one of Toradol, an anti-inflammatory, one of Reglan, an antinausea drug, and one of Benadryl, which is meant to put her to sleep but doesn't. Every night, she watches three or four or five episodes of *Frasier* with no sleep in sight. When she's not watching *Frasier*, she binge-watches reality survival shows and tells herself she's lucky to have a roof over her head and running water and no bugs crawling on her body and all the food she wants, even if she has no appetite. Protein smoothies and pureed soups become her sustenance, like she just had her tonsils removed. She remembers learning tonsils play an important role in the immune system, defending the body and keeping it safe. Which is what Cara did—kept Ali safe. Or at least made her *feel* safe. And now it feels like Cara has been surgically removed from Ali's body, and she doesn't know how to make skin grow over the wound.

Her anxiety, which somewhat hibernated during the

time she was with Cara, crawls out of its dark hole, ravenous. Her neighbor's house gets broken into, so she becomes
obsessed with checking the locks and peering out the closed
blinds, and when she showers, she brings a steak knife in
with her. She considers getting an alarm system but decides
she wouldn't be able to trust the men who'd come to install
it—she's obviously a single woman living alone, and what if
they programmed in an override so they themselves could
break in to rape/murder/steal? So she goes to the hardware
store and buys about fifteen of those window and door sen-
sors and installs them herself, but she always forgets to turn
them off before opening the windows or doors, and the unexpected blaring almost gives her a heart attack every time,
making her anxiety even worse.

Speaking of heart attacks, a woman Ali knows from
college posts on Facebook about how she had a heart
attack but didn't know it—she thought she just had acid
reflux—and almost died. The symptoms for a heart attack
in women are chest pain, shortness of breath, nausea,
lightheadedness, and pain or discomfort in one or both
arms, the back, neck, jaw, or stomach. The symptoms are
so far ranging, people might as well say, *If you are a woman
who is alive, you might be having a heart attack.* She goes
to the walk-in clinic two different times—once when she
has pain in her left arm and nausea, and once when she
has pain on the right side of her jaw, shortness of breath,
and lightheadedness, but neither time turns out to be a
heart attack. The nurse tells her she can take a daily baby
aspirin as a preventative measure, and this makes her feel
slightly better.

One day, while on a walk with Glen, they meet a dalmatian whose owner says it's friendly, but as soon as she and
Glen sniff hello she lunges for his neck and latches on. It

never occurred to Ali that a dog owner would lie about their dog's disposition, or not know their dog well enough to know whether it would attack. Glen's wounds aren't serious, but Ali is so thrown, she stops letting Glen say hello to any dogs on his walks, which is his greatest joy.

A dog and his owner, both without their greatest joy. She decides she has to do something—*anything*—to make life feel worth living again.

▓▓▓▓▓▓▓ is one of Ali's long-time clients, a closeted gay man in his late forties who has established a bachelor-esque persona for himself and usually beards young models in two-year increments. He's reached the age where it's becoming suspicious that he's never been married. A few months ago, Ali told him to consider it, and he's come to Ali's office to talk about getting engaged to the model he's been bearding for the last two years—she's willing to be "married" for two more thanks to the exposure it'll bring to her career, and then they can get a divorce. (Ali thinks it's funny the general public never notices how two-year relationships abound in Hollywood.)

"Well?" ▓▓▓▓▓▓▓ says. "Should we send out a press release?" He has a few more wrinkles these days, and a bit of an endearing beer gut when he's not filming, but Ali can still see the teenage heartthrob beneath it all: the murky blue eyes that tell a story without words, the pouty lips, the angular jaw. She can understand why the Hollywood machine wanted women to go crazy for him.

"I don't think so," says Ali.

He raises his sturdy eyebrows. "What? You don't think Camille is a good fit?"

"No, I don't think you should get engaged, period."

"Why? You're the one who told me I should consider it a few months ago."

"I know, but I've changed my thinking since then. Don't you get tired of all the pretending? Doesn't it take a toll on you and Lucas?"

He furrows his brow. "Of course, but what's the alternative?"

Ali leans forward and blinks at him.

He shakes his head like he has water in his ear. "Are you, my publicist, suggesting I come out? *Now?*"

"Only if you want to," says Ali. "No pressure, of course. But it's what I'm going to suggest to all my gay clients from now on. If you all come out, there'll be so many of you that no single person will take the heat and none of your careers will suffer—the general public can't boycott all the movies or TV shows with gay actors in them, because it'd be most of the movies and TV shows!"

▮▮▮▮▮▮▮ smooths a hand over his closely clipped goatee. "You're actually serious?"

"Dead."

He scrunches his face. "Where is this coming from?"

"Let's just say I recently got an inside look at what it's really like to hide in the way we've forced you to. No one should have to live like that."

His eyes become distant and pained. "I guess I've gotten used to it, kind of like how I imagine people who've lost limbs get used to living without them. You find ways to work around it."

Ali sits back and crosses her legs. "Wouldn't you like to take Lucas to an awards show? Take a vacation with him without Camille there for the photo ops? Go out to dinner and hold his hand?"

"I don't know, Ali." He shifts around in his chair. "Have any of your other clients agreed to do it?"

"You're the first person I've talked to about it, but rest assured I'm just getting started. I'm going to reach out to publicists at other agencies, too, and suggest they give the same advice."

"If a significant number of actors say they'll do it, I'll think about it. Until then, I just don't know."

Ali squeezes the puffer fish stress ball she keeps at her desk. "Somebody has to be the first one to say yes, ███████ ████."

"Well, let me know who that ends up being."

Not five minutes later, Victoria storms into Ali's office. "What's this I hear about you getting everyone in Hollywood to come out?" She has a hand on her hip, but given her polka-dot dress and matching headband, the colored pencil behind her ear, and her mouthful of gum, it's hard to take her seriously.

Ali scowls. "I'm guessing you just saw ████████████."

"Yeah, he stopped by after his meeting with you. What the heck, Ali? You didn't want to run this by me first?" Victoria never swears and only says "heck" when she's extremely angry. Ali is shocked—she's never seen Victoria go into true boss mode, but she's also never done something this transgressive before.

Ali forces herself not to cower and instead sits up straight. "I knew you'd probably tell me no."

Victoria smacks her gum angrily. "You're right, because that's what I'm telling you now."

Ali is usually the one who tells *Victoria* how to do the job.

Namisa did mention Victoria taking on more responsibility while Ali was with Cara on promo tour, but this seems like too much of a jump. "Seriously? We can't discuss it at all?"

"The time for a discussion would have been *before* bringing it up with a client."

"I'm guessing that means you don't want me to mention it to any other clients?"

"Good guess."

"Well then, I quit." Ali didn't plan this; in fact, she didn't even think about what she would do if Victoria wasn't okay with Ali counseling her clients to come out if they wanted to. But in this moment, Ali feels in the deepest coil of her gut that it's the right decision—the *only* decision. She thinks about the chain of events that led her to this moment: If Natalie hadn't died, Ali wouldn't have fallen for Cara, thus Ali never would have known the pain of being part of a closeted relationship, and she probably would have gone on counseling her clients to stay in the closet for the rest of her miserable career. In a strange way, she's glad the harrowing journey brought her here, where she finally has the courage to stand up for herself and others. For the first time in a very long time, she doesn't feel scared. Even though she doesn't have Natalie *or* Cara. It feels like an extremely necessary rebirth. Ali tosses items from her desk into her tote bag: the picture of her and Drew Barrymore (her favorite client) at the People's Choice Awards, her KACL Talk Radio mug, her puffer fish stress ball.

Victoria widens her eyes—now *she's* the one who seems scared. "Ali, what's gotten into you? This all seems really out of character."

"That's kind of the point. I'm tired of being a cog in a homophobic machine, and I can't believe I let it go on this long. Good luck running this place without me."

* * *

Endorphins zip through Ali's body as she skips down the stairs. She's never quit a job before! She's never done *anything* impulsive, really. It felt good to finally stand up for herself and her clients. There must be a few who are willing to take the leap and lead the way. Or she might just have to lie and tell them other actors are already on board. She'll have to get to them ASAP, though—before Victoria calls and says Ali's had a mental breakdown and assures them it's best to stay with the agency. Immediately, she calls ████████ ████, an actress in her early thirties who never had the stomach for bearding and instead opted for total secrecy about her personal life. (Ali thinks it's funny that every celebrity who's known as "intensely private" and rarely grants interviews doesn't come under more scrutiny as to *why* they're so private.)

Thankfully, ████████████ picks up.

"Heyyyyy, ████████████, my girl, how's it going?!"

"Um…fine? What's up?"

Ali pauses to make her voice less manic and sits down in the stairwell so she'll stop breathing heavily. She wishes she had rehearsed what to say, but it's too late now. "Well, I've been doing a lot of thinking lately, and I know my stance has been that actors should do whatever it takes to find the most success, even if it means hiding certain parts of themselves, but lately I've been feeling differently. I've been feeling like it's a terrible, inhumane thing to ask anyone to do. So I'm now advising my clients to come out, if they're interested in doing that. I wanted to see what you think."

"Wow, that's a lot to take in. Um…you said you're advising all your clients to come out? Has anyone else said they'd do it?"

God, actors are such sheep. "Yeah, so far ████████,
████████, and ████████ have signed on, and I still
have a ton of other calls to make."

"Really, ████████ did? Maybe I'll talk to her."

Fuck. "I'm trying to keep things pretty low-profile
right now, because we don't want anything leaking, obviously. So I'm advising my clients not to talk to anyone
about it."

"Hmm. That seems a little—hold on a sec, I'm getting
another call." A windy pause. "It's Victoria. Any idea what
she's calling about?"

"We split up the client list to call about this, and she
probably forgot I was calling you."

"Oh, so this is like an agency-wide thing?"

Might as well dig the hole deeper. "Yeah, kind of. Mostly
my thing, but I'm getting some help."

"Well, let me think about it, okay? I'll get back to you."

The next three clients Ali calls don't pick up, and her
BlackBerry becomes slippery in her sweaty palms. Victoria
must have organized everyone at the agency to start calling before she could get too far. Or it's a coincidence. She
calls three more people, leaves three more voicemails. Then
three more, and another three, until she's gone all the way
through her closeted-client list.

Two days later, with hardly any sleep and a migraine as
intense as Joaquin Phoenix, Ali hasn't received any return
calls from her clients. She worries about how long the
money in her savings account will last, and when her health
care coverage will expire, and whether she's blacklisted herself from the entire publicity industry. She's not qualified

to do any other job—she probably should have thought of that before she quit. There's still the daydream about her own agency for any clients who want to tell the truth, where she could have a strict no assaulters/bigots/assholes policy, and now might be the perfect time to think about it for real. There's a minuscule chance Ali could get into one of the MFA programs she applied to that would take her away from LA, but she can't afford to wait until those decisions come through. If she does miraculously get in somewhere, she tells herself she'll figure it out then—maybe she could defer enrollment, or work remotely while in school. But in all likelihood, she won't get in anywhere yet again, so she needs to plow ahead with her life.

Her first step, hilariously, is googling "how to start your own public relations agency," but as soon as one website mentions administrative tasks like forming a legal entity, setting up accounting, registering for taxes, and obtaining permits and licenses, Ali gets overwhelmed and closes the tab. She remembers Namisa used to work for a boutique agency, so she might know more about what to do. Plus, Namisa is the kind of person who makes an Excel spreadsheet for vacations, so she loves administrative busywork. Speaking of vacation, she's been in Hawaii for the last week and thus knows nothing about what's gone down at the office.

Hey wifey, when are you back from vacay? Ali texts.

Unsurprisingly, Namisa texts right back even though she's supposed to be unplugging. Tomorrow! :(Dreading it so hard.

Wanna meet up for brekkie the day after?

Totes! See you soon, wifey!

* * *

"So how was Maui?" Ali asks Namisa. They're at a bakery/café near downtown that has a breakfast burrito that's Ali's favorite in the city due to its smashed crispy potatoes, braised pork, smoked chili, and sunny eggs.

Namisa rolls her eyes at Ali's question. "I just watched couples on their honeymoon get into fights all day, every day. I even witnessed a breakup not seventy-two hours after their wedding."

"Sounds bleak." Outside, a man in a muscle tank with dreads down to his butt pulls up on a motorcycle with a bumper sticker that says "instant pussy" on the saddlebag, and at first Ali thinks he's another gross straight man until she sees the man on the back of the bike take off his helmet. He has a shaved head and is wearing a black crop top over wide linen pants with furry black sandals. Now Ali realizes the sticker might be ironic, but keeps watching the pair as they enter the café, looking for confirmation about the sticker's tone.

"You know what? At least it reminded me being single is better than settling, which is clearly what all those women did and what I've done before. Speaking of being single, how are you doing with the whole Cara breakup?"

"I don't think I've really laughed since the last time I've seen her. Back to depression city, population of one."

Namisa raises her iced latte and Ali clinks her decaf against it.

"I had to come up with *some* reason to live, which brings me to why I asked you here today," says Ali.

Namisa purses her lips and sits up straight, her curiosity piqued. Serendipitously, the motorcycle pair sit down next to them, and the man with dreads compliments the bald man's crop top, then asks if he can borrow it sometime. Ali relaxes; the sticker is definitely ironic.

Ali lays her hands on the table and leans in. "You know how we joke around about starting our own agency? What if we did it for real?"

Namisa widens her eyes. "Are you being serious?"

Ali recaps her change of heart and what happened at work while Namisa was gone. As she does, an obscenely handsome man in a fitted white T-shirt and vintage Levi's joins the motorcycle pair at their table, and they all kiss hello on the lips. Ali wants to know everything about them and wishes she could eavesdrop on them for the next hour.

"Holy fuck, Ali," says Namisa. "This is all very much a new vibe for you."

"I know." Ali grimaces. "What do you think, though? About starting our own agency?"

The arrival of their breakfast burritos spares Namisa from having to give an immediate answer. They both take huge bites, and Ali waits impatiently as Namisa chews.

"You know I haven't exactly been happy at work lately," Namisa says. "Like yes, I want Black clients, but I don't want *only* Black clients. And I'm tired of being the only Black person in the office. The person people come to only when their client says the N-word or some other racist thing. Victoria keeps saying she hears me, but then never changes anything."

"We could make all the changes we want at our own place." Ali starts listing things on her fingers. "Only take clients we truly want. Let our clients be who they want to be and say what they want to say. And no more manufacturing lies—we could just promote the work, which is supposed to be our main job."

"You make it sound good, but I don't know. It's a huge risk." Namisa looks nervous, but she has that look in her eyes like when there's cake in the office kitchen and she says she isn't going to have any, but Ali knows she will.

"Think about it, okay? If you don't want to settle for a subpar husband like those women in Hawaii, why would you settle for a subpar job?"

Namisa points at Ali and affects her Valley girl voice. "Touché, wifey."

Ali and Dana were supposed to hang out twice over the past month, but Dana canceled both times. The first time, Cayenne had been up all night screaming due to teething pain, and the second time, both kids had lice. When Ali and Dana finally get together, they go to the Norton Simon Museum in Pasadena, one of their favorites since the museum's collection is small but impressive. They're currently admiring Van Gogh's *Mulberry Tree*, with its flaming foliage and rushing sky and hillside—there's so much movement in the brushstrokes, the painting looks like it's about to jump off the canvas.

"Remember when we had to mimic Van Goghs in art class?" Ali says. "You did the one of the wheat field with cypresses and Mrs. Minot told you she liked it *better* than Van Gogh's?"

"Mrs. Minot was so sweet," says Dana. "Which one did you imitate again?"

"The café terrace at night," says Ali. "It looked like a

demented toddler painted it, but Mrs. Minot told me it 'showed promise.'"

Dana laughs. "Oh, high school. What a bizarre time. Thank God we had each other." She links her arm through Ali's as they keep strolling.

"I know," Ali says, seeing an opening. Ever since Ali and her dad had their big talk, Ali has been thinking about having a conversation with Dana about feeling less connected to her these past few years. Speaking honestly with her dad did wonders for their relationship, and she wants to give her friendship with Dana the same chance to rebound and flourish. Maybe Dana is completely unaware of how Ali has been feeling these last few years, and maybe they can find some sort of solution, or at least understanding. Ali's heart thumps harder and faster as she opens her mouth, but she tells herself to push past the fear. Past the fear is the good stuff. "Sometimes I miss our friendship from back then, before life got in the way. You know? I feel like we haven't been able to *really* talk in years."

Dana slows her stroll and unlinks her arm from Ali's. She narrows her eyes. "You mean before Arlo and Cayenne got in the way?"

"No, not *got in the way*," Ali says, her heart beating even harder and faster. "It's completely understandable that your focus is on them now. Sometimes I just miss the super-close connection we had before. Do *you* feel like our friendship has changed?"

Dana stops walking entirely. "You really want to know what I feel?"

"Of course." Ali braces herself—she hadn't anticipated that Dana would be upset with *her*. What could Ali have done to make her mad?

Dana and Ali sit down on a bench facing Diego Rivera's

The Flower Vendor (Girl with Lilies). "I feel like you resent Arlo and Cayenne. Every time we get together, you act like they're such *impediments*. You've never tried to enjoy their company or bond with them. And I feel like I can't talk with you about them, or about being a mother in general, because you think I made the wrong choice. I miss the days before I had kids, too, when I felt like you understood me and weren't constantly judging me."

Ali realizes she was expecting an apology from Dana, not an accusation. But they need this—to see things from the other side. Ali supposes she *has* been feeling resentment toward Arlo and Cayenne, and it shouldn't be surprising that Dana picked up on it. Ali's cheeks burn—she's been blaming Dana for the strain on their friendship, when in fact Ali was just as responsible. How myopic and selfish of her. "You're right; I do tend to see Arlo and Cayenne as impediments to our friendship, but I need to reframe that. And please talk to me about them and about motherhood. I might not understand, but at least I can listen. I'm going to be better about all this; I promise. Can you forgive me?"

Dana reaches over and takes Ali's hand. "Of course. I hope you can forgive me, too. I know I'm less...present with you since the kids. There should be times when I'm able to give you my full attention. Not every time, because that's not realistic, but sometimes. I'll try to be better about that."

Ali squeezes Dana's hand. "Thank you."

"Thank you for bringing all this up. I'm pretty surprised you did, actually. You're usually not the type."

"Yeah, I'm trying to do more things that scare me lately."

Dana tilts her head in curiosity. "Tell me more!" She reaches into her purse and sets her phone to "Do not disturb," then turns the screen so Ali can see. "You have my undivided attention."

*   *   *

A few days later, Namisa texts Ali: Victoria just interviewed
her tenth white woman for your position. Fuck it, let's start our
own agency.

For the next few weeks, they're so busy Ali doesn't have
time to be lonely or depressed. They get no after no from
current clients, but eventually they get a yes from one of
Namisa's biggest stars—who's straight but says she's tired of
being silenced about all the racism in Hollywood. After they
announce she's signed on, they get just enough yeses from
other clients—mostly people who simply want to keep working with Ali and Namisa no matter the reason—to pay their
monthly bills. Ali tells herself to be patient, that eventually
clients who are ready to come out will come.

Ali and Namisa form a legal entity with the name
Frankly PR, to highlight their differentiator of frank discus-
sions, with a nod to Clark Gable's final line in *Gone with the
Wind* and another nod to Clark Gable's likely closeted sexuality. That night, they get together at Namisa's apartment in
the Hollywood Hills to celebrate the milestone.

"I'm proud of us," says Namisa as she pours them each
a glass of champagne. They're on her balcony, looking out
at the twinkling city sprawled below them. The sun is setting, turning the sky nectarine. Silhouetted palm trees rip-
ple in the breeze, and it's just cold enough to need a coat.
Glen is wearing a snowflake sweater and lying on Ali's lap
underneath a blanket. A few balconies over, someone plays
"Check on It" by Beyoncé.

"You know what? I'm *really* fucking proud of us," says
Ali. "It took a lot of guts to quit and start our own company.

And who knows how it will turn out—there are so many unknowns ahead of us—but instead of feeling terrified, I feel excited. I've literally never been excited about work before!"

"Same," says Namisa. "And I know there are parts of the job that'll still feel stupid and annoying, but at least our goal now is to enable our clients to *speak* instead of staying silent. To Frankly PR, baby." She raises her champagne glass. Ali clinks her glass against Namisa's, and they both take a bubbly sip. "So how are you doing, a month and change post-breakup?" Namisa asks. "Like, *for real* how are you doing?"

"Still really sad, but also weirdly empowered? Like, I'm proud of myself for honoring my feelings and letting it end instead of enduring something that was slowly killing me. I feel kind of…strong. And independent."

"Okay, Miss Independent!" Namisa sings to the tune of the Kelly Clarkson song. "Miss Self-Sufficient. Miss Keep Your Distance."

Ali laughs. Somewhere nearby a coyote yips, and from underneath his blanket, Glen growls. Ali pets him until he quiets down.

"You know what? I'm kind of feeling the same way," says Namisa. "I haven't been on a date for months. For the longest time I felt like I had to find a new husband stat, but now I'm like, maybe I'll never get married again, and that's totally fine. I can make *myself* happy." She pours more champagne into both their glasses. "Speaking of, ever since I quit, I've finally had time to start choreographing again. I got in touch with this little contemporary dance company downtown, and they're letting me choreo a piece for their show this spring. It's totally small time, but I'd love it if you came."

Ali slaps Namisa's thigh. "Of course I'll come!" Ali holds up her glass. "To you choreographing an amazing piece!"

Namisa smiles and taps her glass against Ali's. "It just lights up my soul, you know? Speaking of, have you heard back from any MFA programs?"

The champagne in Ali's stomach fizzes. "Not until the end of March. I'm trying not to get my hopes up too much."

"Girl, get your hopes up!" Namisa points at Ali. "Sometimes I think that's the only way shit happens—if we get our hopes up and imagine it and *manifest* it, you know?"

"Uh-oh. Manifest it? You're starting to sound a little Los Angeles woo-woo. Next thing I know, you're gonna tell me you need to recharge your crystals in the moon."

"Oh yeah, I do need to do that!" Namisa pretends like she's about to get up to get her crystals, then sits back down and laughs. "But wait. If you do get into an MFA program somewhere that's not in the LA area or remote, what will we do about Frankly?"

"I could definitely work for Frankly remotely, part-time. So we'd probably have to hire someone else in LA. But let's not think about that yet. We'll cross that bridge if we get there. That's basically what I'm telling myself about everything these days."

Namisa holds up her champagne glass. "To crossing that bridge if we get there."

Ali clangs her glass against Namisa's, then swallows the last of the champagne.

February fifteenth, the long-awaited date of Ali's neurologist appointment, finally arrives. Ali is relieved when Dr. Joyce has the same kind smile Ali remembers from the photo on her website. She also has brown hair in a center-parted ponytail and dry flaky skin on her chin (which makes Ali feel like she's a real, relatable person) and seems to be Ali's age, which surprises her—she assumed most neurologists would be older.

Dr. Joyce asks Ali a lengthy list of questions about her migraines—when they started, what they feel like, if she's noticed any triggers, etc.—then prescribes triptans to treat them, which she says are extremely effective for most people, but you can only take a maximum of nine pills per month. To try to prevent the migraines, Dr. Joyce instructs Ali to take B_2 and magnesium supplements daily.

"In addition to medication and supplements," says Dr. Joyce, "I'm one of the few neurologists who advocate acknowledging the mind/body connection. Studies show when people experience a really traumatic event, like the death of their partner, for example, the parts of the brain that are activated are the exact same ones activated by a physical injury. So emotional pain can create physical pain, which is why it's so important to process traumatic events. Can I ask if you've talked to a therapist about your partner's death?"

Ali would normally lie about insurance problems or months-long wait times, but this doctor makes her want to tell the truth. "Talking about it feels too terrible."

"I completely understand why you would want to avoid it. But when we stuff down emotions instead of processing them, they essentially become stuck in our body. Processing them lets them out, so to speak. I know it sounds like Los Angeles pseudoscience, but it's true. What do you think is worse—talking about your feelings for one hour a week, or having four to five debilitating migraines per week that last for hours?"

"Well, when you put it like that..."

Dr. Joyce hands Ali a lavender business card with the name Tiphaine Laurent written in a calligraphic font. "Dr. Laurent is a pain psychologist, which is what it sounds like—a psychologist who specializes in chronic pain. Part of it will be talking about your feelings, but another part of it will be training your brain to stop having migraines."

Ali narrows her eyes. "I'm confused. How can you train your brain to stop having migraines if it's a physical thing happening in your body?"

"Not a lot of people know that *all* pain originates in the brain—we only feel it once our brain has decided we'll feel it. When you experience a certain kind of pain several times, your brain gets used to it and can essentially get stuck in a cycle of creating pain signals even though there are no physical problems in your body. So you have to train it not to."

Ali glances at a brain anatomy poster on the wall, imagines herself teaching her brain to sit and roll over and shake for treats. What would her brain like best? Squares of dark chocolate? She remembers hearing it's considered brain food. "Can you give me an example of *how* you'd do that?"

"Awareness is one of the biggest factors, so learning this information—that it's possible to train yourself not to have migraines, that this is a problem *you* have the power to solve—is one of the biggest steps. An example of an early technique you'll use with Dr. Laurent is coming up with a 'pain pep talk' to give yourself whenever you feel a migraine starting. It's essentially you saying to your brain, 'Hey, we're not going to do this right now!' You'll be amazed how well your brain will listen to you."

Ali guffaws. "So I just have to *tell* myself not to have a migraine? I can't really believe that."

"I know it sounds far-fetched right now. I'll leave you with this: My patients who start seeing Dr. Laurent usually resolve their migraines within a few months, using almost no medication whatsoever. My patients who don't see Dr. Laurent usually go through a yearslong journey of trying medication after medication with nothing ever really working. It's up to you which journey you want to take."

Ali leaves the appointment with Dr. Laurent's business card at the bottom of her bag, debating whether she'll call. She can't decide if Dr. Joyce was a total quack or if she was onto something profound—the connection between emotional and physical pain *sounds* like it makes sense, and it's extremely tempting to believe Ali could stop having migraines simply by telling her brain to stop, but Ali has spent most of her life feeling completely powerless over her worst-case-scenario brain and the havoc it wreaks on her body. If she could control it, wouldn't she have figured out how by now? Or has she simply never thought it was possible and so never tried?

33

Before Ali knows it, it's the night of the Oscars. After she texts her clients a million times to make sure they'll be on time, secures interviews with the right outlets on the red carpet, and orchestrates a hopefully viral group picture in the theater during a commercial break, the moment she's been equally dreading and looking forward to happens: She sees Cara. When their eyes meet, Cara instantly blows her a kiss and Ali's chest kindles. They're close enough that it would be awkward not to say hello, so they smile and walk toward each other.

Cara is wearing a phenomenal outfit that's a cross between a suit and a gown: The top is a black satin belted suit jacket, under which Cara is of course wearing no shirt, then just below the belt, the jacket opens up into the royal train of a gown, the inside of which swirls with sparkly rainbow colors. The open train shows off Cara's form-fitting, cropped black trousers and black heels. It's the perfect outfit for her, saying everything Cara can't. Ali is wearing the standard forgettable black gown most publicists wear.

Once they've closed the distance between them, they take a second to take each other in: Cara's makeup is understated and flawless, but the whites of her eyes are bloodshot, and underneath them, dark circles linger beneath concealer. Ali wonders how she looks to Cara—if it's written on her face how little joy she's experienced since saying goodbye.

"Motherfucking shitballs, I've missed you." Cara hauls Ali into a tight hug. They hold it a few seconds longer than they probably should, considering where they are.

Ali begs her eyes to stop watering as they pull back. "You too."

"I hate that I have to ask you what's new, like you're an acquaintance."

Ali shuffles around the four clutches she's holding for different clients. "Well, I quit my job."

Cara gives Ali an Elaine Benes shove. "For real? What are you doing here then, looking all publicist-y?"

"Namisa and I started our own PR place. For clients with nothing to hide, so let me know if that's ever you." Ali winks, a signal to Cara there's no hard feelings.

"Wow, Ali. I'm really proud of you." She squeezes Ali's arm and gives her a painfully genuine look. "That takes clit."

"What?"

"Instead of saying 'balls' to mean brave, I'm trying to make 'clit' catch on."

A laugh explodes out of Ali's mouth—the kind of laugh she hasn't had since last seeing Cara. "I like it. I'll start using it, too. What about you?" Ali affects a coworker-at-the-water-cooler tone. "What's new?"

"Actually, almost nothing. It's kind of weird when all the promotion for a movie dies down and you're back to being just…a normal person left with your own thoughts. Kind of makes me feel like I should focus a little more on the normal person part of my life and less on the movie star part."

"Well, you're probably about to win an Oscar, so—"

Cara slaps Ali's arm. "Don't say that! You'll jinx it!"

The lights flash, signaling the commercial break is almost over.

Cara squeezes Ali's hand and gives her a despondent look. "This wasn't enough."

Ali squeezes back. "I know."

As usual, the award for actress in a leading role is presented second to last, and by then everyone is tipsy and crispy around the edges. As Charlize Theron, looking amazing as ever, reads out the nominees, Ali tries to decide whether she hopes Cara will win. If she does, Cara will have fulfilled a lifelong dream, but it will further reinforce the benefits of staying in the closet. If she doesn't win, she'll be devastated, but she might consider coming out, and then they could get back together. Since seeing her, Ali's whole body has been throbbing like a fresh wound.

Seeming to read Ali's mind, Namisa asks, "Are we rooting for her or not?"

Ali tsk-tsks Namisa like she wasn't just having the same thought. "Rooting for her, of course."

"And the award goes to…" Charlize rips open the envelope. "Cara Bisset, *Real Love*!"

Despite having hoped she'd feel happy for Cara, Ali feels her heart sink into her stomach. Across the room, Cara jumps out of her seat. Davi clamps his hands on either side of her face and kisses her—simply a forceful press of the lips, no tongue. Then Cara strides to the stage, shaking her head back and forth like she can't believe it.

She hugs Charlize, takes her statue, and steps up to the microphone.

"Wow, I fully feel like I'm going to pass out." She fans herself with a hand. "I've been practicing my Oscars speech in the shower my whole life, basically, but suddenly I'm speechless." Everyone laughs. Cara's smiling but—and it could just be the shock of it—her expression is flat, her eyes hollow. She seems, bizarrely, disappointed. She blinks a few times, then takes a piece of paper out of her trousers pocket and goes down the list of all the people she has to thank. At the end, she thanks her mom, then pauses, opening and closing her mouth like a fish after being caught, and for the briefest moment, Ali thinks Cara might be about to say something about her, something that would mean all hope isn't lost, but then Cara simply thanks the Academy and her fans and runs off the stage.

Ali sends her a congratulations text with a million exclamation marks to make up for how she really feels, but Cara never responds.

Ali goes to bed feeling utterly decimated. Now she can admit she was holding out hope that Cara would change her mind after a few weeks and agree to come out. But you don't win an Oscar and simply turn your back on everything that can do for your career. Ali has to accept that Natalie is gone, and Cara is gone, and that this is the nature of life: for people and places and objects and even ideas to one day disappear.

"When I die," says Roz on Ali's computer screen later that night, "I want it to be on my one hundredth birthday, in my beach house on Maui, and I want my husband to be so upset that he has to drop out of college."

Ali wakes up at 7:00 a.m. to her doorbell ringing, which

sends Glen tearing down the hallway and barking at the top of his lungs. She hates that when you have a dog, you never have the luxury of ignoring the doorbell—your dog will just keep barking and barking. She shuffles to the door, a migraine knifing the back of her head. *Please stop it*, she says to her brain dubiously. She inserts a finger into the blinds and pulls the slats down, hoping it's a delivery person and not a Jehovah's Witness or a canvasser, but it's Cara, still in her suit gown from last night, looking noticeably disheveled. Ali's heart thumps hopefully as she opens the door.

"What are you doing here?" Ali asks. "Is everything okay?"

"Yeah, everything's fine," says Cara. "Can I come in?"

Glen stops barking when he sees who it is and switches to jumping on Cara, launching himself into the air.

"Hey, buddy, I missed you." Cara squats down and lets Glen lick all over her face, which is still covered in faded makeup.

"Have you been up all night celebrating your win?" asks Ali. "Congratulations, by the way. Your lifelong dream came true!"

Cara grimaces and crawls to the couch. "It didn't really feel like that."

"Too surreal to sink in?"

She splays out on the chaise and hugs Glen to her. "No, not surreal. More like…it felt shitty."

Ali sits down on the couch and raises her eyebrows. "Winning an Oscar felt *shitty*?"

"I thought if I won, it would justify all the shady choices I've been making. To not come out, to lose you. But standing up there holding that gold statue didn't feel as good as being with you. It didn't feel worth all the hiding and lying. It just felt bad."

Is this going where Ali hopes it's going? She feels terrible that the moment Cara had dreamed of her whole life didn't feel amazing, but it might mean she's come around. "That's really depressing, Cara."

"No, it was actually a good thing. Because now I know what I need to do."

Ali's heart thumps harder. "What?"

Cara smirks. "I need to schedule a gynecologist appointment."

Ali smacks the couch. "Stop!"

"I need to...clip my toenails."

Ali buries her face in the couch and screeches, which makes Glen jump over to her, trying to figure out what's wrong. "Oh my God, I'm going to kill you!"

"You know what I'm going to say, Ali."

"For the love of God, just say it then!" Ali sits up and gives Cara a pleading look.

"I need to come out," Cara says. "And I want you to help me do it. And if you'll have me, angel, I want to be with you." Cara crawls to her and stops when she's nose to nose with Ali.

"Yes—to all of that." Ali wraps a hand around the back of Cara's neck and pulls her into a kiss that feels like pressing play on a song you had to pause and step away from but were dying to hear the rest of. The beat and the bassline and the chords and the melody resume, pulling Ali back in, enveloping her completely. When Cara's tongue swishes against hers, Ali winces into Cara's mouth with gratitude that she gets to feel this again. All the days they weren't together dissolve like sugar in coffee, turning it sweet.

Cara pulls back and Ali assumes she's about to comment on her morning breath, but then Cara presses her thumbs into Ali's cheeks and stares into her eyes and says, "I love you. I'd rather have you than all the success and fame in the world. That's what I realized last night while I was giving my acceptance speech."

Hearing "I love you" now feels like the actual first time—Ali's heart feels like it's rocketed out of her body and busted through the ceiling and is soaring in the blue sky like a bird, buoyant with joy. It's a phrase Ali never thought she'd hear again, at least not romantically. And while she still wishes she never had to lose Natalie, it feels like a magical, cosmic gift to know she can love again, and be loved. "I love you, too," says Ali, and they start kissing again, and now it feels like the song is turning into a whole album. Ali isn't naive enough to use words like *forever* anymore—it might last for a few months or years or decades, but right now, she doesn't want to worry about that. She just wants to be here, in this moment, experiencing every part of it. Cara's wet lips sliding against hers, Cara's thumb softly caressing her cheek, the fingers of Cara's other hand tickling Ali's back.

Cara pulls away again. "I'd really like to sex you up properly, but I feel like I have to get out of these tight-ass clothes, brush my teeth, and wash off all this makeup and hair spray."

"Let's start with the tight-ass clothes." Ali begins unbuttoning Cara's silky black suit jacket, giving Cara's bare skin a kiss after every button she frees. There are only a few before the belt, which Ali unclasps unhurriedly. The jacket hangs partially open, revealing the tempting swell of Cara's breasts up until just before her nipples. Ali caresses only what she can see for a few seconds, then slips her hands under the fabric, finding the hardness of Cara's nipples before slipping the jacket off her shoulders. Then Ali stands Cara up to unbutton and unzip her skintight trousers and is surprised to be met with Cara's pubic hair instead of underwear.

"They literally wouldn't fit with underwear on," Cara says, and Ali laughs as she struggles to yank them down.

After a few unsuccessful attempts, she lowers herself to her knees for a better angle, and the pants skid down Cara's legs. Ali helps her step out of her heels, then pulls the pants all the way off, past Cara's hideous, callous-covered feet, which she missed terribly. She gazes up at Cara's body, remembering all her favorite features like the gangliness of her legs, the straightness of her hips, the fullness of her pubic hair, and the speech bubble–shaped birthmark coming out of her belly button.

Ali stands up and takes Cara's hand, leading her to the bathroom, where she opens a drawer and hands Cara the purple toothbrush she used to use when she slept over.

"Aw, you kept it." Cara cradles the toothbrush like an infant.

"I was hoping you'd be back."

Cara pulls her into a hug, squeezing tight before abruptly pantsing Ali, underwear and all. "If I have to brush my teeth naked, so do you." Obedient, Ali raises her arms and lets Cara tug her T-shirt over her head.

As they brush their teeth, their naked breasts jiggle slightly from the back-and-forth motions of their arms. Ali lets blue foam drip down her chin, and when Cara tries to say something Ali can't understand, Cara does charades, thrusting her hips, rolling her eyes back into her head, then bringing an imaginary fork to her mouth and chewing.

"You want to eat me out?" Ali guesses, and Cara collapses laughing.

Once they spit, Cara says, "Yes, I always want to eat you out, but I was asking if you want to get breakfast after we give each other a bunch of O's."

"Ooh, yeah, I want pancakes." Ali imagines going out to a meal with Cara and holding her hand and kissing her with no fear. It all feels so giddily quotidian.

They get into the shower then, their skin goose-bumping before the blissfully hot water makes contact. Ali is more grateful than she's ever been for the immense rain shower head that came with her fancy apartment. They wash each other's hair with Ali's favorite coconut shampoo, discovering Ali prefers to scrub vigorously with her fingertips whereas Cara mostly just smooths the shampoo over her head with her palms. Then Ali squeezes a dollop of tea tree body-wash onto her loofah and they exfoliate each other's backs, their skin tingling wonderfully. Ali almost kicks like a dog when Cara hits the spot in the center Ali can't reach herself. They're unselfconscious when it comes time to wash between their legs, spreading their cheeks and leaning forward, then spreading their labia and leaning backward.

As Ali rinses her face one last time, Cara comes up behind her, pressing her breasts into Ali's back and reaching around Ali's front to caress her while biting the side of her neck. Ali lets her head fall back, and Cara slithers one hand down Ali's wet body to find the other wetness between her legs.

Ali inhales sharply. "Christ on the cross, I missed you."

They both laugh, and then they get down to business. Cara's hand moves down, dipping inside the tiniest bit, then moves up, making a few tight circles before sliding back down. Up and down and up and down until Ali's thighs burn. Ali pushes her butt against Cara, backing them up until they hit the tiled bench at the end of the shower. She sits on Cara's lap, both of them facing front, and spreads her legs wide. She lets her head fall back as Cara continues to conduct an orchestra with her hand. Ali presses her heels into the tub's edges for leverage and her hips thrust upward, hitting their final resounding notes.

After Ali's breathing and heart rate have returned to

relatively normal, she folds a washcloth lengthwise and sets it on the tub's bottom, in front of the bench, then kneels on it and pushes Cara's thighs open. Ali looks up at her, Cara's skin pink and moist. Strands of wet hair fall in front of her face, and her eyes look like a misty morning ocean, currents of desire moving underneath the surfaces of her irises. Ali can't believe this movie star, this *Oscar winner*, thinks being with Ali is more important than anything else.

"I love you," Ali says.

"I love *you*," Cara says, and pleasure reverberates through Ali's body. She laps droplets of water from Cara's thighs, getting closer and closer before inching back out.

Cara releases a frustrated growl.

Ali only teases her a bit longer before flicking her tongue where Cara has been waiting. Ali licks and kisses and *mmm*s her way through Cara, all the way to her tissues and bones and cells. Ali wishes it were possible to get that close, but in lieu of that, she looks up and finds Cara watching her— holding eye contact during cunnilingus is its own kind of cellular intimacy. Ali loves how Cara's face reacts to everything she does: Languid up-and-down strokes make her moan softly, hungry kisses make her release a low growl, quick tongue flicks make her yelp, circles make her bite her bottom lip, and firm pressure makes her throw her head back, finally breaking eye contact, until she shudders and yells, "Good God almighty!"

They blast themselves with a stream of cold water to rinse off all the sweat and stickiness, then run to the bed, laughing. Ali thinks what nonlesbians don't understand about lesbian sex is that it can go on for hours and days and years and eons, with uncountable bountiful orgasms like ripe berries hanging from a bush—it just depends how many you want to pick, or more likely how many you have time to pick before life beckons. In this case, it's before Ali and Cara's stomachs start to protest.

They go to Millie's, a bustling sidewalk diner on Sunset Boulevard in Silver Lake, and as they approach, Cara takes Ali's hand. At first, on instinct, Ali pulls her hand away, but then she looks at Cara, who gives her a giddy smile and once again threads her fingers through Ali's. A tingly thrill travels up Ali's spine. This is the quotidian, monumental moment she's been waiting for ever since she and Cara started dating. She thought it was never going to happen. Grateful, euphoric tears fill her eyes. As they approach the host, a few people do a double take, their forks full of eggs or pancakes paused midair. Two women wearing beanies over sharply angled bobs and leather jackets over flannels even screech. Others, like a Hispanic family and an elderly couple who either don't know who Cara is or don't care, continue eating, unaware of the historic moment unfolding before them.

The host seats them two tables away from the lesbians in leather jackets, who keep looking over and giggling. The sun is shining in a blue sky dotted with puffy *Super Mario* clouds, which reminds Ali of their very first lunch, when Cara was flirting with the waitress with the cloud tattoo on her wrist, and Ali was jealous but refusing to recognize it, and Cara was saying she didn't want to lie about who she was. Everything feels like it's come full circle to the way it was always supposed to be.

When their server, a Hispanic guy in his twenties with a mohawk and a no-nonsense attitude, asks them what they'd like, Cara says, "I'll have the breakfast burrito, and my *girl-friend* will have the huevos rancheros, and we'll split some blueberry pancakes." He writes down their order with no reaction whatsoever, then hustles off to take another order. But Cara and Ali are grinning at each other and celebratorily shimmying in their seats like they're in on the world's greatest joke.

"This is absolutely wild," says Ali. "I cannot believe we're out to breakfast as an actual couple."

"About damn time, huh?" Cara winks, poking fun at herself, before reaching across the table to take Ali's hand once again.

All the lesbians in leather jackets swivel their heads at the same moment. One takes out her phone and pretends to snap a picture of her omelet, but Ali knows it's of them. She wonders if it will make its way to the internet and whether anyone will speculate about it. Probably just Perez and one or two other gossip blogs—the legit magazines wouldn't publish the photo without publicist approval. "The publicist in me has to ask…do you want to make an official announcement?"

"Duh squared!"

Ali laughs, relieved. "What are you thinking? A social media post, a speech at an awards show, a TV interview, a print interview…?"

Their food arrives in record time, and Cara considers the question while she takes a gargantuan bite of her breakfast burrito. She swallows, then says, "I really liked that bitchy journalist, Jason, who wrote the profile of me for *Vanity Fair*. He deserved better than what we gave him."

"I think he was pretty furious about that. We'll see if he even picks up when I call." Ali licks guacamole from her fork. "And you're *sure* you're ready to do this? You're not worried about what it might cost you, careerwise?"

Cara dumps an inordinate amount of syrup over the pancakes. "I feel like we're at this tipping point right now, and as an Oscar winner, I have way more cachet than I would

have had before. Trust me, honey, I'm willing to lose everything, but I'm not sure I will." Cara takes a face-stuffing bite
of pancakes.

"I hope you're right. I'm really proud of you, you know."
Cara has a smear of syrup on the corner of her mouth. Ali
points to the spot. "You have some syrup."

"Oh, do I?" Cara takes another bite, purposefully smear-
ing more syrup around her mouth. "Where is it? Can you
show me?"

Ali laughs and Cara leans across the table, her eyes glinting mischievously. She gives Ali a sticky, smacking kiss, and
Ali eats it up, feeling like in this moment, she couldn't ask
for anything more.

34

CARA BISSET IS OFFICIALLAAAAAY GAAAAAAAY!

Let me be emo for a sec and just tell you I cried LITERAL TEARS when I read **Cara Bisset**'s coming-out interview in *Vanity Fair*. It was literally one of the best days of my life. I've been telling you hos she's a lez since day 1 and almost no one believed me! Remember my **post** with the picture of Cara and her high school friends standing in front of a partially obscured sign that says "gay" and pointing at Cara? What about the interview where she slips and literally mentions her "ex-**girlfriend**?" Remember how you all just told me she was talking about a female friend? Yeah, I KNEW her publicist Ali Larson wasn't just her "gal pal." I could go on...NEwayz, this is all just really validating. I'm not cray-cray! I WAS RIGHT! And it's a huge deal for someone who just won an Oscar to come out! It's gonna help so many gay people feel less alone. And hopefully it's gonna inspire other celebs to do the same! OK it's getting way too earnest up in here...Back to our regularly scheduled bitchy programming!

Ali feels more empowered than she ever has before—so much so, she thinks maybe she *does* have the power to control her migraines. Over the past few months, she's done enough reading online about pain science and the mind/body connection to prove Dr. Joyce is not a quack. When Ali feels a migraine coming on, she gives herself a little speech about not going down that road. Sometimes it doesn't work, but sometimes it bizarrely does, which could be a coincidence, but she's finally ready to believe she might have what it takes to get better.

She even calls the pain psychologist Dr. Laurent, who teaches her a technique called somatic tracking, which is all about focusing on your symptoms without reacting to them or trying to change them. You look at them like a curious, detached observer and assess them, noticing how they change. It goes against all of Ali's instincts—when she has a migraine, she usually tries her hardest to avoid and push away the symptoms, which Dr. Laurent tells her actually adds to the fear and danger signals in the brain. With practice, Ali is flabbergasted to find that somatic tracking actually works. Dr. Laurent tells her it's because the technique teaches your brain not to approach your symptoms with fear, which allows the brain to understand that the symptoms are safe, which deactivates the pain. "Fear is like gasoline for pain. You stop supplying the fear, and the pain has nothing to run on," said Dr. Laurent at Ali's latest appointment.

This is what everything in Ali's life seems to be telling

her right now: Nothing good comes from fear. Talking honestly with her dad and Dana, quitting her job, starting a new company, applying to MFA programs again, helping Cara come out, being with Cara period—all these good things came from pushing through fear. She hopes she can keep doing it.

Despite so much going well in Ali's life, MFA rejections have been rolling into her inbox almost daily. When she gets the final one, old Ali would have gone into a depression as deep as the bottom of the ocean and doubted herself so much she might have stopped writing forever, but new Ali lets herself mope for a day or two, then tells herself she'll apply again next year, and the year after that if she still wants to. In the meantime, she'll keep writing her stories, which she no longer thinks of as stupid.

Ali starts a story that's unlike any she's ever written before, based on the dream she had a while back about flying through the sky with her mother. Ali tries to let go of her fear and her desire to control the story, and instead lets the story control itself—she just sits back and sees where it takes her. Ali sends the story to ten lit mags, and after just one month, she gets an acceptance—from one of the smaller, less well-known ones, but it's still her first acceptance. She wonders if it's a coincidence that her first accepted story is the one she approached without fear. Probably not.

One day, Ali calls her dad while chopping herbs for Persian noodle soup—she and Cara ate the last frozen Pyrex of it weeks ago, so this time when the craving hits, Ali has to make it instead of simply unfreezing it. (These days, her freezer looks much less like a doomsday prepper's.)

Gene picks up after three rings. "Ali! I'm still getting used to *you* calling *me*!"

Ali laughs. She's still getting used to the feeling of

genuinely *wanting* to talk to her dad. "I know, it's pretty wild."

"You know what else is pretty wild? I just left Wendy's house, and we bought plane tickets to Rome!"

Ali cuts into a bundle of parsley, releasing its bitter, grasslike scent. "Oh my God, Dad! Your first trip to Europe! How on earth did she convince you?"

"She's been convincing me to try a lot of new things. Starbucks coffee, sushi, one of those phones with the keyboard you can text from...I'm realizing maybe I've been a little too set in my ways."

"What did you think of the sushi?"

"I had something called a dynamite roll. There was avocado and mango and jalapeno in it! With fish! I never would have thought to put all those things together. It was a little strange, but not bad."

"Would you try it again? Maybe I'll take you somewhere the next time you come to LA. The sushi here is probably astronomically better than in North Dakota."

"You said you had the best sushi of your life in Tokyo. Maybe we'll have to go there!"

All the parsley is chopped, and Ali moves on to the cilantro, with its earthy, citrusy smell. "Whoa, I'm sorry. Who is this and what have you done with my father?"

"Call me Gene 2.0," he says. "How's Ali 2.0 doing?"

"Pretty good," Ali says. "Namisa and I found an office space in Hollywood we really like for Frankly. We're going to put in an offer this week."

"How exciting! I'll keep my fingers crossed for you. And how's Cara?"

Ali smiles. "She's good. It's been nice spending more time with her, since promo for *Real Love* is finally over and *Star Wars* hasn't started shooting yet."

"I still can't believe my daughter is dating the star of the next *Star Wars* movie! It's nice being able to brag about that now. It was hard having to keep it a secret."

Ali laughs as she moves on to chopping dill, the most pungent of the herbs with its sweet, licorice aroma. "Tell me about it!"

"I'm really proud of you, Ali. For soldiering on after Natalie's death and finding ways to still be happy, for starting your own company and helping all these celebrities tell the truth about their experiences. I wish your younger self could see how brave you've become."

Ali stops chopping, her knife held midair. "Brave? That's a word I never thought I'd hear to describe myself."

"Well, hear it again! You're brave, Ali!"

"Remember the ACT UP movie I auditioned for a few months ago but didn't get?" asks Cara, joining Ali in the checkout line at the grocery store. She had just gotten a call and stepped outside to take it. "That was Ilene Chaiken on the phone. She said they had decided to cast mostly openly gay actors for the movie, which was why they hadn't offered me the role. But now that I'm out, they want me!"

"Oh my God, Cara, that's amazing." Ali kisses Cara before placing a carton of organic strawberries and a package of ground turkey on the conveyor belt.

"The one catch is it's filming at the same time as the *Star Wars* movie." Cara grabs two Snickers bars and adds them to the belt. "So I think I have to give up *Star Wars*. The ACT UP movie means way more to me."

"Are you sure? You should give yourself time to really think it over."

"I'm positive. I feel it in my gut. Speaking of—" Cara pauses to burp, then grimaces. "I still feel kind of nauseous."

Ali shakes her head. "I told you not to get ceviche from that food truck."

"Hey look, it's us!" Cara points to the cover of a gossip magazine, where there's a photo of Ali and Cara kissing at a restaurant next to the headline "Out and Proud."

Ali smiles, relieved the truth is partially out there. On the cover next to theirs, though, is one of Ali's old clients who didn't follow her to Frankly. He poses with his beard wife, and the headline announces her pregnancy. *Oh well—you can't out 'em all*, Ali thinks.

As they're loading groceries into the trunk of Cara's VW Golf, Cara bends over and puts her hands on her knees. "I think I'm gonna—" Instead of saying the word, she actually pukes, light-pink chunks of raw fish splatting onto the concrete.

On instinct, Ali turns away, claps her palms to her ears, and hums, then acknowledges that probably isn't the most empathetic way to behave while her girlfriend is puking. She forces herself to remove one of her hands from her ear and uses it to half-heartedly rub Cara's back, praying she won't also puke as her own throat constricts and her stomach churns acid.

"You okay?" she asks when it seems like Cara is done, at least for now.

"I don't think I can drive." Cara wipes her mouth with the sleeve of her hoodie.

"All right, I'll call a cab and we can come get the car later," says Ali.

"I'd really prefer not to vom in a rando's car," says Cara. "I bet they would also prefer I didn't."

"Well, that's kind of the only option," Ali says. But when she calls the usual cab place, it rings and rings.

"We're less than two miles from your apartment, angel," says Cara. "You know the route. No highways, no unprotected left turns. Couldn't you do it?"

Ali hasn't driven in four years, but an unexpected feeling whips through her body. It might be…bravery? Just like her dad said. She closes her eyes and pictures the route. A left out of the parking lot onto Griffith Park Boulevard, which will probably be the worst part, but it's not terribly busy, so she should be able to find an opening. Then straight through the light and straight again through a few stop signs. A left at the four-way stop onto the steep hill of Effie. After the hill, the two-way street is narrow enough that cars generally have to pull over a bit to let each other pass, and that makes Ali a smidge nervous, but she'll just be the one to pull over. Then down the super-steep hill that's semiblind at the summit—that'll be the second-worst part, but she'll just go slow. Then a right onto Berkeley and straight through a few more stop signs, and she's home. Hopefully there'll be enough open spots that she won't have to parallel park, because that's a whole other battle. But she'll cross that bridge if she gets there.

Ali looks at Cara, who's giving her a hopeful but nervous look. "Okay," Ali says, and holds her hand out for the keys, surprised it isn't shaking.

Cara squints at her in disbelief. "Seriously? Are you sure?"

Ali nods once, decisively. "Give me the keys before I change my mind."

Cara pulls them out of her pocket and slowly places them in Ali's palm. "Well, that's a weird feeling."

Ali laughs. "It'll be okay," she says. "I can do it." She instructs her brain to believe it, like she's been instructing her brain not to have migraines, which is working more and more lately. She unlocks the car and slides into the driver's seat's warm leather, scooting it forward since she's shorter than Cara. Then she adjusts the mirrors, clicks her seat belt closed, turns the key in the ignition, and shifts the car into drive. She takes a deep breath and presses her foot to the gas.

Acknowledgments

Thank you to my agent, Alexa Stark, for successfully selling this gay smut and for keeping me levelheaded all these years. It felt like destiny to finally work with this novel's first editor, Seema Mahanian, who opened up the story in all the right ways. The thoroughness and specificity of your feedback was such an immense gift. I was lucky enough to have two additional editors this time around, so thank you also to Rachael Kelly for taking over this project and helping me polish it until it gleamed; and to Jacqueline Young for never letting small details fall through the cracks! Thanks to all of you for never telling me to tone down the extremely steamy sex scenes. Thank you to everyone at Grand Central, including Bob Castillo, Liz Connor, Lauren Sum, Leena Oropez, Kamrun Nesa, S.B. Kleinman, and Lynn von Hassel, for making this book a reality.

Thank you to my amazing blurbers Steven Rowley, Amy Spalding, Diane Marie Brown, Camille Perry, Karelia Stetz-Waters, Cecilia Rabess, Laura Kay, Susie Dumond, and Ashley M. Coleman.

Thank you to Brandon Cardet-Hernandez for being the first person to tell me about a certain closeted celebrity. That knowledge truly changed my life and rewired my brain and inspired this book. Thank you to everyone who has listened to me endlessly blab on or gossiped with me about closeted celebrities in the ensuing years.

Thank you to Casey McQuiston for writing *Red, White & Royal Blue,* the book that turned me on to queer rom-coms and thus gave me the idea that maybe I could write one too.

Thank you to my Slackers author group (the most ironic name for us): Laura Warrell, Jasmin Iolani Hakes, Tracey Rose Peyton, Diane Marie Brown, Ashley M. Coleman, and our honorary member Greg Mania. Finding community with you all finally made Los Angeles feel like home. Thank you to Liv Stratman for starting and managing the larger author Slack that connected us and so many others.

Thank you to other LA author friends Gabrielle Korn, Amy Spalding, Ilana Masad, Hannah Sawyerr, Anna Dorn, Carolyn Huynh, Rufi Thorpe, and others I'm sure I'm forgetting. I'm so grateful to have found you!

Thank you to Deborah Brosseau for sharing your publicist knowledge.

Thank you to my parents for never making me feel like I had to hide who I am—but please skip *Cover Story*'s sex scenes, okay? That goes for all my relatives.

Lastly, thank you to all the celebrities who have bravely come out, and for those who haven't—we still see you and celebrate you.

About the Author

Celia Laskey is the author of *So Happy for You* and *Under the Rainbow*, a finalist for the 2020 Center for Fiction First Novel Prize. Her work has appeared in *Catapult*, *Guernica*, *The Minnesota Review*, and elsewhere. She has an MFA from the University of New Mexico and currently lives in Los Angeles with her dog, Whiskey.

Questions for Discussion

(This Section Contains Spoilers)

1. From the very first page, Ali's dog, Glen, is a significant character. Discuss the role he plays in the novel. (You might think about when he was attacked, when Ali takes him to the emergency vet, or when he waits by the door for Natalie to return the night of her accident.) As a reader, did you enjoy his presence or not? Can you think of other books/movies/TV shows where dogs play a significant role? (Hint: *Frasier* is one!)

2. Ali works as a publicist, but her dream is to write and publish short stories. Do you think most people have a dream that's different from their day job? What do you think stops them from pursuing it? Do you have a dream? Have you pursued it or not, and why?

3. Several pop culture references from the early aughts are peppered throughout the text. Did any of your favorite films or actors make it into the story? If so, which one(s)?

4. Similarly, snippets from fictionalized versions of early 2000s gossip blogs appear throughout the text. They use extremely vulgar and crude language to speculate on Cara's sexuality, even going so far as to draw semen on her face. Did these snippets make you reflect on the sexism of celebrity coverage in the early 2000s? How far do you think we've come since then?

5. Discuss the inner turmoil Ali faces throughout the novel, trying to reconcile her own identity with the painful necessity of keeping her clients closeted. Contrast this with the situation in which Cara finds herself: an actor about to get her big break. Do you agree with her following Ali's advice and pretending to be straight? Do you think it's true that actors would have been less successful if they came out in the early 2000s? What about today?

6. In chapter 3, Ali describes her experience of anxiety as a "rubberized running track you visit at predictable times, looping around and around." Ali's experience of grief, however, is a "dark, endlessly meandering tunnel you can fall into any time you're not looking." How else is anxiety and grief given shape throughout the novel, and how do the author's depictions resonate with your own understanding of these emotions?

7. The author breaks down a lot of what happens behind the scenes between stars and their teams (publicists, agents, managers, etc.) and with the media. Did anything surprise you? If so, what?

8. Ali has strong feelings about motherhood, which often arise after spending time with Dana. Ali frequently feels like she and Dana aren't as close as they used to be because Dana's kids hoard her attention. Do you think it's possible for someone with kids and someone who doesn't have kids to maintain a deep friendship? Why or why not? How have your own relationships with friends and family been affected by decisions about children?

9. In chapter 3, Ali learns she has chronic migraines, which started after her partner Natalie died. What do you think these migraines are meant to represent? Do you think they're connected to Ali's grief and anxiety? In general, do you think our minds and bodies are connected or separate? Have your mind or emotions ever impacted your physical body?

10. The first time Ali learned an A-list celebrity was gay and hiding it, she was twenty-three. It triggered a grief response, because she felt if she had known how many people were actually gay in the world, she would have realized her own sexuality sooner. Through the lens of this scene, and many others throughout the book, why do you feel it's important for people of all identities to see themselves represented in popular media?

11. Growing up, Ali had a difficult relationship with her mother as well as with her father. How does Ali's childhood impact her sense of self? How do you feel about the steps Ali takes at the end of the novel to heal her relationship with her father?

12. Ali watches *Frasier* to calm her mind. In your own life, what do you lean on for comfort or distraction? Is it related to pop culture? An object? A memory? Explain.

13. The author observes it can be difficult to know whether something seemingly innocuous can cause genuine hurt to another person. For Cara and Deb, Christmas is a sore spot: "All those expectations like expensive presents, the picture-perfect family...We never had that." Ali also touches on "loaded questions": *Are you close with your parents? What are you doing for Mother's Day? Do you have a significant other?* How did you feel reading these lines? Did it make you rethink how you'll approach certain topics with strangers (or even friends) in your own life?

14. At the end of the Christmas Day celebration with Cara's friends and family, Ali feels grief and joy "sitting on either side of her." Have you had moments like this in your own life when you experienced both grief and joy at the same time?

15. As Ali and Cara get closer, they both share their traumas: Cara tells Ali about being raped, and Ali tells Cara about when Natalie died. Do you think this is a necessary step for falling in love? Have you ever shared your trauma with a lover? How did it make you feel? How did they respond?

16. Ali and Natalie had been together for over a decade when Natalie died, and they had a very happy relationship. Ali is "convinced no one will ever be more right for her—she might find someone who ticks a few boxes, but Natalie ticked them all. No one could find that more than once in a lifetime." But then Ali falls in love with Cara. Do you believe it's possible to have more than one soulmate?

17. Ali breaks up with Cara when she can no longer take the secrecy. If you were in a relationship that had to be hidden for one reason or another, how do you think it would

affect you? Would you be able to live with it, or would it tear you up? How would you try to resolve the situation?

18. In chapter 31, Ali reflects on her journey throughout the novel and is thankful she's gone through what she's gone through because without those experiences—good and bad—she wouldn't have found the courage to stand up for herself and others. Discuss this idea of "rebirth" in relation to the novel. (Potential examples: Ali starting her own PR firm with Namisa, the driving scene at the end of the book, Cara's ultimate career decision, etc.)

19. At the end of *Cover Story*, Ali realizes how much good in her life has come from pushing past fear. When was the last time you went outside of your comfort zone or pushed past fear? What was the result?

20. In *Cover Story*, Cara is one of many closeted stars. Do you think things have changed since 2005 in terms of public figures coming out? Do you believe there are still celebrities who are closeted today?

Blind Item

If you were to look at my internet search history on any given week, it would go something like this: "Taylor Swift gay," "Will Smith gay," "How to tell if blue cheese has gone bad," "Leonardo DiCaprio gay," and so on and so forth. When a friend asks what I'm doing throughout the day, 50 percent of the time my answer is "gaygling" (or "gay googling," a slang term I invented that I'm hoping will spread more than "fetch"). The urge to gaygle usually hits around 2 p.m. when I'm in bed, laptop on lap, halfway through my work and a box of Cheez-Its. It's a midafternoon pick-me-up, like a cup of coffee or a protein smoothie. Fortifying. Energizing. Very necessary.

I usually start by going to an anonymous Twitter account called *Beard Club*. A beard is a person who agrees to be in a fake relationship (sometimes even including marriage and children) to cover up someone's sexuality. Frequently it's symbiotic—the beard may also be trying to cover up their own sexuality—but not always. If the beard isn't also queer, they're usually gaining fame (which leads to more work opportunities) by fake-dating the person. The relationships tend to be contractual and are set to end after a designated number of years. Hollywood is full of them. Many of the "couples" you see on the covers of magazines are not actually in a romantic relationship at all. *Beard Club* is dedicated to exposing these faux-mances.

If *Beard Club* mentions a fake couple I didn't previously know about, I do some gaygling. The results are usually mixed: Sometimes you can actually find hard evidence, like a photo or video of a celebrity kissing someone of the same sex; or an interview where they once came out but then their rep denied it the next day; or a lawsuit pertaining to an alleged lover. But more often it's just quotes the celebrity has given about the speculation, saying something like "Don't assume anyone's sexuality," "My sexuality can't be labeled," or "I prefer to keep my private life private."

Then I move on to "blind items," pieces of gossip in which the details of the event are reported but the identities of the people involved aren't. Currently, the biggest place for blind items is the *DeuxMoi* Instagram account, but in the past you could find blind items on Reddit or any of the celebrity gossip blogs like *Perez Hilton* or *Lainey Gossip*. Usually, one out of four blind items is about someone who's secretly queer. They'll say things like "Which sexy bad boy rapper was caught with his pants down with another man in a hotel bathroom?" or "This pop star was so afraid she was about to be outed...that she suddenly married a guy she met only a few weeks ago!" The comments tend to reach a pretty quick consensus about who these people are, but I investigate a little more just to make sure. Generally, there's at least one picture of a closeted celebrity looking *very* gay, based on some long-forgotten haircut or outfit choice, and I'll text it to a friend with something like "Dyke alert!" They'll always write back "You are OBSESSED." Yes, that would be a pretty accurate word for it.

* * *

I wasn't always this way. Here's my own blind item: About a decade ago, I had friends over for our monthly-ish potluck dinner and dancing party. As we sat around the living room eating various quinoa salads and drinking bourbon punch, our Very Fabulous Gay Friend—who's married to a man who, at the time, was the editor of a popular fashion magazine—let us in on a big secret. He and his husband had recently attended a red-carpet event where they saw an older, A-list actor with two Academy Awards kiss another guy when the cameras weren't around.

I'm not naming this actor because, obviously, I don't think anyone should ever be outed. I also don't believe anyone is required to come out. I do think it's important, though, that the general public understands closeting is still a reality for many celebrities (and many people in general), which reveals that LGBTQ+ acceptance is not nearly as far along as they'd like to believe. Sadly, homophobia has not yet been eradicated. And to anyone who says we shouldn't discuss closeted celebrities or speculate about sexuality, that's just another version of "Don't say gay" or "Don't ask, don't tell." Because if you say it's harmful or disrespectful to speculate about someone being queer, what you're saying is that it's harmful or not respectable to *be* queer. Thus, you just want to keep assuming everyone is straight. Speculating about sexuality actively challenges heteronormativity, which we must continue to do if we ever want to live in a truly egalitarian, inclusive world.

Anyway, back to my friends who saw an A-list actor kiss another man. They were puzzled, and they asked an industry insider, "Who is that with Actor X?" The insider casually replied, "Oh, that's his partner. They've been together for-ever." It seemed that everyone in Hollywood knew this actor was gay, but somehow it had never gotten out to the larger public. This actor had cultivated a playboy persona through-out his career, achieved by having two-year relationships with C-list actresses or models. He'd "married" a woman almost a decade before and now has children with her. Everyone in our living room was thoroughly shocked and entertained by this revelation about Actor X. At first, I was too. But when I started to think about how Actor X was just one of many closeted celebrities, I started to feel really devastated, for him and all the others and for me.

Because none of these celebrities were able to be visi-ble as their true selves, I spent twenty-two miserable years thinking I was straight: "miserable" meaning I never had a boyfriend, I puked every single time after having sex with a man, and I was still like, Oh yeah, I'm definitely straight! Much like *Cover Story*'s main character Ali, I thought I was just really picky, or hadn't met the right person yet, or was commitment-phobic, or had some kind of emotional prob-lems, or just wasn't a very sexual person, or was asexual, or had been molested when I was younger: All of these things occurred to me, but the simplest and most obvious option did not. I've come back, over and over, to the question of how I couldn't have known. And what I always come up with is visibility.

When I was growing up, there were almost no openly queer celebrities. When I was twelve, Ellen DeGeneres was the first one to come out—then she was blacklisted for years. When I was seventeen, Rosie O'Donnell came out (after her talk show wrapped); when I was nineteen, Cynthia Nixon came out (after *Sex and the City* wrapped); and when I was twenty, Portia de Rossi came out. Then I was twenty-one, an adult, and there were a grand total of four celebrities who I could see as gay role models.

Over the years, a few more celebrities came out, but I learned about even more closeted celebrities from people who had hard evidence like my friend. Sadly, only a small percentage of them are out. Yes, even today. When I originally wrote *Cover Story*, it was set in the present day. But when my agent and I tried to sell it, the feedback was: No one is closeted anymore! That's a thing of the past! In 2013, the *New York Times* said, "The culture has moved on...A person's sexual orientation is not only not news, it's not very interesting."

But I don't understand how people can think no one is closeted anymore if there are only *maybe* ten A-list actors who are openly LGBTQ+. Right now, make a list in your head and see if you can name more than ten. Neil Patrick Harris, Elliot Page, Kristen Stewart, Jodie Foster, Angelina Jolie...That's usually where the list ends. And people must understand that ten people out of all the A-list actors is not statistically representative of the population at large. A Gallup Poll shows that the average American believes one in four people are gay or lesbian, which I'd say is roughly accurate. But if one in four A-list actors and actresses were queer, there'd be a lot more than ten of them.

Regardless, I couldn't fight against public perception, so to sell *Cover Story*, I had to set it in 2005, when it was "believable" that public figures were still closeted. But I want readers to know that it's still very much a reality today. People want to believe we've reached full LGBTQ+ acceptance, especially after same-sex marriage was made legal nationwide. But book bans, "Don't say gay" laws, and bills seeking to ban or restrict gender-affirming health care for transgender youth are flooding our recent news cycle. According to the Trevor Project, 41 percent of surveyed LGBTQ+ youth considered suicide in the past year. Celebrities' agents, managers, publicists, and studios are still counseling them to not come out; the language they use might not be as blatant as it was in 2005, but the underlying message is the same. So please know that it's still difficult to come out. It still takes a lot of courage. And that shouldn't be minimized.

GRAND CENTRAL

Your next great read is only a click away.

 GrandCentralPublishing.com

 Read-Forever.com

 TwelveBooks.com

 LegacyLitBooks.com

 GCP-Balance.com

A BOOK FOR EVERY READER.